An
AMERICAN
WIFE IN
PARIS

BOOKS BY CHRYSTYNA LUCYK-BERGER

SECOND WORLD WAR

The Girl from the Mountains

The Woman at the Gates

Souvenirs from Kyiv

THE DIPLOMAT'S WIFE

The American Wife

THE RESCHEN VALLEY SERIES

No Man's Land: A Reschen Valley Novel Part 1

The Breach: A Reschen Valley Novel Part 2

Bolzano: A Reschen Valley Novel Part 3

Two Fatherlands: A Reschen Valley Novel Part 4

The Smuggler of Reschen Pass: A Reschen Valley Novella – the Prequel

Chrystyna Lucyk-Berger

An

AMERICAN
WIFE IN
PARIS

bookouture

Published by Bookouture in 2023

An imprint of Storyfire Ltd.
Carmelite House
50 Victoria Embankment
London EC4Y 0DZ

www.bookouture.com

ISBN: 978-1-83790-032-9
eBook ISBN: 978-1-83790-031-2

For Ursula.
This one is on you.

PROLOGUE

JANUARY 1941

London, England

The Travellers Club in London was where powerful men exchanged secrets like currency, and concocted global schemes. It was one of the reasons Nils Larsson had invited Major "Wild" Bill Donovan to meet him there.

Huddled against the wind and rain pelting down from the steel-gray skies, Nils disembarked at Charing Cross and walked past Trafalgar Square to St. James's. After dodging a double-decker bus, he found refuge in the club's lobby. The traffic noises were shut behind him as he headed up the carpeted stairs to the second floor. He peeked into the smoking room. Nils's size alone garnered the same attention as a dusty stranger entering a western saloon, except the Brits were much more subtle about staring. When he did not find Donovan there, he moved on to the library.

The American major was standing before a bookshelf and scanning the leather-bound titles with a crystal glass of Scotch or bourbon in his hand. Nils couldn't remember which the man preferred. Donovan was dressed in a civilian suit geared for fighting in Washington, D.C. rather than on a battlefield. His dark, bushy eyebrows were knitted in concentration, and with his wide stance, he reminded Nils of a quarterback, waiting for the football.

At the sight of him, Donovan waved his glass, his voice booming across the otherwise hushed room. "Nils Larsson, good to see you!"

A man behind a newspaper cleared his throat. A waiter, setting drinks before two silver-haired, pinched and piqued men, shot them a chastising frown.

"Bill, how's it going?" Nils greeted, keeping his voice low. Years of living abroad—in Germany, in Japan, now in England —had dropped his usual volume a few decibels.

Donovan clapped his shoulder and steered him toward a couple of mahogany and leather armchairs near a window. "Senator Larsson sends you his greetings. Specifically, he wants to hear from you about how your sister is *really* doing."

Nils had expected that. His father never quite believed that Kitty told the whole truth, and for good reasons. But Nils was going to remain silent on this one.

"She's just as she says she is. You can tell him that. I need to talk to you about her, anyway."

Donovan waved a passing waiter in. He ordered a Scotch on the rocks for Nils.

"So, what can I do for you? What is Kitty up to these days?" Donovan's expression bloomed into fondness.

"You saw her last year."

"I did. After she left Austria. Shame how that meeting in D.C. went, but she'd be proud to know that we now hold regular joint military conferences with Great Britain. You can tell her that."

The waiter returned and Nils gratefully took the Scotch,

then settled into the high-backed armchair. He clinked glasses with the major.

Nils rested his drink in the palm of his hand. "Kitty also told you about the O5 resistance group in Vienna, didn't she?"

"That's right."

"You were in Greece," Nils pressed. "On this junket."

"I was. And I looked into their resistance movement, as your father had suggested I should. I studied Italy, too. Quite a bit stirring up there. Let's not forget General de Gaulle's undertakings here in London, and his Free French Army."

"And? What do you think? Because Kitty believes we should be supporting resistance groups deep behind Axis lines, too."

"Look, Nils, arming Germans—or Austrians—is out of the question. But Roosevelt will appreciate any efforts made against the Nazis." Donovan pronounced the *a* like in *Nancies*. "He'll certainly be interested in seeing these resistance groups transform into surrogate expeditionary forces. If we supply them with the weapons and intelligence, local guerrillas could help prevent our American boys from having to fight their battles."

"You don't really believe that, Major," Nils said testily. "We're talking about defending the free world, here. Since when would Americans—whose country is founded on that very principle—just stand back and watch from afar?"

Donovan shrugged. "That's what Kitty tried to tell us, too. You know what I told her? This all takes time."

"Time? At the cost of how many lives?" Nils shared his sister's frustrations. In Berlin, in the Thirties, he'd prepared diplomatic briefs, including stark warnings, about Hitler's regime. "Kitty was in Austria right when the Anschluss happened. Both of us have experienced Nazi brutality up close."

The major sighed and placed his empty glass on the side table between them.

Nils forged ahead. "The president sent you across the Atlantic to get the big picture of the war. And? What do you make of the Allied situations?"

"The compromise is for me to talk up a lend-lease program. It's our way of offering military assistance."

"You can't possibly mean that America will stay out forever." Nils waved his glass around the room. "Not after you've seen what Europe is up against?"

"I know it's skirting the issue, but a promise is a promise," Donovan said. "Roosevelt ran on the promise of not putting boots on the ground."

"He also ran on the economy." Nils rested the glass on the armrest. "There's money to be made in conflict. We all know that. We could boost economic growth by manufacturing better weapons."

"We." Donovan eyed him. "We are not in the fight."

Nils opened his hands. "Lend-lease."

"Of our existing supplies, yes."

It was time to stop tiptoeing. Nils leaned forward.

"You and I both know it's a matter of time before we're up. Roosevelt won on an ideal, but you're here to report on the realities. More often than not, the two things don't mix. You can't try to fool a fellow diplomat, Bill."

"I'll give you that." Donovan tipped his head. "There's campaigning on promises, and then there's policy. The thing they have in common is they both need to be sold to the public. But right now? That public is divided."

Nils swirled the Scotch thoughtfully. "All right. Then sell it. Europe needs America's attention. Those resistance groups— even the ones in Austria—will need intelligence and can provide intelligence. So, let's campaign for that support. I know people here who can help write the propaganda."

Donovan studied him. "I know what you're alluding to,

Nils. I'll take it into serious consideration." He leaned back and steepled his hands. "Is this on the record or off?"

"Off." Nils picked up his glass and drank. He'd delivered the message. He was pretty certain he had set the wheels in motion. "Can I order you another one?"

Donovan agreed. Nils rose and found a waiter. When he returned, the major reached over and pounded him on the shoulder once. "What about you? I heard you've moved up the ladder again."

"Diplomatic counselor."

"The Senator must be proud."

Nils nodded appreciatively. "I suppose he is."

"So, where is Kitty now?"

Nils shrugged, sticking to the story. "She's traveling. Doing what she does best."

"Playing cards and cleaning house?" Donovan quipped. The waiter returned with their drinks, and Nils raised his glass to Donovan.

"How old was Kitty when she beat us at poker?" the major asked.

Nils chuckled affectionately. "Sixteen, maybe? She did walk away with quite some cash that night."

"She cleaned us all out." Donovan smirked. "I take it that's exactly what she's doing, then. Still playing the game."

"Something like that." Nils nodded into his drink to cover up his smile.

PART ONE

CODE NAME: ELIZABETH HENNESSY

1

APRIL 1941

Istanbul, Turkey

The ballroom of the Pera Palace Hotel was lit up by magnificent chandeliers, but the last of Istanbul's natural light was filtering through the ceiling's glassed domes. The eclectic and tasteful mix of Neo-classical, art nouveau and oriental styles made the space feel both grand and cozy with its plush carpets, and dark, warm furniture. It was the place to be for those traveling on the Orient Express and it was the place to be for anyone who meant anything. The hotel's regular events and soirees meant that writers and artists could rub shoulders with heads of state, politicians, diplomats, and royalty—the perfect ingredients for cobbling together spy networks and cultivating intelligence sources.

Perched in an Ottoman chair, her ankles crossed, and eyes darting quickly around the room, Elizabeth Hennessy was one of the hotel's many American guests. Her pale green gown complimented her sea-green eyes. She was a gregarious, extroverted redhead from Boston. Her tall and athletic stature both fascinated and intimidated men. It was this combination that provided her certain advantages.

Coolly sipping her gin rickey, she pretended to pay attention to the Swiss financier who'd approached her. Behind her was a French aide-de-camp and a Belgian businessman. That was the discussion she was keeping track of since they'd dropped the words *gold bars* and *special deliveries*. She had positioned herself with the Swiss financier in a way that allowed her to continue picking up bits of the conversation. She was now quite good at piecing together information. After nearly a year in the field, she'd also gotten good at being able to discern chicken feed from real nuggets of intelligence.

As "Herr Geneva" droned on about the impact the war was having on the money markets, Elizabeth subtly tracked the movements of three Nazis in uniform across the room, one in particular, whom she knew to be a diplomat. He was standing in front of the arched windows and speaking with the host of the party. Behind him, the sun tugged out its last strands from the surface of the Bosphorus. The diplomat turned his head slightly, as if he could feel her watching him, but did not stop talking to the Turkish statesman—a pasha with numerous business interests throughout Europe and whose file Elizabeth had read.

The man she had her eye on had short brown hair. He was attentive, his smile gentle, reflecting nothing of the Nazi brutality she was familiar with. Though he commanded respect, it was through grace.

"And you are from New York, Mrs. Hennessy?" the Swiss financier prodded.

"Boston, Massachusetts," she said automatically, her accent clearly marking that East Coast city. "My husband was a New Yorker."

"I really love the United States. Many things in common with Switzerland, you know?"

The diplomat suddenly faced her and indicated her side of the room. The pasha he was with smiled and ushered the man in her direction.

Quickly downing the rest of her drink, she coughed into her fist. "I'm so sorry."

Alarmed, the Swiss financier reached to clap her back, but she waved him off.

"Would you please excuse me for a moment?" She made as if to escape into the corridor but the pasha reached her first. The party's host took her hand and she thanked him for inviting her.

"Mrs. Hennessy, allow me to introduce you to someone." The pasha turned to the Nazi. "This is Dr. Edgar Ragatz. He is an official with the Reich's Foreign Ministry in Berlin."

Dr. Ragatz smiled at her, revealing deep dimples. His green-blue eyes were alight with interest. "I'm really from Vienna. Have you ever been to Vienna?"

"No, Dr. Ragatz. And it certainly has not been on my list of places to see since the Anschluss." Elizabeth tensed her jaw and eyed the uniform. "I thought I was in Turkey, not in one of your occupied zones. Do you not have a tuxedo for such occasions? Or do you enjoy drawing attention to yourself?"

The host looked aghast.

Dr. Ragatz bowed his head. "My apologies if I offend you."

"Offend?" she scoffed. "You can only offend someone who cares."

The pasha's eyes bulged and he brushed a hand over his white mustache, stammering apologies.

But Dr. Ragatz had taken a step toward her, effectively closing out their Turkish host. "And you do not? Care, that is? How could I rectify the situation?"

Elizabeth sniffed, her emotions churning. She raised her empty glass. "I do like a good gin rickey."

The Austrian beamed at their host as if he'd just won a toss at a football game. The Turkish statesman's bafflement transformed into relief.

"Good, a drink for the lady!" The pasha snapped his fingers in the air at a passing waiter.

"I'll see to it, Pasha," Dr. Ragatz offered. He turned to Elizabeth. "Care to join me at the bar?"

Elizabeth could not suppress a quavering smile. "Very kind of you. Thank you."

At the bar, she waited nervously as he ordered her cocktail and a brandy for himself.

He faced her and leaned forward, keeping his voice low. "I caught you watching me earlier when I was speaking with General Stülpnagel."

"The man in charge of Paris? I assume you two were comparing the best years of French burgundies and German Rieslings."

Dr. Ragatz raised an open palm. "I see that I make you uncomfortable, but if you would just give me a chance. I knew your husband quite well."

"I highly doubt it." She snapped up the gin rickey from the bartender.

"There is a matter I'd like to discuss with you."

"You have two minutes." She turned her shoulder to him.

"Join me outside?" Dr. Ragatz indicated the balcony ahead. She moved with him but did not take the arm he offered, although she very much wanted to. She could hardly wait to touch him.

Several guests grinned slyly as they passed by. The room sensed the sparks that were flying between the Austrian and the American and everyone was listening in. That was what Istanbul had become: a place for public pillow talk.

Elizabeth allowed him to lead her onto the balcony and watched him close the French doors before taking his position against the banister opposite. Electricity shot through her and a longing tugged at her so hard that she had to put a foot forward to balance herself.

He tipped his glass toward her, his eyes turning dark with desire. "Cheers."

"*À votre santé*, Dr. Ragatz." She raised her drink in the air, forcing herself to stay on her side of the balcony.

"You're radiant as a redhead, I'll give you that," Edgar said. "*Ich habe dich vermisst, meine* Kitty Larsson."

"And I have missed being your Frau Ragatz."

"One more hour of this," he murmured. "And the whole party will know that Dr. Ragatz has seduced the rich American widow, Elizabeth Hennessy."

Kitty cocked her head at him. "Or the other way around."

2

APRIL 1941

Istanbul, Turkey

The early morning was hot, and the cicadas were already filling the air with their song. Turtledoves cooed somewhere on the roof. Across the Bosphorus, the minarets and domes glowed in the sun. There was a sense of permanence, of stability in that morning that shoved the world's conflicts so far away it made Kitty feel guilty.

Her skin was coated in wisps of dust and salt. Draped in the cornflower blue bedsheet, she leaned against the stone landing of the second-story terrace. Between two umbrella pines, her husband, or not-husband, appeared, pulling powerful strokes as he did the crawl. His body had just been over hers, and she relished the lingering deliciousness of it. After making love, he'd invited her to join him for a swim, and as much as she enjoyed the cool sea water on her body, she was feeling luxurious and lazy. And most certainly enjoying the sight of him now.

It had been much too long since they had last seen each

other. For months they had planned one clandestine meeting after another, only for those plans to stall. In the end she had told her British supervisors she would quit if they did not succeed in putting her and Edgar in one place together. Finally, General Stülpnagel's junket to Istanbul gave them both a reason to be in Turkey.

She glanced into the room. Her ballgown was draped to the right of the bed. Lying on top of the dresser was the falsified American passport identifying her as Elizabeth Hennessy, a widowed American socialite who'd been married to a wealthy New York businessman. As opposed to Kitty's fluency in several foreign languages, Elizabeth came across as more shallow and naïve. This gave people the confidence to say things in front of her that they might otherwise not.

It was the British Foreign Office that had concocted the cover story with her. After leaving the States for a "tour around the world," she set up shop as Elizabeth Hennessy in Bern, Switzerland. There, in the lap of luxury, she held soirees and functions, felt out new talent and reported her findings. She was not authorized to recruit those potential spies; her job was only to supply their names and other soft intelligence.

Her operational officer was delighted by how well she buttered up even the toughest nuts, and scrutinized who was likely using their diplomatic status as a front for espionage. She had agreed to do it on the condition that she and Edgar could occasionally meet on neutral territory: Lisbon. Morocco. Madrid. Bern. But after nearly a year, only Istanbul had panned out.

Now that she and Edgar had a moment to shed the cloaks and daggers, she realized how worn out she felt. She wanted her husband back. And peace. But with Hitler's armies and brutal thugs having swept across Europe, the Nazis were proving that they were growing stronger. Which meant Edgar's determination to continue working from within the German Foreign

Office was cemented. While he'd remained on the inside, she'd fled and reinvented herself.

Kitty tightened the sheet around her as the unbidden memories of her work with the O5 resistance network assaulted her. Her friends in Vienna were dead or scattered. She'd been driven to the group because Edgar had posed as a passive regime supporter. Unaware that he was supplying valuable information for the British and leading a small resistance group, she had not been able to stand by and watch the Nazis destroy the city—and the man—she loved. She'd nearly and unknowingly blown her own husband's cover in the process of defying him.

She turned and leaned in the doorway of the balcony, taking in the uniform Edgar had worn to the party last night. It hung on the door of the wardrobe. Kitty shivered. When she had discovered Edgar was a spy, she'd reeled for weeks, unable to fathom how she had not seen what was before her very eyes. Then MI6 had suggested the two of them get divorced. For Edgar's sake; so that he could return to Austria and continue working undercover. So that he could shake off the nuisance she had become.

She had fought the idea, but espionage did not allow for such indulgences as love. She had signed the divorce papers. Over a carefully prepared and painful PR campaign, Nils—the only family member privy to her secret life—made sure the story got published in all the right places.

Back in Minnesota, Kitty's youngest brother Sam waited with flowers, a cocktail, and a good, long hug.

"Welcome home, Kit," he'd said. "You really blew this one and I wasn't there to see it."

He'd been referring to the divorce. Lying to her family was torturous, especially when it came to Sam. She'd gritted her teeth as her mother—with peppered-in French exclamations—claimed that she had always suspected that not everything about Edgar had been right. The Senator had simply hugged Kitty and told her he was glad to finally see his daughter back on American soil. Even then, in the safety of the Larsson mansion, Kitty had not been able to tell him why she had not fled Austria sooner. People had depended on her—people she had now left behind.

It had not been difficult to duck her head in shame and make Kitty Larsson Ragatz disappear. Elizabeth Hennessy grew in her stead. It was sometimes easier to play someone new.

Watching Edgar kick onto his back from the buoy, she corrected herself. Lying to her family wasn't the hardest part. Indeed, it had become her profession, and she had grown remarkably good at it. The hardest part was the distance between her and Edgar, because she longed to continue redis-covering the man she loved passionately. As far as the two of them were concerned, their divorce was only on paper.

"Think of me as your lover," Edgar had whispered into her hair last night. "It might even be sexier that way."

"Sexier?" she had protested, tracing his dimples then his lips with her finger. "How is it possible for you to be any sexier?"

After they had publicly continued their seductive dance at the Pera Palace, Edgar had driven her to the seaside villa he'd rented across the strait. They'd arrived, pretending to be tipsy and full of desire for one another. That desire had not been an act.

Edgar had swept her up the grand staircase into the suite and checked for bugs as they kissed and flirted. Only when they were both certain that they were safe, did the two of them undress each other and remove their disguises. Blissfully, they were husband and wife again. Soon—too soon—she would have to leave her "lover" and be Elizabeth once more.

Kitty watched her husband slide out onto the beach, stride to his towel and begin drying himself off. He'd cut his brown hair so short that she could no longer run her fingers through his curls. He was thinner, but still powerful and muscular. At that moment, he looked up toward the villa and beamed up at her. Even from that distance, his smile was a brilliant beacon.

She pushed herself away from the landing. She should get dressed. Edgar had bought her a choice of dresses to relax in. They would have breakfast soon, and she desperately wanted a coffee.

The spacious suite was decorated with warm-colored tiles of orange, bright pink, and soft blues, like the sky now. A bronze sun-shaped clock hung above the bed, the hands stuck at 7:22. They had joked about time standing still for them. If only it could be true.

She opened the wardrobe, effectively hiding Edgar's uniform. She pulled on a flowing white and turquoise dress before padding into the marble-tiled bathroom. There, she examined the woman she was supposed to be, not the one she truly was.

Like Edgar, she'd also cut her hair short. It was chin-length now, and her blond waves had been violently straightened then dyed red. The freckles she'd had hennaed on two weeks ago were just beginning to slowly fade. Her eyes were like Edgar's now: his naturally switched from green to blue the way the sun changed the color of the Mediterranean. She reinserted the glass contacts that covered up her own blue eyes and turned them green.

She blinked the discomfort away, resigned to the fact that her diet of deception and lies would have to sustain her until the end of this war.

As Edgar was heading up through the olive grove, there was a knock on the door. Checking outside, Kitty found Nasir, one of the servants, waiting in the corridor with a silver tray of Turkish coffee and a sealed envelope. The envelope was addressed to Edgar at the Sunrise Villa.

She took both and thanked him, set the coffee on a tiled table and brought the envelope out onto the balcony, gently thumping it against her other palm.

Edgar looked up, his white towel slung over his shoulder. She lifted the envelope into the air. He dropped his head as if the pathway had grown too steep.

She dreaded the message herself. Nobody knew where to find him except his case officer. Either it would mean she would have to abandon her husband or he would have to abandon her. It wasn't fair. Just one night together was not fair.

He disappeared beneath the roof of the terrace and a few moments later he was in the bedroom. She held out the envelope, but he plucked it away. It fluttered onto the bed as he drew her in for a kiss. Scented by the sea, he peppered the nape of her neck and she wrapped her hand around the back of his head.

"I want to come wherever it is you are going next," she murmured.

Edgar held her tightly against him and whispered back. "I haven't been this happy in a long time. Right here. I just want to stay here. Promise me that when it's time we'll return to this spot."

"Don't go." She nibbled his earlobe, kissed his jaw. "And then you don't have to worry about a return at all. We could stay here. Forever stuck at seven twenty-two."

He groaned and pulled away. "There is a war on. And reasonable evidence to believe that Germany will—"

She put her hand up. "Go on. Open it."

Edgar grimaced but plucked the envelope off the pile of bedsheets. He slit the top with a finger. Kitty took his towel and hung it over the line on the balcony to dry. Edgar's back was to her when she returned, the message at his side.

"I'm to meet with Masterson at the Café Istanbul this evening. Kitty..."

She bit her lip when he faced her. She sensed what was coming next and dreaded it.

"When General Stülpnagel learned that I'd studied in France, he asked me to join him in Paris as his aide-de-camp. I've done everything for this to fall into place. Masterson has to bring me up to speed about the circuit there. Kitty, I'm going to see that you are posted in Paris. It's time you were doing more than acting the spoiled socialite."

Her heart somersaulted. "If I move to France..."

"I could say I want my lover near me, and we can continue this affair."

"They won't agree to it," Kitty protested. "You know I break too many rules. It's already a stretch that I'm working for anyone again after what I pulled in Vienna."

Edgar smiled tenderly. "They underestimate my determination, Kitty. And yours. I've been saying all along, you're going to waste gathering soft intelligence. I'll try to strike a compromise. MI6's greatest concern is security."

Hers as well, but she wanted to be where Edgar was. Very badly.

He laid a palm on her cheek and she leaned into it. His tone turned bitter then. "I'm behaving the compliant diplomat but all I feel I'm doing is saving my own life. If I can do something that will stop the regime in France, then I will. And I want you to be there."

She nodded but was unconvinced. The truth was, she was not sure she trusted herself any longer. Edgar had worked as a spy right under her nose. Collecting information in a neutral country was not the same as working in the midst of Hitler's regime. What if she was caught and the Gestapo recognized her? She'd once again risk exposing Edgar.

He was waiting for her response. She tightened her hold on

him. "More than anything, what I want—*all* I want—is for the war to be over and to have my husband back."

"For that, Germany must lose. Hitler must be destroyed." Edgar took both her hands. "It's time we help make that happen, Kitty. Together."

She pressed herself against him. "You talk to them, and I'll hear them out. When do you have to meet Masterson?"

"Half past seven."

She glanced at that silent bronzed clock. "Then you only have eight minutes," she teased, but she could not smile.

His gaze was tender. "I have all day with you, yet. And then you're coming to Paris. It's going to be like the old days."

She knew he meant like the days of their courtship, but Kitty shuddered, remembering the sorrow and terror of those last years in Vienna.

I certainly hope not, she thought.

3

Paris, Nazi-Occupied France

Paris, the City of Lights, was dimmed by the dark shadow of the Nazi regime. On her arrival on a warm summer afternoon, and to Kitty's utter dismay, the city she'd studied in, partied in, celebrated the discovery of herself in, had become entirely German. There were virtually no differences between Paris and Berlin— a transformation she had also witnessed in Vienna after the Anschluss.

Gone were the artsy posters, the street musicians, and that atmosphere of gaiety and liberty. The colors and details of art nouveau were covered by German banners and German signs. The Reich's flags were stuck on every building along the expansive avenue, left and right, up and down.

Where once there had been posters for every imaginable creative forum, now there were bilingual announcements screaming threats. The one Kitty read—like a personal warning

—outlined the penalties for any resistance or sabotage against the Third Reich in three large bullet points:

- *All the close male relatives of the accused, in the ascending and descending line, as well as the in-laws and cousins above 18 will be shot.*
- *All the women of the same degree of kinship will be sent to forced labor*
- *All children 17 and under and related to those found guilty will be interned in a reformation institution.*

Signed, the highest order of the SD—the German security division. End of story.

Kitty turned away from the crass announcement, even more awful because the border of it was in red, white and blue—the colors of liberty.

She looked around her, having not gone much further than the square in front of Gare de Lyon. German Wehrmacht walked about in tailored uniforms in shades of gray and green, their black leather belts cinching their waists as if to hold them together.

Although Paris appeared to be on its knees, Kitty suddenly realized there was something going on among the people that passed her by. The local women were chic and carried their heads high. She took a moment to observe everyone coming and going; but, yes, roughly every other woman was dressed in French flair. Two women, linked at the elbow, wore matching outfits save that one was in vibrant pink and the other in bright green. An Asian woman, her dark hair done in a high pompadour, wore a striking black-and-white plaid dress with a full skirt, red belt, red shoes, red hat and red handbag, as if to mock the parade of gray Germans. Another woman stepped delicately down the stone steps in high heels, in a flared summer dress with splashes of peonies. Her hat and her purse had matching appliqués. It was like sitting on the side of a catwalk and observing a silent protest.

The effect was so strong that when a group of women, speaking German, passed Kitty by, she realized that she could pick them all out from the crowd. The austere, straight-cut outfits ranged from shades of gray-gray to gray-blue to gray-green and the most vibrant was a washed-out rose. These women, who'd likely giddily moved to Paris only to wash out the French colors, were no match for *la femme française rebelle*.

Paying attention to all the details, Kitty headed for the metro. The ticket booths for many of the cabarets and cinemas warned that only Germans were allowed. Others were closed down entirely. Signs pointed the way to air-raid shelters, others reminded the population of the latest curfew. Rationing was on for food, tobacco, coal and clothing. Kitty made a mental note to register herself so that she could pick up some ration cards.

German propaganda was everywhere she turned, except for the propaganda trying to convince the French that Marshal Pétain—who'd "saved" southern France and now headed the puppet government in Vichy—was really someone to be admired. On a billboard, two children greeted his likeness with a bundle of wheat and flowers, but someone had scribbled devil's horns onto Pétain's head.

Kitty smirked. The surface of Paris had changed but the freedom-loving French were still here, and they were at work.

She got out at the Opera House station. On the corner of Rue du 4 septembre she found the building she was looking for. A banner hung over the original French sign and now read *Platz Kommandatur*.

She had to register with the local authorities before she could go to the house Edgar, with MI6's approval, had located for her.

"Madame Hennessy? American?" The registrar raised one dark eyebrow, and his eyes traveled the length of her.

"*Oui.*"

"What brings you to Paris?"

"As you see here, I've volunteered to work with the Ambulance Corps at the American Hospital."

"I do see. But... Madame Hennessy, if you do not mind my pointing it out, it is a very dirty job for a woman of your... status."

She easily slipped into the story she had prepared for such scrutiny. "I had a friend who once volunteered at a camp for the homeless. He was already thinking of studying to be a doctor. He could only go on the condition that he take his sister with him. She told me it was one of the most eye-opening experiences of her life. I'm looking for my eye-opening experience."

The official sighed heavily and muttered something about the luxury of wasting time.

"The address of your residence?"

She produced her letter of invitation, the details of her address listed clearly. He handed over her ration card and she read that the allotment of meat was 250g per week.

"Welcome to Paris." He tapped the side of his nose. "*Et bonne chance*, Madame Hennessy."

Kitty easily found the terraced house. It was nowhere near as lavish as her apartment in Bern had been, but it would suit. Edgar had suggested nothing too fancy, to avoid attracting any unwanted attention. The neighborhood was quaint even if a little impoverished. More importantly, she was located away from the heavier trafficked areas of Paris, and quite the opposite end from German headquarters.

Her address was part of a row of terraced houses. Inside, there was a sitting room, a cozy dining room, and a kitchen in the back facing a tiny garden. She found two bedrooms and a bathroom upstairs.

After unpacking her things, she still had a few hours before Edgar was to visit. To kill time, she walked from her neighborhood toward the Seine. The trees along her street were still a young green but the atmosphere was that of the drooping tulips in the park. The buildings on the main avenue were gray, hidden behind the bright scarlet of Nazi wallpaper. Disgusted, she turned around and headed back the way she'd come.

That evening, when she finally heard someone coming up the narrow garden walk, she leapt to her feet and peeked behind the blackout curtain.

Edgar.

He was dressed in civilian clothing. She hurried to the door and opened it, throwing herself at him as soon as it was shut. He had a basket of goodies for her. She took it from him and placed it on the floor.

"How was your—?" he started.

But she was kissing him.

"I take it," he chuckled, "you'd rather we talk later."

Later came too soon anyway.

Candlelight flickered over their bodies as they lay facing each other. She had put the blackboards up on the windows earlier, mostly as a way to seal them from the outside world. Kitty refilled their wine glasses then nibbled on a slice of cheese from the platter between them. Edgar picked apart a day-old baguette and fed it to her.

"When do you start at the hospital?" he asked.

"Tomorrow. At the grueling hour of seven."

"I live only twenty minutes from there, in Neuilly-sur-Seine." Edgar popped the crust of the baguette into his mouth. "You could come to me after your shift."

"So soon? Is that wise?"

He shrugged and stroked her face, his eyes drinking her in. "Probably not."

She rolled onto her back, pulled the sheet up to her chin, and studied the plaster detail on the ceiling. Tomorrow she would begin working with a group at the hospital who helped smuggle in necessary goods to the POW camps, among other activities.

"How is this going to work, Edgar?"

"You mean the meager rations?"

She chuckled. "No."

"Because I brought extra rations for you. I miss your cooking."

She laughed and playfully punched his shoulder.

He propped himself on his elbow. "You'll drive the ambulance. The supplies will be provided irregularly. Medicines. Food. And on occasion..."

"On occasion..." She fluffed her pillow and sat up. On occasion she would courier messages and illegal contraband and stores to a depot near the Gobelins metro. It was rather like the old days. She'd done similar work with the O5 in Vienna.

"OK," she said.

He reached for a strand of her hair. "I'll go over the codes with you. The channels of communication."

"And in an emergency?"

Edgar clicked his tongue. "We work alone, Kitty. Those are the conditions."

She turned her head to him, silently pleading.

"I'll give it some thought."

"Anything else?"

He sat up as well. "Many things. But everything will be done on—"

"A need-to-know basis," Kitty chanted. "I know."

He stroked her bare arm. "Security is of the utmost importance, Kitty. That's what we agreed to. It's why you're allowed to be here. For your sake and the sake of all the others on this line."

"And yours." She slipped her hand into his and squeezed. If he was ever discovered, there would be no question what would happen to him. *All male members of the assailant's family will be summarily shot.* But she and Edgar were divorced. And she was Elizabeth Hennessy.

The clock in the next room chimed midnight. Kitty looked at her husband expectantly. "You missed the curfew."

Edgar set aside the platter and the glasses of wine. "Then maybe we should get some sleep."

Grinning, she blew out the candles and turned to him. "We can sleep when we die."

Zara Tolomei was a dark-haired, olive-skinned Frenchwoman from Reims, with two perfectly proportioned ears, a sharp chin and aquiline nose. She was very serious. She was volunteering because the *boche* had imprisoned her husband, and she was hell-bent on making sure she made the prisoners' lives easier and the Germans' lives harder.

Carrying a clipboard, Kitty's partner strode over to the truck and waved for her to get in. "We have a package to retrieve this evening. At the mechanic's."

Kitty's stomach did a little flip. It was not the first time they would be picking up a "package"—that was what it meant to take the truck to the mechanic's after their shift—but each time she did, Kitty had to battle with her anxiety. The "package" was usually a person on the run.

She went around the front of the truck and got behind the wheel, started the engine and pulled out onto the street. "We've got food deliveries to three of the POW camps, and medicine."

Zara nodded, settling back into the bench. "All right, then. Let's make our first drop at Austerlitz."

Half an hour later, they pulled up to the camp gates and Zara jumped out, tugged down the jacket of her uniform and went to the back. The woman was about to deliver the first box of food to the camp guards when she halted and scanned the area. Kitty glanced at her. Zara's gray eyes were taking it all in—

the dark, oppressed atmosphere, the walled-in enclosure, the stiff German guards.

Her nose wrinkled and she sniffed. "*Putains de boches.* I will never forgive them if Gaston does not return alive."

Kitty took in a sharp breath. She understood the woman's anger and also knew it was futile to argue with her. The first time, Kitty had suggested that there were many Germans who were very much against the regime—men and women who risked their lives to sabotage Hitler's efforts.

But Zara spat and muttered, "There's no such thing as a good German. Otherwise, they'd never have let this happen. May they all rot in hell."

Elizabeth Hennessy had never lived in Vienna, so there was no way Kitty could convince Zara that was untrue.

As they headed to the second POW camp, Kitty slowed down and glanced at her partner to see whether she saw the checkpoint up ahead. "Don't say anything, do what they say, and there won't be any problems."

Zara narrowed her eyes. "'Do what they say, and there won't be any problems.' See where that kind of mentality got us here in France?"

Three Wehrmacht soldiers were waiting for them. Kitty showed them their documents; they mechanically checked the ambulance. Zara was staring straight ahead, but Kitty could feel the woman's anger simmering on the surface. She was glad when the soldiers quickly let them through.

"Zara," she started gently. "You will have your day, I promise. This cannot possibly be the state of things all our lives. But I'm telling you, the best way to defeat the Germans is to keep your wits about you and outsmart them. Not to provoke them."

The woman turned a little and began to say something but then clamped her mouth shut.

"We have a 'package' to pick up tonight," Kitty reminded her. "Our job is to get him or her to safety so that they can finish doing the job they're supposed to be doing." She reached over and patted Zara's arm. "This is what we can do. It is what we are doing. Now we do it right under these bastards' noses and keep our cool."

The "mechanic" was in the sixth arrondissement. Kitty pulled into the garage and turned off the ignition, jumping a little when two men threw open the back doors of her ambulance. She and Zara sprang out and watched as their "package" ducked inside.

"A British airman," the Frenchman nearest to Kitty said. He cupped his hand around the end of a cigarette and lit it, then plucked a piece of tobacco off his lip. "Shot down in the north. He had a pretty bad sprain. Still limps."

The pilot was tall—enough to draw attention—but was dressed in a slightly rumpled, French-styled suit, the shoulder pads making him look enormous. Kitty greeted him and introduced herself and Zara.

"Ask for Dr. Max," her French contact said.

Grimly, Kitty checked the rising panic in her chest. Dr. Max was the code for an emergency. It was the same "Dr. Max" Edgar had provided as her contact if she were ever in deep trouble. He'd shared a set of codes to get various messages through, and in cases of urgently required documents, they had the dead letter box at a spot on the Seine.

"Our man here is Aidan Alloy," her counterpart told her. "But his French name is Élliot Ardoin." He made Kitty repeat it.

"This is all we could manage." He handed her an official transfer to the hospital and Élliot's French documents. "Tell them he was in a bicycling accident outside of Paris and you're transporting him for an emergency surgery. Dr. Max will see to it he gets out."

Dr. Max, and Edgar's network of forgers, couriers and safe houses.

"How's his French?" Zara asked.

The man rolled his eyes. "These Brits have only the rudimentary. If he needs to order at a restaurant, he might pass. If you run into gendarmes, you're going to have problems."

"There were new checkpoints en route," Kitty warned. With his bad leg, she thought, Aidan would not be able to run.

The man glanced over her shoulder. "Then he had better play unconscious if he goes up against our bastard collaborators. He might pass under *boche* scrutiny. Maybe."

Kitty rubbed her neck, a sharp pain going straight to her temples. She faced the garage doors that the two Frenchmen opened for her to drive out of, and held up her hands. "Stop."

They shut the doors again. She turned to Zara. "I don't have a good feeling about this."

Kitty went to the back again, Zara following, and queried the Brit in English.

"Aidan, how bad is your leg? Could you make a dash for it if need be?"

"I could try."

"Not good enough." The extra checkpoints were a real concern. They were either controlled by the Wehrmacht, German security service, or French gendarmes. More often than not, French gendarmes.

Kitty nodded at Zara. "We're going to have to knock him out."

She reached up and Aidan helped her inside. She opened the locker with the sedatives, withdrew one of the drip bags, and looked at the Brit. He was young, with a boyish face, and reddish-brown hair. She smiled reassuringly though her nerves were taut.

"I'm going to give you some sodium amytal. It's going to knock you out. I can't risk them making you speak. All right?"

"Do you know what you're doing?" the Frenchman asked her. The second one lingered off to the side, his dark eyes mopey. She could tell he did not trust the operation either.

"My brother is a doctor," Kitty replied. "I helped him practice..." Sam had let her try it out on an orange. Once. She glanced up from the drip bag she was preparing and switched back to English. "Aidan? Are you ready?"

He grimaced as she wrapped a rubber tube around his upper arm and tapped for the blood vessel. She swore to herself at the sight of her shaking hand, held her breath and said Aidan's name again.

"Here we go."

He nodded and she inserted the needle. She'd watched Sam do it a hundred times, especially in Des Moines when they worked at the shacktown during the Great Depression, but her insides flinched as she pushed deeper. She attached the tube and hung up the bag, then secured the intravenous site.

"You have a lie-down, now. You're going to sleep and when you wake up, I hope we're at the hospital and can make you into a bona fide Frenchman."

"Do you know how much he needs?" Zara whispered when Aidan's eyes began falling closed.

Kitty watched the drip, switching back to French. *Enough to knock him out*, she thought. "I'm hoping these have already been measured out."

"And if they aren't?"

She took up his wrist and checked his pulse. "Then I might kill him."

4

OCTOBER 1941

Lyon, Non-Occupied France

It was Edgar who came to Kitty's home two days later and told her that she was going to escort Aidan out of the occupied zone. The pilot had survived her dose of sedative, and "Dr. Max" was so impressed with her quick thinking that Kitty was made his guide.

Southern France was occupied by Pétain's government, but was Nazi-compliant enough to make it dangerous for Kitty and Aidan to travel through. The police were mostly corrupt bullies and easy to buy off with bribes. However, they were on the lookout for traitors and dissenters and ostracized them quickly, especially if there were Germans around to observe.

The address in the Terreaux district was tucked behind a cobblestoned alley and adjacent to a hotel, which Kitty guessed was more a brothel by the number of grinning gendarmes coming and going. The apartment building of their safe house had wrought-iron bars on the windows on the lower level. The ones above were mostly sealed behind wooden shutters, some so narrow they were like an afterthought.

After having watched the building for a while, Kitty finally determined it was safe to go in. She and Aidan entered the atrium. There was no concierge, which was rare and put her on alert. It may very well be that the people running the safe house had purposefully chosen an address where nobody would know about the comings and goings of strangers.

Kitty and Aidan climbed the circular stairwell to apartment 12 where she rapped softly on the door. The pilot went to the landing and scanned the staircase as they waited.

After a moment, a woman's voice asked who they were.

"I'm looking for Guinevère. It's Madame Hennessy," Kitty replied, then gave the password: "You requested an interview."

The password worked because there was the click of the lock, and the woman appeared before them. She was stunning. Her chestnut hair was tied back, but wisps fell around her Hellenic features as if she'd just been doing physical work. She had muscular arms and a strong jawline. But it was that unwavering gaze that lent Kitty the feeling she was in competent hands.

"Your interview was at ten o'clock," the woman complained.

Aidan released a huge sigh at the confirmation of their password and stepped forward. "I'm so glad," he said. "I've been—"

"Not here," the woman interrupted. She waved them inside and shut the door. "I'm Guinevère. This is Stanley."

A man came into the room from the back. He was carrying something in his arms, covered over with a cloth. He lay the bundle down, and it clattered onto the table.

"What do we have here?" he said in English, barely looking up in acknowledgment. He had a British accent. "Are you here for the training?"

He uncovered several weapon parts and mechanically began putting them together. Kitty counted three magazines.

Guinevère scowled at him and hissed in English, "Keep your voice down, Stanley, and speak French, for Chrissakes."

He looked only mildly chastised, but Kitty beamed at Guinevère. "You're American."

Guinevère eyed her. "So are you." She stuck out her hand and shook Kitty's. She had a firm grip.

"Where are you from?" Guinevère asked in French.

Kitty shook her head, forming the accent she had adopted for her cover. "For the purposes of your story, Boston."

Guinevère's lips flicked up. "Boston it is."

Kitty felt she had just passed an assessment. She turned to shake Stanley's hand, who then took Aidan by the shoulder.

"Congratulations for surviving this far," he joked.

Aidan immediately recounted the story of how he'd come to be in Lyon, including being drugged by Kitty. In the meantime, Guinevère led Kitty to a table and offered them a glass of water, then pulled the cork off an already opened bottle of red wine. She poured four short glasses and handed two to the men, then placed the other two down for Kitty and herself.

Guinevère patted the table. "Have a seat."

Kitty lowered herself onto a wobbly stool.

"You can't be too careful," Guinevère said. "We just got reports of several brutal clampdowns, both in the non-occupied zone and in Paris."

That caught Kitty off guard. Was Edgar safe now that he was working so closely with the new government? "Reprisals? What happened?"

"I'm not sure, but they're targeting Polish refugees," Guinevère said. "Apparently, some officers from the Home Army have escaped from the east and organized themselves here in France."

Guinevère tossed a meaningful look at the back of the room where Aidan and Stanley had vanished. "Also, it's been raining too heavily with airmen up north. Then, last week we had an assassination here in *zone nono*. A German officer was shot, and the Nazis murdered forty-eight villagers in reprisal."

Kitty looked down at her glass. "Polish refugees and Jews. You've certainly heard about what's going on in Paris with the Jewish refugees, too. But how is it here? Are the French here as anti-Semitic?"

"There are plenty here uncovering their deep-seated hate for Jews," Guinevère said acidly. She studied her glass. "I was hunting once in a... well, let's just say, an exotic land. A land where men are not really allowed to mix with women. Do you understand? A man approached me in one of the villages we were passing through. I was shocked that he came directly up to me, and cupped his hands as if to cradle my face. It was a rather disconcerting gesture, I'll admit, but he didn't touch me. He was very earnest, and just started talking. I was curious, so my guide translated. The stranger said, 'There are angels walking this earth and there are animals. You can tell which are which by their faces. You have the face of an angel. But do not doubt it, the animals will come. Then the hunt is on. That is what you will chase after: evil.' He was so sincere that I knew it was not some cheap attempt to seduce me or scare me. His words haunt me, because that's what is happening all around me right now: the unleashing of wild animals."

Kitty understood what this woman was saying. That lawlessness. That loss of morality. The days following the Anschluss, the Nazis did not march in as much as they had risen up and crawled out of Vienna's woodwork. Unleashed. It was a good way of putting it, but at the memories of her friends on the run, the fear that stalked them everywhere they went, Kitty had to bite the inside of her lip to keep it from trembling.

"Hey? Are you OK? All the color's drained from your face."

Kitty ground the heel of her hands into her eyes. "I've just seen a ghost."

"Where?"

She pointed to her head. "Here. Friends of mine, and one especially. He fled to Paris over a year ago. I don't know whether he made it. I don't know if he's in the non-occupied zone or..."

That ghost was Oskar Liebherr. As soon as she knew she would be in Paris with Edgar, she had pleaded with her husband to look for her friend—the only one she was certain had gotten out of Austria thanks to his help. Edgar was reluctant to search for him, which was typical. Her husband never did anything that did not serve a purpose, and nothing that caused unnecessary security risks.

"Your friend is Jewish," Guinevère guessed. "If he went to Paris, a lot of them fled to the south of France. Especially the refugees. They recognized the warning signs."

The men suddenly reappeared from the back room. Stanley announced, "I'm going to escort our Élliot here to the next safe house after the show."

Kitty frowned. "What show?"

"I'm doing Sten gun training at a local club." He indicated the three guns he'd assembled. "You should come."

"Stanley!" Guinevère glared at him.

"What?"

"You can't just go about..." She gritted her teeth. "Inviting *anyone*."

"She's not just anyone. She's one of us." At least he was no longer speaking in English.

"But she's not," Guinevère bit back.

Stanley was not apologetic. "Well, maybe she should be? Her French is perfect."

Guinevère's jaw clenched, and her eyes narrowed. "Shut the hell up. That's an order."

Stanley swung to Aidan. "And we thought the Yanks were more laid-back than we are."

The pilot threw Kitty a sheepish look before following Stanley to the back of the apartment again.

Guinevère, her chest rising two, three times, turned back to Kitty, contrite. "Not everyone is cut out for this job. And yet... you know how it is. Men like Stanley know the right people, and they get to pull strings. He thinks this is all fun and games. It's going to be a whole different story when he gets caught and the French or the Germans torture him for information. He won't last the forty-eight hours."

"Forty-eight hours?" Kitty asked. There were a dozen questions she had about what had been said, but this question seemed safest.

Guinevère gazed at her steadily. "That's how long we have to hold out without getting the rest of us killed."

The rest of us. Did she mean the four of them, in this apartment? And if not, this group Guinevère alluded to, how many of them were there exactly? And if Kitty did not belong to Guinevère's group here, then who did Guinevère belong to?

"He's right," Guinevère interrupted.

"About what?"

"Your French is flawless. Better than mine, I think."

"Why is that so important?"

Guinevère shrugged. "Airmen aren't the only ones raining down on France." But her look stopped Kitty from asking what she meant.

"Let's get this interview going, shall we?" Guinevère rose and went to the couch, glass in one hand, the other plucking a notepad off a sideboard.

Her mind reeling, Kitty joined Guinevère in the sitting room.

"What do you want my article for the *Post* to focus on?" the woman asked. "What is Elizabeth Hennessy doing in France?"

"I thought we could talk about the American Hospital, and the volunteer corps," Kitty suggested. "They could use some more help. So I might as well make myself look good and promote that at the same time."

"Good. London relies on my articles for insider information, just the day-to-day things to evaluate what's really happening here. The mood, the morale, everything. The more details, the better."

"I can share anecdotes. About the POWs, for example. How the spot checks are menacing, even when all your documents are in order, that kind of thing."

"That's good. Yes." Guinevère shot a look over her shoulder where the men were in the next room, then examined Kitty for a moment. "How long have you been doing this?"

"You know I can't answer that."

The woman flicked her another smile. "Right. But I meant, how long have you been volunteering?"

"Good God. I certainly need to be on my toes around you, don't I!"

"Good God," Guinevère teasingly mocked. "I think that must be why I'm the first woman they sent out here."

Though Kitty laughed, she didn't consider the comment a jest. It was likely very honest. Suddenly, she was struck with an idea, and it was thrilling and terrifying at the same time. If she was right, then the British Foreign Office was testing out women for covert operations in France. Which made perfect sense. Women in France were free to move about. According to German ideology, women were to stay at home, raise the children, tend to the hearth and home. That mentality meant that the Germans were far less likely to suspect women as secret operatives.

"Is something wrong?" Guinevère frowned.

Kitty returned her focus to her but couldn't share her suspicions. It would get her nowhere with this woman. "Let's go on."

Guinevère looked down at her notes, but not before Kitty saw that furtive flick of a smile once more.

.   .   .

As tempting as it was—she desperately wanted a closer look at those three guns—Kitty did not take up Stanley's offer to attend the Sten gun training. Instead, she stayed with Guinevère, helping her to formulate the news report that would also double as an insightful and informative message to London about conditions in Paris. Aidan assisted with some choice bits from his own mission that had ended on a field in the north of France. Time flew by, and when Stanley returned, Kitty hugged Aidan goodbye and wished him luck.

"Thank you for everything," he said and placed his other hand on Guinevère's shoulder. "You're both incredibly brave. Imagine what the fellows will do when they see me coming back to the hangar. You've just helped boost the morale tenfold."

"Next time, just stay in the air," Kitty teased.

He laughed appreciatively and shook her hand again, then slipped out of the apartment.

Kitty turned to Guinevère. "How will I know whether he's made it?"

The woman frowned. "You won't. You'll just have to believe he has. That is, if Stanley returns without getting himself caught."

"Wait. Do you think—"

"Forget I said that." Guinevère looked apologetic. "We've sent four men down the line recently. Stanley's got it. He just finds all this to be a big game sometimes, and he's got too big of a mouth on him."

As much as she liked Guinevère, Kitty shared the woman's reservations about Stanley, whom she suspected had little common sense about security. It did not bode well. Lives depended on discretion. Though she had to admit that she was very intrigued about what the two were up to in Lyon, Kitty wanted to get back to Edgar.

"I'm taking the couch," Guinevère said. "Stanley will have

the floor. You can have the bedroom."

Kitty followed her and the woman began clearing the bed of her personal belongings.

"You know, I'm a pretty good shot," Kitty said. "Stanley's training might have been interesting."

Guinevère looked at her with renewed interest. "You shoot?"

"You said you hunt. I hunt, too."

"Really? Waterfowl? Big game?"

"Birds. Deer." Kitty hesitated for a moment, but she wanted very badly to know who this woman was. And how she had gotten here. One piece of information might crack open that lid. "And moose."

One of Guinevère's eyebrows curved upwards. "Moose? In Boston?"

Kitty shrugged. "We traveled."

"Uh-huh."

"Is your accent also studied?"

Guinevère shook a finger at her. "That's going a step too far. But no, I'm not trying to cover a Texan drawl beneath this."

Kitty had instead detected an upper East Coast accent in that neutral American.

"Look, I don't know who you answer to," Guinevère said. She handed Kitty a nightshirt and perched on the bed. "And I don't want to know. But I sense that you are very interested in what we are doing."

Kitty undressed and pulled the shirt over her head, then twisted to look back at Guinevère. "I am. But then I'm not. But I am again."

Guinevère leaned on the bed with one arm. "It's just I think Stanley might be right. You would be great at it."

"Great at what?"

The woman narrowed her eyes. "You've got the instincts. Don't kid a kidder."

Kitty relented. "If I'm right about what it is you're doing, then yes, I'm intrigued. But no, I don't think I'd be great at it. I've made a mess of a lot of things."

"Really? Did you learn from your mistakes?"

Kitty pulled her knees up. "I don't know."

"Don't underestimate yourself. I think you've got the right amount of sense and courage to pull it off."

There was also one other thing but admitting it even to herself filled Kitty with dread. If she was to report to a different department of the Foreign Office, she would lose her last line to Edgar. She would not be able to choose where she was assigned. She would likely not see her husband until after the war. If it ever ended.

Guinevère was watching her. "I just want to say, they're looking for good... shots."

"Who also speak fluent French," Kitty added.

"And know France. Enough to be invisible. You know..."

"What?"

"America won't be able to stay out forever. But for now, people like you, people like me, we can pave the way."

Kitty hung her head. "As soon as America joins, however, people like you, people like me, won't be able to stay in France on American passports. We could be interned." Which also meant she'd have to abandon Edgar. It left her cold.

"Nope," Guinevère said in English. "Then we will all have to turn into chameleons and make our French teachers proud."

Kitty studied her. "What are you in this for? I mean *really*?"

The woman tilted her head and raised an eyebrow. "Hating those Nazi bastards isn't enough?"

Kitty laughed and shook her head.

Guinevère smiled briefly. "What about you? I can't believe that your entire socialite story is fake. You're too... authentic."

"You can't kid a kidder," Kitty said. Because Guinevère was

anything but working class either.

The woman smiled slyly. "No. You can't. So then, what's your reason?"

Guinevère had not answered Kitty's question, but she volunteered her answer anyway. "When I first moved to Europe, a friend of mine asked me whether I was doing it for love or money. I said, for love. And it's still love."

Guinevère narrowed her eyes. "For the same person?"

Kitty had to speak softly to control her emotions. "I lost people I loved to the regime. Two were killed... The others... I don't even know whether they are still alive. And one... well... if he doesn't survive this war..." She looked up. "I don't think I could go on, then."

Guinevère sighed and started to leave but turned back to her. "You're not doing this for love. I think it might be part of it. But I think you're doing it on principle."

Kitty frowned.

The American woman opened the door. "Everyone recognizes evil when they see it. That is, if they are not evil themselves. We're here to hunt down the animals."

5

NOVEMBER 1941

Paris, Nazi-Occupied France

November came with cold gusts of wind, and the leaves were nearly gone from the linden tree in her back garden when Kitty recalled Guinevère's words again.

Those first awful crackdowns were becoming the norm across France with reports of police brutality and merciless hunts directed against Jews. Daily, buses and police vehicles rolled into different districts and the thugs, who were meant to protect the population, broke down doors, arrested civilians, stormed into cafes and businesses and dragged their victims out. Nine times out of ten, the victims were Jewish, ratted on by neighbors, by collaborators, by people who'd been offended by a simple affront. Guinevère had been right. The animals had been turned loose and handed a license to inflict pain and misery.

Those arrested landed in the notorious headquarters at 84

Avenue Foch, which was a copy of Hotel Metropole in Vienna. Every incident made Kitty grit her teeth, made her blood boil, and steeled her determination to do all she could to destroy the Nazi regime.

The Germans had no qualms about advertising their activities either. After mock trials, the names of those sentenced, their ages, home addresses as well as their occupations were posted on the walls in both German and French. Bright orange posters hung outside the police station.

Bekanntmachung!

For spying, sentenced to execution and shot to death today!

Frau Blanche Josephine PAUGAN

Sentenced to prison. Sentenced to a concentration camp. Sentenced to hanging. Sentenced to execution. The latter two were the most frequent ends for the accused.

But violence fed violence, and secret police bred clandestine activities to resist them. It was an all too familiar cycle for Kitty. In Vienna, Edgar and she had been instruments in the O5. Whereas the resistance group's call letters appeared in chalk around the city, in Paris, Kitty discovered postal stamp-sized messages slapped onto walls and the posts of streetlamps. Their sources and the messages varied but all of them were calling on the population to resist. And as in Vienna, it seemed to be a mixed bag of politics and beliefs coming together to fight one vision: destroy the common enemy. Hunt down the animals.

The one thing that kept Kitty sane, that returned her to some semblance of humanity, were her rendezvous with Edgar. They did not meet in public; neither wanted that. But he also made no secret of having a mistress he called on regularly. It was not unusual, and therefore nobody questioned him. Regardless, they laid down one law: no messages, no supplies for the network, no discussions about their clandestine activities entered her little house. Unless he called to ask her to cook chicken fricassee. Then he was coming to share intelligence, and she had to check for bugs.

Sometimes Edgar would be gone for days or even weeks at a time, unable to visit her, although she received frequent messages with instructions for various operations.

On one routine visit to a pharmacist, as "Elizabeth Hennessy" picked up her "usual" bottle of vitamins the woman behind the counter presented Kitty with a secreted packet of henna and a small tube of toothpaste.

"It's a sample," she said of the latter, and put it into Kitty's bag.

Kitty anxiously muttered her thanks. Toothpaste messages came directly from Edgar and they were rare. So rare, they were like receiving notes from a secret admirer; whenever she got one, she was thrilled and embarrassed. Then the yearning for her husband would grow so strong that she felt sick to her stomach.

Back at the house, she hurriedly extracted the message from the tube. She read the sheet. It was the code they'd agreed upon regarding Oskar:

What was once lost has now been found.

Edgar had found her friend Oskar Liebherr. And she would have to face him; she would have to face the circumstances of his mother's death all over again.

Kitty's chest constricted as she recalled Judith Liebherr. The little woman with the big, brown eyes and the most generous heart had offered Kitty a sanctuary from the ultra-conservative, upper-crust Viennese elite. Judith had become a second mother to her, especially in the aftermath of the Anschluss when Kitty had become estranged from Edgar—before she knew he was spying for the British.

Kitty stared at the brief line of text for a long time, her tears and her shame rising. She'd played a part in Judith's murder at Hotel Metropole. And now she would have to beg Oskar Liebherr for something she could never give herself: forgiveness.

It took weeks for Edgar's call to come, and when it did, Kitty's heart raced with anticipation at the sound of his voice. Formal. A little solicitous, which was appropriate for someone having an affair.

"Madame Hennessy, I wonder whether you are free tonight? I'm in the mood for your chicken fricassee."

Kitty gripped the phone. He'd be coming over on official business. Probably to tell her where and how to meet Oskar. "I'd be happy to see you. And to cook."

"Would six o'clock suit you? I don't wish to impose."

"Six o'clock is just fine."

"Set the table for three," Edgar suddenly added.

Kitty frowned at herself in the mirror opposite. *Three?*

"I'm bringing a friend I'd like you to meet."

To announce this publicly was a risk. The central operators, who connected their calls, had a German standing over them, able to tap in and listen at any point. It was what necessitated their codes between one another. But why was he bringing Oskar to her? *Was* he bringing Oskar?

"Madame Hennessy?" Edgar sounded impatient. "There is a reason I secure extra rations for you. I'm in the mood for chicken fricassee and so is my friend."

"It would be my pleasure," she answered quickly. "I look forward to it."

She hung up, unnerved and anxious, and hugged herself when she conjured up the last time she'd seen Judith's son. Oskar had been a stunning man. A bit flamboyant in his coat-tails and the red roses stuck in his buttonholes. He sometimes pomaded his long wavy hair. He wore top hats. Kitty had adored him from the first moment, and loved watching him rule the roost at Der Keller, the Vienna nightclub he and his lover had established for an array of the city's subculture. At the memory of Artur's murder, her chest tightened.

Oskar and Artur.

Artur and Oskar.

Artur used to perform as Agnes at the underground cabaret. But on Kristallnacht, he had been brutally murdered by storm troopers. As police inspectors snapped photographs, Kitty had slowly approached the makeshift stage. She'd first identified the blond wig, then the red satin gown, and finally the bullet hole that had blown open Artur's head.

She remembered Oskar's expression as the police had stuffed him into the car. He was screaming—in French— warning her to leave the scene. But she had stayed.

That was when the Gestapo began asking questions about Kitty's association with Oskar and Artur. Two homosexuals. Both Jews. A double whammy, as far as the Nazis were concerned. And, those two factors alone made it an easy crime to pin on Oskar. On false charges, they sentenced him to a prison camp in Dachau. She found out much later how Edgar had helped him to escape certain death.

She was nervous all morning, brushed the house for bugs twice, and changed three times. She checked her freckles, re-did her makeup. Dressed for her role, she reviewed—as she did every day—her cover story. Every detail of it.

Just in case. Just in case.

At half past five, she paced up and down the sitting room, peeking out from behind the blackout curtains and onto the empty road. When a black Citroën pulled up, Kitty was immediately on alert. What was going on? Why was Edgar being so brash? So obvious?

Two uniformed officers got out. One was obviously Edgar. She recognized that gait from miles off. But the other? He was dressed in a Wehrmacht uniform, his face hidden beneath an officer's cap. Was it possible that Edgar was really bringing another German to her apartment for entertainment? Her heart leapt and her mind reeled out all the possibilities that might have led her to misinterpret her husband's information. Had he been caught and was being held hostage? Was he being forced to lead German secret police to her? Was she trapped?

The knock at the door was louder than usual. Whatever was about to unfold, it was too late for her to escape.

Edgar came inside, whipped off his cap and leaned in to peck her cheek but she was waiting for some kind of signal from him. Too quickly, Edgar indicated the man directly behind him.

"Madame Hennessy, let me introduce my guest. This is Sergeant Major Franz Vogels, an old friend of mine. We were in school together in Vienna."

Kitty froze as the second officer stepped up. His hair was white on the sides of his head. His angular face was sharp and rigid, like a battle-hardened soldier's. But those dark brown eyes were just like his mother's. She took a step forward, Oskar's name on her lips, but Edgar maneuvered between them as he handed her his coat.

"Sergeant Major Franz Vogels." Edgar firmly closed the door behind them. "This is Mrs. Elizabeth Hennessy."

Kitty hesitated, then extended her hand, and did not slip out of her disguise as Elizabeth. She looked down at the hard grip. Was this Oskar? His hand used to be warm and soft. She gazed up at him.

Edgar then signaled to her, asking: *Bugs?*

She lifted two fingers, glanced at Oskar. Everyone was pensive. Edgar scanned the street from behind the curtains, nodded at the two of them and Oskar slowly opened his arms.

"Kitty," he mouthed. His smile reached his eyes this time. They were filled with a mixture of joy and sorrow, and when he beckoned to her, she welcomed his embrace.

Shedding her Elizabeth Hennessy persona, she sobbed quietly against her old friend as Kitty Larsson.

When Kitty was composed once more, she led the two into the dining room and placed a serving dish of fragrant chicken between them on the table. She dished up three plates, passed out the bread, poured white wine, then took her seat next to Edgar. She grasped her husband's hand beneath the table, relieved that he was all right, and desperate to pull him to her, to have him as near as possible, but it was Oskar's story that she was to pay attention to.

As her friend sliced into his chicken, Edgar began that tale. She watched his profile, noticing the satisfied gleam in her husband's eye.

"It took me a long time, but I finally tracked him down." Edgar revealed. "He had a very good cover."

Kitty smiled uncertainly at her friend. "As a Wehrmacht officer?"

"That's Edgar's doing." Oskar patted his mouth with the napkin before continuing. "I was working for a book publisher, and according to my documents, I'm from Alsace, which explains my accented French."

"He is also a full-fledged Catholic," Edgar added.

Oskar nodded. "After Edgar's friend helped get me out of Dachau, they gave me French identity papers so that I could at least get to Paris. And the name of a French priest should anything happen. When the Germans occupied Paris, it was the first thing I did. He got me the job, my new birth certificate, integrated me into the community and by the time the local police were taking down our names, I was essentially a very proud and devout Catholic."

Kitty looked at him in amazement but then her thoughts darkened. "But if it was working so well, why are you here in the occupied zone again? Why didn't you stay where you were? If Edgar can find you, Oskar, then surely the Gestapo can as well?"

"I'm here to help some friends." His eyes darted to Edgar. "They are Jews."

Kitty dreaded what was coming next.

"I'm going to get them through the non-occupied zone and out of France. But there are so many, Kitty."

She grasped the stem of her wine glass, her sorrow and a sense of futility overwhelming her.

Oskar beckoned Edgar with his fork. "Show her."

Kitty released her husband's hand and he reached into his trouser pocket. He produced a small green ticket. "They began appearing this past spring."

She read the words printed on the ticket. It was a summons, signed by the Paris police commissioner, and instructed the recipient to present himself at seven in the morning on the date shown.

"And then?" Kitty asked, bracing herself. "They went there and then—"

"Anyone who went, vanished," Oskar said.

"Good Lord," Kitty muttered. "Those sons of..."

"We're guessing about four thousand Jewish refugees at least," Oskar continued. "All of them had fled Hitler's other occupied territories. The Parisian authorities rounded them up with these tickets and told them they were only verifying their status. A simple formality," he said bitterly. "But when they arrived, two of my friends, who were suspicious, watched as the authorities led the people into buses."

It was Vienna all over again. In the Thirties, German Jews had flooded the Austrian capital, fleeing Hitler's regime. After the Anschluss, they were herded into ghettoes within Vienna.

Kitty turned to Edgar. "Do you know where they are?"

"Loiret," he said. "About ninety kilometers south of Paris."

"Some people have managed to escape," Oskar said. "That's how we first heard of it. When Edgar found me... Well, he assured me he has a secure route."

Kitty grasped Edgar's hand again. "The escape line?"

Edgar squeezed back. "We're going to activate it, *Elizabeth*..." He looked at her pointedly. "And funnel them out. Oskar, too."

"I know what I have to do. But him? Dressed like that?" Kitty pointed to Oskar's uniform.

Edgar scratched his head. "This was only so I could get him here, to you. We needed a safe place to talk."

"Please excuse me." Oskar rose. "Where can I freshen up?"

Kitty directed him to the toilet and watched him walk out of the room. He had a limp; she had noticed it on the last day she'd laid eyes on him in Vienna.

"This is outrageous," she said, turning to her husband.

"I know, Kitty." Edgar suddenly leaned into her, and kissed her.

She lay her hands around his face, brushing every part of him with her fingertips, focusing on the fact that they were together. At least for a moment.

"I've missed you so much," he said. "It's getting harder to get away. Things are developing so quickly, I can hardly keep up."

"I heard about the reprisals." More so, she'd heard about the assassinations of German officials.

Edgar's jaw tensed. "I'm afraid, every single day."

"Is there something I should know?" She pulled away, anxious.

He tugged at his tunic collar. "I feel like I'm being watched. Maybe because of my relationship with you. But, this is why I put Oskar into that uniform. I made him take a train from the east, so that it looked legitimate when I met him. I told the office I was picking up an old friend on leave. There's also..."

She looked questioningly at him.

"Kendrick is no longer my handler, and my new one... Well. He doesn't seem to believe in 'good' Germans."

Chilled, she caressed Edgar's face again. Small lines had begun to form in his brow that did not go away even when he smiled. "I know you're trying to prove yourself, but promise you'll take your foot off the pedal a little?"

He nodded, but she knew he would not.

"By the way, when I was in Lyon, I caught wind of something you should know about." She shared her suspicions that the Foreign Office was planting female special operatives in the non-occupied zone. She hurried through the details. "What do you think?"

Her husband looked pensive. "I'll try to find out more. If London is even free to tell me, that is."

"But, Edgar, if I don't have to be reassigned anywhere else, I'd be happier. I like being where you are."

The door opened and Oskar strode back in, effectively covering up that earlier limp. He took his seat and something about his movements—careful, choreographed, the control he had over himself—made her sit up.

"Actually, Oskar, your disguise is perfect." She faced Edgar. "You had to put together documents for Vogels, right?"

Edgar narrowed his eyes. "Yes."

"Can you get all of them for him, under this Vogels name? All twenty or thirty that you officers need in order to move freely about?"

Oskar frowned. "What are you getting at, Kitty?"

"I'm thinking you ought to prepare for the performance of your lifetime, darling." She reached for his hand across the table. "Imagine how many people you can help if you can transport them in the open. For example, in my ambulance..."

6

DECEMBER 1941

Paris, Nazi-Occupied France

It was a few weeks before Oskar could return to Kitty's. Meanwhile, she was making plans at the American Hospital on how to smuggle out four refugees on the run.

The evening when Edgar returned with Oskar—disguised as Vogels again—Kitty had set the kitchen table in the back and cooked a vegetable stew. She was disappointed when Edgar announced that he could not stay.

"I've been summoned back to the office," Edgar explained. "I'll come later and hear about your plans."

Kitty kissed him goodbye and led Oskar into the kitchen. The back of the house felt more secluded. She served two heaped bowls of stew and broke off pieces of a stale baguette she'd rewarmed in a damp towel.

Oskar dipped his spoon into his bowl. "I'm glad we've got some time alone, Kitty. I didn't want to bring it up last time, but Edgar told me that you went to the Gestapo after they arrested me and my mother. That you demanded to see us. He said it was the second time you drew the authorities' attention."

Kitty embraced the familiar stab of grief. "After Artur's murder, yes. I shouldn't have done that. I feel it's my fault that Judith was tortured. My showing up likely provoked them even more."

Oskar placed a hand on hers. "It's not your fault. My mother could not withstand pain." He fanned his face and swallowed hard before continuing with a wavering smile. "What about Khan? Big Charlie? Bella?"

"Like you, the rest of the gang scattered. When the Gestapo took me in, Edgar involved the American consular. They got me to London. I went to Washington after that. I reported on the events in Vienna, the pogroms in particular. I told them what I saw, what I lived through. The brutalities on just about everyone. I also vented my frustrations with the immigration policies, especially on the blockade they put up to prevent Jews from getting visas."

"And has America taken any action? Raised the refugee quota? Anything?"

Kitty scoffed. "The administration talked only about obstacles. Not solutions. Now Congress is dealing with a Fifth Column. My dad says his opponents are fomenting fear in order to keep America out of the war."

"But how are we going to help anyone get out of France if nobody will take refugees?" Oskar sighed. He put his spoon down, his stew untouched. They were silent for a moment. "Edgar is taking a great risk exposing himself to me like this."

Kitty had thought the same. "I *begged* him to. He would normally not do it. And meeting you out in the open is not an option."

Oskar's expression hardened. "You said the last time we came that if he can find me—"

"So can the Gestapo," Kitty finished gently. "Then it's better this way. Better that Edgar found you first."

They ate in silence for a while before Kitty said, "Edgar tried to locate Khan and Big Charlie, too. The police got so close. The authorities found some ink and the papers we'd used to produce ration cards. I'm not sure whether they found any of the forged documents, but it was enough. A cellar in the Vienna Woods on the Ragatzes' property..."

She paused. How much did Oskar know? "Edgar's whole family was questioned."

Oskar squared himself. "Even his parents? They're Nazis, aren't they?"

She nodded.

"What about the mission I directed you to?"

"So you did know about the attempt to bomb the Gestapo HQ."

Oskar kept his eyes glued on her. "Was that what you were up to? All I knew was that I had to give you a message through that newspaper in the tavern."

Kitty grasped her wine glass tightly. She had said too much.

Oskar fell pensive again. He tapped his spoon on the side of the bowl and laid it down. "Has it ever occurred to you that a person who is prepared to betray his country would have no difficulty betraying the other side?"

"What do you mean?" she asked sharply.

Oskar shrugged. He broke off a piece of bread. "I'm not comfortable with Edgar."

This rankled Kitty. Neither Oskar nor anyone in the gang had ever been. "It doesn't seem you have a choice now, do you?"

A shadow passed over his face. "If you'd seen the things that I have, witnessed how easy it is to turn someone with torture, to draw out someone's treacherous side with threats and fear—"

"I have," Kitty bit back. "I have. Edgar nearly sacrificed my love for him—"

"Nearly. But not entirely." Oskar leaned back and lifted his hands. "Sorry. Kitty, I'm really sorry. I've become quite the suspicious little bitch, I know. Forgive me."

"Edgar risked his life to reveal himself to me. Like he did to you," she stressed.

She crossed her arms, but her anger simmered. It had grown dark outside. A few dried leaves from the linden tree scampered silently across the small terrace. "Help me with the blackout boards, will you?"

Oskar rose quickly and helped her to seal up the windows.

"I wonder whether the rest of the gang are still working," she said as he drew the curtains closed in the sitting room.

"Khan and Big Charlie?" He frowned a little. "If they have found a way to do so as free men, yes. I can't believe either of them would sit passively hoping for the end of the war. If I know them—"

"And you do." She was trying to compensate for the sharpness earlier. "You knew them better than me."

"You know them better now. You were the ones who brought my ideas to fruition. Mine and Artur's." Oskar's face fell. "Anyway, I'd be willing to bet that those two are out there wreaking havoc on the Nazis."

He glided over to her and brushed a hand over her hair and face. "You look different, Kitty. The red hair. The freckles. You've grown into our lioness."

She took his hand and kissed the palm. "You always believed in me. Believe in my trust in Edgar."

Oskar closed his eyes briefly and steered her back into the kitchen, where she topped off their bowls with warm stew. It was not like Oskar to avoid a truce. Something was really bothering him.

"Can you tell me what happened in Dachau? How you got that limp?"

He cleared his throat. "They broke my leg, and it never healed properly."

"The guards?"

Oskar's gaze turned stony. "It'd be easier to accept if it had been the *verdammte* Nazis. But it wasn't. It was a gang of inmates. We had pink triangles, all of us. They were people... people who, I thought, were like me. But I was the fresh meat."

Kitty stared at him, hating what he was suggesting. "*Verdammt.* Oskar, I'm so sorry."

She stood up and went to him, pulling him against her. Oskar's mistrust of Edgar made sense. How could he believe in anyone any longer?

He quickly swiped at his eyes and pulled away. "It's no use wallowing, Kitty. I need to move on. I need to get out of France."

After cleaning up the kitchen, they moved into the sitting room. It was nearly midnight when they finished welding together a good plan to get him and four others out of the country. Two men, a sister of one and her young daughter would be their companions. Kitty would transport them by ambulance from the country to the nearest train station and lead them to the first safe house along the escape line.

"The plan is nearly perfect," Kitty declared. The bottle of wine was empty.

For the third time, Kitty peeked from behind the blackout curtain out onto the dark street, wondering what was keeping Edgar so long. Just then, the black Citroën pulled up to the curb, rolled to a stop and the headlights went out. Kitty squinted at the dark shape in the car and jumped when music began playing. It was jazz. Ella Fitzgerald.

Oskar sidled over to her from the phonograph. "A dance, darling?"

She turned her attention to the car again. "What is he doing out there?"

Oskar peered over her shoulder. "Who?"

"Edgar."

"Are you sure it's Edgar?" he asked ominously.

"Yes, of course it's him. But what is he waiting for?"

Suddenly, the car door opened and Edgar, his cap under his arm, came slowly up the walk. She hurried to the foyer and let him in.

"You two shouldn't be peeking outside," Edgar muttered as she closed the door sharply behind him.

Kitty moved to him and folded her arms. "What's wrong?"

"Is it that obvious?" he asked.

She dropped her arms at the hangdog expression. "Edgar?"

"Who died?" Oskar joked drily.

Edgar's jaw clenched before he answered. "So far? Over a thousand Americans."

"What?" Kitty stared at him. "What happened?"

Oskar stepped away and Edgar looked mournful. "The Japanese attacked the navy air base in Hawaii."

"No," Kitty whispered hoarsely. "On American soil?" Minnesota was thousands of miles away from Hawaii. But her father would be headed to D.C. if he was not already there. What if the attacks were not limited to the Pacific? What if...

Kitty tore away from Edgar as if he were the menace. "When? When did this happen?"

He clutched his cap against him. "Early this morning local time. There was an air raid. Right after the church services. You can imagine... They destroyed ships. Airplanes. Manned. Unmanned..."

"*Verdammte Scheiße*," Oskar whispered.

"My family!" she sobbed and spun toward the telephone. "I need to call my family!"

But Edgar stepped in front of her. "You can't do that, darling. Claudette and the Senator don't even know you're in Paris. You're going to have to wait until you get into Spain. Or when you're in England. But you can't call now."

England? She protested, but Edgar squeezed her arms, his eyes piercing her.

"You are Elizabeth Hennessy. Now, more than ever, you are not allowed to forget that."

"But this means..." Kitty began. "This means we'll declare war. America will declare—"

"On Japan to start with," Edgar agreed.

Oskar shot her a grim look. "They'll join the Allies in all the theaters after this."

"I'm setting the escape procedure in motion," Edgar interrupted, urgent now. "For both of you."

Kitty frowned. "I don't understand."

"Kitty, you do understand."

Edgar pulled her into an embrace. This time, she allowed him. It was just as Guinevère had warned her. Her time was up. She would no longer be safe running around as some innocent socialite-cum-volunteer.

"What about my friends?" Oskar looked dejected. "We just put our plans together."

Edgar stiffened and Kitty drew away.

"We can't, Oskar," he said. "You both should leave as soon as possible. Any delay will be too dangerous."

"I'll decide what's too great of a risk for me," Kitty objected. He had to help them. They had a good plan. "At least Oskar's friends. And then we can figure out how to bring the rest."

"The rest?" Edgar sighed, brushing a hand over his head. "What were you hoping to do?"

"If you can train Oskar on his cover story. Make him into a

convincing Wehrmacht officer. An officer on rehabilitative leave. Finish his cover story. Make him believable."

"Yes," Oskar pressed. "Please."

Edgar strode away from them, then spun to face them, but said nothing.

"Listen, I'm still Elizabeth," Kitty hurried. "I'll take Oskar and the group through the non-occupied zone," Kitty said. "And then I'll find a place in southern France to stay until you can get to me."

"No." Edgar pointed at them both. "If you're going to do this, you're returning to England. Take Oskar to Barcelona first, to the British consulate, tell them he's an asylum seeker but he has information for the Foreign Office." He was all business now. He strode back to Kitty and grasped her shoulders. "I want him to go to Kendrick. You hear that, Oskar? You're to see Colonel Thomas Kendrick in England. He'll know to expect you."

But Oskar looked dubious. "I'd rather go to America, Edgar."

Kitty was worried about something else entirely. "You can't mean that, Edgar. Me? Go to England? I'll never see you again. I could go to southern France, though."

Oskar backed away. "This is a lot, *Liebling*. I'm going to give you two some privacy, and help myself to some of that ersatz coffee you have in the back."

Kitty watched him for a second before whirling back to Edgar. Surely he had to have a plan B. But the grim set of his mouth told her he did not.

She cupped his face in her hands. "Did you speak to Kendrick? About what I told you? Is this why?"

"London won't tell me anything. But Kendrick did say that if you ever have to leave Paris, you should call him." He pinched his nose with his thumb and forefinger. "I know what the regime intends to do when America declares war. You will no longer have the clout, not even as a senator's daughter. And if they discover you've been parading about—my ex-wife, Kitty Larsson Ragatz—in disguise as my lover... They won't hang me, Kitty. They will shoot me. On sight."

She tightened her grip on him, but he was right. Yet, if she left now, the Foreign Office would never send her back to work with him again. Theirs was a one-off exemption; as soon as she left Paris, she would lose access to her husband. By Edgar's expression, she knew he was aware of it, too.

Tears welled as she peppered his face with tender kisses. It was never enough. Their time together was never enough.

His voice was hoarse. "Darling..."

"I don't think I could bear it," she whispered against his chest.

He made her look at him. "Don't underestimate yourself."

Kitty spoke rapidly, protesting: "They'll never take me. Look how unperceptive I was in Vienna, and I was sleeping in the same bed with you. I am too blind. Too rash when I get emotional."

"Hey," Edgar said. "Look at me. That's simply not true. You've learned your lesson. I watched you, at the Gestapo head-quarters a few months ago. When I sent you to Lyon with the airman. Even with Oskar a few weeks ago, when he first appeared, you didn't even flinch."

Kitty blew softly. "You have no idea. My heart was hammering when I saw your 'companion'. I didn't recognize Oskar at first. Not even Oskar. Right before my very eyes."

Edgar tilted her head so they would see eye-to-eye. "Kitty, you didn't even know about the game. You didn't know there was one being played. You landed right in the middle of it. But now you do. Now you know not only what the stakes are, but what the rules are. Hear Kendrick out. You can always decide against it."

"I don't have to decide anything right now."

He stroked her face. "No, you don't have to decide anything right now."

She leaned against him again, wishing he was correct. But America was under attack. She had much to decide now. "A thousand Americans dead."

Behind her, in the kitchen, her friend was waiting. He had to be as devastated as she that their plan was not going to work. Not like this. But she could come back. She could find out what this Guinevère was doing. And she owed her friends to give it her all. Now was not the time to shy away. At least for Judith. At the very least for Judith.

"Edgar," she pleaded. "Let me take his friends. We won't even be leaving them stranded in Spain. They will get visas for Portugal."

Edgar was shaking his head but she gripped his arms.

Slowly, he raised his palms in the air. "All right. I'll do it. But Kitty..." His tone raised goosebumps on her arms. "There's something you need to know."

7

DECEMBER 1941

Marseilles, Non-Occupied France

Traveling by train with Oskar as a German officer attracted the kinds of stares Kitty had expected: looks of disgust directed at her when she spoke in English to the officer on the platform next to her; looks of fear and loathing at the sight of Oskar's uniform. His presence sucked the air out of the corridor while they sought their carriage in first class.

Edgar had prepared him well for the officer's role, hammering in the etiquette, the mannerisms, the dangers of slipping up. It had taken nearly a week, and Edgar had made sure that Kitty drilled Oskar on his entire identity. Together, they invented their love story, how Elizabeth and Franz Vogels had met, where they had fallen in love, and why they were now traveling to the non-occupied zone. It was an enormous amount of work for the short trip from Paris to Lyon. Because as soon as they crossed the demarcation line, Oskar would have to transform himself back into a French national to avoid harassment from the French.

"It's an awful and macabre game of dress-up and make-believe," Kitty remarked.

"Darling," Oskar whispered close to her ear, "I've been playing make-believe all of my life. To be honest, this is the first time I've felt like I might have some power over my own fate."

When they arrived at their compartment, four other people sat in the padded seats: Oskar's four friends, smuggled to the train by Zara with the help of two railway workers.

Kitty knew the group only by the names on their forged identity cards: Jean-Paul, a man in dark-framed glasses and whom Kitty secretly referred to as "Professor," was sitting across from her. Next to Professor was Leopold, a middle-aged man who wore a red scarf and had a large mole on his right cheek. His black beret was tilted toward a little girl on his right. In real life, she was Jean-Paul's eight-year-old niece, Anna. Today, however, she and her mother Hélène were related to Sergeant Major Franz Vogels. Hélène sat next to Kitty at the window. She and Anna had left Germany when Hélène's husband passed away and returned to her native France. Her daughter was, therefore, bilingual, and this provided the group a great advantage.

Nobody spoke as the train pulled out of Paris, and all the way to the demarcation line. There was no need to. They had rehearsed, practiced, and prepared for the border control for hours before they'd left. When they halted for that check, all eyes shifted to Oskar and Kitty.

Two German guards approached their carriage. Kitty had earlier instructed that, should the procedure appear to go awry, liable to create trouble for any—or all—of the four Jewish companions with them, Oskar would have to interfere as an authority figure.

Closest to the corridor, his eye was on the German making

his way toward them. The official slid the door open and snapped a salute to Oskar.

"Sergeant Major Vogels," he barked after examining Oskar's initial identification card. "With all due respect, may we check your remaining documents?"

Oskar nodded stiffly. "*Natürlich.*"

Edgar had warned him not to ask whether there was a problem. The French did not want Germans in the non-occupied zone. It would be routine for the German to stall someone like Vogels.

Instead, Oskar reached into his coat pocket and withdrew the thick leather booklet containing nearly twenty different documents. He handed it over with a confident nod.

It had been a painstaking process for Edgar to arrange the papers. Some were very poor forgeries, Edgar had warned. They'd not had a lot of time to prepare after America declared war on Germany.

As the guard flipped open the book, Oskar casually indicated Kitty, Hélène and her daughter. "These are my companions." He passed their documents over to the guard. Leopold and Professor, meanwhile, also held theirs at the ready.

Kitty brushed Oskar's arm possessively. The guard rifled through Oskar's thick book first, but examined Kitty's American passport more closely. Oskar seemed about to say something, but Kitty gently squeezed his arm. This was not a problem. She would pass through. Many Americans were now leaving the occupied zone. Oskar should save any indignation or interference for their fleeing companions.

The guard now looked at the other documents in his hand and peered at Hélène and Anna. "You're from Stuttgart? My mother is from there."

Kitty's blood chilled.

Oskar smiled pensively and leaned over to Anna, placing a hand on her knee just as Edgar had choreographed. "*Liebling,* tell the guard what you learned to recite for the Führer." He nodded at the German. "My niece here was personally invited to one of the Führer's last visits."

Anna looked doubtful, her eyes flitting to her mother. Kitty prayed silently that she would do as they had taught her. To her relief, the girl took in a breath and, with wide eyes turned her head to the guard.

With practiced German, Anna recited, "I know you well, and love you as I do my father and mother. I will always be obedient to you as I am to my father and mother. And when I am bigger, I will help you, as my father and mother do, and you will be proud of me, as my father and mother are!"

Hélène's hand was shaking in her lap and Kitty quickly covered it up with her own, beaming at her then the child. "You must be so proud."

The German guard thrust their documents back at Oskar, but his eyes were on Kitty. "Madame, the attack on your country is most unfortunate," he said in English. "I really did enjoy America when I visited it."

Kitty inclined her head, genuinely surprised. "*Danke.*"

He clicked his tongue, his light gray eyes cold. "Perhaps, when Germany has occupied all of Europe, we will have victory over America. Then I shall move to California permanently."

Without waiting for Kitty's response, he turned his attention to the two men. "*Papiere!*"

Oskar indicated the two men, his voice an octave lower and smooth. "We've been talking to them this whole way. I found nothing suspicious."

The guard glanced at him, then handed Jean-Paul and Leopold back their documents.

Leopold had a slight grin on his face. "We've been talking to Sergeant Major Vogels here as well. He seems to be in order, too."

Kitty's fake smile melted but Oskar chuckled and flashed a grin at the two Jewish men.

"It's all right, it's all right," he assured the guard, and clapped Leopold on the knee. "That was amusing."

The official finally left and Kitty was holding her breath just as everyone else was. Moments later, the train proceeded over the demarcation line.

Everyone moved swiftly. Kitty bent down and retrieved the bag of civilian clothes, and pressed them into Oskar's hand just as Hélène pulled down the shade over their window. Oskar leapt up, and unbuttoned his uniform jacket, slipped off the boots and pulled down his trousers. Jean-Paul held out a fresh pair of French-made trousers from the bag. Leopold was helping him into a suit jacket. Oskar brushed himself off as Kitty bundled the German uniform up and Hélène handed Oskar his original French documents.

Everyone resettled in their seats, the German uniform safely tucked away, the German documents with them. Oskar cleared his throat, put on a hat and settled back into his seat.

By the time the French gendarmes were doing their own border control, all six passengers in the compartment were quiet. They were out of occupied territory, but there was a long way to go before they were out from beneath the regime's heel.

First, the group had to get to a safe house in Marseilles. What would happen after that, Kitty did not know. This was the other danger: their reliance on an invisible system run by strangers. Not all the French people were thrilled with Allied interferences, but the escape route Kitty was using was all they had. It was like free-falling in the hopes that someone would be there to catch them, and that those catching them would *not* be collaborators.

They got off at Gare Saint-Charles in Marseilles and

walked the long steps down to the Boulevard Flammarion. Although they could not see the Mediterranean, the air was filled with the smells and scents of a coastal city. Bicycles were lined up along one side of the road. A woman sold crêpes and hot coffee from a pull cart. Kitty fished out her sunglasses, adjusted her hat and took the lead into the city.

Their instructions were to go to Café de la Place near the market and wait there for further instructions. As they neared the sea, the port was blocked by industrial installations. Large ships loomed on the horizon. The Professor and Leopold, followed by Hélène and Anna, tailed behind. Kitty was leading them past the first market stalls when the sight of a woman in a navy-blue coat made her freeze.

Oskar spun to her with a questioning look, but Kitty was staring straight at her aunt Julia.

From beneath the woman's coat peeked out a chartreuse and black skirt. Her dark hair was streaked with white now, but there was no doubt it was her. Kitty's mother's sister was chatting to another very well-dressed Frenchwoman.

"Please give me a moment," Kitty whispered to Oskar.

Their four companions lingered in the background, but Hélène's frightened look made Kitty flash her an assuring smile. The woman turned into a shop and pulled Anna in with her, darting a look out the window.

Oskar muttered, "We shouldn't be late."

"Pretend to be browsing. I just need a second."

Kitty adjusted her sunglasses and hat, then sidled over to a nearby stand selling onions and cabbages. Next to her, Aunt Julia was choosing carrots and chatting away.

"I'm not sure if there is a market for any artist right *now*, but what I can do is offer to write some of my contacts and see whether anyone would be looking for such a piece outside of France. Oh, Adèle! It would be such a shame if you were to get rid of it."

"What else am I to do?" the woman named Adèle replied. "After Pierre's—

"Well, we're all in a bind, aren't we?" Aunt Julia tutted.

"May I help you, mademoiselle?" the vendor asked Kitty.

"Just browsing," she said in her East Coast accent.

She stepped right next to her aunt as the two women continued chatting about the painting.

"May I dare ask?" Kitty asked the woman called Adèle in English. "Which artist are you looking to sell?"

Aunt Julia narrowed her eyes at her. Kitty wanted to fling her arms around her, to hug her and tell her how very glad she was that her aunt had gotten out of Paris. But Kitty could not possibly break her cover. Not here.

"You are an American?" Adèle cried gleefully. "You collect paintings?"

"May I ask who you are?" Aunt Julia said, halting Adèle.

"Excuse me for eavesdropping." Kitty offered her hand to Adèle first, her heart pounding as her aunt limply took it next. "I'm Elizabeth Hennessy."

Adèle gazed at Elizabeth: from the hat and sunglasses, to the fur stole and her American shoes. "How wonderful."

Aunt Julia looked more suspicious now. She blinked at Kitty and frowned. "Do I know you from somewhere?"

"You might," Kitty said coyly, tipping her head a little lower. "My husband, the late Charles Hennessy? He was a big supporter of the arts back in New York."

Aunt Julia frowned at her. "Never heard of him."

"And you, dear?" Adèle was solicitous. "Are you interested in the earlier works of Raoul Dufy?"

Kitty smiled at Adèle. "I'm afraid I am just passing through." She glanced at an anxious Oskar. Behind him, Leopold was watching warily. Returning her attention to Aunt Julia again, Kitty hurried, "I will be back in France sometime soon. Do you have a gallery? That is, if you are the broker?"

"I had a gallery. In Paris." Aunt Julia folded her arms, her basket dangling from the crook of her elbow. Her eyes bore behind Kitty's sunglasses. "You remind me of someone."

Kitty ducked her head. She had to go. Now.

"Madame Hennessy," Oskar called behind her. "*Liebling*, do you mind?"

Kitty jerked at the German and so did the other two women.

"I must go," Kitty hurried. "Where might I find you if I were interested?"

"Julia," Adèle said sharply, "I think I've changed my mind. I won't be selling after all."

But Aunt Julia was not listening. Her eyes slid between Kitty and Oskar and back to Kitty. "I don't have a gallery. But you can ask for me."

"And the name?" Kitty pressed, remembering to ask, or she'd really give herself away.

Her aunt narrowed her eyes. "Madame Julia Allard."

Kitty turned aside. "I hope to see you again very soon."

When she returned to Oskar, he muttered, "I'm so sorry. What the hell was that about anyway?"

She did not reply. She had an idea. A very good idea. If she was going to come back to France, to do something like Guinevère was doing and rouse up resistance, then she already had a good contact she could begin with.

And Marseilles was absolutely reachable for Edgar.

A woman of few words received the six of them at the cafe in Marseilles and gestured for them to follow her. On a quiet street, she directed Kitty to a Dr. Reboul and his wife in Rue Roux de Brignoles.

"It is near the Palace of Justice," she said and left them.

When they arrived, a middle-aged couple ushered all six of

them to various rooms located in the lavish apartment building. Afterwards, Kitty met with the couple in private.

Dr. Reboul was a genteel man with a dark handlebar mustache. His wife was graceful and gracious with small, soft hands. When Kitty discreetly asked the doctor whether the escape line was safe, he assured her that he was the least suspected man in Marseilles.

Unsure about what he meant, Kitty asked warily, "What kind of doctor are you?"

"The kind who knows everyone's secrets. Especially from those who would lose a lot of influence if those secrets were aired out."

Kitty could appreciate that very much and she decided to trust him.

"There's something I need to speak to you about," she said as he poured her a cup of coffee. "I've been informed that not everyone along the route is... how should I put this delicately? They are not all doing this for a noble cause, not involved because it's the right thing to do, but because it is lucrative."

Dr. Reboul replaced the coffee back onto the tray and turned to her, his chin pressed in against his chest. "It's a war, Madame Hennessy. One of the least noble activities in the world. But I take it you mean they are risking their lives because of the generous sum they receive for each airman they safely see through?"

Kitty flushed.

He sighed and slowly sat down. "This is true."

Her heart fell. Edgar had been right to warn her.

"I assure you, madame, I am not one of them. But why do you ask?"

"We want to send through... other types of people. With little monetary reward. In comparison, that is."

He held her look. "Your friends here, do they at least have visas?"

Kitty blinked. "They will get them."

He pushed himself from the table. "I'll make you a list of people I know that you can trust. And you tell them that I sent you. You also tell them that if there is anyone they suspect would turn Jews in for money to any authorities, they are off the line. My orders. Is that clear?"

Kitty smiled cautiously. "Absolutely clear. I'm so grateful."

The next morning, he quizzed her on the three people and their addresses until she had them all correct. Then he shared the phrases that would open their doors.

Kitty grasped his hand, her heart swelling with admiration. "I won't forget this. Ever."

Later, she, Oskar and the others boarded the train again, and Kitty instructed the group about their next stop. "Oskar and I will check into our hotel in the town. You four are to make your way by bus to Françoise's house. This is where you will wait until we are directed further. I'll visit her tomorrow to see how you are all doing."

A few hours later, she and Oskar checked into a small hotel in the center of Perpignan. Over dinner, which they had served in their suite, the two of them finally had time to catch up in peace.

Oskar pushed the last slice of potato through the thin sauce on his plate. "So, you and Edgar, how are you? This happened all so fast, you hardly had a moment alone."

"It wouldn't be the first time we parted without a proper goodbye," Kitty said miserably. It hurt to even think of him.

"What do you mean?"

"We met in Tokyo in the spring of thirty-seven. We were supposed to motor down to the sea, and our lives were interrupted. I couldn't even see him off. That's why I went to Vienna."

Oskar smiled. "To get your goodbye kiss."

"Something like that," she scoffed.

"You two have been through a lot."

Kitty nodded ruefully. "I nearly divorced him because I thought he had no scruples."

"I nearly left Artur once," Oskar said quietly.

"You did?"

Oskar pushed his chair away, picked up the bottle and their glasses, then offered his hand. He went to the sofa. She took the armchair across from him.

"It was in Paris," he said, pouring them each another glass of wine. "He and Leopold—"

"Wait, you all knew each other before?"

Oskar nodded. "He and Leopold were being very secretive and shady. I was certain the two were having an affair. So, I spent a lot of energy trying to catch them at it. Well, after one show, Artur had an encore performance as Agnes..."

"He had such a beautiful voice."

"Yes, he did." Oskar sighed. "Anyway, he took off with Leopold afterwards. I followed. All the way to the Eiffel Tower. The park was alight with hundreds of candles. It was my thirtieth birthday and the two of them had arranged all those candles to form the number thirty. They had planned to take me up the tower; Jean-Paul was supposed to bring me, but he'd lost track of me. All Artur was doing was trying to surprise me. I never doubted him again."

"Huh," Kitty said.

Oskar looked at her and brushed a hair from his forehead. His eyes revealed regret. "What I said to you about Edgar and trust? I was wrong, Kitty."

She inhaled sharply. "Thank you."

"Love hurts no matter what. But always trust yourself. Trust your instincts."

"I thought I could, but I'm not sure anymore."

"You can, *Elizabeth*." He grinned slyly at her, then his eyes went warm—that old warmth she'd yearned for, that old warmth she remembered of Judith, too.

"Kitty, you have a huge heart but sometimes you bowl right over everyone in your determination to set things straight." Oskar's eyes twinkled mischievously. "Besides, I haven't seen passion like that in a couple since Mary Pickford and Douglas Fairbanks. You are both very brave. Very, very brave."

Kitty laughed sadly, thinking of how he'd been in Dachau. "It's what we have to do. A small sacrifice."

"You forget that I was desperately in love, too. I know the pain of not being able to be who you are, what you are, in the open."

Kitty moved to the sofa and dropped next to him. He watched her carefully as she set down her glass, turned to him and took him into her arms. Oskar leaned into her. She held him.

They dozed like that, their fragile selves pressed up against one another.

8

DECEMBER 1941

Perpignan, Non-Occupied France

The following morning, Kitty dressed in a wool suit, pinned back her red hair, slipped in the green contacts, and thus into Elizabeth's persona.

She left Oskar at the hotel and took the bus to Port-Vendres, getting off at the stop just before the town. As promised, she would check in on Oskar's four friends at the farm run by a woman called Françoise.

She walked down a lane, beneath mostly-bare oak trees with acorns scattered about on the road, and followed it to the sprawling Bastide ahead. Kitty straightened her wool coat before knocking on the white-painted door. A very large red tomcat sprang onto the stoop and meowed, winding his way around her ankles.

A woman, white-haired with a beautiful face of fine wrinkles, high cheekbones, and bright green eyes, opened the door to her.

"I'm Madame Hennessy," Kitty said and spoke the code Dr. Reboul had given her. "I'm looking for the man who makes cognac."

"There is no man. It's a feminine touch that makes my brand renowned," the woman replied correctly. She stuck her hand out to Kitty. "I'm Françoise."

"Elizabeth."

Kitty followed her inside, into a tidy, airy home with stone walls and a large fireplace in the kitchen that opened on the other side into the living room. She offered Kitty coffee and then poured a generous shot of cognac with a mischievous smile.

"To hell if the Nazis get their hands on my best years," she winked. "So, I drink a little every chance I have."

"Is that a lot, then?" Kitty smiled.

The woman gave her a thin smile and tipped her head. "Quite."

"How are the... mice?"

"The four mice are just fine. They're comfortable in the haystack." Françoise looked at the red tomcat. "Old Gingembre here has been a comfort for the little one. Otherwise, no other cats prowling about."

Kitty understood the reference to the coast being clear. "How long then before we can get a guide to take us over the border?"

"Two, three days at most."

"We'll inform our concierge the day after tomorrow that we'll be taking a day-trip to the Pyrenees."

Françoise pushed herself up and opened a drawer at the hutch before returning with a map. "Tell the concierge you're going to Banyuls. It's a popular spot for hiking the foothills. You'll take the bus there. Go to the post office and ask for René. He'll pick you up and take you to the safe house. It is where you will wait for the rest of your group. We'll get the others to you over the next few days."

"That's good," Kitty said. She cupped her mug, the fumes from the cognac warm and fragrant. "It's gotten very chilly."

Françoise tipped her head toward the window. "I'll make sure they're dressed for it."

"In case our guide doesn't show up..."

"The people there have maps for you. It's a climb. It could be dangerous for the child, so make sure she has layers. I'll pack extras of whatever I can. But it's rare for a guide not to show up. I'm happy to say that I've had over two dozen airmen pass through my house since I started."

Kitty balked. "That's a lot."

"Yes."

They raised their glasses to France then to America.

Kitty stroked the cat, who now sat next to her chair. "I spoke with Dr. Reboul in Marseilles."

Françoise smiled warmly. "How is the good man?"

"He is well. He told me that you are his most trusted person."

The woman's cheeks turned a soft shade of pink.

Kitty shared her request about vetting out the members of the escape line. "Our concern is whether everyone is open to Jews. If not, they're out of the network completely. Is that clear?"

"I don't believe you're going to find anyone here against that idea. We are loyal to the Free French and General de Gaulle. It's the way we can spit on Pétain without getting shot."

Kitty raised an eyebrow and Françoise waved a dismissive hand.

"You understand what I mean by that. But you're right to take precautions. I will take this upon myself and make sure that the people on my end of the line do the same."

"Good."

Not every Jew she and Oskar were hoping to help could be escorted over the demarcation line with a disguised Wehrmacht officer in tow. But if she could let Edgar know it was safe, he would see to it the network assisted more refugees out of France.

That day, Kitty and Oskar made two more stops to meet with safe house organizers along the line and confirmed the same: the route would be opening up to help Jews flee the country. Either they were in, and set fair prices, or they would be cut out.

The following day, they went to the concierge and explained their plans for hiking near Banyuls in the Pyrenees. They abandoned their luggage in the room, hid money on themselves and struck out with only their backpacks, and a few spare items of clothing.

They found René, a goat herder with a rather large family. Kitty and Oskar dressed into more sensible, local clothing, including heavy wool jackets, scarves, mittens and caps, then René's eldest son led Kitty and Oskar to a shepherd's hut in the foothills of the Pyrenees.

They expected Jean-Paul, Leopold, Hélène and Anna to join them soon afterwards. In fact, Kitty was hoping that they would make it to Barcelona just before Christmas, but when the weather turned bad and a storm raged all night outside, Oskar and Kitty became anxious about whether they would get out at all. It took nearly five days before the other four arrived at the hut with provisions and more clothing and it was another two days before their guide showed up.

He introduced himself as Xavier. He was from northern Spain and shorter than Kitty, had a balding head beneath his country cap, and dark, arched eyebrows, as if they had been penciled on with coal. He appeared perpetually surprised but proved very competent.

In French, he explained that he would get them over the

border then drive them to the next big town, where they would catch a train to Barcelona.

The hike was strenuous but not unpleasant as the sky was bright blue and the sun shone warm, melting the snow enough so that they could make snowballs. Oskar and Anna started it, and Kitty quickly joined in. Soon, everyone except Xavier was laughing and playing, involved in the battle. Their guide patiently watched from a distance, as if he knew that this was the kind of simple abandon none of them had been able to feel in days, if not years.

The landscape was beautiful. On the south side of the mountains, they descended into Spain over sage-green brush, surrounded by red earth. The snow had only sugar-coated the highest peaks here.

Xavier led them to a small truck hidden at the bottom of a path. They climbed in and motored down the side roads to avoid the risk of being seen or stopped.

In the next town, their guide gave them specific instructions and Kitty found the rail workers who were to help them. The group had just been smuggled onto a grain car when the Spanish authorities showed up at the train station and started randomly questioning passengers. Hiding behind the door of the wagon, Kitty watched through the crack.

"What are they doing?" Oskar whispered behind her.

"I think they're pulling anyone out who doesn't have entry papers," Kitty muttered.

"Do we happen to have anything like that? Fake ones, even?" Oskar asked.

"Nope."

"Great," Oskar whispered.

Kitty shuffled away from the door. "Let's just try and relax."

At the sound of barking dogs, the group looked at her in disbelief, but when the train jerked forward and began rolling along the tracks, Oskar and his friends released a muffled cheer. She grasped each of her companions' hands.

"We're going to make it," Kitty assured them. "Barcelona first, then we're on our way to the free world."

Barcelona's palm trees were draped in fog. Spanish national troops milled about in the city's cafes and along the broad avenues. Oskar purchased two coffees and two pieces of cake from a street vendor and handed Kitty one of the cups.

"What will become of me if England doesn't accept me?" Oskar asked as they reached the British consulate.

He let the policemen check their identity papers and Kitty showed her emergency certificate. The policemen directed them to the consul's office. She and Oskar stopped at the door.

"They will have to walk over my dead body before they leave you in the lurch. I promise, everything will be fine. You have plenty to offer," Kitty insisted.

"Like what?" Oskar asked. "What do I have to offer?"

"The Foreign Office could use your Parisian contacts sympathetic to the cause. The details you know about the Jews' plight, for example."

Oskar patted her shoulder. "All right. Let's get you back in touch with your people, first."

The sadness was instant. Her people had included Edgar, but if she went through with this, she would likely not see him again for as long as the war was on. Sensing her hesitation, Oskar stepped forward and rapped on the office door.

The chief met with her alone, and after a call to the Foreign Office, confirmed that she could be put onto a submarine from Gibraltar to England. Because they would need more time with Oskar, Kitty said she would return for him. She had another stop to make.

At the American consulate, Kitty asked the foreign officer to notify her brother Nils in London and tell him where she was, then requested they put a call in to Minnesota. She checked the calendar. She'd lost track of the days, and was glad to see it was Saturday. There was a greater likelihood that her dad was at home. He answered the phone.

"Kitty? Is that really you?"

In the background, her mother repeated the question excitedly.

"I'm in Barcelona," Kitty told them. "How are you all? What news do you have?"

"Roosevelt declared war, Kit. It's time to come home."

Kitty winced. "Dad, you tell me that every time we talk. You know I can't do that. I'm on my way to London, though. I'll be staying with Nils and Rose, so I'll be safe."

Suddenly, Claudette's shrill voice came through on the line, her mother already talking before she had the phone to her ear. "London still has air raids all the time. Nils told us so."

Kitty braced herself for the stinging guilt that followed when she had to lie to her parents. "Maman, I'll be fine."

Claudette made a smacking noise, then Kitty heard Sam asking for the phone. His voice came over the static.

"Hey, Kit. Are you giving them hell over there?"

"I'm doing fine. And you, Dr. Larsson?"

The increasing static was making it difficult to hear her baby brother. She had to press the phone hard against her ear.

"The hospital's a mess. Lots of us doctors are signing up. You've heard, haven't you? We're in the war, now. What did you say you're doing over there?"

She hadn't. "I've been volunteering at a hospital, Sam. You'd be proud of me. I'm taking this all to heart. Maman? Dad? If you can hear me, I'm out of danger."

"I'm taking it to heart, too," Sam shouted back into the line.

Kitty had a sinking feeling. "You're not joining up, are you? You just said the hospital won't have enough staff."

"I'm a doctor. Our boys will need me. Of course I'm joining up."

"Of course," she repeated quietly. Sam always did the right thing. And if Nils and she were already involved one way or another, then what would stop Sam from serving his country? She looked up and blinked back her anxiety.

"Kitty, we've got to do everything we have to do right now. This is about liberty. You're the one who impressed that on me. Remember, when you returned from D.C., how furious you were when you got no reaction? You were the one who said, if we do nothing, then we are complicit."

"Yes." She choked back her sadness. The costs were so high. "I know I'm being selfish."

"It doesn't hurt to think about yourself once in a while. You're going to do the right thing. If that means staying in Europe, then stay in Europe."

Again, her mother protested in the background, but Kitty spent another minute reassuring her parents before hanging up and returning to the British consulate.

Oskar was outside with his four friends, waiting for her.

"Now what?" he asked. They were standing a few feet away, watching the group he had helped get out of France as Jean-Paul paid for cake and coffee from the street vendor.

"It's time to regroup. I have to go to England. They'll debrief me when I get there."

"Then I'm coming with you."

"They granted you a visa?"

"At least a temporary one. And an invitation to meet with your friend, Colonel Thomas Kendrick." Oskar smiled as Anna, on her toes, turned beneath a palm tree. Leopold and Hélène laughed. "We're doing this for my mother. For Artur. For our friends. And Kitty, this is just the start."

Kitty sighed heavily, her heart melting as Jean-Paul took Anna by the hands and danced with her around the trunk.

She did not want this to be the start. She wanted this to be the end.

9

JANUARY 1942

London, England

Now a colonel, Thomas Kendrick pulled on his pipe as Kitty waited impatiently for him to tell her something—anything—about Edgar. Her trip from Paris to London had taken her and Oskar nearly four weeks. The Foreign Office put them both up at Trent Park for the duration of their debriefings, but Kitty waited ages for Kendrick to finally have time to see her.

The estate was remote with comfortably appointed rooms. She and Kendrick were sizing one another up in the Blue Room, his office now.

"I remember when you first brought me to the manor here," she said. "And the surprise at finding you here, waiting for me."

Kendrick clicked his tongue. "It must have been a shock to discover that Edgar was our spy, Pim."

"It was." She looked around the room. The satin sofa. The fireplace that gave off only a little heat. It was just over two years ago that she had been here. "Things have changed."

"We made a few updates to the décor, but not much as you can see."

"I'm not referring to the room."

He pulled his pipe out and studied her. "No. Of course you're not."

She could not put her finger on it, but the whole house had a certain sense of urgency in the atmosphere. Of being busy. There were lots of people at Trent House now, including an entire wing that she had no access to.

"We have set a number of things in motion since your last visit."

And she would never be privy to it, Kitty thought. "I just want to know whether he is all right. I know you are no longer supervising him, but..."

Kendrick looked down at the coffee table between them. "He is concerned."

"About?"

Edgar had said it to her as well. But she wanted to now know whether something had happened since.

Instead, Kendrick stuck the pipe back into his mouth. "Kitty, Edgar is right. You're going to waste with soft intel. I'd like you to consider meeting some colleagues of mine."

It was pointless trying to get information about her husband. Kendrick was now running a different department, and Dr. Edgar Ragatz did not exist as far as the colonel was concerned. Most especially when it related to Kitty.

"Fine," she said. "Then I'd like you to consider my colleague."

"You're referring to Mr. Liebherr?"

"He wants to do something to help the resistance. He's done with hiding from the Nazis. We have established an escape route and we could help bring Jews across into Spain."

"Illegally," Kendrick reminded her. "See here, Kitty, I know how hard you worked to help those in Vienna. The fact remains, Great Britain has yet to open its borders to more refugees."

"I know how you circumvented the barriers to help bring Jews to Palestine," Kitty said. "I really admired you then."

"Then?"

Kitty flushed. "I mean, it was one of the times I really admired you."

"Well, I'm grateful for that."

"Don't you have contacts there that can help?"

Kendrick chewed on his pipe, non-committal. He didn't have to say it: she was overstepping her bounds. Again. She switched gears.

"In Vienna, Oskar wanted to set up his own resistance group. He initiated our involvement with the O5. He motivated me to do more and push past the bureaucratic red tape."

"I'm aware of Mr. Liebherr, but I'm not aware of all the details." Kendrick seemed to ponder something. "There's an interesting idea we've been tossing around in my new department. I assume your friend is fluent in German?"

"He's an Austrian national. Of course."

"And he came across with Edgar posing as a German officer? How did he do?"

"Remarkably well."

Kendrick pulled on his pipe and narrowed his eyes before pointing it at her. "I plan to speak to him about it in any case, get him involved in some way."

She flashed him a grateful smile.

"What about you? Edgar's afraid—rightly so—that you'd be interned in occupied France, but you want to be sent back into *zone nono*."

Kitty crossed her legs, and decided it was time to test the waters. "I met an American agent working for the Brits. She goes by Guinevère?"

Kendrick showed no recognition.

"She implied that the Foreign Office might be organizing new British ops in France. And that fluent French speakers would be needed."

Kendrick grunted. "And ones who know the culture. But it's not the Foreign Office. It's the Ministry of Economic Warfare. Special Operations Executive—SOE for short."

Kitty felt the sting of disappointment. She would not even be working for the same entity if she did this. But if there was any chance that she could return to France, she had to at least explore her options. "Like Oskar, I might have some ideas for assets in the south."

"Very good." Kendrick shifted in his seat. "I'll get you an appointment and make my recommendations."

"Thank you," Kitty said. "I only want to hear them out."

"You're still so uncertain. What is stopping you?"

"From what?"

"From going back in. That is, besides the incredible risk that, if you're caught, you'll likely be tortured or shot."

Kitty gripped the arm of the sofa. *Tortured, like Judith.* "Besides that?"

"Yes, besides that."

"If I work for a different department, I'd lose contact to... you know."

"There is that. But you don't have that much contact with him now."

"What little I did have sustained me. What if I lose him for good this time? He gets captured. Tortured. Executed..."

"Yes, Kitty. It's all possible." He gestured to the air around him. "Nobody here signed up for this without knowing what could happen."

They were quiet for a moment before Kendrick spoke again. "I can set up a meeting for Monday and get you introduced." He paused. "Kitty, do you regret anything so far?"

She leaned on her thighs and faced the fire so he would

not see the emotion in her eyes. "With Pearl Harbor, it all moved so fast. My husband and I didn't even have a proper goodbye."

Kendrick grunted. "In war, there is never time for a proper goodbye. I'm afraid you'll have to leave the rest up to Fate."

Having recently returned from another junket himself, Nils arranged to meet her for lunch at Claridge's after Kendrick's meeting.

She was shocked to see her brother had visibly aged in the past year. His hair was thinner; he would soon end up looking like their dad. Despite his Viking-sized stature, she noticed the weight he'd put on in his middle, too.

They hugged warmly, and as if he'd read her mind, he said, "Looks like I put on the pounds you lost overseas. Kitty, you're tiny."

Which was not something many people ever said about her. Like Nils, she had a Scandinavian frame, but he was right: the stress, the rationing, the lack of sleep had thinned out her face and melted her curves.

The maître d' led them to their table beneath dangling crystal chandeliers, past potted palms, and along the shiny marble floors. There were layers of petits fours on tiered trays. Kitty cast them a hungry look. It had been a long time since she had eaten for sheer pleasure rather than necessity.

Nils pulled out a chair for her. "Are you moving into our place this weekend?"

Kitty opened the menu. "Next week. I have a meeting on Monday."

"A meeting." Nils looked over his menu.

"*Mmhm.*" She pretended to be studying hers.

Nils's eyebrows shot up and he laid the card off to the side. "All right, Kit. I won't ask any further questions. So, besides the fact that you are now a skinny, half-freckled redhead, what else is new?"

"I'll be shedding this personality, I guess. More than that, I can't say."

"Well, this is going to be a short conversation," Nils quipped. He snapped the napkin into his lap.

Kitty laughed. Nils knew a lot, but he could not know everything. "I don't want to talk about the war anymore. Please, tell me about the family. How is everyone?"

After they took a moment to order, Nils switched to updating her on events back home. The Senator was planning on retiring after his term was up. Maman was still working at the University of Minnesota but the board had passed her over for promotion. Her plans to take a sabbatical in Japan for a few months had also been put on hold due to the war.

"She told me she's going a little stir-crazy," Nils reported. "But then the Met contacted her and asked whether she would assist in curating a new show on Asian art for next fall."

"Claudette jumped on that, I presume," Kitty said. "I can see her doing something like that. She should really get out of lecturing."

The waiter brought their food and Kitty eyed her brother's plate with some envy. She had the sole with a bordelaise sauce, boiled potatoes with parsley, and steamed carrots. Nils had ordered roast beef with gravy and Yorkshire pudding.

"Did you hear Sam is joining up?" she asked.

Nils's eyebrows shot up. "Yep. I think he's supposed to go into training next month. They miss you."

Kitty nodded and stabbed a piece of carrot. "I know."

"They have no idea what you're doing. Other than the lies on those postcards your various British embassies put in the mail for you. By the way, before Paris, you were in Rome. Just in case they ask you."

"They have no idea. And neither do you. But thanks for rubbing in the guilt."

"Don't take it like that, Kitty. It comes with the job. A healthy dose of deception is one of the requirements. And selfishness."

She bowed her head.

"Either way, they know you're not stationed in Bern. But do you know who is?"

She looked up from her fish. "Who?"

"Millie Hoffmann. See? If you were in Bern, you would have known that."

"Millie?" Kitty declared fondly, but she grew instantly suspicious. Her old friend from Vienna was supposed to be in Washington, D.C. "That's a step down from the Department of State. What happened?"

"She got married and her husband took a position with the legation there."

Kitty smirked. "A diplomat's wife? Poor Millie."

Nils guffawed. "It's a cushy number. Attending parties, being the fly on the wall. My wife doesn't complain about it."

"Rose and you are pretty well settled in London, so no, she likely has nothing to complain about. But she was not happy in Tokyo."

"Rose never said that."

"She didn't want you to know."

Nils huffed and wiped his mouth of gravy. "Anyway, Rose knew—"

"What she was getting into when she married you, yes." There was one more little secret between Kitty and her sister-in-law. Rose was at least partially responsible for Nils's position in London, thanks to her wily charms and ability to call in favors at the right time.

"You'll at least come to dinner tomorrow?" Nils prompted.

"Rose is making her famous Sunday roast. Come around at about six."

"Absolutely. I wouldn't miss it for the world." Kitty forked a potato, reached over and dunked it into Nils's gravy before devouring it with relish.

When Nils opened the door to her at his comfortable terraced house on Sunday evening, his daughter rushed into the corridor. Kitty exclaimed how much her four-year-old niece had grown.

"Molly Larsson!" She beamed down at the girl. "Is that really you?"

Molly skirted behind her mother and stared up at Kitty. Her big, serious dark eyes had definitely been passed down from Claudette's side of the family, but the rest of Molly was very much Rose's: the little upturned nose, the spatter of freckles, the dark chestnut hair. Kitty embraced her sister-in-law next and shrugged out of her coat, shivering.

"I forgot how cold and damp London can be," she said.

Smiling, Rose briefly examined Kitty's new look: the red hair, the faded freckles. Kitty left out the contacts while in London.

Instead of mentioning her appearance, Kitty's sister-in-law ushered her in. "There's a fire in the parlor. Let's have a nip before supper, shall we?"

Molly slipped her hand into Kitty's and promptly began showing her some of her toys. Kitty admired them, and just as a grandfather clock chimed six, Nils came in carrying a tray of sherry.

Kitty rose from the floor and clinked glasses with the others, feeling a little outside of herself.

"Something wrong?" Rose's smile wavered with concern.

"It's nothing. It's just all the changes of hours, maybe," Kitty said.

But Nils gave her a knowing look. At Claridge's over lunch, she'd told him how exhausting it was to shift between what felt like different lives and worlds all the time. Here, snug in the comfortable home, she felt thousands of miles away from immediate danger, though air-raid sirens could go off at any time in London. She was thousands of miles away from the Larsson mansion, and hundreds from Edgar. With the cozy family around her—Nils, Rose and Molly—Kitty's homesickness was sharp, and it hit her with a sense of vertigo.

By the time they sat down to supper, Molly insisted Kitty sit next to her. Looking around the table, Kitty could hardly fathom that she was here with her family. If only Edgar was with them; he should meet his niece, be here playing and laughing with her. If only there wasn't a war on.

The ringing of the telephone interrupted Rose's delivery of dessert. She strode past the console in the hallway and tossed Nils an annoyed look. "It's for you, anyway."

Nils politely admired the apple pie first, then rose and went into the hallway. Kitty heard his voice booming into the line then suddenly dropping so low she could not make out what he was saying.

"Can I slice it, Mommy?" Molly asked Rose.

Kitty strained to hear Nils, but Rose came over and handed her the pie cutter. "You mind helping your niece?"

"Not at all."

Rose nodded in Nils's direction. "He never stops working."

Kitty smiled sympathetically.

"And neither do you." Rose rubbed her arms.

"Neither do *you*," Kitty put an arm around Molly. "She's gorgeous. And you've got your hands full with that brother of mine."

"I certainly do."

Nils appeared in the threshold and Rose straightened. Kitty paused in slicing pie with Molly.

"I've got Bill Donovan on the phone, Kitty. I just told him you were here."

"Wild Bill?"

"He wants to talk to you. You've got a minute?"

"Jesus, Mary and Joseph, Nils," Rose complained. "Can't it wait until after dessert?"

"I'll just be a second," Kitty promised.

She took the receiver from Nils, who leaned against the wall, arms folded, shirtsleeves rolled up.

"Kitty Larsson, this is very serendipitous."

"Hello, Bill. How are you doing? *Where* are you doing?"

"I'm in Washington. Listen, young lady, now that we're in the game, Roosevelt has made me one of his quarterbacks for a new department. I can't go into details on the phone, but I think, after talking to you last spring, it's something that would be of interest to you."

"Really?"

"Yeah."

Kitty cocked an eyebrow at Nils and cupped a hand over the mouthpiece. "Choices. It's good to have choices," she whispered. "Who said that to me, once? You or Sam?"

Nils shrugged. Or was it Edgar? No, he always said, *Der Qual der Wahl*—the agony of choice.

Unaware that she'd been distracted, Wild Bill was talking a mile a minute, but he said something that made Kitty return her attention to him.

"Wait, did I just hear you right, Major Donovan? You want me to be your personal secretary?"

"That's right."

She rolled her eyes and shook her head at Nils. Guinevère was right before her face, that steely gaze, those muscular arms. That grit and determination inspired Kitty to say what she said next.

"It's a nice offer, Major, but no thanks."

Nils pushed himself away from the wall, smirking.

"I thought you wanted to serve your country?" Donovan said.

"It's not what I *want* to be doing. It is what I *am* doing, Bill. And for quite some time, as a matter of fact. Maybe not directly, but for this war, here, I have been giving it my all to be on the side of good. Whether it's for the U.S. or our Allies, who have been essentially entrenched for years, Major, it doesn't really matter where I am serving, does it?"

"Are you sure, Kitty? I mean, if you change your mind, my offer still stands."

"Nah, thank you, Bill. I'm going to stick with what I'm doing."

"Poker?"

"What?"

Donovan laughed drily. "I asked your brother what you've been up to and he said you've been winning at cards. Monte Carlo or something like that."

Kitty shot Nils a scathing look. He shrugged.

"Thanks again, Bill. Good luck with what you're doing."

"If you change your mind, Kitty—"

She handed Nils the phone. She wondered how her meeting would go the following day and hoped that the SOE held her in higher regard.

Besides, going back to the United States and putting even more distance between herself and Edgar was absolutely out of the question.

10

JANUARY 1942

London, England

The note that Kendrick had given her told her to report to Room 055A at Whitehall. On that Monday, the weather was so frosty, the wind whipping off the Thames, that Kitty was reminded of the bone-chilling cold of a Minnesota winter.

She was shown into a room where there was a major in uniform and a woman in a herringbone blazer and matching skirt. The officer shook her hand and introduced himself as Major Maurice Buckmaster. The woman, who was the quintessential stiff-upper-lip Briton, was Vera Atkins.

Miss Atkins explained that she was the major's assistant. She was very pretty but had a no-nonsense quality that commanded Kitty's respect, if not a little intimidation.

Major Buckmaster, on the other hand, was more relaxed. He had wide eyes, arched eyebrows and a high forehead. His upper lip jutted out slightly.

Kitty was directed to a seat across from the major's desk. He offered her a cigarette, but she declined. Miss Atkins positioned herself to his left and took one.

"I'm only here to find out what you're all about," Kitty said as they lit up.

Major Buckmaster looked up in surprise. "You mean to interview us, then. I was not aware."

Kitty backpedaled. "No, I mean... I didn't mean it that way. I'm just..."

Miss Atkins came to her rescue. "I can understand that you are nervous. I was told your real name is Gertrude Larsson. Is this correct? Tell us how you came to be called Kitty."

"My family called me Gertie, and my younger brother, Sam, couldn't pronounce it, or he thought they were saying Kitty. So that's what he called me. And it stuck."

Major Buckmaster looked amused. "That's what I call a long and winding road."

Kitty smiled. She had not even tried to deliver the story with her regular punchline, the way she'd always made people laugh. Like she'd done with Edgar when they'd first danced together in Tokyo.

"Tell us, Kitty," Miss Atkins continued, "Captain Kendrick says you speak flawless French. How is that?"

Her voice was soft and friendly. Both of them were relaxed, which made Kitty all the more nervous.

"My mother, Claudette, was born in France, and moved to Boston when she was a little girl. But she traveled to Paris each year to visit her relatives. Her sister moved back, eventually."

"Is her sister there now?"

Kitty nodded, harboring the secret idea she had should this all go as she believed it might. "In Marseilles, to be exact."

"We understand," the major said.

"And where do you come from, exactly? Can you tell us a little about your family?" Miss Atkins asked.

Kitty suspected that both of these people already knew the

most basic things about her. That she was Senator Arne Larsson's daughter. That she was the sister of a U.S. senior diplomat in London, but she told them anyway, knowing that they were only weighing her up. She braced herself for the inevitable question about Edgar. To her disappointment, it never came.

When she was finished, Major Buckmaster shared a look with Miss Atkins. The personal assistant tucked in her chin.

"So, Miss Larsson, have you ever flown?" the major blurted.

Kitty frowned. "Yes, sir. Many times."

"And do you believe you would have the stomach for jumping out of an airplane by parachute?"

Kitty suppressed a laugh. Was he serious? Was this how Guinevère came into France? She could suddenly imagine it.

"I haven't given that any thought, sir."

Miss Atkins was watching her with anticipation.

"But, yes, now that you say so. Why not?" she hurried. "I mean, it's all a bit derring-do, isn't it?"

Buckmaster scratched his chin and smiled before lighting another cigarette. Again a look passed between Miss Atkins and him. "It does sound it, I'll give you that. It's how we get our agents into France."

Kitty felt a thrill run up and down her back. This was already a lot of information. It sounded like she had her foot in the door.

"You would say, then, that you are courageous." He exhaled off to the side.

Kitty held her breath. He'd said it so matter-of-factly, as if he were asking, *So, you like red wine?*

"I suppose I might." Oskar had called her the kitten that threw the shadow of a lion. "I mean, yes. I know I am."

Miss Atkins took one of the cigarettes from the open case but did not light it. She pointed it at Kitty. "If you are dropped into France and get caught, things will be most unpleasant for you. Torture, prison, a painful death."

"This is a volunteer job," Major Buckmaster continued. "But Captain Kendrick assured us that you would do it if we offered you a spot on our team."

"Do you mind if I just think about this?" Kitty asked.

Miss Atkins arched one eyebrow briefly. "If you decide not to go ahead, of course we shall understand. But..."

Kitty waited.

Miss Atkins turned to the major. "Do you mind if I have a moment alone with Miss Larsson?"

He exhaled and stubbed out his cigarette. "Not at all." He rose and grasped Kitty's hand as he shook it. "It was a pleasure meeting you. Nice to know that Yanks are so open to working with us."

"Yes, sir," Kitty said.

She sat back down, as did Miss Atkins. The door shut behind her. Biting the inside of her lip, Kitty returned her attention to the woman, who was watching her silently.

Her heartbeat was maddeningly unsteady. "You said torture, Miss Atkins. Do you already know of such situations?"

Miss Atkins remained still and Kitty swallowed.

"If I go in, it would be the third time. I'd be in the wolf's lair again, so to speak. I ask myself how many chances does an ordinary person get?"

"I don't know," Miss Atkins said matter-of-factly. "But you're not ordinary. None of our agents are. Do you have a high or low pain threshold?"

"I might take that cigarette now," Kitty said. Her nerves were fraying rapidly.

Miss Atkins held the light over the desk for her and Kitty inhaled delicately. It had been a long time since she'd had one.

Kitty sat back down, propping her elbow in her other hand. "Psychologically, high threshold. Physically? I don't know."

"The concern is how quickly you could betray your circuit under duress."

"I know that all too well, Miss Atkins."

"Call me Vera, please."

They were quiet for a moment as Kitty continued smoking, her head turned to the window that faced another brick wall. "What is it? Forty-eight hours is what one has to endure, at the absolute minimum? Forty-eight is the magic number so that the others can try and make their escape?"

Vera nodded slowly.

"There were so many times I thought I would break, where I didn't believe I could go on. Not with what I was witnessing. Not with my heart breaking over and over again. But *I* never broke. If I've learned one thing, it's this. My will has a very high threshold. Maybe that is what gives me the courage."

"They pull fingernails."

"Electric shock," Kitty agreed. Her voice grew low as she listed the Gestapo's known techniques, imagining what had caused Judith's heart to finally stop. "Beatings. Water torture. Extracting teeth. Rape. I know."

"Personally?" Vera asked tacitly.

"From friends. From reports." From Edgar, but she wasn't going to reveal that.

"Captain Kendrick has already told me much about you," Vera said. "Your work is admirable. We could use someone like you. We'd train you. You'd be prepared."

"My experience with preparing myself for just collecting soft intel was kind of like shooting ducks in the dark. Nobody knew what to expect when they sent both me and my..."

"Your husband. Yes, we are aware of him."

Kitty looked up sharply. She tried to relax. "Do I get to pick my own team?"

"What do you mean?"

"I met one of your agents, Guinevère."

This time Kitty did see a flicker of recognition. Vera nodded. "Another Yank. She told us about you, too."

Kitty flushed. "She's why I made inquiries. Before the States declared war... Well, I haven't had much patience for how slow things are to start up. The resistance work in France—in Austria, even—is already years ahead of U.S. intelligence ops. I don't want to move back to square one. So, do I get to pick my own team?"

"I assume that when you're asking that question, you have a reason for it."

"I do. I think you should consider Oskar Liebherr. He knows his way around Paris and is tremendously resourceful, especially good with people. I know he wants to do something. Especially now. We feel a bit cheated."

"Cheated. How so?"

"We had plans. To help people get out of France. The pogroms against the Jews are nothing short of a crime against humanity." Kitty put a hand beneath her ribs, but her voice still shook. "I've been carrying quite a load with me. For years, I've had to keep secrets from my family about what it is that I'm doing here, and what I did in Vienna."

Vera sat back, her gaze steady on Kitty. "And now you want to tell me all about it?"

She had not realized how much. Something was building up in her and she knew she was on the verge of quite possibly imploding if she had to keep everything in. Vera Atkins, with that see-all gaze, her bluntness, her steadfastness, was someone Kitty knew she could trust. Moreover, she wanted to win the woman's confidence. Whatever she said next would determine whether the department would give her a chance. And send her back into France.

"I worked for the American consulate in Vienna. It was only a legation when I started, but after the Anschluss, it became a fully operating consulate. And that's when things really got started, when I began seeing that the world was not prepared for Hitler's determination. He wants to rid the entire world of Jews. I think even more than that, he wants to conquer it."

Vera cleared her throat.

"I had friends," Kitty said mournfully. "Before it all happened, I had friends whom I adored and loved. Who were already forced to live beneath Vienna's rigid surface. They had carved out their own subculture, and they were a beautiful bunch of diverse, intelligent, dynamic people. Oskar is one of them. They were the first ones who accepted me as I was, who made me feel at home. And one in particular..." Kitty smiled sadly. "Judith. She became my confidante, my dearest friend. Like a second mother."

The woman across from her folded her hands on her desk.

"She was Jewish," Kitty said, looking up as her throat constricted. "A fashion designer. She designed my wedding dress. Back then even I knew that it was a problem for my husband's family. Anyway, she was Oskar's mother."

"Was."

Kitty bit her lip. "She was arrested by the Gestapo after Kristallnacht, tortured, and murdered."

"Bloody hell," Vera murmured.

"Oskar had the idea of sabotaging the regime's activities, and to help his Jewish friends out of Austria. None of the other countries were prepared to raise their immigration numbers to take them. I was so angry with them all—with Great Britain and my country in particular—because they were dragging their heels while my friends were dying. And if they were not dying, they were being persecuted in every humiliating way possible."

Vera clicked her tongue. "Yes."

Kitty told her about Big Charlie and Khan, about the Vienna Woods cottage and how they had turned the root cellar into a veritable factory for falsifying documents, and printing ration cards. How they had helped to get people out of Austria on forged passports, fake visas, and falsified work permits.

Vera was leaning forward on her desk by the time Kitty finished her story.

"How many?" Vera asked. "Not that it matters. It doesn't matter. One is enough. None, even. The fact of the matter is, you did what you did. But do you know how many people you helped?"

Kitty glanced out the window. "Dozens and dozens. Hundreds? That is, if they made it."

Vera placed her hands flat on the desk, her eyes lowered. When she looked up, they were filled with emotion. "I was born in Romania. My family, Kitty, is Jewish. The fact that I'm even able to work for the SOE might seem miraculous to some. It has been anything but easy to win the trust of my colleagues. And I still have to fight. Every day." She held Kitty's gaze. "Like you."

Kitty reddened. "Thank you."

"I don't believe your luck has run out yet, Kitty. I believe you have faced your mortality. How old were you when you began this impossible journey?"

"Twenty-four. Twenty-five."

The woman nodded. "Young. But you have been scathed by reality. You've seen the inside of a Gestapo headquarters. Loved ones have died. You might lose your husband. For good this time."

Kitty looked down into her lap, her emotions welling. They knew everything they had to know about Edgar and her.

"It's your mortality, Kitty, not luck that you see at the end of the road." Vera was quiet for a moment. Kitty was afraid to look up. "This Oskar Liebherr. He is now here in London?"

"Yes."

"Does he speak French fluently?"

"If you say he is from the Alsace, yes."

"But he is an Austrian national?"

Kitty confirmed that he was, and Vera winced.

"That's going to be a problem."

"How do you mean?"

"We've had an incident. It turned out tragic for our agents. A German we had trusted double-crossed us."

Kitty frowned, remembering how Edgar had said his handler did not believe in "good" Germans. "I'm so sorry."

"But you say Mr. Liebherr is well connected in Paris."

"In Paris and in the non-occupied zone. The people he was with are reliable, even tested."

"Brilliant. We could use that."

Kitty hesitated a moment before saying, "How soon would I return to France?"

Vera shook her head a little. "I can't say. First we have to accept you as a candidate to this department."

"This department you won't tell me the name of."

"Exactly. You'll know when it's time."

"So... what now?" Kitty asked.

"If we summon you, you'll be sent to training. Not everyone makes it through. But we always have work for those who want it. The training will allow us to see where your talents are. Though..."

Kitty waited but Vera seemed to have changed her mind. "Let me see you to the door." She rose and came around her desk.

Kitty followed her. They shook hands warmly, and Vera narrowed her eyes.

"You'll hear from us. Soon enough. But sleep on it. At least do that for yourself."

The following week, Kitty received a letter inviting her to appear at a meeting at 2 Orchard Court in London a fortnight later. If she wanted it, she was in.

In the corner a handwritten message in a feminine hand. As Kitty read the lines, she felt herself grow taller.

It is in extraordinary times that we discover either the best or the worst in ourselves. I believe you are on the road to discovering the former. My hairdresser is Janet Greymoor in Marylebone High Street. She will expect you. Get back into your own skin, at least for a little while.

I look forward to witnessing your transformation.

V.

11

MAY–JUNE 1942

Hampshire, England

Raymond Henry was the kind of man Kitty could imagine swinging an axe in Minnesota's Northwoods, like Paul Bunyan. He was broad-shouldered, with muscular arms, and enjoyed a healthy girth. He did not have the cutting-edge fine-boned features of British aristocracy. He had the build of a man of the land, except that he was not.

Raymond—that was the name the French Section of the Special Operation Executive gave him—came across as well-educated, well-spoken and calm. Whereas the rest of the SOE prospects in Kitty's group looked as normal as could be—just a bunch of people who might meet for a beer in the local pub or attend a concert together at the town hall—Raymond was the only one who might have passed as a spy. He had that look: a broad forehead, deep-set eyes so that they were hard to read at times, and powerful hands. Kitty had felt them on her neck during training when they'd practiced how to defend against strangulation.

Except for their trainers and commanders, Raymond Henry was also one of the few who wore military fatigues to their courses. The rest of them were in civilian clothing, like her.

On the day the F Section teams were brought to a new site to train on sabotage missions, Kitty's commanding officer ordered Raymond to put a team together. He picked Kitty for the fifth time, and that was when she realized that she would be passed up for circuit leader. Their CO ordered Raymond and his team to march up a country road and find the bridge they were meant to detonate.

Kitty fell in step with the other two members of her team. It was the fifth time Raymond had also picked Vladimir and Marie. A White Russian-English-French national, Vladimir Gurevich was proving to be a talented wireless operator. He was in his early thirties, average height, had gray eyes, and a mustache. He also had long fingers and Kitty discovered that he played piano quite well and liked keeping to himself.

Marie Sourisseau was the complete opposite of Vladimir. She only came up to Kitty's breastbone, and looked more like a child, with her wide hazel eyes framed by long, dark lashes. She had a gregarious personality. But those innocent features and personality traits were exactly what would fool people because, below the surface, Marie was smart as a whip and her French was as good as Kitty's. She also had a sharp sense of humor, and really liked to blow things up.

Kitty had met all of them on the first day at Orchard Court, and over the weeks, the four had gravitated to each other. They trusted one another, despite the fact that the only truths they knew about their fellow team members were those that could be gleaned from observation. And even that meant very little, because before they'd all been thrown together each of them had been groomed and briefed in detail about their new identity.

From her commanding officer down to Marie, Kitty was known to F Section as Yvette Archambeau.

Vera had promised a transformation. But on the first day Kitty had shown up at Flat 2 Orchard Court, she had no idea what awaited her. The block of modern flats had a large entrance hall. The interior was all very upscale with thick carpets and uniformed porters. As instructed on the invitation, Kitty had taken the lift to the third floor and rung the bell.

Vera Atkins and Major Buckmaster met her in a room that did not fit with the rest of the building. There were no carpets. There was only a desk, two chairs and two full-length mirrors. Blackout boards were leaning against the wall below the windows. Was the Special Operations Executive—the department responsible for spying, for collecting intelligence from around the world—operating on a shoestring budget? Or only F Section?

Vera first provided her with a section leader uniform of the First Aid Nursing Yeomanry. It was Kitty's entry ticket for all the going back and forth between the various SOE properties: it got her in with only a few questions, and it got her out with even fewer.

Next, she met her commanding officer. Colonel Simon Martin had a gold tooth and a Belgian accent. Kitty and the others quickly learned to anticipate that whenever he had new orders, he would blow into the room, utter instructions in a hurry, and blow right back out. It earned him the nickname, "the Mistral."

When it came time to meet the others, Kitty was put together with a group of eleven prospects. One of the men, who introduced himself as Antoine and was obviously a French national, joked that they were like the apostles at the Last Supper. Then he winked at the group of three women that included Kitty, Marie and a woman with a Liverpool accent named Nadine, and said, "Except..."

"Except what?" Nadine's cigarette bounced angrily in her mouth.

Standing next to Kitty, Marie laughed. "Except that Mary Magdalene wasn't invited."

Antoine shrugged. "Someone had to serve tea."

When Commander Martin blew in again, he explained that the course was set up for the purpose of evaluating them. "Not all of you are going to make it."

"What do they do with the ones that don't?" Vladimir muttered next to Kitty.

"Shoot them out back," Nadine quipped.

Kitty stifled a laugh, but wondered, really, what would they do with the people that didn't pass muster, because they were about to become privy to a lot of intelligence.

The Mistral shrugged. "They'll decide in the end whether you're fit to survive France."

"Oh, *they* again," Marie retorted under her breath.

"The mysterious 'they,'" mumbled Vladimir. "I've been hearing about them for weeks."

"They," Kitty agreed, smirking at them. "The secret force that determines our fates for ever more."

Kitty Larsson Ragatz was blond and blue-eyed. And that was exactly the description on the Gestapo's books. From the get-go, she therefore decided that Yvette Archambeau would have green eyes and wear glasses, but keep the blond hair. It was getting harder to find quality dyes in any country. She wondered what Edgar would think of the dark frames.

Training began in London, learning how to make up false

identities and names, and fabricating a life to cover that new name. For every manufactured identity, an expert was assigned to find holes in their stories. Kitty had thought the exercise would be a breeze. Edgar had already taught her very well, but her trainers were ruthless.

In one instance, she was asked about her birthdate, and she had provided Yvette's date, and then the conversation heated up, got intense as the trainer fired one question after another. Kitty struggled to keep her cool, but suddenly he slipped in the question about her birthdate again, and on reflex, she gave him her birthdate, not Yvette's.

He cocked a finger at her and pulled an imaginary trigger. "You've just earned a bullet to your head."

"Damn it," Kitty cried. She hit the top of the table with an open palm. "I thought I was so relaxed."

"That's it," he stressed. "That's what we're trying to tell you. You have got to be ready for anything. You have to remember the details so well that your memory reflexes are giving the false information. You have to believe these details with every cell in your body. Your survival depends on it." He tapped the side of his head. "You need to convince your brain who you are."

"Who am I going to be when I'm done with this war?" Kitty implored. It was not the first time she had asked herself this question.

He looked sympathetic but shrugged.

From London, she and the other eleven prospects were sent south to Hampshire, to the small village of Beaulieu. The training regimen was meant to showcase the trainees' "stuff," as Kitty called it. She was so busy that she hardly had time to think of Edgar, but when she did, it was with a pang of guilt. Because, in all honesty, she was enjoying her time with the men and women in the English countryside, and could understand how

Guinevère's man in Lyon had landed in France, believing he was a swashbuckling musketeer.

Whereas Edgar had dived into a dangerous game of espionage with only his wits and instincts to rely on, here she was in some obscure countryside blowing up bridges for practice. She was not in the thick of things. Not yet. Even this bridge she now had in her sights led to nowhere special. There were no Germans on the other side, threatening to go over it, and still, she felt a thrill for what was about to happen, and this thrill was followed by sheer loneliness. Because every time she succeeded at doing something extraordinary, the first person she wanted to share it with was Edgar.

She lowered her binoculars as Raymond scurried over with the spool of detonating cord. She held the controller as he wrapped the wire onto the knobs. Marie and Vladimir were making themselves scarce in the tall grass after affixing the explosive charges to the bridge. Marie had a cigarette dangling from her lips. When she sprinted back to Kitty and Raymond, her dark hair bounced beneath the bright red beret.

Raymond sighed. "Jesus, Marie, the enemy could see you a mile away with that red beret, and that cigarette. Put that thing out."

"How else is she going to send smoke signals to the Indians over yonder?" Kitty drawled.

Ever since the parachute jumping class, she and Raymond always bantered back and forth like this. Vladimir scurried up the bank next and reached them, grinning in anticipation. Raymond pushed the bar down.

Boom!

The explosion sent everyone ducking for cover. Kitty looked from beneath her arms, then slowly stood back up as the smoke cleared. There was a nice, crumbled gap in the middle of the bridge.

Vladimir released a long, low whistle and yanked his tweed cap off his head. He mopped his mustache with it, laughing.

Raymond lowered his binoculars, put his hands on his hips, a tight-lipped smile on his face. "Well, that was very satisfying. Very satisfying indeed."

It most certainly was.

Marie clutched her hands and stretched her arms over her head before spinning to Kitty. "Can we do that again?"

"I'd love to," Kitty said. "Raymond?"

"We've got to report in. The Mistral will be waiting. Next time, lads and ladies. Next time, we must leave something for the others."

On the morning of June 21st, the Mistral blew into their quarters, spread his legs apart, put his hands behind his back, and nodded at them.

"The Germans have blitzed into the USSR. Ukraine, Belarus, and Russia. You're all on the truck in the parade square in fifteen. Full kit."

And then he left.

"Are we heading to the East Front?" Kitty called after him, frustrated by the lack of information.

Vladimir kicked at his bunk.

He must have had relations in the east, Kitty guessed. "Are you going to be all right?"

He shook his head, his brow furrowed. "Not until every last German is down."

"We're off to Bournemouth," Raymond suddenly called from his bunk. "We've got a mission. Antoine found out at breakfast."

As soon as they had packed up their kit, they set off for the waiting army truck. A window was open in one of the nearby offices and Kitty heard the BBC announcer going through the details of Germany's latest invasion.

"So much for that pact they signed," she muttered to Marie.

"Mesdames and mademoiselles!" Raymond called. "Let's go!"

Kitty and Marie hurried to their ride, threw in their kit and let the men help them in.

"Did you catch the news report?" Vladimir asked.

"Sounds like the Germans have blitzed into the east," Marie declared.

Raymond growled. "They just don't stop, these bastards, do they?"

When they arrived in Bournemouth, the Mistral was surprisingly more verbose with his instructions.

"We're going to test your training on passing messages, remembering codes and instructions. You are to consider this a real site of operation. You are also to make sure that you are never followed. Essentially," he raised his head to address all of them, "you'll be delivering messages or supplies around town, locating possible airfields, and organizing reception committees for drops. It's just as if you were in France. So if you're going to make mistakes, you make them now. But there will be consequences."

He looked at Marie, Kitty and Nadine in turn, and beckoned them to him. He was holding a map of the town. "You're my couriers today. Your headquarters is this hotel here. You're going to get yourselves checked in under your names. You'll find instructions hidden in your rooms."

Studying the town's map and the bus schedules, Kitty reviewed the protocol of what to do if she suspected she was being followed. She could take that bus that just passed by them and then get off at the fifth stop to quickly catch the one going the other way. She could walk into Selfridge's, normally a busy department store, take an elevator to one of the floors, walk up to another, then take an elevator down and find a back door. Raymond had told her that usually did the trick, though he did not elaborate as to how he knew that information.

At the hotel, she waited until Nadine had checked in, walked around the block once more and noted the faces she passed. Finally, she received her room key and found an envelope inside one of the pillows containing her instructions. She was to meet her asset at a cafe across town. He would have a green pocket handkerchief. Her task was to make her own invisible ink, and write the message on a sheet of paper.

Antoine had been provided with a pipe where he could roll a message into a hole. She, Nadine and Marie had been taught to stick their notes into their hair, clip them into barrettes or bobby clips, or into the ribbons of hats.

When it was time, she left her hotel room. Not one of her colleagues was in sight. Outside on the street, she halted and fumbled in her purse.

"Shoot," she muttered. "I forgot to turn in my room key."

She walked back to the hotel, watching all the people who were coming in her direction, popped into the lobby, and went to the front desk.

"Here you are, sir," she said to the clerk. "I nearly forgot."

Except she hadn't. It was this trick that gave her the opportunity to observe both streets and see who was about, and whether any of them would be someone she'd catch tailing her later. The instincts were already there. Edgar had taught her a good many things that she had repeated in the F Section training course. Still, and especially after many slip-ups, she did not let up, never let herself relax.

Yards from the cafe, she spotted her man. She did not recognize him, but the bright green handkerchief was her signal. Then she saw another man with a light green handkerchief. Kitty's heart skipped a beat, and she swore to herself.

She passed by the cafe, took note of the patrons and the

surroundings. It was now that she would look for anyone suspicious—Gestapo or police—note where they were and, if she were going inside, take a seat with a wall against her back. But her man was outside. Both of them.

Then, the one with the light green handkerchief suddenly rose, collected his things and left the cafe. Kitty released her breath slowly. By waiting, she'd hoped to eliminate a problem, and then, as if Edgar was standing right next to her, she heard his warning, "He might have just had reason to believe you would not show up and got nervous."

Kitty steeled herself. There was nothing she could do but try.

She strode over to the table and fanned herself as she looked at the cafe window. "It's almost too warm for tea today."

Bright Green Handkerchief man lifted his head and looked around. "They make a refreshing lemonade here."

That was her password and his reply. Remaining impassive, she chose a table kitty-corner from him and removed her hat and, at the same time, the pin that held her message. She hovered it over the table, first, slipped the rolled note beneath her napkin, and then lay the hat on the chair next to her. She then crossed her ankles, and turned away from the man, calling the waiter's attention.

A moment later, a chair scraped against the pavement and she saw her contact from the corner of her eye. He packed up a newspaper and his briefcase, and came very close to her table as he passed by. When the waiter arrived, Kitty smiled up and ordered a lemonade, then put a finger over the edge of the napkin. Her hatpin and her message were gone.

She had two more missions that day, including being part of a reception committee that night, and picking up a drop in an airfield. Late that evening, Kitty and her friends received word that all but three SOE prospects had been successful.

"What will happen to them?" Kitty asked the Mistral.

"They'll likely go to the cooler. But we're not done yet."

The group looked at one another quizzically before Antoine, rolling a cigarette, sidled up and stuck it behind his ear. "The cooler. They'll be working for the war somewhere where it's damned cold until the intel they got is obsolete."

Tired and thrilled by her successes, Kitty went out for drinks with Raymond, Vladimir and Marie. As music played in the background, she scooted over next to Raymond on her bar stool and propped her heavy head in one hand, realizing she was getting quite drunk.

"Hey." Raymond grinned. "You did good."

"Am I always going to live like this? Looking for escape routes? Instinctively sitting with my back to a wall? Always watching faces?"

"Yes."

She pushed herself up. "Is that it? Just *yes*?"

He opened his hands around his glass. "What do you want to hear?"

"You like this, don't you?"

Raymond lifted an eyebrow and studied his lager. "Maybe."

She laughed and drooped over the bar again. "You're a terrible liar. I hope you do better than that in France."

He chuckled and raised his glass. "Me too."

Six months and two weeks after she'd crossed the French-Spanish border, Kitty Larsson, now firmly Yvette Archambeau, passed the training. Eight of them would be going to France. The others were sent to the cooler.

PART TWO

CODE NAME: YVETTE ARCHAMBEAU

12

JUNE–JULY 1942

London, England

Gertrude "Kitty" LARSSON
Field name: "Yvette Archambeau"
Operational name: "Huntress"
DOB: April 21, 1913
Planned date and method of entry: July 20/21, 1942,
felucca
Circuit: SCULPTOR
Role: Courier

Kitty studied the slip on the file. She was in the bone-bare room at Orchard Court again. Across from her, Vera Atkins was waiting for her reaction.

"So, I'll be with Raymond, Vladimir and Marie?"

"You and Marie will work as couriers," Vera confirmed.

"And where?"

"Not too far from Marseilles."

Kitty felt relief. She would not be connected to Edgar but she was at least somewhere where he could reach her, and maybe, just maybe, Fate would be kind to them. But she had another issue to raise with Vera.

"There's something I want to talk to you about."

Vera nodded, indicating she should go ahead.

"I have an aunt. She doesn't know where I am, only that I'm not in the United States. I saw her on my way back to England. She's in Marseilles. She's an art dealer."

Vera tipped her head. "I'm listening."

"A lot of the *bourgeois* fled Paris when the Germans invaded and she's still got contacts around the Côte d'Azur."

Vera raised her chin slightly. "You'd like to vet her? Use her? Integrate her into the escape line and the network?"

"I'm thinking about it."

"Good. You'll let us know whether it works. Does she have a gallery in Marseilles? Because something like that would be very valuable."

"I don't think so."

"Find out first. If she doesn't, you'll need to find a physical storefront for her. You'll let us know. But first, Kitty, you are to study her; tail her. Watch and observe. Be certain she is not only on your side but willing to commit. And you do not approach her as Kitty Larsson, or even as Yvette Archambeau. Are you two close?"

"I lived with her for a few weeks when I studied in Paris. That was nearly a decade ago, but I wouldn't say we were close-close." Kitty folded her hands. "I approached her in Marseilles as Elizabeth Hennessy. She was suspicious, but it did work, especially with sunglasses."

"You'll need a wig, then. Disguise yourself well. Until you are *absolutely* certain that she is not a collaborator."

Kitty frowned. "But she wouldn't be. I know at least that much."

Vera reached for the cigarette case on her desk, tapped one out and just held it, studying Kitty. "People are predictable, I'll give you that. They tend to fall quickly into habits, they repeat patterns. You might forget that as an agent you can easily fall into that very trap yourself. See who she meets. What she does. Who her contacts are. And only when you are sure that this is an asset you will be able to trust—I don't care how much you love your aunt, she's an asset first—then you go to her. Understood?"

Kitty agreed and checked the time. "We've got to go. The final debriefing is in five minutes."

They took the stairs to the next level and entered the room where the remaining seven agents had already gathered. Two men Kitty had only seen in passing were taking them through the final preparations for France.

The first stranger was Théo, and the way he was speaking rapidly with Antoine, Kitty figured he was quite possibly a member of the Free French. The second introduced himself as Guy. He was a large man with a mustache, sideburns and a balding head.

He stood in the middle of the group and looked around him. "We've had some interesting developments in France this past week, most especially in the *zone nono*."

Everyone stilled.

"The BBC broadcast an announcement. They called on the French to begin resisting. It seemed to have worked. Masses gathered in the non-occupied regions, including in Marseilles. The good news is, the French have signaled that they are prepared to take a stand. We are therefore going to help them get better organized. So far, we've been collecting soft intel from our operatives already there; now, we need to show the French that we aim to make it really difficult for the Germans to achieve their ambitions. We'll be supplying you and them with weapons, explosives, clothing, other essentials—"

"Chocolate," Marie said. "I saw one of the canisters."

Guy grinned at her and turned to Nadine. "And cigarettes."

"Now yer speaking my language," Nadine declared.

They began running through the general procedures of what to expect upon arrival. The Circus and Sculptor circuits would rarely have contact with one another save in emergencies. Nadine and Antoine would connect with agents already on the ground for Circus. The remaining two agents were heading into Paris and Lyon respectively, the latter joining Guinevère's Prospect circuit.

Guy moved on to the next topic. "As far as mobility is concerned, you're to stay away from automobiles unless you, or a local asset, is in possession of the necessary permits."

Jean pointed to Raymond and Antoine. "The two doctors in your circuits have those permits, but go to them only if absolutely necessary."

Guy warned them to carry their identification on them at all times. "If you don't have them on you, the authorities will escort you to wherever your papers are. Which means, the whole pension or the safe house that you are staying in will be compromised. And that means, you'd put your hosts in danger should the authorities—or the Gestapo—find anything out of sorts."

Jean took over again. "We want you to continue rousing the rebels. However, printing materials are restricted. This is because the Germans are rationing paper as a way to crack down on the forgers, on underground papers, and propaganda."

Kitty shot Vera a fearful look. Edgar had warned that the Gestapo were going undercover to root out resistance efforts.

"Next," Guy said, looking specifically at Nadine. "Women are no longer allowed to smoke in public."

"Come now, lads," Nadine cried. "I can't just go cold turkey."

There was a round of sympathetic chuckles.

"Not in public," Jean stressed.

"I'll find you a cellar you can smoke to your heart's content in," Antoine said with a smile.

"A bunch of beauts. They can all do one," Nadine muttered. "And you can't have your tea," she said to Raymond.

Guy's eyebrows shot up. "One way to make sure the police descend on you is to order tea in a restaurant, and then with milk. All of you, if you're going to drink anything it's wine and ersatz coffee."

"All right," Jean took over. "Let's move on to management. The circuit leaders are the organizers. You are responsible for choosing your native assets and additional couriers, whoever you add to your circuit is your responsibility. You'll also decide as a group who the commanders are. You'll choose them before you leave to make sure everyone is on the same page."

"If we can't smoke, are women at least allowed to be commanders?" Kitty half-joked.

Jean sniffed. "They are. We do have one."

He looked at the agent who would be joining Guinevère in Lyon. But the look on Raymond's face made it clear that Yvette Archambeau—Kitty—would have to go up against him. She decided not to even try.

Jean continued, his hands on his hips. "You're also responsible for maintaining contact with London, arranging that arms and stores are delivered by the RAF. You need to scour the countryside and locate drop zones. You've been trained on what to look for so our boys can land safely or drop the canisters without detection."

The group nodded, understanding.

"If you come into contact with anyone you think could organize local groups, we're prepared to train them, supply them with what they need. Including providing finances," Guy added.

Everyone looked silently at one another before Vera stepped up and interrupted another one of Antoine's attempts at a smart alec comment.

"Until we get that kind of insider support, however, you're going to become chameleons. Everything and anything that you have in your possession that is not French-made is banned from now on."

She issued everyone with three changes of clothing. Their civilian outfits looked reasonably worn as new clothes could only be bought on the black market and would attract attention. The men's suits had square shoulder pads. The women were provided with dresses and skirts, wooden block heels and boots.

"For the weekday and the weekend woman," Marie joked, holding up both sets of shoes in turn.

Next, the men were given French matches, lighters, and cigarette paper.

"In France, you never throw away the dog-end," Jean instructed them. "You keep it in a little box and re-roll it later."

Other items included a pocketknife, fountain pen and pencils, all engineered to squirrel away messages or microfilm. They were going in with all of the essentials. Vera warned them that they would be thoroughly searched just before leaving for France.

"If you think I'm joking, I'm not," she added. "We've lost a handful of operatives just because they did stupid things, like throw on a tweed blazer or, in the middle of the street, brag about having gone to Eton."

She then fitted each of them with a money belt.

"How much is this?" Kitty muttered to her, fingering the padding.

"Enough to pay off your life, if need be."

"Any questions?" Guy asked the whole group.

Kitty raised her hand. "How are we going in? Raymond sprained his ankle in the last parachute training."

"You will all go by plane except the Sculptor group. A lovely submarine awaits you, will take you to Gibraltar, then a felucca will pick you up and sail you to the coast."

Jean and Guy then turned to Vera, who came forward once more, her mouth set in a grim line. She first stepped up to Antoine and handed him something. Then each individual down the line received the same thing. Kitty was last, and she put out her hand as the others had. Vera dropped a white capsule and a small tube into her palm.

She gazed at Kitty but spoke to the whole group. "This is your cyanide pill. In a pinch... If you think you're not going to make it."

The room became oppressively quiet as each person handled their pill. Raymond popped his into the vessel without another look. Vladimir held his between thumb and forefinger and eyed it. Marie's face fell and she cupped hers in her hand as if it would explode. Kitty turned hers in her palm. It was shaped like a white bullet. Deadly, it would kill her in a moment.

They were dismissed, and Antoine strode over to their group with Nadine.

"Well, you were wrong about one thing," he said. "Despite this bare room, SOE is not running on a shoestring budget."

"Nope," Kitty said. "They are not."

The waiting was excruciating but Sculptor was on hold after Vladimir fell ill, and the department decided to wait before sending the group in.

Kitty spent time with Rose and Nils, went to the park with Molly and tried to keep her mind off France. Again and again, she was struck with an awful yearning to have her own family, to be with Edgar, and to rebuild her life with him, which then made the waiting for France hard once more. It was a vicious cycle.

When Oskar suddenly appeared in London at Nils's town-home, Kitty was grateful for the distraction. They decided to have lunch at one of her favorite pubs not far away and sat at a snug corner table at the back.

"How are you?" she asked him earnestly over a plate of bangers and mash.

Oskar waggled his head a little. "I'm all right."

"Are you still at Trent Park?"

He pursed his lips for a moment. "This is going to be a difficult conversation."

"I know. You signed the Official Secrets Act, but is there a hint you can drop?"

"I have access to that zone we did not have when we arrived there together." Oskar reached for his ginger beer.

Kitty leaned back and folded her arms. "Wow. Can you say what you're doing?"

He shook his head. "But I can assure you it's important work."

She smiled. "I am happy that they took you on, Oskar. Very happy. I know how important it is for you to be doing something, *anything* that might make a difference."

"What about you? You look like you're about to fly off in a shot, like a partridge in the bush."

"Is it that obvious?" Kitty cut into her sausage and covered it with the mashed potatoes.

Oskar chuckled, but his eyes were grave. "Wherever you end up next, promise me you're going to be careful."

"I'm always careful," she said with a smile. "They've prepared me well."

Her friend gazed at her for a while, the questions between them thick. They both tucked into their lunches at the same time and concentrated on their plates. What she wanted to tell Oskar was that the SOE might have attempted to prepare her, but she and the other circuits could never possibly be ready for everything that awaited them.

She was going to be carving a trail into unchartered territory for future operatives—the next group of candidates was already in training—and it was going to be like walking into a jungle full of dangerous beasts with only a machete at hand.

13

SEPTEMBER 1942

Bédoule, Non-Occupied France

The Chastain family was very security conscious and not amused when the Sculptor Group turned up, unannounced, according to them. The sons unceremoniously shoved the four of them into a narrow room in the attic and argued with the parents downstairs, where Kitty kept her ear to the floorboards.

"You'd think they'd be happy to see us," Kitty muttered to the others.

Marie rolled her eyes. "We schlepped chocolates all the way from England. I'd jolly well expect at least a thank you."

"What if it's like this everywhere we go?" Kitty asked nobody in particular.

Vladimir rubbed his thigh with one hand. He was twitchy. He'd hated the submarine, and Kitty suspected that he was a little claustrophobic, the close quarters having been simply too much for an introvert like him.

Raymond was on the ground, leaning against the wall

where the roof sloped. It was hot as Hades, and sweat rolled down the side of his face. At the sound of the head of the household banging about and shouting profanities, he pulled up his knees, his eyes dark. "We stick to the plan. The Chastains will have to deal with it. But damn it if they don't shut up, the whole neighborhood is going to hear them complaining."

Kitty smiled to herself. They were in the middle of nowhere, surrounded by salt marshes. She doubted anyone could hear the arguing French family.

The next morning, the youngest son opened the attic door, and beckoned the group downstairs. Monsieur Chastain scrutinized them all beneath thick eyebrows while Madame Chastain handed each of them a small wheel of sheep's cheese wrapped in wax paper, a loaf of bread, and two jugs of wine. She pressed the second jug into Kitty's hands and smiled up at her.

But Monsieur Chastain spoke gruffly. "Madame Keller is expecting you in Bédoule. She runs a family pension and has room for you there. My son will bring you to the nearest train station in the wagon this night." He glared at Kitty and her companions in a way that left no room for arguments. "We wish you good luck from there."

Kitty glanced furtively at the youngest son and he gave her an embarrassed smile back.

In comparison, Madame Keller welcomed them warmly, though she too seemed to be on pins and needles. Nobody in the group could blame her. This was new, all of it, and she was a young widow with the pension her only source of security. Harboring spies and operatives who were to rustle up a rebellion was life-threatening.

As she handed out their keys, Madame Keller was discreetly taking measure of them. They were shown to their accommodations and she informed them that only three bicycles were at their disposal, but a bicycle shop not too far away might have extras to sell.

"Breakfast and dinner are included. Please inform me whether you will not be taking one or the other meal on any particular day, at least a day in advance. Everything is becoming more scarce," she explained. "*Il n'y a pas de petites économies.*" Waste not, want not.

She then handed Vladimir and Raymond their work papers. Raymond had a job at a small warehouse where he would be noting down supplies and goods distributed within the occupied zone. London had managed a restaurant job for Vladimir with "old friends."

Kitty and Marie settled their scant things in their shared room. Vladimir was next door, but Raymond had a separate apartment in the adjacent building, and Kitty and Marie crossed the courtyard to meet with him as arranged.

Vladimir was to report to London with his wireless from the pension's attic, but a few moments later he joined the rest of the group in Raymond's apartment. His brow was furrowed, and he tossed something small onto the side table next to Raymond.

"These got wet," Vladimir said. "Must've happened when we were in the dinghy. But they're not working. One of the wires is also frazzled."

Raymond scratched his head. "What do you need? Repairs? Parts?"

Vladimir shrugged. "I'm a cook, not an electrical engineer. What am I going to do? Walk into a TSF repair shop and say, 'Hey, can you manage to get me this part for a two-way wireless radio I happen to be hiding in the attic of a pension here?'"

Marie got up and paced the room. "We have to report our arrival to London. They need to know we've reached our base. How are we going to do that?"

Kitty and Raymond looked at one another. She knew what had to be done.

"I'll have to go to Paris," he said.

"I could go," Kitty offered quietly.

None of them had any idea about Edgar. But the thought—even a glimmer of chance—of seeing him, even from a distance, left her breathless.

But Raymond shook his head slowly. "It's my responsibility. I'll do it. It's the protocol and I'm the organizer. I've got to arrange dead letter boxes anyway, and establish contact with our couriers up north. I'm just going sooner than I thought."

"You're going to be stopped and checked," Kitty warned. "It's inevitable."

"Then it's a good thing nobody knows me yet," Raymond said.

Marie had been in deep thought and now she sat up, her nose scrunched the way it did when she was worried. She was about to say something when Vladimir interjected.

"If you make the Paris operator send our message, he'll be at the radio twice as long."

Marie clicked her tongue. "Exactly what I was thinking. Remember what they told us about the German detection vans."

Vladimir shot her a look of admiration, but Raymond sighed and paced between them.

"Until we either get a spare part, or a new wireless set, I don't have a choice. I'll head to Marseilles tomorrow morning and hope to be back in the next two days."

"And what are we supposed to do in the meantime, Chief?" Marie asked.

Raymond shrugged out of his jacket. It was hot in the room. "You all need to check in with the police. Let them know you're here. We practice our cover stories again. As always." He then pointed at Kitty. "I need you to go meet with the forger, Henri."

"Henri?" Kitty was still disappointed that Raymond would not send her to Paris.

"Yes, he's in Carnoux, and you need to let him know that we are in operation. Madame Keller has her hands on some false identity papers, but they need to be stamped. She assures me Henri is our man for that. Get it done, and then come back. Hand the papers back over to Madame Keller. She knows where they need to go."

Kitty agreed. "Can I take Marie with me?"

Raymond shook his head. "Marie, you'll take a bike ride out into the country, locate an airfield. Vladimir, you'll head off to the coast and find us a place to meet agents and supplies by sea. And all of you check in with the gendarmes. You need the certificates for the three bicycles Madame Keller has for us. I don't want any incidents."

Marie flopped onto the settee. "I am not looking forward to that."

Kitty smiled reassuringly. "Baptism by fire."

Vladimir was still examining the part that had fried in the seawater, muttering something in Russian.

"I already registered with the authorities," he suddenly said.

Raymond was surprised.

"I went straight away," Vladimir said. "They were desultory. But, I'm registered. And I won't be surprised if they knock on my door several times a week to ask further questions. But take it as routine. I'm a foreigner in this small town. And I've got an accent."

Raymond threw his hands up in the air. "All right. One down. Three to go. No radio. And an unplanned trip to Paris. Fantastic start, lads and ladies." He turned to Kitty. "I hope this Henri checks out."

Her eyes widened. It had not occurred to her that he would not.

Raymond lowered his chin. "Lesson number one. Don't take anything for granted."

Kitty puffed out her cheeks before slowly releasing her breath. "I won't."

. . .

It was a drizzly day and the earlier heat was swept away by a stiff breeze from the sea. Carnoux was about half a day away by bicycle. Kitty bundled up into a raincoat that Madame Keller found for her, and hid the ID cards in her underwear and brassiere. There were six in total.

"Come on," Marie offered as she pushed off. She had one foot on a pedal before swinging her other leg onto the bicycle. "I'll ride a ways with you."

Vladimir said goodbye to them, waiting in the dripping doorway of the shed. He would give them time to get on the road before breaking off in the opposite direction.

By the time Kitty arrived in Carnoux, her thighs and back were taut and burning. She was perspiring beneath the raincoat, and felt the paper cards sticking to her body. She decided it wasn't so bad. They should be a little worn by the time they reached their new owners. At the address she was given, she walked past the building, observing the environment first, but the street was empty. Madame Keller had warned all of them not to leave the bicycles out on the roads, but to always carry them into the apartment buildings. Theft was a real problem, and a bicycle was of great value now that nobody could drive.

Henri's apartment was on the third floor. Kitty lifted the bicycle, pausing on the second landing, out of breath. There was not a hint of life behind the doors she passed. She was relieved, however, that there was a set of back stairs leading to a second door, and that the way was clear. Just in case. Always just in case.

She heaved the bicycle up one more time and reached the third floor. It was the top of the building, but Kitty saw no way to reach the roof should she need a second escape route. But when she walked up to the door that supposedly belonged to Henri, there was a sheet pinned onto it.

Will the owners of this flat come at once to the police chief's office on their return. We have called twice today and received no reply.

Kitty stared at it. It was signed by an officer and bore the stamp of the local police. Henri was of interest to them. Not something anyone wanted in a forger. She glanced down the stairwell, her pulse beating rapidly at the base of her throat.

"*J'étais sûre que ça arriverait,*" she swore softly in French.

And then, the sound of movement behind the door opposite. She clutched her chest, the bicycle between her and whomever she was going to face.

"What did you know was going to happen?" a muffled man's voice asked.

Kitty took a step back. "Who are you?"

"Who are *you*?"

Kitty quickly remembered her password. "*Boulestin.*"

"*Écu de France,*" came the correct reply, to her great relief.

The door opened. A dwarf of a man beckoned her in, bicycle and all. She found herself standing in the middle of the most untidy apartment she had ever seen. Henri had a bulbous nose, deep-set brown eyes, and a pair of spectacles hanging around his neck. His face was unshaven and he reeked of body odor and cigarettes.

"Madame Keller sent me," Kitty said.

He wiggled chunky fingers at her. "Hand them over. Let's get this over with."

She gladly did so. She reached into her brassiere, reddening as he watched her with a flat smile. She turned around to reach into her skirt and retrieve the documents.

"I... I thought the other apartment over there was yours," she stammered as she handed the six identity cards to him. "The address..."

"It is," Henri said simply.

Somewhere, from another room in the apartment, there came a knocking sound.

Kitty's heart tripped in her chest. "What is that?"

But Henri paid her no mind. He took the cards, opened each of them, scrutinized them, muttering to himself. Finally, he went to a side table in the living room, reached beneath, and produced a stamp. *Bam, bam, bam. Bam-bam-bam.* And it was over. But the knocking in the other room continued.

He handed the ID cards back to her, his mouth twitching. Kitty turned around and, as discreetly as she could, tucked them against her body again.

Henri, in the meantime, waddled to a counter piled with old plates and cups and looked for something before exclaiming victory. He came back to her, pulled two glasses off the messy table and poured red wine.

"You'll need your strength," he said.

Knock. Knock. Knock-knock.

Kitty turned her head to it, but Henri pushed the glass beneath her nose. It had lipstick on the rim. His had the dredges of old wine now floating about. Kitty's first thought was what a sacrilege it was, then how disgusting it was.

"*À votre santé*," Henri said.

Kitty raised her glass, closed her eyes and drank. She had to admit, it was exactly what she needed, but after the long bicycle ride and no food, the wine went straight to her head.

Henri snatched her glass and held it aloft, as if he would beat her with it. "Now, go back to where you came from. Go on, then. They'll be back." He gestured over her shoulder. Beyond the door was the apartment with the police notice on it. "Next time, I won't be able to keep my neighbor quiet."

Kitty's eyes widened and he giggled. She suddenly had an image of a woman tied to her chair in that back room, with a rag stuffed into her mouth.

Dashing out, Kitty bounced the bicycle down the stairwell

and out onto the street as fast as she could. She was not going to wait around to see whether she'd be Henri's next victim.

The fact that the authorities were looking for Henri meant that Sculptor would have to find another forger. Using him again would be too risky, and she wondered during the bicycle trip back whether he'd really tied up his neighbor to escape the authorities.

She reached the outskirts of Marseilles just before seven and, remarkably, without further incident. She wondered how Raymond was faring in Paris when a building caught her attention. A *"For lease"* sign hung in the window with information indicating that inquiries would be taken at the local post office.

Kitty looked around and coasted to a stop. She slipped off her bicycle and wheeled it back to the building. It was on the main road but when she studied the wide-open space, she could see the promenade and the sea on the other side.

It had been a clothing shop by the racks and hangers that had been left behind. An old lounging chair was propped up against a large mirror. It brought back a flood of memories of her time in Judith's *haute couture* studio in Vienna.

Kitty pulled away from the windows and noted the instructions on the sign. Could it be this easy? Could Fate just leave this at her feet?

When she wheeled her bicycle around, she realized something else. The local police headquarters was right down the street. Kitty smirked to herself. This was too perfect. Hiding in plain sight. She climbed back onto the bicycle, making her plans.

It was time to go to Marseilles and find Aunt Julia.

14

SEPTEMBER 1942

Marseilles, Non-Occupied France

Raymond returned from Paris without any problems, but was shaken. He was brusque and annoyed when Kitty announced that Vladimir would have to send a message regarding the storefront for lease.

"It was in the plan," she argued. "London knows about it."

"Well, you're going to have to wait until the first canisters arrive and Vladimir can radio the message."

A week later, Kitty was not on the reception committee for that first Lysander from Great Britain. Marie was, and she returned, still charged up over the operation. Their first drop contained the parts and instructions that Vladimir would need for the radio, and he immediately set about fixing the wireless.

"I'm a chef," he muttered again. "Not an engineer or electrician." But he was immensely proud of himself when the radio not only worked but successfully transmitted Kitty's message about the storefront.

The response was for Kitty to confirm that "Buyer"—the code for Kitty's aunt—was certain to commit. Only then could they use the francs at their disposal to pay the rent. As arranged, Kitty would track down Buyer in Marseilles and observe her for some time until she had a good feel for her aunt's comings and goings, but most of all, her leanings toward the Vichy government.

She would tail her aunt disguised as Yvette Archambeau, and Marie would assist with tailing her. None of the group knew that Aunt Julia was related to Kitty; they only knew her as Madame Allard, or as Buyer. Nothing about anybody's real life was shared by the group.

"What's the asset like?" Marie asked that night, folding her clothes.

Kitty smiled ruefully to herself. Aunt Julia was a lot like her mother, Claudette. "She appears to be a self-made expert in her field. I think that makes her suspicious of others, which makes her come across as haughty." She shrugged. "Other than that, patriotic. Determined. And quite possibly damned stubborn."

Marie plopped down on her mattress. "Those all sound like they could be beneficial if Buyer decides to work with us."

Kitty could not disagree.

But then Marie grabbed her toothbrush and squeezed Kitty's shoulder before heading to the sink.

"You two are going to get on like a house on fire."

Café Central in Marseilles, with its round-back rattan chairs and the red-and-white striped awning and green lettering, was busy with late coffee drinkers, and newspaper readers. In a smart pale green Chanel suit, her red wig coifed beneath a white straw hat, Elizabeth Hennessy took a seat at a table near the far edge of the cafe. The bells of St. Joseph rang eleven just as the dark-haired woman glided from around the corner, smiled tightly at the waiter, and ordered her usual coffee at her usual table facing the street.

She was in her early fifties, wore a white dress with gold trim, high-heeled shoes with straps, and a broad-brimmed hat. Elizabeth reached into her purse and placed money on the table, then rose. She walked to the opposite end of the cafe and stopped before the woman.

"Pardon me," Kitty said in Elizabeth's Boston-accented English. "Are you Madame Allard?"

The woman looked up and shaded her eyes. Her brow furrowed as she examined the woman before her.

"Who is asking?"

"I'm Elizabeth Hennessy. We met last year. At the market. Are you not the one who ran an art gallery in Paris?"

Aunt Julia was still suspicious. "How did you find me here?"

Elizabeth moved away from the sun and smiled patiently. "You told me I would. Do you have a moment? I would like to discuss a business opportunity."

Her aunt stiffly tipped her head at the empty chair across from hers then raised her chin, waiting.

Kitty unraveled Elizabeth's story about her late husband, his love of art, and how she was looking to add to her collection.

"I understand that many of the more wealthy Parisians have fled to the south, like you," she finished. "It must have been awful."

Aunt Julia pursed her lips but her eyes hardly left Kitty's face. "It was indeed. For many of us. Some never made it. I was only lucky that I already had friends here with an apartment. Where is that German you were with?"

Kitty's insides flinched, remembering how Oskar had slipped up and called her *Liebling* in public. "You don't actually believe that I was serious about him?"

"That would make you a traitor now, wouldn't it?" Aunt Julia was testy.

Leaning over the table, Kitty whispered, "And the Vichy government? Are they not the worst kind of traitor?" She had been tailing her aunt for some time, listening in on her conversations at this very cafe, and both she and Marie had determined that Aunt Julia was most certainly a fan of the Free French, and not the Vichy government.

Kitty's aunt darkened. "It would be wiser if we remained on the subject of art." Her eyes bored into the American widow and her expression wavered.

It was time.

"Is there a problem?" Kitty touched her hair, then brushed a hand over her lap.

"I apologize," Aunt Julia muttered, and dropped her look.

"Last time I met you, you said I look like someone you know. A friend?"

"My niece." Her eyes darted to Kitty's again. "She is in America. But your face, your height. The similarities are really most disconcerting."

Kitty inclined her head. "I apologize for the confusion. I simply wanted to let you know that I am interested in purchasing paintings. I could offer you twenty percent for your troubles. But if I am making you uncomfortable, I completely understand."

Twenty percent was a generous commission, and the way her aunt grabbed Kitty's hand to stop her from going, the money was needed.

"It is I who must apologize," the Frenchwoman said. "As for your request, I do know quite a few people here in Marseilles and all along the Côte d'Azur. Some very good clients of mine, as a matter of fact, who might be open to letting you examine their collections. Of course, today's prices..."

"I understand. Completely." Kitty slid a note across the

table. "This is what I'm looking for."

The woman picked it up and reviewed the list. Her eyes grew wide when she hit the bottom of the page.

"Is there a problem?"

"No. It's an impressive list. It's just that this... Well. This Japanese artist here... He's my sister's favorite."

"I'd like to get my hands on his cherry blossom tapestry."

Aunt Julia stiffened and Kitty swiped a finger over her lips quickly, as if she were wiping something away.

The woman's eyes revealed the satisfaction that her suspicions had been correct. They both knew that the cherry blossom tapestry was hanging at the top of the stairs at the Larsson mansion back in St. Paul.

Lowering her voice, Kitty spoke slowly. "I would very much like to speak to you about a business opportunity here in Marseilles. You see, Mr. *Hennessy* has left me some money and I'd like to help you set up shop. Before I return to America, that is."

Aunt Julia was frozen. She blinked rapidly. Kitty had not dropped the Boston accent, and now she reached over to take the list back. In the exchange, Kitty pressed a small slip of paper into her aunt's hand. The woman did not resist.

"Meet me at this address next Tuesday. Six o'clock."

Kitty stood up, blocking the sun from her aunt's face once more.

Julia Allard was still speechless, but grasped Kitty's hand and squeezed it tightly.

"Six. On Tuesday. I'll be there."

It was nearly seven o'clock the following Tuesday when steps approached the shop and someone tugged at the door handles. Kitty, now back in her Yvette Archambeau persona, had put up brown paper in all the windows and it was dusky inside, but from a space between the pavement and the window, she recognized the strapped shoes that her Aunt Julia had worn at the cafe. She opened the door to her.

"I was expecting..." Aunt Julia said as Kitty maneuvered around her and shut the door. "Where is..."

The woman did not trust herself. Kitty removed the dark-framed glasses. Her eyes were still green instead of blue, but she was blond again.

"Aunt Julia, it's me. But you are not to call me by my name. *Never.* Do not let it even enter your mind." She stuck out her hand. "Yvette Archambeau. Delighted that you've come."

Her aunt's expression wavered and she tentatively opened her arms. She clasped Kitty's hand instead, but Kitty drew her in for an embrace.

"This is the last place I would expect to see you. In France, Kit—" The Frenchwoman stopped herself and bit her lip. "Mademoiselle Archambeau."

Kitty kissed the top of her aunt's head. "I am very glad you got out of Paris. Come to the back room with me. And pardon if I do not turn on the lights. Fewer lights, fewer prying eyes."

She led Aunt Julia into the back room, the woman still studying her. On the rickety wooden table the previous renters had left behind, Kitty had arranged a small plate of charcuterie and bruschetta, and some apples she'd found along the way. She poured glasses of white wine from the Loire Valley and then indicated the second crate for her aunt to sit down on.

"I still can't believe it's you. I mean... I thought..." Her aunt patted her hair. "You had me. You nearly fooled me with that red hair, but then..."

"I have a lot to explain," Kitty agreed. "But first, tell me what's happened with you. How did you come to Marseilles? When did you come here?"

Aunt Julia rocked back a little and sighed heavily. "I fled as soon as I heard the Germans were north of Paris. It all happened so fast. There was positively no resistance, and the authorities opened up the city to them. Neighbors of mine offered to take me with them to Marseilles. They have a summer home here."

Kitty reached over and covered her aunt's hand. "I wanted to tell Maman that I saw you last winter. But... Well, you understand that she does not know that I am in France. Or what I am doing here."

Aunt Julia took a large gulp of her wine. "And? What are you doing here? What is this place? What is this disguise of yours?"

Kitty lowered her head. "I'm here to help."

"Whom, mademoiselle?"

She steeled herself. "You mentioned that there was no resistance in Paris when the Germans marched in. Wouldn't you have preferred it another way?"

Aunt Julia stared at her. "Who is behind this? You can't possibly be working alone."

Kitty held up her hand. "I cannot tell you the details, Madame Allard. For your protection, you must not know a thing about what this place will be doing outside of your gallery hours."

"Gallery?" she whispered.

"Yes. This is yours. It will be your front. I am Mademoiselle Archambeau, your personal assistant. The gallery is your front and it is my back, so to speak. Whatever goes on after hours, you will not be privy."

"Unless..."

Kitty frowned. "Unless?"

"Unless I want to be." Aunt Julia rocked back and folded her hands into her lap. "I happen to know quite a number of people who would be more than happy to have a hand in liberating France once and for all."

"Let's not rush into anything. Before I even ask you to do

what I am about to ask you, I need to know: are you willing to risk arrest and interrogation by the police should any suspicion be aroused? Are you willing to lie about my true identity? About how you found this place? That Elizabeth Hennessy is your beneficiary?"

Her aunt chewed on something and looked toward the window before she set her determined gaze on Kitty again. "Yes. All of it."

"Madame Allard," Kitty warned. "Should I ever get caught, you will be the next person they come to. You can ask no questions. You cannot follow me. You cannot ever, ever call me by the name of the niece you believe me to be. Because I am no longer she. Is that clear? You are Madame Allard to me, at all times now. That is all."

Aunt Julia bobbed her head up and down a few times before she breathed in deeply. "Anything I can do to help, I will do it."

Kitty grinned, filling with pride and relief. "I had a very good feeling that I could count on you. All right. Do everything you must to get the gallery off the ground. All the paperwork, licensing, whatever it is that is involved. Call on all your favors. And tell me which of your patrons you can trust the most. I need help. The more influential, the better."

Her aunt pursed her mouth, then reached to take Kitty's hand. "I've been waiting for something like this! I've had enough of these traitors and bystanders. I'm French, and old, and will do what I have to in order to help France. But you are an American, Kitty. You are young. Is what you are doing... Is it worth it?"

Kitty closed her eyes. This had nothing to do with one's country. Guinevère was right. It was about the principles of the free world. And it was about Edgar. About having a life with the man she loved.

She squeezed her aunt's hand, more to reassure herself than

her. "I have to believe it is."

Every new gallery had to have a grand opening, and Kitty made sure that invitations were sent to a number of the contacts she had in Paris. Including a particular diplomat in Paris.

Kitty prayed that Edgar would recognize her mother's maiden name. He would come if he could. And she, if even only one more time, would be able to see him again. She kept Raymond and the rest of her network abreast as to the gallery's progress but did not mention that she had invited Edgar. They knew nothing about him, and she was relieved that they stayed out of her way during the set-up.

To make certain that the storefront was as legitimate as possible, the invitation list did contain prominent members of the Nazi government. Kitty explained to her aunt that the idea was to open the doors to them and work right in front of their faces. It would quite possibly cause some sparks among the French population, but Kitty assured her that it had to be done. It would give them an aura of leverage.

The gala was arranged for late September. Aunt Julia had assembled her own network of influential patrons, colleagues whom she believed would be good assets to the cause. They would pool their resources to help supply paper for flyers and newspapers, or fashion artwork and faux backs on paintings to hide leaflets that they would later use to rally resistance among the locals.

Raymond fashioned a hiding place in the floor of the office, and Marie found a large oriental rug for the room. There, they could hide some of the tools and weapons they would use to sabotage communication lines and any other efforts made to halt German ambitions.

On the day of the gala, Kitty stuck to the back of the room, her dark-framed glasses on, and maintained a mousy demeanor.

It was completely the opposite of what she had done in Vienna, in Bern, or in Istanbul, but was just as effective for her purposes now. Barely anyone paid attention to her as she lingered in the background. But every time the door to the gallery opened, her heart somersaulted in hopes of seeing her husband.

And then he was suddenly there, dressed in civilian clothing, and looking dashing. And annoyed. Kitty could not catch a breath. Her pulse raced. He pulled off his hat and frowned, scanning the room. Aunt Julia turned sideways and shot Kitty a terrified glance. Kitty realized that her aunt would have certainly seen photos of her and Edgar at some point, but she gave Aunt Julia a curt nod. Annoyance flitted over the older woman's face.

She glided over to Kitty, grasped her elbow firmly, and whispered, "I don't like surprises."

Kitty looked down at the woman's hand. "Then you will have to get used to them. Please trust me."

Aunt Julia grumbled but patted Kitty's arm before smiling and moving to another guest. It was something Kitty appreciated about her: she asked very few questions.

When Kitty returned her attention to Edgar, she realized he had spotted her. His eyes bore into her, his jawline worked for a moment. He didn't like surprises either. She knew this, but if he had truly not suspected she was here, he would not have made the trip. She was certain he wanted to see her as much as she wanted to see him.

Someone came up to him, greeting him by name. Edgar shook the man's hand and flashed that diplomatic smile, but his eyes darted in her direction.

Kitty slowly made her way to the back room, stopping to ask guests if they needed anything. She did not look back as she reached the office. Her hand was shaking when she turned the knob and went inside. She prepared to introduce Edgar to Mademoiselle Yvette Archambeau.

15

SEPTEMBER 1942

Marseilles, Non-Occupied France

Edgar walked into the gallery office without knocking, allowing the background noise to seep in before sealing the room in silence. Kitty turned away from the wall and faced him, her arms crossed in front of her, unsmiling. He looked her over once, shook his head slightly, and walked slowly to the edge of the table between them. He spoke German.

"This is—under the espionage code of conduct—illegal. To call for me for no reason other than..."

"*Ich weiß es,*" Kitty said. I know it.

"What the hell were you thinking?" Edgar sat on the edge of the desk and something cracked. He leapt up as if he'd just been shot, and lifted the gallery's catalog that had somehow knocked over the photo of Marshal Pétain. For appearances, Aunt Julia had placed the portrait of the Vichy government's head on her desk.

"*Scheiße,*" Edgar swore.

"That he is," Kitty said. "A real shit."

Edgar looked taken aback. A slow grin then crept across his face, revealing his dimples. Kitty cupped a hand to her mouth and giggled, her eyes on the man before her. He stifled a cough, but his shoulders began shaking. It made her laugh harder, and she pressed her hand to her mouth.

He was trying to put the broken fragments back into the frame. "*Ach, du heilige Scheiße!*" Holy shit!

This made Kitty giddier, and she held on to her sides, trying hard to remain silent. On her next intake of breath, she took a step toward him. He took one toward her. Another two steps. Then she was in his arms, and they were holding on to one another, laughing into each other's shoulders.

Edgar was suddenly at the nape of her neck and whispered, "Who the hell am I kissing?"

Kitty held him closer. "Mademoiselle Yvette Archambeau."

She lifted her chin so that he could kiss her throat, her cheeks, her mouth.

"A pleasure to meet you, Mademoiselle Archambeau," Edgar said. His voice was deeper. "Please don't tell my wife."

Kitty stifled another laugh and clung to him. She wanted to crawl into him, and now her chuckles were turning into sobs of relief.

"I am at a hotel in Marseilles," Edgar said, still at her ear. "The Louvre et Paix. Room 302. Come to me tonight. You don't have to tell me anything. Tell me nothing. But I want you to take delivery of something."

Kitty pulled away. His eyes were serious. She was disappointed that he had an alternate reason for being here. He was working.

"All right," she said. "I'll be there. Tonight."

He stroked her hair, a sad smile deepening the lines on his face. "I missed your blond hair. You look good. You look really good."

She reached up and kissed him again, remembering when they first met in Tokyo; they had also parted without a proper goodbye. She put a finger to his lips. "I invited you here because I needed to tell you something..."

He lifted a finger, as if he were prepared to reprimand her, but suddenly she saw recognition bloom on his face. He smiled sadly. "I love you."

Fresh tears threatened and she clutched his lapel, burying into his neck. "Yes."

He'd remembered, too.

Kitty excused herself from the gala shortly after that. Aunt Julia kissed her cheeks in goodbye, but her eyes darted across the room. Edgar was standing with three other Germans. One was a statesman, the other two were from security services. Edgar held a wine glass in his hand but was not looking her way. It did not matter; Kitty knew he saw everything.

"Trust me," she mouthed to her aunt again, then parted.

Raymond wanted a report. She had promised she would not stay at the gala for too long, only to make sure that everything was going smoothly. But he had something up his sleeve and she was to check in with him that evening. She just hoped that, whatever it was, she would not be required to join him at all hours of the night. Not this night. Not when she could be with Edgar this evening.

When she found Vladimir and Marie at one of the out-of-the-way spots they used to discuss operations—an old shed in a field—or to meet potential French locals they could build into their network, Raymond was nowhere to be found.

"What's going on?" Kitty asked the other two.

"Raymond said we're to form a reception committee. We've got agents to meet at our coastal point tonight. But I don't know where he is," Vladimir said.

Marie folded her hands and stretched them out in front of her like a cat. "Maybe we should be patient, huh? We can't just walk away from a—"

The door of the shed opened and they turned to face Raymond. He pulled off his cap, and mopped his brow.

"Chief?" Marie called.

"Hey. Sorry I'm late."

"I just got here myself," Kitty said.

"How was it?" he asked.

"The gallery front is going to work," Kitty said.

"Anyone there we should take note of?" Marie asked.

Kitty blushed a little, thinking of Edgar. "No. Not at all. Except…"

Vladimir raised an eyebrow. Raymond put his hands on his hips.

"Except," he said.

"I need to go to Marseilles tonight."

"For what?" Vladimir and Raymond asked at the same time.

"I need you here for the reception committee. We've got a felucca coming this evening with agents and materials," Raymond said.

Kitty looked at Marie, then the two men. "I can't tell you why."

"Why the bloody hell not?" Raymond demanded.

She nervously licked her lips. "I need you to trust me. Only…"

Raymond's expression turned dangerous. "If there is something going on, I'm in charge. I'm the one who gets instructions. What the hell are you going on about, Yvette?"

She looked at Marie and Vladimir pleadingly. If she said that someone approached her with information, it would open up a whole new discussion. She was on a slippery slope.

"I don't know myself. I just know that I need to go to

Marseilles; something I heard at the gala. It's really important. I know that much. It's just really, really important."

Raymond towered over her, glowering. "You get yourself into trouble, Yvette, you get yourself out. You're on your own. We don't know you. You don't know us."

"Yeah," Kitty said. "Of course. I'll take the cyanide pill with me."

"What the fuck, Yvette?" Vladimir's eyes were bulging out of his head.

"I won't need it. I promise. Let me go, let me go find out what it's about. Raymond?"

He threw his hands into the air. "Yeah. Go on. We'll pick up the canisters ourselves. No problem."

They left her there, and Kitty wrestled with her conscience but the guilt was winning. What she had done was not only wrong, but could pose problems for the group.

"Once," she whispered to herself. "Just this one last time."

One proper goodbye.

The night sky was pitch black beyond the wrought-iron banister of the hotel balcony. A light breeze caressed Kitty's skin, and the tide strummed the shoreline. In the corner, on the round table, a large uneaten baguette with cheese, and a bottle of red wine. They had not touched any of the food or drink. Never got around to it. A small lamp on Edgar's side of the bed cast a shallow, dim light.

It was worth it. All of it. She and Edgar made love, abandoning their cares if only for a little while. Afterwards, they lay together, her husband behind her, his hands cupped over her breasts. He kissed the nape of her neck. She wished they could simply disappear, leave the war behind.

"We can never do this again," Edgar whispered near her ear.

Kitty squeezed her eyes tightly.

"But I'm glad we did."

Not trusting her voice, she pulled his arms tighter around her.

"Do you know what I've been dreaming of?" he whispered. "Of that villa in Istanbul. I don't think of us reuniting back in Vienna. Or America. Or anything like that. I think of Istanbul. I don't know why. But this night, it reminds me of it. The sea. The air."

Kitty clicked her tongue. Her voice was groggy when she finally spoke. "I know why. It was the last place we found each other. We had a plan. We were going to be together." But they had learned that plans were futile in war.

"Remember that clock?" he asked.

"Time stood still," they both said. "At seven twenty-two."

Edgar sighed heavily. "I have to tell you some things."

She pressed her head into the pillow. Even as he was trying to prop himself up, she clutched him. Eventually, he slipped away and Kitty turned to him. She did not want to talk. But he did.

"I was in Berlin in February," Edgar began. "I had a very disturbing meeting with some old acquaintances."

Kitty's ears pricked. *Which* old acquaintances was he referring to?

"Several from the high command and a number of exclusive businessmen met in Wannsee. The topic, it turned out, was what to do about the Jews."

Mute, Kitty dropped her hand flat onto his chest to keep him quiet. He didn't.

"A final solution. That's what they called it." Edgar brushed his hands over his hair. "I wanted you to know this because this spring, we got directives to send forced laborers to Germany and out east. I don't know whether those two things are connected. Maybe that's where we've—"

"They," Kitty said sharply. "You, no, *we*, don't have anything to do with that."

He swallowed, but corrected himself. "Where *they* have been sending the Jews. But my source did say that the chemical compound discussed at Wannsee is now being mixed on an industrial scale. And shipped in very large quantities to the east."

"What compound?"

"Some kind of pesticide. But that can't be what it will be used for."

Kitty pushed herself up, her eyes on Edgar's face, remembering the poison gas the French used in the Great War.

"Then, late this spring, a Polish officer escaped from the concentration camp in Auschwitz. He was captured in Paris. The Gestapo seized a report from him."

Kitty held her breath as she listened.

"It described the conditions in the camp, and stated that a massive influx of Jewish prisoners arrived in Auschwitz. A whole committee of Polish officers—POWs—listed their grievances. They were addressing the Polish government in exile and calling on international courts to intervene."

"Where's the report?" Kitty asked flatly.

Edgar rubbed his face, and she leaned forward, waiting. After a moment she laid her hand on his arm.

"What happened to him. The Polish officer?"

He looked at her with such sadness, she knew the answer before he opened his mouth but he said, "*Nacht und Nebel.*"

"*Was?*" She shook her head, confused. "What does that mean, night and fog?"

"Shortly after you left for England, Hitler decreed *Nacht und Nebel*. It orders that spies and traitors have no rights to records. They should disappear. This Polish officer... They determined he was carrying sensitive German intelligence. They treated him as a spy."

Kitty gasped. Spies. Traitors. People like her and the Sculptor circuit. People like Edgar. If caught, they would simply vanish? No orange posters announcing their execution. No records of their incarceration in a concentration camp. No way for their families to ever really know what had happened to them.

"What do you want me to do?" An old anger stirred in her chest. "What can I do?"

His voice was filled with sorrow. "I don't know where they take these people. Where they took the Jews from Paris. I no longer..."

"What?" Kitty's pulse throbbed at the base of her neck.

"I no longer have clearance for that kind of information."

Terrified, she asked, "Do your superiors suspect you, Edgar?"

"Which ones?" he asked acidly.

"What do you mean which ones? The Germans, of course."

"Or the Brits?"

"What are you talking about?" Her voice was high-pitched with the growing panic.

He gazed at her, his head shaking slowly. "I've been thinking about it. The high command has ordered internal changes. I'm not the only one in Paris who has been affected by the level of access. But it does not make me feel more confident." He sat up and looked at her expectantly, but she did not know what to say.

"I really wasn't going to come here," he said. "But I need your help."

She clutched the bedsheet to her.

"Those British agents that were murdered in Norway, lured by false information—"

"I heard about that," Kitty said quickly.

He did a double take, then pursed his lips. "Suddenly

London is cold with me. They doubt everything I report, and are slow to respond."

Kitty tried to have a better look at him.

"I'm closing my London lines of communication for now," he said urgently. "I feel a noose..."

"Edgar—"

"I need you to get some photos to London." He was all business now.

He swung his legs over the bed, and lifted the end of the mattress. He steered her chin in his direction, his gaze intense even in the half-light. "Kitty, listen carefully, I needed a bird's-eye view on this. And I got it. I found a little bird who could help me."

He withdrew something and placed a white envelope on the mattress. "Look inside."

Kitty edged closer to him but she did not reach for the envelope. Something had changed. She did not want it. Impatiently, Edgar withdrew four small photos protected in wax paper. One was taken from a great height, the others were quick-and-dirty images of a construction site in progress. There was also a map pinpointing the site.

He pointed at the details as he spoke. "It's a top-secret construction in Watten. Northern France. Nobody could work out what it was, but when I saw it, I started thinking about the intelligence I've been getting from Berlin and from Vienna."

She looked at him, then back down at the photos.

"The Germans are building these types of facilities in a number of cities. I don't know if they're for developing new weapons, but they are definitely aimed at supporting the military. A chemical bomb maybe? Either way, the Nazis are building something. And it's made of poisonous pesticides. I think they're using the Jews, and other slaves, to build this new weapon. Or weapons." His gaze pierced her. "My meeting in February, Kitty—"

"Edgar, I—"

He put a finger to her lips. "It won't happen again." He held the photos out to her. "One of my recruits is the foreman. But even he said the Germans are being very hush-hush. Guards are keeping sightseers away, his workmen are checked and double-checked. Whatever this place is, the Allies have to know about it."

He pulled away from her, the question in his eyes. She placed a hand on the small pile of photos. Just once, she had said. She had gotten her chance and gotten in a proper goodbye. It was no use trying to drag out the inevitable.

"I can get them out," Kitty said. "I'll get them out for you. But it has to be tonight."

16

SEPTEMBER 1942

Marseilles, Non-Occupied France

Brushing mosquitos away, Kitty held the binoculars steady and searched the waters for a sign of the felucca, but the boat was nowhere to be seen. Below, somewhere on the calanque, Marie and Vladimir were hidden. Raymond was close enough that she could smell the lavender soap Madame Keller had put into each of their rooms. She could also sense his resentment oozing. Her commander had made it clear he did not appreciate her last-minute arrival.

Suddenly, Kitty tensed. The smell of cigarette smoke was so faint that she had to turn her head several times before catching it again. Just then, the wooden sailboat appeared, bobbing against the pre-dawn sky. At the same time as she caught the cigarette smoke again, the boat flashed its green light. Kitty stepped closer to Raymond.

"Smoke," she whispered to his shadow. "Could be patrols."

"The national police don't have enough men for random patrols," he hissed.

And then a man's voice around the corner from the promontory, a tone of outrage as he swore in French. "And what can I say to that? I told her there was nothing to worry about. The money will come in..."

The voice drifted away on the crash of the next waves. A second man's voice responded but Kitty could not understand him. She looked down at her dark lantern, then at Raymond again. She could not possibly signal the felucca that the coast was clear.

"We need to return," Raymond whispered angrily. "Tell the others to back away, and we'll meet at the safe house."

But Vladimir and Marie appeared, panting.

"Patrols," Vladimir whispered.

"We heard them," Marie said. "On the other side of the rocks."

Kitty looked regretfully at the felucca. It flashed its green light once more. She gave it no response. The boat then veered to the east and sailed away.

She was dejected, but not overly surprised. One thing that she had learned was, regardless how well an operation was planned, it rarely went as hoped. It took painstaking time for the pieces to fall together and failure was just around the corner. The felucca would have to try again tomorrow.

Four exhausted and hungry agents reached the safe house. Sculptor was staying with an artist and his wife. Olivier and Angelica were discreet, did not ask many questions, and kept the wine and liquor flowing, food on the table, and warm blankets to fight off the chill. Angelica made sure the group was settled in before she and her husband returned to bed. The rest of them were too wound up to sleep.

Raymond rubbed his dark, greasy hair until it stood on end and poured himself a cup of hot water, threw in some dried herbs and a shot of cognac. Vladimir drank straight out of the bottle. Marie nipped at it next. But Kitty, dejected, sat at the table and dropped her face into her hands.

Edgar and she had left the comfortable hotel room, and he had managed to get her past a spot check, so that she could hike out to the meeting point with as little trouble as possible. As much as it pained her, she had led him astray as to where her rendezvous point was. She had no sooner caught up with the others than they struck out.

"So what is it that made you come running back to us?" Raymond asked her now.

Kitty withdrew the sealed envelope from where she'd hidden it against her middle. She pulled out the photos, now in a small waterproof bag Edgar had given her.

"I made contact with someone on my old route," she explained, now having a good story for it all. "A person I'd met when I used the escape line. He was at the gallery, so I approached him and he asked me to meet in Marseilles. He told me there is a large facility being built in northern France. Likely a chemical factory. He has reason to believe that the Germans are producing some kind of new, poisonous weapon."

Vladimir pushed himself from the wall he'd been holding up and squatted on the stool next to her. He poked at the bag. "Can I look?"

Kitty glanced at Raymond. He shrugged.

"Go ahead," she said.

Vladimir freed the photos and delicately lifted one after the other up to the light. Marie turned them to her from across the table and bent over them.

"They're all blurry," she complained.

Raymond waited until Vladimir had looked at all of them.

"Those are chemical tanks," Raymond said.

"They certainly are not wine vats." Vladimir looked admiringly at Kitty. "That's going to be very interesting for London."

"If I can get them to someone who can deliver them."

"You will." Raymond reached for them. "Mind if I hang on to these?"

Kitty put a protective hand over them. "You bet I do."

He looked stunned, then angry.

"You have no idea what I had to do to get these," she argued. She realized what she was alluding to, and allowed him to think what he wanted to think.

He threw his hands up in surrender. "All right, it's your show. But until the felucca lands, I'd get them off your person."

"How do you mean?"

"I mean, hide them. And not on your person. Got it?"

Kitty frowned. Marie raised an eyebrow. She was leaning over the table, her feet—like all of her—always in motion so that the table rocked back and forth on its slightly shorter leg.

Raymond pointed at Kitty's hand. "You can't just give them over like that. If they get stopped by patrols, the first thing they're going to want to know is what's in the protective bag. You understand?"

Kitty did. "OK. I'll find another way to deliver these."

When a storm blew in, they were set back another four days before they were able to try to meet the felucca once more. Raymond scouted the shoreline before having the rest of the group take their positions. There was a soft thud next to Kitty and Raymond swore beneath his breath.

"I can't see a bloody thing."

This time, Kitty saw the flash of green light before she even noticed the felucca had sailed into the harbor. She was able to signal back with her red lamp. As soon as the dinghy landed in the inlet, the group scurried down to receive it. Kitty went to the man with the paddles.

"We're taking in water," he said in English. "The cases are too heavy."

She was shocked to find that the two agents had been sitting on six very heavy cases.

"I'm Davide," the first passenger said as he stepped out.

Kitty cringed at the sight of him. He may as well have shot off fireworks, that was how loud his bright white suit was. Did he think he was arriving as a tourist to Gibraltar?

The second one gave his operative name as Luka. He spoke French with a hint of a British accent.

"I'm Yvette," she said, pulling them both onto shore.

Marie was struggling with one of the cases and Raymond plucked it out of her hands. She turned around and tapped another one on the beach with the tip of her shoe.

"I don't know how we're going to manage all these," she said. "We've got a rocky slope to maneuver. And the main road is quite a ways up. Your first attempt didn't go over because there were patrols about fifty feet from us."

Davide looked around. "Is there somewhere else that we can land the dinghy? Closer to the road?"

The man who'd rowed them in groaned. "We can't take those cases any further."

Raymond considered this for a moment. "Follow the coast, west. You're going to see a big cliff, and on the other side of it, there's a narrow beach. We'll signal you from there."

"But," Kitty called after him, "that's wide open!"

Raymond agreed. "Do we have any other choice?"

Vladimir sighed and shrugged in the dark. Marie scampered off after Raymond.

Kitty turned to the man in the boat. "Listen, in case I can't ask you then. I need you to get this to London."

The sky had lightened enough that anyone could see the outline in the wax paper bundle.

He looked up at her with a miffed expression. "A sandwich? You want me to take a sandwich to London?"

"It's not just any sandwich."

He sniffed it and made a face. "No, I'd say not. What is that?"

"Cheese."

He gagged. "Why?" he insisted.

"It's what's *inside*." She unwrapped the paper a little and lifted one side of the baguette. Hidden between the lettuce and the cheese was the protected package. "This needs to get to London. Do you understand? Hide it on the boat however you want to, but it gets to London."

He looked up at her and she could see his teeth. He was grinning. "You've got it, Yvette."

Relieved, Kitty grinned. "We'll meet you at the shore."

"Sand or rock beach?" Davide asked.

"There's a sand beach, but don't land there. You'll have to land at the rock."

"Luka and I will go with you," Davide said.

Kitty protested. "You can't go like this in your white suit..."

"Get in!" the rower cried hoarsely. "I'll get them there!"

Luka then handed Kitty something. It was long and made of canvas. "It's our money belts. Take them. Just in case."

The SOE mantra, *Just in case*, left a whole lot of room for catastrophes.

The rower deftly negotiated the dinghy out onto the water again. It took nearly twenty minutes to get to where she could skid down the slope to the pebbled beach. Raymond and Marie were already helping the two men out of the water. Vladimir was lugging one of the cases onto land. The new agents were both drenched.

"What happened?" Kitty asked. The tide was coming in quickly.

"We took in too much water," Davide said. "I hurt my leg, too."

"We lost one of the cases," Luka added. "I have no idea which one but let's hope it's not the one with the luxury goods."

"What about the cheese sandwich?" she pleaded.

But neither could answer her. Kitty scanned the water in disbelief, then spotted the dinghy heading back to the felucca. With Edgar's photos, she prayed.

Between the six of them on shore, they lugged the five remaining cases to the safe house. Kitty's arms and legs were sore and she was exhausted, but she was most certainly better off than the two wet agents.

When they reached Angelica's and Olivier's, they found the table set and Angelica cooking a large pan of eggs. There was fresh bread, and wheels of marinated goat cheese. A few shots of cognac in their coffee and herbal drinks, and the Sculptor team headed back to Bédoule and the pension.

Luka and Davide would go on to a network in the Savoy. Their mission was to deliver weapons and begin training a group of French rebels in sabotage and reconnaissance. The white suit, to Olivier's delight, was strictly ordered to be left behind.

As soon as Marie unlocked their bedroom door, Kitty pushed through it and slumped onto the bed. She wrapped the corners of her bedcovers over her, and fell into a deep sleep.

Some time later, Vladimir reported that London thanked Raymond for the cheese sandwich.

Kitty read the message and went to Raymond with it. "Why are they thanking you for it?"

Raymond scratched his head. "Bloody hell if I know. But I am your leader, so..."

He stalked away into another room and Kitty frowned over at Marie, who looked down at the table for a moment. She scratched the surface with her fingernail.

"The chief was poking around that envelope," she muttered.

Kitty couldn't believe it.

"I didn't think he was doing anything," Marie defended. "But he'd written something on the envelope. Just after you put it into the sandwich."

Kitty narrowed her eyes and glanced at Vladimir, who was working on something, and oblivious to their conversation.

"Son of a..." Kitty whispered.

She'd been through this before in Vienna. Stabbed in the back. Her initiative taken and the credit given to the man who was supposed to be her ally. It infuriated her even more because it was Edgar's hard work she'd turned in. And likely the last coordinated effort she'd make with her husband, the one who should be lauded for the intelligence in the first place. She recalled Edgar's misgivings about the Brits trusting him any longer. Here was proof he was doing all he could for them, and Raymond's stunt was in bad taste.

Marie grasped her elbow and tilted her head toward the door. "Want a cigarette?"

Kitty huffed angrily. "Yeah, I do."

She followed Marie out of the apartment, slamming the door hard behind her.

17

OCTOBER 1942

Bédoule, Non-Occupied France

Kitty groaned as she heaved another load of cold dirt and dumped it onto the pile.

She used the bandanna around her neck to mop her brow, then leaned on the shovel, scanning the recently cut lavender fields around them. The leaves of the surrounding oak forest had turned to a burnished orange. The lavender grower had given the Sculptor Group permission to dig pits where they could hide the new stores they would soon be receiving. With the resistance growing at a rapid rate, Raymond had put in a request for twelve more containers of guns, ammunition, and supplies.

Vladimir and Marie were just a few feet away in another quadrant, near the trees. The White Russian was swinging the shovel in a healthy rhythm while Marie leaned on a post and watched him.

Kitty glanced up at her chief. Was Raymond catching on to

what was going on? The flirtations? The stolen glances and lingering touches? If he was, he wasn't letting on. He stood smoking a cigarette near the processing building, surveying the landscape. She jabbed the shovel into the dirt and threw another good lump onto the pile.

"How big do these need to be?" she called to Raymond.

"Six feet long, four feet deep. Big enough for at least two canisters."

Vladimir suddenly appeared over the rim of his pit and handed Marie the shovel. Marie set it on the ground and began placing branches a few inches below and across the hole. Vladimir jumped out and strode over to Raymond and Kitty.

"We're ready with ours," Vladimir said. "Brush and branches, some turf, and they'll be camouflaged."

Raymond was looking up at the sky. "The Lysander won't come tonight." He turned to Vladimir. "Let's test these out first and we can continue tomorrow."

Kitty breathed a sigh of relief, and measured out the pit. Raymond had done most of the hard work, but it was still grueling. As it turned out, he was right not to dig the other eight pits. Rain came in and did not let up.

The delay of the Lysander dragged on. A week later, Vladimir returned from the lavender producer with more bad news.

"Both of our holes were discovered."

Kitty gaped. "You are kidding me."

"A gamekeeper fell in."

Marie stifled a giggle. Raymond grunted.

"What happened?" Kitty asked.

"He went to the authorities and the French police examined the scene. They found the second one, too." Vladimir brushed a hand over his mustache, hiding a sly grin. "Now there's a rumor going around the village that the authorities discovered gravesites for some murder—already taken place or planned."

Kitty dropped her head in her hands and groaned.

Raymond coughed into his fist. "I'll get some of the locals to help us carry the stuff. We need a hiding place though. I can't just bring twelve containers here to the pension."

"Maybe we can ask some of the locals to store them until we can get them to the gallery," Marie suggested. "They can cart the canisters away on the same night."

"If it even lands in the right place," Kitty reminded them all.

Marie raised her eyebrows. "Seven miles," she started.

"Off target," Kitty finished, and they smiled at each other.

"Let's hope that doesn't happen again," Raymond said. "That drop was nothing but a disaster."

"I'll say." Kitty laughed. "My body is still taking a toll thanks to that airman."

In truth she had great respect for the pilots who flew their agents and supplies in. It was a tough job, but sometimes—just sometimes—they created sheer chaos. On the other hand, those brief contacts with London kept the group buoyed.

Each of them had changed quite a bit since arriving in France. They'd fallen into their roles and rituals and were an effective and tight group. Vladimir often changed locations to send and receive messages, and quickly discovered that he indeed had talents beyond just playing piano, reading heavy literature and cooking. And something else. Although they were complete opposites in nearly every way, Kitty believed that Vladimir and Marie were conducting secret operations of their own; a romance had definitely blossomed between them.

And why not? A capable woman was sexy indeed, and Marie was hands-down the most enthusiastic sabotage expert. She spent her time drawing up plans for possible targets, such as depots, bridges, factories, anything that would go *boom*. She then delivered her directives to their Provencal contacts.

In the meantime, Raymond was now busy, vetting and organizing resistance cells. To establish a truce between them, Raymond assigned Kitty to conduct weapons training and shooting, stating he had great trust in her abilities. He sent her to the more rough-and-tumble areas and she met with young and old guerrilla fighters alike. The French rebels quickly agreed that the Sten gun was a fine close-range weapon.

But what dampened all of their advancements was the news that trickled down to them from occupied France. Reports of assassinated German officials, followed by news of heavy and brutal reprisals reached Sculptor like pieces of a puzzle, and the more Kitty fit them together, the heavier the stone of dread grew in her middle. SOE agents disappeared, and she recalled Edgar's warning about the *Nacht und Nebel*—Night and Fog. She told Raymond about what she knew about the decree without giving away her source. Each time another German officer was attacked or killed, Kitty went cold with terror. She knew that Edgar could either be caught by the Germans for sharing intelligence with the Allies, or he could just be in the wrong place at the wrong time and be liquidated by those very Allied agents. Either way, the memory of how he'd used the word "noose" in Marseilles gave her nightmares.

When the Lysander was finally able to fly over the Channel, the reception committee now included three locals.

The drop was also decently accurate. Kitty and Marie rushed to the canisters and cut the chutes, then quickly buried the silk and string in the woods. Meanwhile, the men loaded the canisters into handcarts and into a bicycle trailer and parted ways. Between the seven of them, they had found places to hide the stores on various properties, but one member of Sculptor went with a local to conduct a full inventory.

Kitty went to the processing building with the lavender

grower. Together, they popped open the two canisters they'd taken with them and Kitty let out a low whistle. She had the most precious stores: warm clothing, blankets, several Sten guns, and cigarettes.

And then the Frenchman raised the lid on the next canister. There was a hint of almond in the air and he unwrapped one of the packages.

"*Ça alors!*" he exclaimed.

"Holy smokes." Kitty laughed, delighted. "What a cache!"

She was looking at Nobel 808 explosives. A lot of them. They were green plasticine, easy to mold and easy to use.

The Frenchman pointed at the stash with his cigarette. "*Boom.*"

Kitty waved him off, joking about the dangers of smoking. There were also chargers, wires and everything else they would need to perform Marie's favorite hobby.

Raymond had told each of them to keep an eye out for the shipment and waited until everyone returned to the lavender farm to announce her find.

Marie tiptoed around the canister. "How? How are we supposed to deliver all of this to the gallery?"

Raymond rubbed his hands over his head.

The farmer raised his eyebrows and looked away, as if to say, "Not my problem."

"I can do this," Kitty said.

"How?" Raymond probed.

"I have an idea." She waved Marie over and whispered into her ear. "You know those underpants I hate wearing?"

Marie pulled back, her eyes and smile widening. They both looked into the canister. Marie snapped her fingers at Raymond to make him back away and said, "This is ladies' stuff now."

· · ·

With all of them busier than usual, they needed a fourth bicycle. Kitty found one for sale, paid the extortionate amount of francs for it, obtained the certificate for it from the authorities, and pedaled back to the lavender grower's, where Marie was already busy affixing the explosives into a pair of bloomers.

Raymond and Vladimir watched from a distance. "Make sure you don't break wind, Yvette."

Vladimir chuckled into his chest. "Don't let anyone get into your pants."

"Do you two have anything better to do than make stupid jokes?" Marie challenged.

Raymond raised a bottle to his lips. "Who me? I'm not making fun. But if anyone tries patting you down, Yvette, don't explode from all that attention."

And the crassness went on.

Kitty gingerly stepped into the bloomers and pulled them up to her waist before dropping her skirt over them. She turned around for them all. Raymond whistled and clapped, his cigarette dangling from his mouth. Vladimir paced around her, pursing his lips in admiration.

"Looks good," Raymond said, this time meaning it. "You're a little more padded, but it suits you."

Vladimir chuckled again, then excused himself to radio London from his new hideout.

Kitty had quite a ride to Aunt Julia's gallery ahead of her, so she struck out at dawn the next day. Marie held the bicycle steady for her as she mounted it.

Raymond patted Kitty's shoulder. "Look after yourself. Come back in one piece."

She scoffed. "Very funny."

But she gave Marie a long, careful hug before pushing off toward Marseilles.

. . .

Days before, Raymond had reported a conversation with the lavender producer.

"He warned that, with the Americans in Africa now, the Nazis are just waiting for the Vichy government to display one moment of weakness, one hint of defiance," he'd told them. "If they do, the Germans will move fast to occupy the rest of France. The only ones really left doing the Nazis' bidding are the real bastards who get a kick out of helping them. They'll move aside if need be, then ask for a job."

Which was why Kitty's heart nearly leapt out of her throat when, on the country lane she was cycling, a checkpoint appeared ahead. She swore under her breath, and only slowed down a beat. There were two gendarmes—one tall and broad, the other small and round—leaning lazily against their barricade, smoking cigarettes, rifles slung over their shoulders. The smaller one glanced her way and poked the other, grinning. He pinched the dog-end off his cigarette. His companion was already striding to the middle of the road to block her way.

Kitty coasted to a stop. In her bicycle carrier was her handbag, and her documents. In her bloomers, enough plasticine to bring down a power station and two locomotives.

"*Bonjour*," she said. She straddled the bicycle between her legs, feet firmly planted on the ground.

The larger of the two began circling her. He reeked of alcohol.

"Good day. Where are you going?" the smaller man, blocking the road, asked.

"To work. At Madame Allard's gallery in Marseilles." She handed her documents to him.

The one behind her tapped her bicycle with the barrel of his gun, and she flinched.

"You need air in your tire."

She glanced at the back wheel. He was right. It was low. "Thank you. I'm nearly there."

"But I have something for you here." He grinned at his companion and hitched his trousers up. "We could fill you up right now."

Kitty willed herself to stay calm. She reached into the bag in her bicycle carrier and patted it. "I have a pump with me."

He extended a hand to her. "Give it to me. Let me do the honor."

The other one was pretending to ignore their conversation, still studying her documents with a smirk. He pressed the papers to his chest then and indicated his companion with a toss of his head. "Give him the pump."

The bigger guard was now looking her up and down.

Kitty did not want to move away from the bicycle. She did not want to lift her leg over it. She did not want to be here—alone—with these two gendarmes. Suddenly, Raymond's and Vladimir's jokes were menacing and bode no good.

"Look," Kitty said sharply. "I know you two are bored out here, but I have to get to work. I got this far, and I can manage the rest of the way just fine. Thank you."

The big guard scoffed. "We are just trying to help a lady who needs our... help."

"Messieurs," she said angrily. "Do I need to see Captain Roux when I get into town?"

At the mention of the police captain down the street from Aunt Julia's gallery, the smaller one stepped back. He jerked his head to the road behind him and thrust her papers back at her.

"Go on. Get out of here."

"Thank you," she said. "And good day."

"*Bonne journée!*" the bigger one taunted.

She pushed off, keeping her eyes straight ahead. The skin on her legs was burning as she coasted down the hill and into Marseilles. She had made it, she thought, and then reminded herself not to count her chickens until they'd all hatched.

. . .

After Kitty pumped up her tire, she went inside the gallery. Aunt Julia greeted her with a kiss in the back office. She stuck to her agreement and never called Kitty by her real name, but her expression read that she was concerned for her niece.

"You look piqued. I'll make you something to revive your spirits."

A bowl of fruit was on a corner table, glowing in the sunshine. Kitty, still shaken by the close call with the gendarmes, let her aunt dote on her a little.

"I received a telegram from... my sister," Aunt Julia said. She handed Kitty a cup of ersatz coffee.

Kitty looked up in surprise, her head reeling. Word from her mother. She would know where Sam might be. "What does she say?"

Aunt Julia laughed drily. "She told me I should come back to America. She says she's lonely. Your..."

Kitty looked at her sharply, and Aunt Julia drew up.

"You're probably not interested, though," she said dismissively.

"No. Do tell."

"Apparently, her *daughter* is in Casablanca. And Sam—her youngest—is stationed in Africa."

Kitty softened her gaze, grateful for the news of her family.

Aunt Julia rose from behind her desk. "Anyway, I'll let you get to it. I'm going to the cafe in town. I'll be back after lunch."

"Madame Allard?" Kitty called. "Is there any word from... Paris?" *From Edgar?*

Her aunt peered at her. Kitty had shared only enough information to assure her that Edgar was not to be feared.

"No. Nothing," Aunt Julia said.

Kitty's heart sank. She glanced at the fruit bowl. "Do you mind if I have one of the lemons?"

"Whatever you need."

After Aunt Julia was gone, Kitty found a knife, as well as a thin paintbrush. She then pressed the office door closed and locked it.

The storage space beneath the floor was located to the right of the table. Kitty rolled up the first half of the Ottoman rug and ejected the board, then pulled off her bloomers. She carefully removed the plasticine and tucked them into the hiding space. Marie had done a masterful job of fashioning the bloomers to carry the packets. When everything was stored away, she closed the trapdoor, and took a step back. It looked good. She rolled the rug back on top of it, and then went to the desk.

Before it got cold, she drank the coffee and rinsed her cup with a bit of water from a pitcher. She then cut the lemon and squeezed the juice into her cup. She reached for the first piece of paper and dipped the paintbrush into the lemon juice. She preferred using baking soda and water; it dried better than the juice and did not bite into the paper, but she would have to make do with what she had available.

She wrote the first message, dipping the brush in every few letters. She would courier it to a dead letter box in the next town. A local from the circuit would pick it up, understand her reference to *Boulestin* and arrange delivery of the explosives.

She carefully cut the slip, rolled it up and put it in the bottom of her sock. Outside, she checked the tire, and kicked it with frustration. It was low again. There was definitely a hole in it.

It was going to be a very long day.

When Kitty finally returned to the pension, she rummaged in the shed for tools and extracted the inner tube from her bicycle. The group was sitting around the table in Raymond's apartment, and he pushed himself away when she walked in.

"We've got news."

"So do I." She dangled the rubber tube from her wrist. "My bicycle tire has a hole."

Vladimir got up and took it from her, then examined it. "I can do that. Some linen and glue, and it'll be as good as new."

"See," she teased. "You're not just a cook any more. You're a poet, too."

Before Raymond could interrupt her, Kitty sat down and made her report. "I'll be at the gallery four times to help pack the sculptures," she said, referring to the explosives.

She then told them about the spot check and the patrols that had stopped her.

Vladimir was dunking the tube in a small tub of water. "So they wanted to blow up your tire. And that really set you off?"

Raymond laughed abruptly, but Marie scowled at both men. She stretched out her arms, her nails scratching the surface of the table. "Enough with the jokes, Vlad. She was in real danger."

"Right," Vladimir said, his smile disappearing. "Sorry about that, Yvette. Very insensitive of me."

Marie looked satisfied.

Kitty turned to Raymond. "Sorry, what did you want to share?"

Raymond darkened with his bad-news expression. "Prosper is on the run."

Kitty's heart fell. That was Guinevère's network in Lyon.

"Stanley was arrested in Paris," Marie added. "But not Guinevère, that we know of."

Kitty pictured the man who had casually invited her to the Sten gun training; how irritated Guinevère had been with him for his lack of security.

"So, with Prosper out of the loop," Raymond went on, "we've been asked to take over an operation."

"What operation?" Kitty asked cautiously.

"One of us has to go up to Paris and meet a runaway the Prosper agents were supposed to take in."

Her stomach lurched at the mention of Paris. "An airman?" Kitty guessed.

"I don't think so," Vladimir said. "This is an order from the top. They're calling it Operation Austerlitz. The man we're supposed to escort goes under the cover name Bonaparte. We're to take him down the Pat Line but from Clermont-Ferrand."

"I'll go," Kitty hurried. "I want to go. Can I go?"

Raymond scowled. "Why?"

"Because I've used the escape line on two other occasions. I know the people. The network knows me. And I know Paris like the back of my hand."

"I was planning on going," Raymond said. "It's apparently important enough that—"

"That we need to double down on security," Kitty stressed.

Marie was watching her with interest. "Let her go, Chief. I think Yvette has a good point. Besides, you owe her a cheese sandwich."

Raymond's neck grew pink. Kitty put her hands on her hips, copied his wide stance, and cocked her head at him. "You do, don't you?"

He growled before he blurted, "I'll ask London. But I'm not promising anything."

Satisfied, Kitty turned to Vladimir. "When are you wiring the next message?"

"Day after tomorrow."

"Ask London if Huntress can go," Raymond muttered, using Kitty's code name. He faced her. "If they say yes, then you'll go. If not, I'll go."

After Vladimir messaged London two days later, he brought back the response. He brushed his hand over his mustache, but Kitty had already seen the grin. "Says here, if Raymond orders Huntress to transport explosives in her bloomers, and she does so with brilliant success, Huntress can have what she wants. Huntress goes to Paris."

Raymond capitulated.

"You told them about the bloomers?" Kitty demanded.

Vladimir's grin slid off his face. "Yes."

"You made jokes about the bloomers to London," she said flatly. "Tell me you didn't."

Raymond shrugged. "What? It's a sensational story. Anyway, you are the one going to Paris. Finally you get to go to Paris, for whatever reason you always want to go to Paris."

Kitty looked incredulously at Marie.

Her friend took her by the elbow and threw Raymond a dirty look. "That's another cheese sandwich you owe her, Chief."

"Both of us," Kitty added.

"How so?" he demanded.

Kitty whirled on him. "It was a lot of explosives, Raymond. Enough to blow up a lot of things. And it was my idea. And Marie's ingenuity."

"Are you sulking?" Raymond mocked.

"No," Kitty bit back. "But if you're going to give me credit for doing something brave and crazy, then give me—and Marie—credit for the whole damned thing!"

18

OCTOBER 1942

Paris, Nazi-Occupied France

According to the brief Kitty read, Operation Austerlitz entailed meeting and escorting a POW escapee from Paris to Barcelona. She was to refer to him as "Bonaparte."

"Where did he escape from?" she asked Raymond.

"Poland, as far as I know. What's wrong?"

Kitty shook herself off. "Nothing." But she was recalling Edgar's story about the last man who'd escaped from Auschwitz carrying a report about the awful conditions in the camp and the crimes the Nazis were committing—the man and the report intercepted by the Gestapo.

Raymond interrupted her thoughts. "You'll get on a train and make contact with a courier at this library. They'll let you know how and when to meet Bonaparte. And Yvette?"

"Yeah?"

"No funny business. You double down on security. Is that clear?"

"Yes, sir," Kitty said. "I understand."

Two days later, she was on her way. As usual, the train to Paris was packed, and she was checked, not just once, but three times, nearly at every stop. Having befriended one of the rail workers, Vladimir had been able to get Kitty's double-sided suitcase hidden in a secret cavity of the baggage car. She had nothing on her except for her identity papers and a rucksack and easily passed through the checks.

When she arrived in the capital, she tensed at the sight of the luggage cart standing on the platform. There were more German patrols milling about than she had previously seen in Paris, and two of those guards were at the stack of baggage. She waited a moment as passengers retrieved their suitcases. Hers stuck out like a sore thumb, though Kitty chided herself about being paranoid. It was not unusual in any way; not to the uncritical eye in either case. Suddenly, a man appeared with another cart piled high with official boxes. As he passed the first cart, he grabbed two of the cases from the first one and placed them on the other. One of those bags was hers. He positioned it near the entrance.

Kitty did not hesitate. She quickly walked over, gripped the handle of her case and walked out of the platform and into the station. A moment later she was on the street, and hurrying to her hotel in the Latin Quarter. She checked in, and left that suitcase beneath her bed as Raymond had instructed. All she knew was that there was equipment, francs, and messages to be picked up, and when she returned, that suitcase would be empty, save for her clothing.

Kitty left the hotel and headed to the Mazarine Library, the hollow clop of her heels echoing off the atrium's tiled floor. She took the stairs to the second floor and requested the reading room, waited for permission to enter, and took a seat with two titles on French history. She ran a finger beneath the floral scarf she was wearing around her neck; the signal to the courier.

A moment later a young woman approached her table and switched on the reading lamp. "That should help." She was a pretty brunette with her hair in marcel waves. She was wearing a rust-colored dress and a floral scarf.

"There's a draft in the room," she said.

Kitty perked up at the password. "The weather has turned."

The woman nodded at her and handed her a book. "I think this is what you are looking for."

A History of the Napoleonic Wars.

Operation Austerlitz. Bonaparte.

"You'll find what you are looking for on page two hundred and one. It's due back tomorrow by 11 a.m."

Kitty thanked the woman and watched her go, before turning the book face up. On the page the courier had told her, she found a piece of blank paper. Kitty bit her lip. Invisible ink. But she already understood that she would meet Bonaparte tomorrow, at eleven.

Later, back at her hotel, Kitty was about to go into her room when a German soldier and a curvy woman wearing an indigo dress stumbled past her. Kitty froze as the German, a long scar on his right cheek, leered at her.

"*Mademoiselle*." His head turned as he passed her. "Come, join us. For a nightcap."

The brunette giggled and leaned into him, her smile solicitous.

"*Merci*," Kitty said. "Have a good evening."

She quickly let herself in, and listened at the door. The two went into the room a couple doors down, the woman's giggles ceasing. Kitty locked her room, clicked on the light next to her bed and let the lightbulb warm up. Gingerly, she held the paper to the glowing heat and the letters appeared in light brown.

Café Blanc in Montmartre, red tie. 1 p.m. departure.

She lit a match and burned the note, then turned off the lamp. She tried to get some sleep, but thoughts of Edgar kept running through her mind. Being in Paris was sheer torture. He was right *here*, in *this* city. Her hotel was in the Latin Quarter. It would take her just under an hour to walk to his apartment.

She reminded herself of Raymond's warning. Guinevère's circuit was now dispersed. Under the Night and Fog decree, agents were disappearing and nobody knew their whereabouts. Kitty reprimanded herself. Marseilles had been a big rule-breaker already.

Kitty flopped onto her other side. The loneliness, the futile fantasy of Edgar showing up at her door, was so painful, she had to squeeze her eyes shut but nothing kept the tears back.

Waiting at a bistro across the street from Café Blanc, Kitty did not remove her sunglasses or her hat, but sat at the window facing the slanted autumn sun and the street. The cigarette smoke was pungent, and she pretended to ignore the two German men who walked in. Unfortunately, she was acutely aware of their every move and even recognized that one had an Austrian accent. They were in civilian clothing, and talked loudly about the German army's successes over glasses of beer.

On the street, Kitty caught sight of a man coming around the corner. He was in a gray trench coat, hunched beneath a brown hat. He suddenly straightened, his face pale, and though he wore spectacles, even from this distance she could tell he was glancing nervously about. That was when she spotted the scarlet tie.

He yanked at the door of the cafe. It took two attempts before he slid in and disappeared inside.

Kitty cleared her throat and downed her cold coffee. She would have to make sure Bonaparte learned to relax, and fast. She went to the bar and smiled wanly at the two Germans.

"*Fräulein*," one said, raising his beer to her, as if he'd been waiting all this time for this very opportunity.

Kitty gave a non-committal smile and hid her hand beneath the bar. A ringless finger attracted unwanted attention.

The man winked at her and turned back to his partner, who was muttering something about how French women only played coy.

Kitty quickly paid and gathered her things. She walked toward the cafe on the street opposite, her handbag pressed against her. The glass etchings on the windows practically hid all the patrons from view. She crossed the road and caught sight of Bonaparte sitting at the last booth, a wall to his back. She faked a double take, returned to the window, and waved at him warmly. Poking out of her handbag, the floral scarf. If the two Germans at the bistro happened to be watching her, they would think she had just spotted a friend.

Bonaparte's eyes widened and darted about as if he were searching for an escape before landing back on her. Kitty went inside.

"How are you?" She took his hand when he stood up to greet her, and leaned in to peck his cheeks. Near his ear, she whispered, "Sit down and relax. I'm Yvette. Yvette Archambeau."

"*Bonjour*, Yvette," he said. His accent was Polish.

The waiter was quick. She ordered two coffees, checked the time and waited until their order was delivered. She then watched as Bonaparte nervously stirred his coffee. There was no milk or sugar to be had.

"Our train leaves in just about an hour," she said chattily. "Take your time, and then we'll head to the station. It's a fifteen-minute walk from here." She clutched her handbag. "So, tell me. How is the family?"

Bonaparte replaced his cup, and pushed up his wireless glasses. He looked shabby, but his clothes were French. This was good. Wherever he'd been staying had at least tried to dress him as a local.

"I've had a long journey," he said. "They are fine."

She nodded. "Good, and Eva?"

He looked confused for a moment but replied, "She's fine."

Kitty decided this was not going to be easy but she had to say something. And he had to play along. "Michael is certainly looking forward to seeing you, in either case. It's been too long. Much too long."

He gulped down his coffee and cast her a pleading look.

"What do you think," she said, relenting. "Should we go?"

He reached into his pocket and dropped coins on the table, then looked sheepishly at her. "I am a gentleman."

They left. Just around the corner from Montparnasse station suddenly two trucks sped into their street. Kitty jumped against the building, yanking Bonaparte with her. The vehicles squealed to a stop and four Wehrmacht soldiers jumped out.

Kitty froze. She was about to throw up her hands in surrender when she realized that the Germans were not hunting them. Instead, they quickly surrounded the entrance of a building opposite. Two rushed inside, the other two were keeping an eye on the street. Soon, one of the soldiers reappeared, dragging a middle-aged man out. Another one tripped the man, who fell, sprawling across the pavement.

"Get up! Get up, you dirty Jew!"

A lump in her throat, Kitty remembered being tossed out onto the sidewalk in front of Hotel Metropole. She silently pleaded for the man to get up. He did, but the Germans immediately grabbed him and shoved him into the vehicle. The second soldier who'd gone into the building reappeared with an older man. He had a gray and black beard, and his glasses were askew on his face.

Bonaparte snatched Kitty by the elbow and tugged her down the street. It was empty, but they passed people huddled in doorways, faces peeking outside windows before shutting the curtains when Kitty looked in their direction.

"That's how it is there…" Bonaparte said it so quietly she'd thought she'd misheard.

"Where?" she whispered.

But he did not answer.

Gare Montparnasse was right ahead of them now.

She pressed the train ticket into Bonaparte's hand. "We'll board the train separately."

He nodded and they approached the hall where gendarmes were checking everyone's identities. Bonaparte queued ahead of her. Suddenly a man protested loudly, and arguing broke out at the front of the line. Kitty craned her neck, her gut clenching, but it was not Bonaparte. The man in question was exasperated and began patting his coat pockets furiously.

"Where should I have this on me?" he shouted.

The gendarme motioned to two other officials, who stepped on either side of the passenger and hauled him to an office at the end of the station.

The woman ahead of Kitty turned to her, eyes clouded by anxiety. "I'm so glad I got my new identity card yesterday."

"New identity card?"

"Yes. The damned Nazis changed them again."

"For Paris?"

"For Paris," she confirmed. "For all of occupied France."

Kitty stood on tiptoe and looked for Bonaparte. She spotted him just as he turned to her, his brow creased with worry. She waved him over.

"Let me see your identity papers," she whispered to him when he arrived.

Bonaparte handed them to her. Her heart sank. His had a Paris address.

"Excuse me, madame." Kitty tapped the woman ahead of her. "What does your identity card look like?"

The woman frowned, and Kitty explained. "My friend here lives in Paris. I don't want any trouble."

The woman showed it to her, and Kitty closed her eyes tightly. She sighed, thanked the woman and pulled Bonaparte out of the line with her.

He followed without protest. She went to the waiting area and sat down on a bench in the corner. He sank down next to her. She looked in despair at the clock. Their train was leaving in less than twenty minutes.

"You can't travel with those papers. You'll have to wait for new ones to leave the city."

"What does that mean?"

"It means we need to find a safe house, and we need to find a forger," she said quietly.

He pressed his glasses to the bridge of his nose. His right eye twitched.

"Where did you get these?" She meant his identity papers.

"Here, in Paris."

She had no time to think that through. Another pair of gendarmes strolled by the waiting area. There was an idea in the back of her mind, but first she had to find a safe house. She would have to track down someone from the SOE network. She knew of an "Alex" Raymond had told her about. And the woman at the library. She could possibly find her there again. But until Kitty could make contact with them, she needed to get herself and Bonaparte to safety. Her thoughts were split in six different directions.

Back in London, Oskar had given her three addresses. The nearest one was about a twenty-minute walk from where they were.

"Let's go," she said. "We're on plan B now."

"Isn't it dangerous?"

"There is always a plan B, and if not B, then C, and D, and

so on. You're going to have to stay on your toes a little longer with me."

The one thought that would not let her go as she steered Bonaparte to Oskar's friend's home was making her queasy. It was the one thought that dug into her, clawed at her heart—the one thought that would create the most trouble for her, and it was this: Edgar was the only one she trusted and who could obtain forged paperwork. Fast and accurate forgeries. He was also absolutely off limits. Except, perhaps, in an emergency.

And for that, Kitty had Dr. Max.

19

OCTOBER 1942

Paris, Nazi-Occupied France

The corridor in the apartment building in Passage de la Tour de Vanves was dark when they arrived, but that meant nothing. The blue and green paint was flaked and peeling. She knocked at the door number Oskar had given her. A woman answered.

"Madame Tourneau?" Kitty stuck out her hand. Bonaparte shuffled behind her.

"*Oui*. What can I do for you?"

"I'm a friend of Oskar Liebherr. You once helped four of his friends."

Her eyes widened. She looked at Bonaparte, and opened the door wider. "Come in. Come in."

When they were inside, Kitty finally allowed herself the luxury of anguish. She had a lot of work ahead of her if she was going to get Bonaparte out of occupied France. After convincing Madame Tourneau of their need, the woman left to prepare places for them to sleep.

Kitty turned to face Bonaparte. "I think it's time you tell me how, and where, and why you're here."

Bonaparte looked startled. "Which question would you like me to begin with?"

"Where did you come from?"

"Auschwitz."

"You too?"

Bonaparte's brow knitted together. "Me too?"

Kitty would not give him the benefit of the doubt. "You must be awfully well organized, you Polish officers, for one person after another to find their way out of a prison camp." Her thoughts were on the Polish officer Edgar had told her about, who'd been captured by the Gestapo in Paris. That man had also been in Auschwitz.

Bonaparte's neck reddened. "If you people already know about us, why hasn't anything been done? We've been begging, for years, for the Allies to put an end to it. And now..." His face radiated anger.

"Is this what an ally does?" he went on hoarsely. "Nobody moved when the Germans invaded Poland. Nobody. We risk our lives, and suffer those Nazi beasts, so that you can sleep well at night, or what?"

Kitty shook her head. "We do not sleep well. We do not sleep well at all."

He leaned forward, his eyes blazing behind the spectacles. "Then do something about it."

"I am," she said measuredly. "That's why I am here, in Paris, with you."

Bonaparte shrank back and whipped off his spectacles. He rubbed his face. "I'm sorry. Of course. I don't mean you..."

"Listen, I understand you're anxious. But why are you in occupied France? Why didn't you go over Switzerland and the non-occupied zone?"

"Because Sweden was where someone could receive me," he said glibly. "Beggars can't be choosers."

Kitty muttered her apologies. "It's just that the man who came before you... He didn't make it..."

Bonaparte sighed and closed his eyes. "Stanislaw. We had a feeling. Because if he had, I would have died under a carpet of bombs."

Kitty had a dozen more questions now, but it was obvious that Bonaparte's group—whoever they were—were trying to warn the world of something important. And horrible.

She stayed on task. "How did you get out of Auschwitz?"

He shrugged. "I got released in August."

"But it's almost November," she exclaimed.

The Polish man scoffed. "And I've been on the run the whole time. I managed to get into Sweden, but the man I was with was arrested right after I arrived. I narrowly avoided being snatched by the police myself. They seized the personal documents I had to leave behind. I had nowhere else to turn. I couldn't go to Holland, so I came to France, where I knew someone. He got me to your people here. But then the people I was staying with disappeared and the Gestapo showed up to search their apartment. I remained hidden for quite some time before someone came and got me out.

"She brought new papers, and assured me I'd get swiftly over the border. But then she realized the Gestapo were closing in on her, and had to call for help. We had no idea the identity cards were being changed."

"She?" Kitty said.

"Guinevère. She went by Guinevère."

Kitty leaned back. Guinevère was in Paris, or had been. "Is she all right?"

Bonaparte considered for a second. "Last I saw her, she was as good as someone on the run can be."

"You're right. She couldn't have known that the Nazis

would change ID cards," Kitty muttered. The only one who might have known was Edgar, and F Section certainly did not have contact with him. "What are you carrying on you? Weapons? Papers?"

"Information."

"In paper form?"

He looked down at the floor and tapped his head. "Most of it is in here. But yes, I have a version on my person."

"Is it something we could wire over to London?"

He shook his head. "We've been collecting data for years. It would take much too long."

"So you are the information," she determined. "You are the package I need to get across the border. We're going to manage that. All right?"

Bonaparte looked around the room but did not look convinced.

"I had a friend from Poland," Kitty said. "A good man. He returned to fight, with the Home Front, I think."

"There were many of us who were good," Bonaparte said.

"I don't know where Jerzy is," Kitty said. "He had a wife and child in Warsaw and he felt the need to protect them. His wife is Jewish."

Bonaparte looked sorrowful. "Then he has much to grieve over."

Madame Tourneau appeared to show them to their room. Kitty thanked Bonaparte for being forthcoming and told him she would return soon. He looked nervous as she slipped back into the living room.

"I'm going to have to make a phone call," Kitty said to their hostess.

"I don't ask questions. I don't want to know," she said. "Go do what you need to do. The post office is open in the morning and is just around the corner."

The room that Madame Tourneau had put them in had a

second exit and a window where they could easily get out onto the roof. Kitty searched for other hiding places, including a large wardrobe but the apartment was small and there were not many choices. Yet, she had no reason to believe they had been followed, even suspected, but they were trapped in Paris until they could get Bonaparte new documents. She needed a forger. Fast.

She could try the woman at the library. It would be what the SOE would expect of her; to find the courier who'd already helped her. But if she was to make anything of Bonaparte's report, it was that anyone involved in clandestine operations in Paris right now was not likely to be found anywhere near the surface.

Someone had to know how to get to "Alex," Raymond's Parisian forger. Again, Kitty's foremost thought was Edgar. But calling Dr. Max—the emergency extension at the American Hospital—was not only dangerous but wholly against SOE protocol. Sighing, Kitty admitted to herself that the preferred way, the regulated way, was not always the best way, not the fastest and certainly not always the safest.

The next morning, she went to the post office, pulled the door closed and asked the operator to put her through to the American Hospital. A woman answered and Kitty asked for the emergency extension.

"Who are you looking for?" the woman asked sharply.

"Dr. Max, please." There was a pregnant pause on the other end and Kitty nearly hung up before the woman snapped again.

"Who?"

Kitty did not trust herself to repeat the name. Then a man's voice came on the line. She could not place the accent but she sensed the suspicion.

"There is no Dr. Max here. Who is calling?"

Kitty bit her lip, looked out the phone booth and froze. Two men in Fedoras walked in through the door. Dark winter coats.

Gestapo? One shot her a cold glance before going to the post office counter. The other stopped at a rack of cards, rifled through them, then stepped in line.

There was an intake of breath on the other end. She would lose the man if she didn't hurry.

"Elizabeth," she whispered, turning her head toward the wall. "Please tell Dr. Max that Elizabeth is calling."

"Like I said, there is no Dr. Max," the man growled. "Where are you calling from?"

"The Seine. He knows where."

The receiver slammed down on the other end, and Kitty jumped.

The two men who had walked in together were now at two separate counters. Kitty kept the phone held to her ear until one left. Then the other. Even as she left the phone booth, she was jittery but, out on the street, there was no sign of them. That meant nothing.

Kitty did not return to Madame Tourneau's, though she knew that a long absence could traumatize Bonaparte. He'd lost so many of his guides already. But she could not risk it.

Instead, she went on a tour of Paris to shake off any potential tail, and mulled over her situation. She and Edgar had arranged a rendezvous point on the Seine as well as a dead letter box site should she ever need blank identity cards.

By noon, she was in the Champs-Élysées, and certain that she was not being followed. As she took the steps down to the Seine and hurried in the direction of the Latin Quarter, she reflected on that phone call. Did Dr. Max really no longer exist? Had the extension been discovered? Answered by secret police? And what if she had indeed made an impact? What if she had gotten a message to Edgar? She had no choice now but to show up, to wait on that bench between two and three in the afternoon and hope—quite possibly against hope—that Edgar would deliver. The thought of seeing him—his hand on her shoulder, a caress, a stolen kiss—left her even more highly strung than she already was.

That afternoon, nobody approached her on the Seine.

Kitty began to believe that the worst had happened to Edgar and his network. What if she had created trouble for him? She could try and track him down at his apartment, if he was even still in Paris. She glanced over her shoulder as a man passed her by. Not Edgar. Not even suspicious. But the feeling that there were prying eyes everywhere left her numb at the thought.

With no other choice, Kitty decided to search for the other courier and ask for "Alex." But after two days of attempting to locate the woman at the library, she had no luck either. She was feeling abandoned, and desperately alone.

On the fifth day in Paris, Kitty was frantic. To add to her fraught nerves, Madame Tourneau was reluctant about an extended stay.

"At some point, the neighbors will begin asking questions," Oskar's friend said. The Frenchwoman then pressed a 9mm gun into Kitty's hand. "Take this. Find a place to hide it, but at least you'll have something if you need it."

When Kitty walked into the shared room, Bonaparte sprang up from the sofa in the corner. The gun fit in the palm of her hand and she showed it to him.

"That's a P35. Polish made," he said.

"Do you want it?" Kitty asked him.

He deflated and shook his head, gently pushing her hand away. "I can't. I've always been a pacifist."

"And now you are forced to be a hero." She felt sorry for him. "Don't worry. I know how to handle a weapon."

She went into her room and packed the gun into a hiding place in her rucksack, and had just begun making sure the seam was camouflaged when there was a pounding at the front door.

Kitty jumped up and rushed into the living room. Madame Tourneau spun to her, her face draining of all color. Kitty put a finger to her lips and whispered for her to wait, then quickly retrieved the pistol.

Bonaparte was jumping out of his skin. He was already checking the street and slowly pushing the window open. Kitty waved for him to stay inside and shut the bedroom door. She pressed her ear up just as Madame Tourneau slid the deadbolt.

"Madame? I am looking for Elizabeth." It was a woman's voice. Parisian accent.

Kitty's heart lurched into her stomach.

"Elizabeth?" Madame Tourneau asked with irritation. "I don't know any Elizabeth."

The other woman said something in a low voice, and Kitty steadied her breathing. Bonaparte was starting to climb out the window. She tiptoed over the old floorboards to him.

"I have to go out there," she whispered. She cupped the pistol in her palm, and helped Bonaparte out onto the ledge. He pressed himself against the outside wall and she carefully closed the window. With the gun in hand, she opened the bedroom door and peered outside.

Madame Tourneau backed away from the stranger as Kitty stepped out. She did not recognize the second woman: a blond in her mid-thirties, with high cheekbones.

She gazed at Kitty with interest. "Elizabeth?"

Kitty raised the pistol and cocked it. The woman's expression turned to stone and she slowly put her hands up. Madame Tourneau's eyes widened and she backed into the wardrobe.

"Who are you?" Kitty asked.

"I'm Marguerite. I am..." The woman pursed her lips and Kitty recognized something like regret flashing across the woman's face. "I am not a foe."

Definitely Parisienne.

"I came to deliver something for you. From Dr. Max."

Kitty gripped the pistol, her heart hammering. "Go on."

The woman slowly reached into her coat, and withdrew a brown envelope from the lining.

Kitty waved the pistol toward the table, her chest tight.

"He said this is a final favor," the woman said as she placed the envelope down. "There will be no more."

Kitty swallowed. "I understand." But she did not. Not really. She had obviously been followed. Someone had been watching her at the Seine.

The woman raised a questioning eyebrow at her. "I'm going to leave now."

Kitty lowered the pistol and motioned for Madame Tourneau to take the envelope. "Open it, please."

With shaking hands, Madame Tourneau pulled out documents. She held them up. They were blank.

Kitty looked at the woman, startled. Who was she? Why hadn't Edgar come to the Seine? Where was he?

"Is that all?" Kitty's voice shook.

"No. There was one more message. He said you don't have to worry about a return."

"Pardon?" Kitty frowned. "Return from where? To where?"

The woman's face remained unchanged. "That's all he said."

"He?" Kitty demanded. She wanted to hear his name. If he was telling her to never look for him again, she wanted to hear her husband's name.

The woman cocked an eyebrow. "Dr. Max," she stressed, then turned to the door and without another look—without another word—slipped out.

Madame Tourneau slid the deadbolt into place and stared at the door.

But Kitty was shaken. She went to the window of the sitting room and stepped out onto the small balcony. The woman was halfway down the street already. Kitty went back inside, and found the two blank identity cards and special travel permissions on top of the envelope.

They were not filled in but they were stamped. And they required their passport photos. Kitty could do both. She could do the German cursive. She could give them new names and fabricate cover stories. Best of all, she could get Bonaparte and herself out of Paris.

"I can work with these. We'll be out of your hair in two days. Maximum."

Kitty put the items back into the envelope, but questions about the blond filled her thoughts.

"Where is your companion?" Madame Tourneau suddenly asked.

Kitty had nearly forgotten Bonaparte. "He's out on the ledge."

The woman hurried into his room. It gave Kitty a moment to come to grips with what had just happened, but she was even more confused.

"Edgar?" she whispered. "Where are you?"

20

NOVEMBER 1942

Marseilles, Non-Occupied France

The Rebouls's large and stately apartment in Marseilles was laced with the scents of desperation and relief, of fear and hope; a primitive, almost animalistic odor that lingered in the corners and on the bedding. Or Kitty was imagining it, because she had a fairly good idea how many people had channeled through the home of the good doctor and his accommodating wife.

Mrs. Reboul took Kitty to the side after settling Bonaparte into one of those rooms.

"The American consulate has been referring Jewish candidates to my husband. The ones seeking refugee status," the woman said. "They need official medical examinations to leave the country. They've asked my husband to do them."

Kitty's spirits dared to lift. "And?"

"Just like with the identity papers"—she winked—"he gets things done."

"I am so grateful." Kitty grasped her hand. "Ever so grateful."

Mrs. Reboul told her she had to return to the sitting room. "I have company waiting. Friends of mine. Fine ladies, all of them, and they don't suspect a thing."

Returning to the business of getting Bonaparte out of France, Kitty had already decided that the easiest and fastest way to get him out of the country would be via Lysander. Kitty would find the rest of the Sculptor Group and have Vladimir order the plane from London. She also wanted to check on Aunt Julia. Perhaps there would be a message from Edgar, one that would unravel the mystery behind that strange Parisienne woman's words.

But when Kitty arrived at Madame Keller's pension, she knew at first sight that the place was empty, and when she tested all the doors, they were locked. Fear lodged in her throat. Where were her people?

Certain that the building was being watched, Kitty walked normally past the pension and turned into a side alley, then fled through a narrow maze before catching a bus that was about to pull away. She got off three stops later, and slipped over a bridge, and followed the stream to the bicycle shop. The family there was holding her contraption.

Inside the workshop, there were two other customers: a woman and a teenage boy with a dog. They were gathered around the radio, their faces drawn and apprehensive.

"*Bonjour?*" she called cautiously.

They watched her approach and made room. The owner, a gray-haired man in a green sweater, beckoned her to the side.

"There's just been a radio announcement. The Germans declared that they are no longer accepting the Vichy government's neutrality," he informed her.

"What happened?"

"The French military is scuttling ships in Toulon. The Germans have already crossed the demarcation line."

Kitty's gut rippled with panic. "I need my bicycle," she whispered.

"Sébastien is out back. He'll fetch it for you."

She excused herself and hurried out to the garden. The owner's son was making repairs to the wheel of a bicycle. He saw Kitty and dropped his tools before waving her over to the storage shed.

"Your colleagues," he said as he unlocked it, "have dispersed."

"What do you know?"

"Madame Keller was stopped and found with extra ration cards on her."

Kitty swore under her breath.

"She was arrested early last week."

"That's not long after I left." Kitty looked around. "And now the Germans are headed into the rest of France."

Gravely, he slipped off the padlock, then wheeled her bicycle out.

She pressed some of the last francs she had into his hand. "You did not see me. You did not hear from me. Understood?"

Mrs. Reboul had told her that she and Bonaparte could join a convoy on the way to Spain if nothing else worked out, but Kitty was now certain that she had to escort Bonaparte out on her own. First, though, she needed to see Aunt Julia and check on the gallery.

Only when she was sure that her aunt was alone and the streets were empty did Kitty slip inside.

Aunt Julia threw herself on Kitty and pecked both cheeks. "I thought they had you, too."

"Shhh," Kitty whispered. "Turn on the radio."

After dialing the knobs on the radio, a brass band crackled through. Aunt Julia returned and grasped Kitty's hands. "Marie wanted me to tell you that Madame Keller has been arrested. As has Henri."

The forger. Kitty brushed a hand over her face to hide her expression.

"She said several others have also been taken in for questioning. At least six. Raymond and Vladimir have fled for the hills. Witnesses saw that police were waiting for them while they were on their way to work, but both escaped. Marie arrived and I helped her to bury the stores and Vladimir's two-way radio in the spot you said we should. She's gone to find others from the network. But the money..."

Kitty patted her arm. "I was prepared for that."

Long ago, she had learned not to put all her eggs into one basket. She had another stash, in the plaster statue of a lion she'd acquired from one of Aunt Julia's clients. From the pedestal just outside the office, she carried it to the worktable and tapped around the underbelly. A piece popped out and Kitty withdrew a thick wad of francs.

Aunt Julia watched in wonder. "When you told me I'd never be privy to everything... Well."

"What about you?" Kitty asked, counting out francs for her. "Has anyone questioned you?"

"No." Her aunt rolled the bills together and stuck them down her dress.

"I want to make sure you are safe. If they catch on to any of us in any way"—she shivered at the thought of the men, or Marie, being tortured into talking—"the police will come for you next. And the Germans are en route, too." She considered her aunt. "I should take you with me."

The woman raised her hands. "I'm not running. I would only hold you up. I can go to Toulon. I have friends there, Americans. I'll hang a notice on the gallery that I am taking a holiday. If I get caught with you, the chances are they will find out who you really are."

Kitty choked back a protest. Her mother's sister was energetic. And she was brave but Kitty could not argue with the woman's logic. "Then please. Go, tonight. And try to get out of France. Go to Maman. Stay with the family until the war is over."

"I'll consider it."

Kitty squeezed her arm and turned to go. "Will you please check the street?"

"Wait. There's something else." Aunt Julia hurried to her desk and removed an envelope. "I received this the day after you were last here. It arrived by special delivery from Paris."

Kitty snatched the post from her. *Edgar!* It had to be. Had they crossed paths? Her pulse raced with anticipation. It was addressed, in type, to *Madame Elizabeth Hennessy*, care of Madame Julia Allard. This was odd, but Elizabeth Hennessy was the gallery's financier. Aunt Julia headed outside as Kitty opened the note.

The message made her heart drop. It was written in a feminine hand and echoed the warning she'd gotten in Paris.

Most loyal friends have come to pass. No need to return.

Kitty's hand shook. Something had happened to Edgar, she was sure of it. And she was sure that the handwriting was that of the blond, Marguerite, who'd delivered the blank identity cards.

Aunt Julia returned. "The street is clear now. You have to go." But at the sight of Kitty, her eyes pooled with emotion.

Kitty hugged her aunt before the woman could ask about the message. "I love you," she cried quietly. "Thank you for your courage. I'm so sorry I have to go."

Bonaparte was her first priority, she reminded herself, and

the wolves were closing in. Kitty would have to figure out the rest later.

Aunt Julia squeezed her. "Stay strong. Stay safe..." She pulled away and smiled sadly before mouthing the name, *Kitty*.

On the way back to the Rebouls's apartment in Marseilles, Kitty was mulling over plan C. No group. No Lysander. And no Edgar. She was scared stiff. As far as she and Bonaparte were concerned, there was a safe house some kilometers outside the city. It would be remote enough that they could gather their wits before assessing the safest route to the Spanish border, because by morning, Marseilles would be crawling with Nazis.

Kitty was not wrong to fear the worst. Mrs. Reboul met her in the stairwell and dragged her inside. Her face was pale.

"The Vichy government—"

Kitty grasped her. "I heard. Where is Bonaparte? We're leaving right now."

"Where will you go?"

"To another safe house." She had never been to the farm she had in mind, but she and Bonaparte needed to get their bearings. To rest. To clear her head. To gather her wits.

She rushed to Bonaparte's room to find the Polish man dressed in his coat and hat, pacing. He spun away from the window.

"We have to go. Now."

He pointed to the window overlooking the street. "It's too late. They're here."

"Who is?" At first she thought the Germans. But it could not be. They must still be hundreds of miles from the border.

"Police. They're milling about down in the alley."

Kitty clutched her throat. Had she been followed?

"Mrs. Reboul!" Kitty ran to the front room. "They're coming. We're taking the roof."

Kitty bundled up their things and handed them to Bonaparte as soon as he was on the ladder. Just as he began the ascent, there was muffled pounding on the Rebouls's apartment door. Kitty motioned for Bonaparte to hurry. His foot slipped and she winced, but he quickly regained his balance. Suddenly, she could hear a man's voice right outside the bedroom.

"Search everything!" he ordered. "Mrs. Reboul, where is your husband?"

"At the clinic," the woman answered. "How can I help you?"

Kitty knew she would not make it out the window. She shut it to prevent the police from suspecting someone had fled. The wardrobe. She knew from one of her previous visits that there was a false back. The conversation on the other side of the door continued as she gently tried the panel.

"What exactly are you looking for?" Mrs. Reboul asked coldly.

Kitty heard them enter the room and froze. She had just managed to slip inside the space between the faux back and the real back, but not slide it closed again.

"The concierge of the building has reported a strange-looking antenna," the official said. "Coming from your apartment."

"An antenna? I don't know anything about one."

"Then you won't mind if we look around."

There was the sound of people pacing the room: Mrs. Reboul and the policeman, Kitty guessed.

"What sorts of things would such an antenna be for?" Mrs. Reboul asked.

There was no answer. More sounds of rummaging. The wardrobe knob rattled. Kitty's insides turned liquid.

"Radio. Illegal transmissions of information."

"I beg your pardon?" Mrs. Reboul asked politely. She was being very composed, Kitty thought.

Light seeped through as a mustached man in police uniform glanced over the clothing inside. Hidden in the shadows, Kitty froze.

Mrs. Reboul appeared next to him. "I don't have the faintest idea of what you are talking about."

"We've picked up radio signals in this area." He closed the door again. "And the antenna matches with such a situation."

As their footsteps retreated into the hallway, Kitty cupped a hand over her mouth and released a slow breath.

Then Mrs. Reboul was following the policeman into the dining room next door. Kitty had to strain to hear them.

"Are you talking about music?" Mrs. Reboul asked.

"No, madame. Wireless messages. Do you know this man? His name is Celestin. He's a British national."

Not her, Kitty thought. They were not looking for her.

There was silence. Then, muffled from the wall behind Kitty, Mrs. Reboul continued her calm and innocent charade. "I've never seen him. Not that I know of. He looks like any average Frenchman here."

"He's a wireless operator. British."

"Honestly, I have no idea what that even means…"

They were moving once more. So was Kitty.

She slipped out of the wardrobe, opened the window and got out onto the narrow balcony. Bonaparte whistled sharply from above.

Gritting her teeth, she slowly pulled the window shut then scrambled up the ladder. Bonaparte offered her a hand, and yanked her over the rim.

Neither said a word to each other; they did not have to. They jumped to the next roof easily, found the hatch and were down the stairwell and in the cellar of the next building. This was where Kitty had stored her bicycle. This was where they would wait until dark.

Hours later, Bonaparte was pedaling down a country lane toward the safe house, Kitty perched on the carrier.

It was nearly midnight when they reached the small farm. It was surrounded by woods and—as with Madame Keller's pension—Kitty immediately sensed the emptiness. They coasted to the center of the yard, and she hopped off in front of the barn, everything in her telling her that they were not safe. Bonaparte had crept up to the house. He returned to her.

"The door," he whispered and pointed.

It was standing wide open.

21

NOVEMBER 1942

Southern Occupied France

Nobody was inside the farmhouse.

Kitty shivered, rubbing her arms. She was spooked. Bonaparte had a flashlight and shone it around the room. It was a tidy home, and nothing was amiss. No sign of an interrupted meal, or knocked-over chairs from a violent struggle. It just looked as if the owners had left. To visit family? Friends?

"Maybe they went somewhere safer?" Bonaparte guessed.

Kitty looked at him. His comment had not helped. "I don't want to stay here," she whispered.

Bonaparte stepped out with her into the crisp night. The crescent moon was high in the sky. When they discovered that the barn was also empty—no animals, only the equipment for the fields—Kitty's nerves were not calmed one bit.

"There's nothing for it," Bonaparte said. "We should try and get some sleep. Maybe we can figure this out in the morning."

Kitty announced that she would not sleep in the house

but would fetch food and blankets. Outside, the snap of a branch made her jump. It came from the woods behind the house.

"Hello?"

She strained to hear another sound. Nothing. No dog barking. No cats. Silence. Her gut was telling her to leave, but she and Bonaparte were exhausted. And it was nearly one in the morning.

"Just a wild animal," she muttered to herself. It had to be.

She moved on back into the house and searched the rooms for blankets, bundled them up in her arms, found some fruit compote in a jar, some tomatoes, and a lump of hard bread. It would do.

Bonaparte welcomed the picnic, and after they ate, they began discussing their options, who would stay on watch first, and when they should leave. Both of them lurched onto their feet at the sound of a clutch and a revving engine. Bonaparte scrambled to the barn entrance and immediately ducked back inside.

"Someone's headed up the road," he hissed.

"I should have known it was a trap."

"We don't know that, yet," Bonaparte argued. "What if it's just the owners returning home?"

She shook her head. "It's a trap."

Kitty went to the back of the barn. They could make it to the woods. Run now. But that snap out there. The crack of that branch. She now suspected that someone else had seen them and reported them.

"You should run," Bonaparte said. He reached into the side of his trench coat, and handed her a pen. "Take this with you. There's microfilm inside. You have a better chance of escaping, of hiding than me. You're a woman, and your French is fluent. It's only local police. I can manage them."

"Not with the Germans coming in," she argued. But she

took the pen. "They might hold you and turn you in to prove how very loyal they are."

"You need to go." He was very close now, his eyes drilling into her. "Tell my government in exile that the Polish officers and soldiers in Auschwitz are ready to lay their lives down. They must destroy Auschwitz. Bomb it. Tell the English what I told you. Tell the Americans. Everyone. Thousands of lives depend on you. Maybe tens of thousands now."

His words made her blood freeze. Even as the vehicle pulled into the drive, she could not move. If what Bonaparte was saying was true, she could not abandon him. Because who would believe *her*?

He suddenly shook her and shoved her out the back. "Go. Now!"

She was the last person to run from confrontation, but everything in her body was screaming for her to flee.

She snatched her rucksack from the straw and ran.

Four men got out of the vehicle. They let it run, the headlights pointed at the barn. Their flashlights sliced through the yard on the way to the house.

Kitty followed a narrow trail that brought her between the barn and the home. Bonaparte's pen was still in her hand. She felt for the lining in her rucksack that would allow her to slip it in. The flashlights appeared outside again, along with the dark shadows of three men. They gathered around the vehicle.

"Is anyone here?" a man called out. "We know you're here. Come out and show yourself, with your hands up."

Kitty heard the barn door creak open, and she muffled a gasp as Bonaparte appeared. His glasses reflected the vehicle lamps. He lifted his arms above his head. One of the men drew his weapon. There were words, and Bonaparte answered in mixed English and French.

A second man stepped into the light, and grabbed Bonaparte. "English?"

"*Polski.*"

The police officer had him up against one of the vehicles. The third patrol flung open the door, then called over his shoulder.

"Didi! Bonnet!"

A big man lumbered out of the house and strode over to the running automobile. He spun Bonaparte to face him.

Kitty could not make anything more out, but the big man suddenly shoved Bonaparte into the back of the vehicle. And then the others got in, and they drove away.

She was alone. Who had turned them in? Because if they had, wouldn't they have also been told to look for a second person? For her? Something snapped again, farther away in the woods. Kitty shivered, her heart racing. Either way, she had to leave now.

Mentally mapping out her location, she realized that if she started now, and avoided the roads with her bicycle, there was another safe house she could reach before dawn broke. Exhausted, tense and terrified, she struck out, fervently hoping that the family she helped establish a safe house was still in operation.

Madame Emond and her daughter Lily lived in Larçon, about ten miles from the farm where Bonaparte had been picked up by the police. She found the daughter outside in the gray dawn, wrapped in a scarf and feeding chickens. Blisters searing pain through her feet, Kitty reached the back gate and leaned on it before raising a hand to the young girl.

"Lily? It's Yvette. I once stayed here."

"Yes!" The teenage girl hurried to her. "Where did you come from?"

"It's a long story."

"Come. Maman is making breakfast. You look exhausted."

Kitty relaxed at the sight of Madame Emond in the kitchen. Both she and her daughter were completely trustworthy.

"My friend was taken," Kitty told the woman. "I think by police."

"Where?"

Kitty told her, then, "If it was police, where would they take him?"

Madame Emond wiped her hands on the dishcloth, considering for a moment. "The nearest police station would be in Ditres. I know the mayor there."

Kitty grasped her wrist. "Is he one of us?"

Madame Emond nodded.

"Good, because I know the name of one of the men. Didi Bonnet. Can you check and see whether the mayor recognizes the name? I need to know whom I'm dealing with."

Madame Emond tilted her head. "What do you mean?"

Kitty pulled away. Bonaparte was the package she was supposed to carry across into Spain. He may have given her his report, but he'd said most of the valuable information was in his head. And after what he had blurted out to her, Kitty was not going to move on without at least trying to free him. Before the Germans arrived.

"Let me freshen up first," Kitty suggested. "And then we can talk more."

But the ceiling creaked above and Kitty froze. She stared upwards, and then at Madame Emond and Lily.

"You are not the only one to show up here," the older woman said quietly.

Lily leaned in. "It's all right. We'll let him know."

"Who?"

"He goes by Celestin," Madame Emond said.

Kitty clamped her mouth shut. The police had been looking

for Celestin at the Rebouls's in Marseilles! And he was a radio operator.

Madame Emond jerked her head toward the back door. "Go on. Go to the wash house. Lily will bring you something to change into. I'll talk to him."

She followed Lily to the wash house outside, and did as Madame Emond had suggested. After she splashed water onto her face and brushed her teeth, Kitty examined the pen Bonaparte had given her. She unscrewed it. Inside, as he had said, was the thin film reel. This was enough to get her killed if discovered. And if she was going to risk her life for it, she wanted to know what was on that film.

She carefully unwound the strip. In her rucksack, she had a set of pocket-sized tools, including a tiny magnifying glass. She held the reel of negative to the light with one hand and the glass in the other. There were twelve pages of what appeared to be a typed-up report, all uniform, and in Polish. But the images that came afterwards were what made the hairs on Kitty's arms stand on end. There was a list with names and dates in German cursive, but she could not read the details. Handwritten reports that looked to be deliveries of supplies: food, arms, ammunition, medicines. She held the film closer at the sight of a long list of delivery receipts from a company called Testa. The product on the invoices was Zyklon B.

Again, Kitty recalled Edgar's account of the factories and a particular chemical being produced in mass quantities. And then his bitter message to her. To stay away, to not trust anyone. That their most loyal friends had come to pass. What did it all mean? Who had he meant? Once more, she feared with all her heart that something awful had happened to her husband. Only the blond woman in Paris might know what.

Grimly, Kitty rolled the reel back up and put it back into the pen, screwed the parts together and replaced it within the lining of the rucksack, next to the 9mm pistol.

Just as she finished, there was a knock on her door. It was Madame Emond.

"Celestin knows you are here," she called. "Come in. We can all have breakfast."

At the kitchen table, a man with fine brown hair, a thin mustache and pocked face poured ersatz coffee into small glasses. His long legs were stretched out beneath the table. When Kitty entered the room, he stood up and took her hand.

"Celestin," he said.

"I'm Yvette. The gendarmes were looking for you in Marseilles, at Dr. Reboul's."

He pointed at her. "F Section?"

"Yes. But I've lost track of my group."

"Sculptor."

She did not respond.

"I'm from Circus. I heard about that from my organizer. We had to split right after, as well. I'm to radio in to London in about twelve hours. Do you want me to send a message?"

Kitty could hardly believe her luck. Together, they formulated the news of Bonaparte's arrest, her own escape, the fact that Marie had been last seen picking up money at the gallery, and the rest was unknown.

"Does London know that the French police are trying to prove to incoming Gestapo that they are useful and should keep their jobs?"

"But that's not quite true," Celestin corrected. "I overheard some farmers who claim the local authorities are furious about the *boches* taking over. I don't think they are all as loyal to Pétain as the Nazis had hoped, and they're certainly not loyal to the *boches*."

Kitty studied him. "Is this on good word?"

"It's on experience."

By the time she and Celestin were finished, Madame

Emond returned from her shopping, breathless. She had word from the mayor in Ditres.

"This Didi Bonnet," she blurted triumphantly, "is an *imbécile*, the mayor said. And not a little corrupt."

"What do you mean?"

"There is a small group of policemen who take bribes from the locals whom they accuse of being anti-German and anti-Pétain. For a fee, they look away. They need the money, because they all have gambling debts."

Kitty listened to the details, then asked for a bicycle so she could observe the group for herself. Madame Emond described a high bridge from which Kitty could easily watch the back of the police station where the jail cells were. She mapped it out and Kitty prepared to leave.

"Celestin, don't send that message to London yet. Wait until I return."

"And if you do not?"

"Then you can assume that I have also been arrested. But I have an idea." Kitty had enough experience with how corruption worked. She turned to Madame Emond, examining the woman's dyed blond hair. "Where is the best, most discreet hairdresser you can recommend?"

22

NOVEMBER 1942

Ditres, Southern Occupied France

Just as Madame Emond had informed Kitty, the bridge over the canal provided a good view of the back of the police station and its jail cells.

Kitty spent two days studying the comings and goings of the station in Ditres, her newly dyed red hair tucked beneath a wool cap.

Didi Bonnet, the largest of the four law enforcement officials, stood outside smoking a cigarette. He had a round belly, thick jowls, white bushy eyebrows, and a rolling gait. The way he commandeered and pushed everyone around, she knew he was the pack's leader. His laugh was laced with cynicism.

In the evening, she watched Bonnet and the three other policemen enter a corner tavern. They said something to the bartender, who scowled, and dug into the glasses he was cleaning with more severity before pouring their drinks. He placed the glasses on the bar with a heavy hand.

Bonnet jerked his chin at him, and rapped his knuckles on the bar. "Is Marcel here?"

The bartender rolled his eyes and turned his back on the police. "Go see for yourself."

Bonnet slammed a hand next to his drink. "I said, is Marcel here?"

"In the back," the bartender replied.

Bonnet smirked and tossed down his drink. The three others followed as he headed to the back room. As soon as they were behind the door, Kitty rose from her table and approached the counter. She leaned against it and ordered a pastis. Sulkily, the bartender placed the liquor before her.

"What about you?" she asked. "You look like you could use a drink. I'm buying."

She lay two thousand francs on the bar. The bartender frowned at the money, looked at her, and she tipped her head toward the back room. He placed a palm over the notes and they vanished.

"There's more where that came from. Drink with me."

He poured himself a pastis, then added water to both of their glasses and stirred until they were milky white.

"Your friends—"

"They are not my friends," he growled.

"What's in the back room? Who is Marcel?"

"They take hush money. To pay off their gambling debts and promise discretion for the whoring he does in the back."

"How much?"

"From Marcel?"

"Debts," Kitty said and gulped down the liquor. She was delighted that he was corroborating Madame Emond's information.

"One? One and a half."

"Thousand?"

"Hundred thousand."

She whistled under her breath and looked up hopefully. "Total?"

"He shrugged. Probably a million or two, all together."

She pushed her glass over and laid another two thousand francs on the bar. "You are worth your weight in gold. Give us another."

The bartender repeated the ritual. She raised her glass to his.

"You never saw me," she warned. "Never heard of me. Never answered questions."

The bartender drank to that.

Back at the safe house that night, with Madame Emond, Kitty knocked on Celestin's door.

"When you wire London, tell them Huntress needs two million francs. Do you have a field around here for a drop?"

Celestin looked astounded. "That's a lot of money."

"For Bonaparte and the story he has to tell, it's nothing."

Madame Emond helped them to locate a suitable field. The business was risky but London responded that Huntress would get the money. In the meantime, the fates of Vladimir, Raymond, Marie and Madame Keller were still unknown. And then London added a warning to the F Section circuits over the BBC. All groups were advised to observe radio silence.

She and Celestin met the drop and, by the fourth day since Bonaparte's arrest, Kitty had the money she required. She returned for assistance from Madame Emond.

"I need the best dress you can find. A pair of silk stockings. High-heeled shoes, and good jewelry."

"I do not know if I can get the jewelry, but the rest should not be a problem."

"Do what you can."

Several hours later, Kitty stepped out of Madame Emond's

bedroom, dressed as Elizabeth Hennessy. Kitty understood that what would motivate these men was going to be a well-dressed woman. And money. Lots of money.

Didi Bonnet was loitering in front of the police station, smoking a cigarette. Dressed in a red wool skirt and blazer, high heels and the mayor's wife's fur stole, Kitty lingered in the post office across the street, impatiently tapping her shoe on the cheap tile floor. Finally, Bonnet's three other compatriots stepped out, lit their cigarettes and huddled together. She straightened, and caught a glimpse of herself in the reflection of the window. In a flash, Kitty realized how easily she had transformed herself into a woman who was capable of doing what she had in mind. It was crazy. Beyond crazy. But Elizabeth Hennessy was back, and it made Kitty feel protected.

She took the steps down to the street, and crossed it, bee-lining her way directly to the men. Bonnet saw her first, and she saw the gleam in his eye. He nudged the man next to him and stepped away from the wall. Kitty beamed at him, but her heart was hammering wildly.

"*Pardon.*" She said in heavily accented American. "*Êtes-vous Didi Bonnet?*"

Bonnet grinned slyly and rolled his head to the others, dragging on his cigarette one last time before ripping off the dog-end and tossing the rest. He glanced at her hand. "I am. What can I do for you, madame?"

"I'm an SOE agent, here on a secret British operation," she said matter-of-factly.

The shock on his face, and the way the three others suddenly lined up next to him, was priceless. Kitty, as Elizabeth Hennessy, smiled widely at each of them.

"You are holding my friend inside. A prisoner-of-war who

has very top-secret information for the Allies about German positions on the front."

They jostled one another, their expressions mixed between shock and suspicion. All four were confounded.

Kitty patted her purse. "I have two million francs here, gentlemen. Direct from the British government. That gives each of you five hundred thousand francs." She looked up and down the street. "It's a good way to start a new life, I think, especially when the German Gestapo arrive to take over your offices. I do believe they will be here any day now, if not in hours. What I am offering you is the opportunity to start over in exchange for one foreign POW. What do you say?"

Bonnet was speechless. He shook his head, and Kitty tilted hers at him.

"No? I guess I was wrong about you."

She turned on her heel but a hushed chorus of protests broke out. "Madame, madame, don't go. Stop."

Kitty smiled to herself before turning back to them. "History will judge you for which side you stand on today." She patted the purse once more. "Your choice."

Bonnet checked with the others; all of the men eyed her purse hungrily.

"Let me see the money," Bonnet said, his eyes darting up and down the street.

Kitty stepped up to him, so close she could smell the cigarette smoke on his breath. She opened the purse. The two million francs were there, packaged in four nice bundles of five hundred thousand each. Bonnet jerked his head at the others and wiggled his eyebrows. The others pulled gleeful faces.

"You want to do this on the street?" Bonnet hissed.

Kitty shrugged. "It's the safest I'll feel. There are four of you here. One of you will need to fetch Monsieur Bonaparte and bring him to me."

The shortest of the bunch, with a stiff red mustache, volunteered to go get him.

Kitty turned and waved at the waiting Citroën across the road. The engine started and the automobile pulled up, stopping in front of the station.

Bonnet looked panicked. And why wouldn't he? This was the kind of car German officials preferred above all others in the country. However the hell the mayor—whom Kitty had learned was a fervent follower of the Free French—had gotten his hands on a black Citroën, she neither knew nor cared.

"It's just our ride," she tutted. "You didn't think I was going to *walk* away with my prize, did you?"

Bonnet was still suspicious, but then the door to the station opened and Bonaparte marched ahead of the red mustached policeman.

When the Polish officer saw Kitty, his mouth fell open. She reached into her purse, quickly handed a bundle of money to each of the Frenchmen, then opened the back door for Bonaparte. He stumbled forward when the policeman undid the handcuffs, his eyes behind the spectacles bulging.

She threw herself into the car after him.

"Go," she said to Celestin. There was no time to waste, and she wanted to put these men far behind her.

Bonaparte turned to her, astounded. "I thought I was being transferred to a prison. Or going to be shot. I was sure of it."

Kitty took off her hat and ran her fingers through her newly dyed red hair. In the rearview mirror, she gazed at Elizabeth Hennessy for one last moment before turning to Bonaparte. "We'd never have let that happen."

23

NOVEMBER 1942

Port-Vendres, Southern Occupied France

When Celestin pulled into the long drive to Françoise's house, the first thing Kitty saw was the ginger tomcat. He dashed up the stoop, arched his tail then jumped behind the half-bare bougainvillea bush to the left of the door.

Bonaparte, his usual quiet self, stepped out of the vehicle and helped Kitty out. She rang the doorbell, the two men waiting behind her. The last time Kitty had seen Françoise was on her return to France as an F Section operative. She was the first they had integrated into the Sculptor network.

"Yvette," Françoise said warily. She studied Kitty's companions. "There is trouble, no? All right. Come inside."

They slipped into the comfortable Bastide.

"What do you need and by when?" she asked, turning to them.

"To get over the border, and as soon as possible," Kitty said.

The older woman smoothed back a swath of white hair,

sighing. "The German army is already on the move from the west coast. It won't be long before they set up checkpoints all the way to Perpignan. You can't just cross over."

"Then we really don't have time to linger," Kitty decided.

"You have chosen a very bad time to come," she said. She moved to the chest of drawers where Kitty remembered the woman kept her maps. "There was a terrible snowstorm on the pass. Crossing the mountains will be difficult. And you won't have time to wait for a guide."

Kitty looked worriedly at the two men. Bonaparte appeared resigned. Celestin, on the other hand, bent over the first map and studied it.

"There are mountains everywhere," he grumbled. "Even if we had access to a radio, there'd be no place for an airplane to land."

"We'll have to risk going on foot," Kitty said.

"Submarine? In Port-Vendres?" Celestin suggested.

Françoise shook her head. "The Germans already took the coast." She patted Kitty's arm. "But the snow in the west might delay them. You should rest today, and leave first thing in the morning."

Kitty turned to Celestin. "How are we on fuel?"

He scratched his head, then drew a finger along the map. "I could probably get us as close as here." He pointed to the village where Kitty and Oskar had stayed with the goat herder's family nearly a year earlier.

"This is good. They have a hut in case we need to shelter for a little while longer."

Françoise shook her head and beckoned Kitty away from the table. Quietly, she said, "I have to show you something. I... I have someone else here. And she needs help."

"She?" Kitty frowned, pensive. "What kind of help?"

"She is one of you. But she's had a fever, and a bad cough."

Kitty glanced at the two men. She knew they would go by

car as far as they could, but crossing the Pyrenees with a sick woman would throw a wrench into their works. She followed Françoise out to the adjacent building, a workshop, and braced herself for what the Frenchwoman was about to reveal behind the wooden barricade.

Kitty heard the coughing before Françoise even opened the makeshift door. A body was huddled beneath a pile of blankets on a bed. Kitty only saw a head full of dark hair, but when Françoise bent over her, and whispered something, the woman stretched her arms over her head like a cat.

"Marie?" Kitty hurried to her. Marie was pale and there were dark circles beneath her eyes. "What are you doing here? What happened?"

Marie grasped Kitty's hand, smiling. "Would you look at that," she said weakly. "We meet again."

She let go then and coughed, her chest rattling. Kitty braced her friend's back as she spasmed.

From a thermos, Françoise poured a cup of tisane, its strong herbal scent filling the room, and Marie drank.

"How long has she been like this?" Kitty asked them both.

"Five, six days," Françoise said. "But it's getting better."

"Bronchitis, then," Kitty said. "But it's not pneumonia?"

"She showed up with a fever." Françoise frowned. "I think from exhaustion and cold. But no, not pneumonia."

Marie handed Françoise the cup back. Her face was pale and thin, but her eyes were alight.

"How did you get here?" Kitty asked her.

"Mostly on foot. I ran with only the clothes on my back. I stopped at the gallery."

"Yes, Madame Allard told me. I thought you'd be long gone by now."

"I got sick in Toulon. And the Germans. They arrived in droves. That scared everyone. I ran. I just kept running because

I couldn't find anyone to take me in until I got here." Marie's face fell. "Yvette, Vlad... Vlad and Raymond."

Kitty nodded, and hugged her, helpless to comfort her. Nobody knew their fate.

Françoise then pulled Kitty aside. "She needs to leave before the Germans reach Port-Vendres."

"We all do," Kitty reminded her.

Françoise lowered her voice. "I was going to send her to the hills. There are clusters of insurgents out there now, ever since the forced labor laws were implemented. More and more men began joining them, but they are in rough shape themselves with winter coming. They won't want a woman hanging about."

Kitty studied Marie for a second. That cough. It was hard to control. If they had to hide, Marie could give them all away with that cough. She suddenly eyed the thermos, remembering when Sam had gotten interested in natural remedies.

"Marie will come with us. But I need you to help me. I need citrus juice, cloves, cayenne and ginger. It will help open up her airways, especially the cayenne. Is that something you can help me with?"

Françoise tapped her lips with a forefinger. "I could."

Kitty had no idea how Marie was going to make it over the mountains, but she would sit down with Bonaparte and Celestin to make a plan. She had to come with them. She was sure the men would agree to that.

They could not leave one of their own behind.

"We can't do that," Celestin said angrily. "She'll get us all killed. Can't she hide with the goat herder and his wife? In that hut you mentioned?"

"It's winter," Kitty pressed. "She won't survive in that hut alone."

"She's not going to make the climb," Celestin protested. "She won't survive it."

"She will if we help her. If we are with her." Kitty squeezed the juice of the last orange into a pot, dropped in the cloves, and mulled the chili peppers that Françoise had. She was still searching for ginger.

Celestin frowned at the concoction. "What is that?"

Kitty smiled. "A miracle cure. My brother used to make it for me."

"And how long does it take before it kicks in?" he complained. "We have to get out of here now."

Bonaparte suddenly slammed the table with a fist. Even through his smeared glasses, his eyes bore into Celestin.

"What am I doing this for if we cannot save one of the very people who needs our help?" Bonaparte stared at the Brit. "I am scared, too. I believed I was already dead several times. I escaped Poland in August. *August.* It's now mid-November. And I am *this* close to my goal. So close, I can smell freedom. Do you know what freedom smells like?"

Celestin shrugged.

"Not like this." Bonaparte leaned forward. "Not like piss in your pants." He then pointed at Kitty. "She walked up to those policemen and broke me out of jail. *She* did. And I'm going where she goes and how she wants to go."

Celestin sagged.

Bonaparte was still fuming. "Get her ready, Yvette. She is coming with us. And if I do not make it now, then at the very least, I have died trying."

Kitty blinked away the grateful tears. Delicately, she embraced Bonaparte, and put a hand on Celestin's arm, silently pleading with him.

He slowly shook his head. "I think it's a mistake. But who am I? You were generous enough to let me join you. But then I think we should try to reach a submarine. She won't make the climb."

Kitty gave in. "I'll ask Françoise to locate a wireless operator. We'll go by sea."

She returned to the workshop to find Marie balancing a bowl of soup on her knees. "How are you doing?"

"I'll be fine. I'm a little weak in the legs, but not in here." Marie pointed to her head.

Kitty smiled. "That will be the last thing to go." She perched on the mattress and handed her a cup of the hot citrus drink. "I'm going to be honest with you. Celestin was not for it. He's concerned. Bonaparte is a martyr already. Me... I'm worried. But I won't leave you behind, Marie. You're coming with us."

Marie opened her arms to her. "I'll do my best, Yvette. I promise."

"OK." Kitty stroked her head. "Then let's get you on your feet."

But before Kitty could bring her back to the main house, she spotted Françoise outside with a short, square-shouldered man. He held a cap in his hand and was using it to point in every direction. Though she could not hear what they were saying, his voice was high-pitched, and Françoise's was calm. Kitty ducked back inside and held up a hand for Marie to wait.

When she peeked back out, the man had replaced his cap on his head and was marching back up the driveway.

Françoise turned to Kitty and Marie as they came to her, her eyes grave. "The Germans are here. They are taking over the administrative buildings. My neighbor says they will be holding an assembly this evening and requisitioning homes. Everyone in town will be registered within the next two days. I have to go today; people need my help."

"We need a radio operator," Kitty pleaded.

Françoise raised her eyebrows briefly and clicked her

tongue. "There is an operator, at a refuge in Mont Carrétou, north of Narbonne. If he is still there." She then pointed to the Citroën in the drive. "You can't get to Perpignan by vehicle. You'll be stopped for sure. But take the backroads, leave the automobile at the refuge and I'll see to it that it gets back to the mayor in Ditres."

Kitty put a protective arm around Marie's shoulders and went inside the house to share the news with the men. Celestin and Bonaparte were huddled over the maps but straightened and shook Marie's hand before bending over them again.

"We're going to the coast," Celestin explained. His finger followed the line between land and water. "Françoise said there's a smugglers' path along the clifftops. There are very few coves, no big beaches, but she confirms there is a trail along here. It's rough going, though."

Bonaparte and Kitty glanced at one another.

"It will keep us off the main roads," the Polish officer said. "The Germans won't be fast enough or have enough bodies to set up checkpoints in the more remote areas. If we go now, we might just manage to get there unscathed."

Celestin placed a hand on Kitty's shoulder. "Marie won't make it up the pass. It's our only option if we can't get a boat."

Exhausted by their journey, Kitty looked with concern at Marie, who was swaying slightly on her feet. She steeled herself and put an arm around her shoulder.

"Let's get those legs beneath you," Kitty ordered. "We're going to get you home."

24

NOVEMBER 1942

French–Spanish Border

Kitty watched the dawn horizon between sky and sea, the waves pulsing and crashing against the base of the cliff below her. A trawler was out there, nets at the ready, as if just hauling in or about to drop. It was not unlike the British one that had brought her to the shores of France less than six months earlier.

A cold breeze made her tuck her chin into the collar of her sweater and she lowered the binoculars to look back at Celestin.

"It was real bad luck we couldn't find that radio operator," he grumbled.

Kitty pursed her lips. There was nothing to say. Françoise's contact had abandoned the mountain refuge. When they had tried to make inquiries at the village, she quickly realized that the black Citroën had not infused the locals with any confidence in the four strangers. They'd left the vehicle at the refuge, with a note apologizing for having stolen it from *someone* in Ditres. In this way, the mayor would escape immediate suspicion of being involved with rebels. Now, they had no other choice than to follow the smuggler's trail to the border and hope they did not run into German or French authorities.

"We'll start out tonight," she said. "For now, let's go back to that fisherman's hut, finally get some rest, and hope the good weather holds to give us a clear night."

They rejoined Marie and Bonaparte, waiting in an abandoned and dilapidated fish hut. Along the walls, someone had strung up nets and repair tools. There were dull knives lined up near a trough. The hut smelled of cold sea and fish blood.

"The sky looks good," she said. "The wind is a bit chilly, but I don't think we'll be caught out in a storm. It will be ideal if it holds like this."

Marie smiled briefly, then emptied their sack of provisions, listing the inventory aloud. Six apples, a loaf of bread, goat cheese, almonds and walnuts. Françoise had also given them jars of *vichyssoise*, a jug of wine and one of her bottles of cognac. Kitty inhaled the liquor's caramel warmth, then served out a portion to everyone while Marie cut cheese and bread.

Kitty then put the rest of the things into the sack. "We have no idea how long we're going to have to wait. I say we save as much as we can."

Nobody complained. Nobody disagreed.

At one point, Kitty pulled Bonaparte aside and handed him his pen with the microfilm, which she still had since the police apprehended him.

"You should hang onto it," Bonaparte said.

"Why?"

The Polish man sighed. "You've managed to get me this far. That jailbreak... I wouldn't have even thought of something like that. I thought for sure I'd never see you again. I feel the report is safer with you."

Kitty disagreed.

He peered at her. "Did you look at it? The film, I mean?"

She reddened. "I tried. I only managed to understand some of the delivery notes you had in there."

"I see."

"There is a question, I have," she ventured. "About one of those, or several. The company's name is Testa. They delivered something called Zyklon B. Do you know what it's for?"

Bonaparte bent toward her, his voice low and urgent. "We are only guessing at what might be happening, Yvette. Zyklon B is some type of pesticide."

Kitty's heart tripped.

"It started arriving with an influx of inmates. Entire families of Jews suddenly started coming into Auschwitz. And there is not enough room for them. The Germans first made us repurpose the huts and the bunkbeds. More and more came. They began expanding the camp, and constructed outbuildings. They look like factories. Big rooms, maybe for production or something."

Bonaparte pushed his spectacles up and continued. "One of the Polish prisoners said a Jew told him they were building halls for showers. I didn't think it made sense. What we do know is that it is a miracle to survive that camp. And with more—now women and children, too—it cannot be possible any longer. My friends were dropping dead, right at my feet. Each day that it takes for us to get this report to my government means more and more inmates collapse. And die. Or are beaten. And die. Or starve. And die. The conditions, alone... And now with winter..." His voice wobbled and he swallowed. "Yvette, Auschwitz is where humanity goes to die."

Kitty swallowed the lump in her throat. Oskar's brief recollections of Dachau had been awful enough. She knew she could not fathom Auschwitz.

"Then you must be the one to carry the microfilm." She gently pressed the hand with the pen to his chest. "This is your work. Your story. You need to tell it."

"They will pay for this," Bonaparte said bitterly. "Every single German. Every single Austrian. Every single collaborator who allowed the Nazis to commit these crimes. We will not forget. And we will not forgive."

Kitty wavered. She understood his anger. She understood how easy it was to succumb to the hate. She also knew that there were many Germans and Austrians who were trying to put a stop to it; who were putting their lives at risk to do so. And they would be ostracized by their own countrymen for doing so long after the war. Her husband was one of those people.

They all tried to sleep but, like Kitty, everyone was awake. She was curled up on a bed of rope, facing the wall, her thoughts on Edgar. If he had been discovered by the Germans, he'd have disappeared under the Night and Fog decree. Her mind kept turning back to every word of his that she could remember, and kept coming back to those foreboding messages: *Stay clear. No return needed. Most loyal friends have come to pass.*

As the day wore on, she must have dozed because she grew aware of her surroundings again. The wind had picked up and big rolling waves were crashing on the shore. The anticipation and fear were also rising and cresting within the group. Kitty was not immune to it, and she sat up to assess her companions.

Bonaparte was pressed up against one of the walls, his arms wrapped around him, quiet as usual. Celestin suddenly leapt to his feet, growled, and snatched one of the knives only to whip it at a cutting board hanging on the wall. It stuck there. Nobody moved. Nobody commented.

Marie always muffled her cough, but it had changed. Sam's miracle cure was easing it. Kitty tried to pick up everyone's spirits by pouring them all a cup of wine, but the small talk dwindled back to private, silent musings as the minutes ticked away into late afternoon, and then into evening. When she stepped outside, dark clouds loomed thick over them.

Kitty went back in and put her head down on her arms, trying to really sleep this time but the wind and the waves were not quieting down and she was worried they'd be stuck in the hut for another night and another day. They were so close, and still too far. Darkness fell. They all began stirring.

"I'm prepared for the worst," Bonaparte blurted, voicing the likely conversation he'd been having with himself in his head.

"Discovery?" Marie half-heartedly guessed.

"Being shot on sight," Bonaparte replied.

Their attention turned to Kitty.

"I'm not going to let that happen," she said firmly. "We're going to Spain."

She went outside. The hut was near the beach. Something had shifted. The sky was clear save for wisps of clouds, but the stormy wind had died down some. She went back inside.

"Let's move. With the winds and waves like this, we won't see any boat patrols. It's ideal." But if the sea calmed down completely, the risk of discovery would increase.

Celestin squeezed her shoulder. "All right, boss. We're with you." He then reached over her and yanked the knife out he'd thrown earlier, replacing it where he'd found it.

Kitty glanced once more around the hut. Nothing was amiss, as if they'd never been there.

When she joined the group, Marie patted Kitty's arm. "Let's go, Chief."

"You used to call Raymond that all the time," Kitty remarked.

Marie faced her. "I use that title for people who deserve it. I know you wanted to lead Sculptor before we left for France. I just wish you'd trusted yourself enough to have fought for it."

Kitty reddened. "I didn't think... I didn't think I should."

"Come on." Marie poked her. "You're doing it now. We all trust you to lead us over the border. That's all that counts."

That night, the wind died down and the sea arranged itself into something more genial. The group had been following the rocky coast for some time when the silhouette of a boat appeared. Out of nowhere came the rumble of several motorboats, followed by long searchlights crisscrossing on the water.

"Christ," Celestin hissed.

Kitty froze for an instant then whipped the binoculars back over her head. There were three boats out there, those search-lights doing a 360-degree scan, and scraping the rocky face of the cliff just a few feet away from them.

Celestin swore again and yanked Kitty backwards.

Bonaparte and Marie were right behind her. The Brit dashed over the hard-packed earth and stopped at the edge of an outlook further up. Kitty and the others followed, Marie panting next to her.

"They came from behind us," Marie warned.

But Kitty had a hard time believing that the authorities or the Germans even suspected of their existence. Unless... Unless that radio operator's village had reported them.

"They must know there is a trail up here," Bonaparte guessed.

Celestin grunted in agreement and backed away from the ridge.

"We're going to have to head inland some," Kitty said.

It was pitch black and the ground uneven. Kitty's coat snagged on the weeds and brush, and more than a few times, she nearly tumbled. She was exhausted and cold. The trail had been dangerous, especially at night, and now, a half a mile later, it came to an abrupt end. Between them and the opposite rock face was a ravine. White surf reflected in the deep gouge in the rocks below. A few feet in, Kitty saw that there was a thin inlet. Fighting back her despair, she determined there was no other way but down.

"We'll have to descend down those slippery rocks, go over the inlet to continue on the other side."

"It's too dark," Celestin argued. "And we can't use any lights."

He and Bonaparte discussed it in low voices. Kitty did not intervene. She turned to Marie, whose teeth were chattering.

"How are you doing?"

"Freezing, but good." Marie stifled a cough.

Kitty took off her coat and put it around the woman's shoulders. It nearly dragged on the ground, and she bloused up the waist and tied it tightly.

"Thank you," Marie said. "But what about you?"

"I'm too nervous to be cold."

"Maybe that's why my teeth are chattering," Marie half-joked. But Kitty was afraid for her. When she felt the woman's forehead, Kitty confirmed Marie was running a fever.

Celestin returned to them. Bonaparte was still at the path's edge, looking around.

"We're going to have to turn around. There's no way to get down there tonight."

"How far do you think we are from the border?" she asked.

Celestin squatted and squinted at his watch. "Two hours. Maybe one and a half."

"Let's get some rest," she suggested. "Get out of this wind, and we'll start again as soon as there is enough light to get there safely."

They found shelter a few hundred yards from the coast in the ruins of a stone shepherd's hut. Huddled together against the cold, Kitty and the others dozed on and off. When the pre-dawn sky revealed some of their surroundings, she roused the others. Grimly, they returned to that dead end. The gulley between the two shores revealed that the path did continue on the other side but there was no way to get around except down and go back up.

She began the descent, offering to help Marie. Celestin maneuvered around her, and did the same for her. With Bonaparte at the other end, they created a virtual human chain, taking one careful step after another along the high and steep cliff. It was painfully slow. Once, they thought they heard motorboats again and froze against the cliff wall.

Bonaparte pointed upwards. "It's coming from up there."

Kitty swore to herself and took Celestin's hand to cross over another gap. "Are we that close to a road?"

He nodded. "At one point the trail nearly crosses it."

He reached for Marie then, and she took his hand, but not before her foot slipped and she released an abbreviated shriek. But Bonaparte was on the other side of her and grabbed the knotted belt of the coat just in time. It was Kitty's coat that rescued her.

Everyone took in a deep breath before moving on.

When Kitty reached the bottom there was really no place to stand without stepping into the water and getting wet. She gasped at the shocking cold.

"I don't see a way of getting back up there," she complained. Her boots filled with seawater.

"Check that inlet," Celestin called behind her.

Kitty did and froze. Just ahead of her, on the pebbled shore, was a blue-and-white fishing boat turned over. *L'Ange Bleu.* The Blue Angel.

She cried triumphantly, and whirled to find Celestin and Marie just coming around the bend. Marie spotted the boat and laughed, stretching her arms over her head and doing a little twist before they flopped to her sides again.

Bonaparte was next and it was the first time Kitty saw him really smile. "Is it in good condition?"

Celestin helped Kitty tip *L'Ange Bleu* over, and she quickly checked for damage. There was a sail and a rudder just beneath the boat.

"You know how to navigate?" Celestin asked.

Kitty laughed. "I'm a Minnesota girl."

"I don't know what that means."

"Minnesota is the land of ten thousand lakes. My dad and I sailed a lot. Yes, I know how to navigate a boat."

They put it into the water, watched for signs of any leaks, and Kitty hooted again when the vessel proved to be watertight. She dug in her rucksack and counted out double the amount of francs for a boat of this size before handing them to Marie.

"Put that somewhere where the owner can find it, will you? Mark it some way."

Kitty then pulled Celestin over to her and they studied the map of the coast. The detail ended shortly after the border, but Kitty pointed out a spot at the very bottom which appeared to be a secluded cove.

"This would put us in Spain regardless."

Then she helped Bonaparte into the boat.

Marie returned and climbed in. "I piled up some stones and buried the cash beneath."

Celestin took up the oars and they pushed into the open water. Kitty prepared the little sail, and as soon as it filled with wind, they were off.

25

NOVEMBER 1942

Spain

The sun was a wintry golden orb in the sky when they finally found a protective cove. Certain that they were now on the Spanish coast, they pulled the boat onto the shore. Marie, smiling, and shivering at the same time, decided a portion of wine would have to warm them up.

"A toast to our success!"

She had just pulled the cork when voices shouted at them from the top of the cliff. Shots pierced the air.

Celestin ducked behind the boat. Everyone else scrambled to the rocks. Kitty heard the scrabbling above her and looked over her shoulder. There was no escape, unless they got back into the boat.

"They're Spanish," Celestin called to the others. "Spanish patrols."

Everyone came out of hiding and slowly raised their hands.

Three border guards in light blue uniforms were nearly at the beach.

Kitty's pulse raced. The patrolmen aimed their guns at the group, and Celestin began explaining who they were in rudimentary Spanish.

"English!" he added. "English! American! Refugees!"

The Spaniards spoke rapidly, all at once, demanding papers. Kitty gave them what she had. The others did the same. There were discussions, questions fired at them, but none of her group spoke Spanish well enough, and certainly not the local dialect.

The patrolmen waved them together and marched Kitty and her companions up the slippery path. At the top, Kitty groaned. They had landed right at a border patrol station. Celestin's eyes bulged and he turned to the French border. About a hundred yards ahead, a group of German Wehrmacht were standing about smoking cigarettes. They were, remarkably, not paying attention to what was happening beyond their newly seized border.

The Spanish patrolmen kept the group moving.

"We should have rowed a while longer," Bonaparte said miserably. "We landed right in their nest."

"We saw you coming," one of the guards called in French. "We were waiting for you. You are lucky that the *boches* were not."

The officials searched them, looking through their rucksacks, checking their coats. Kitty tried to remain calm. She still had the 9mm tucked in the lining of the rucksack. She glanced at Bonaparte. Somewhere on him, he had that pen and microfilm.

The guard then led them to a truck and ordered them to get in the back. He dropped the canvas seal closed. No windows, and no way to see where they were going. They traveled for what felt like hours.

Kitty needed a toilet. Marie was coughing a lot now, her hazel eyes wide with fear, her arms so tightly around her she had shrunk to half her already small size. Bonaparte glanced over at Kitty.

"Plan D, boss?"

She shook her head, dejected and unwilling to play the game.

When the vehicle stopped and the guards flung open the canvas flaps, Kitty saw that they were parked outside a low building with a high fence around it. The temperature here was milder, too. They were certainly south of the Spanish border.

"Where are we?" Kitty asked the driver.

He did not answer her, and they were soon frog-marched inside.

"It looks like a prison..." Celestin muttered.

"Internment," the guard who spoke French said. "Until we know what to do with you all."

Kitty took it all in very quickly. An internment camp—with all the people likely escaping over the border as the Germans moved in—would certainly be bigger. This looked like a lonely prison in a remote outpost; not a purgatory for stateless refugees.

The French-speaking guard allowed Marie to divvy up the remaining provisions between the two men and the two women. They took Kitty's rucksack, thoroughly searched their persons again, and then led her and Marie down a dimly lit corridor.

Cockroaches scrabbled across the cement floor. The air reeked of waste and rot. The guards stopped them both at one door, unlocked it, and shoved Kitty into a cold cell. Marie followed. A woman scrambled up from the floor. The door scraped against the cement and slammed shut.

"*Hola*," the woman said. Kitty guessed her to be in her late forties.

Shuddering at the sight of the cockroaches, Kitty turned to

assess the confined space. The walls were scratched up with symbols and writing, including an Orthodox cross and the beginning of the Lord's prayer. There was one dirty mattress for the three of them. One thin blanket. A narrow window with iron bars faced a brick wall and barbed wire. Beyond that was a yellowed, winter landscape of hills, fields, and an oak forest. They were definitely further south, but the room was cold, and Kitty noticed the frost on the bars.

Marie walked over to her. "Do you know where we are?"

Kitty shook her head, now turning her attention to the cell-mate, who was regarding them with some suspicion. She wore a ruffled blouse that might have been white or cream once. She had a colorful wool wrap around her shoulders, her dark hair was matted and dirty. Her long red skirt was also faded. It was tucked beneath her bare legs. Her shoes, however, were remark-able. They were polished, shiny, and had decorative jeweled buckles.

Kitty did not know what to make of them.

"*D'on ets?*" the stranger asked. Then in French, "Where you from?"

"We're English. American." Marie waved a hand between herself and Kitty.

Kitty scowled but before she could reprimand Marie for telling the truth, the woman scoffed and pushed herself away from the wall. She maneuvered in front of them.

"English? American? *Quatre gats*. What are you doing here?"

"We don't know," Marie said.

Kitty gave their operative names, casting Marie a scathing look that made her shrink back as she realized her mistake.

"I'm Linda," the Spanish woman replied. "From Barcelona."

Kitty glanced outside through the narrow window. "How far are we from Barcelona?"

"About forty minutes west of the city by automobile."

"It's all right," Kitty said to Marie, now trying a smile. "That's hours from the border. At least we are in Spain."

The woman in the cell laughed loudly. "Yes. You are in Spain. Surrounded by corrupt *llepaculs*." Then she shouted toward the door, "Franco's and the Nazis' *llepaculs!*"

There was the sound of shuffling behind it. The peephole opened, a dark brown eye glared at them.

"*Puta. Cierra la boca!*" The voice gruffly went on in a tirade before the eye pulled back and the peephole closed.

The Spanish woman laughed again, and looked disbelievingly at Kitty. "He says Franco's men kept me warm and fed all through the war." To the closed peephole Linda shouted, "You men *made* me into a whore."

She turned to Kitty. Still chuckling, Linda drew a slow finger across her throat. "I got my revenge. But I promise you, I will get out of here. You two, though? You are what? Partisans? Mercenaries? Spies?"

Marie shrugged. "What if we are?"

The woman's eyes darted to Marie's bag on the floor. Two apples were peeking out of the opening. "What if you are? What if you are. When I get released, I'll return to Barcelona and tell the American and British consulates that you are here."

Marie smiled uncertainly.

"You're getting out of here?" Kitty doubted her. "How?"

The woman spat toward the door and lifted her bosom with both hands. "Men will do anything for sex. But you?" She pointed to the apples. "I'll do anything for food. And believe me, you want to bribe me before the Germans bribe these Spanish *bastardos* for information about you."

26

NOVEMBER 1942

Spain

Kitty watched the woman devour the first apple. Her stomach grumbled and something was telling her that she would regret giving the fruit to Linda. But she folded her arms and waited silently.

Marie threw Kitty a questioning look, but they were interrupted by the sound of metal scraping against cement. Then they heard voices beyond their cell in Spanish.

"Do you think they put Celestin and Bonaparte next to us?" Marie wondered. She echoed Kitty's own guess.

Kitty strode to the window, and tried to look out. The smell of cold iron was sharp as she grabbed the bars. She heard the door close again in the adjoining cell; keys jangled on a ring or chain.

"Celestin? Bonaparte?" she called.

Linda was watching her with amusement as she popped the

core of the first apple into her mouth and immediately began on the next one.

But there was no response from the neighboring cell. Below her, she could just make out the arch of an overhang. Kitty could see the yard with the stone wall and barbed wire stretched across the top. There was a heavy gate with two metal panels, big enough for a vehicle to drive through. The wall had brick-red smudges in places and she saw scores in the stone.

With dread, Kitty turned to Linda. "What kind of place is this? This isn't an internment camp, is it?"

Linda crossed her arms. "Prison. Torture chamber. The land of the lost."

"You said you were going to get out, Linda from Barcelona," Kitty whispered. "How?"

"You want to know my deepest, darkest secret?" the woman mocked, hands on her hips. "Good, then I will tell you. Our civil war taught me much about myself, such as, I am a criminal right down to the marrow. A thief. A whore." She raised her chin high and stared at Kitty. "A survivor. That is my dignity."

Kitty studied the woman. "You've been in here before, haven't you?"

Linda flipped a dismissive hand. "Dozens of times." She kicked out her foot from beneath the skirt. A cockroach leapt from the hem and scurried away. "See these shoes? My lover accused me of stealing, but they were a gift from another admirer. My lover, however, is a madman, a jealous idiot." Her scowl turned into a smile. "But a rich, jealous idiot and he is *crazy* in love with me."

"How will you get out then?" Marie said from where she was huddled against the wall.

"When he misses me, and he always misses me, he will come and take me away."

Marie broke into a coughing fit. When it passed, she turned her head to look at Kitty, her long, dark lashes framed glassy eyes. They were filled with terror. She suddenly lurched to her feet and heaved into the nearest corner.

Kitty went to her and helped her right herself, but Linda nudged her over and put a hand on Marie's forehead. In a surprisingly soothing tone, she urged Marie to lie down on the mattress. She gave her the blanket and then spooned next to her protectively, throwing the wrap over her, too.

"Is she all right?" Kitty asked, kneeling on the other side of the mattress. She was worried about the vomiting.

Linda was rubbing Marie's arms and legs. "Fever. Bring that water over."

Kitty fetched the small pail of brackish water.

Marie was hoarse. "I'll be all right. I'm only very, very tired."

Kitty felt her forehead, too. It was hot and dry. With despair she looked at Linda. "This is not the place for her to get worse. She needs to keep up her strength."

Linda pursed her lips. "She needs rest."

As Marie's eyes closed, she touched Kitty's hand. "Do you think Vlad made it out? That Raymond and he are..." Her eyelids fluttered, then she focused on Kitty, her face heavy with sorrow. "What if they took the pill?"

Kitty shushed her, then cast Linda a grateful look as the woman dabbed at Marie's face. "Thank you for your help."

Up close, Linda's eyes were alive and bright, but her brow and mouth had the deep creases of worry and hardship. It reminded Kitty of how much Edgar's features had changed since the war had torn their lives apart.

She wondered if she, too, carried the fingerprint of tragedy on her face.

Marie finally slept, and the amount of heat she radiated, as well as the scurrying sounds of the insects, made Kitty uneasy on the very edge of the thin and dingy mattress. Linda must have sensed that she was awake, because she suddenly propped herself up.

"What about you," her silhouette asked. "What's your darkest secret?"

Kitty scoffed to herself. Which of the hundreds could she share? And she was not sure she wanted to at all but she obliged the woman. "I have regrets."

Linda clicked her tongue. "Ridiculous."

Kitty felt the tears gathering at the back of her eyes and pressed the heels of her hands to them. "I got someone killed."

The Spanish woman did not respond immediately. "On purpose?"

"Of course not."

"Of course not," Linda mocked. "That's not a dark secret. Regrets and guilt? Those are not dark. They are heavy blocks of sharp, white ice all of us carry."

Kitty did not want to speak to her anymore.

Later, wedged between them, Marie suddenly muttered and tossed her head side to side. The water pail was empty. Kitty's repeated poundings on the door had brought nothing save for a plate of some hard bread and gruel. They had eaten the last of Françoise's provisions together.

Linda was singing something in a low alto, stroking Marie's hair. She touched Kitty's hand, her tone more gentle now. "She will be all right. She is in shock. It's one way the body deals with it."

It had to be the middle of the night when Marie seemed to be doing better.

"This must be the worst day of your life right now," Kitty said to her and gently wiped her forehead with the cool rag.

Marie sighed. Her voice was groggy. "I think the worst day might have been when I set my parents' house on fire."

"You set your house on fire?" Kitty smiled sadly.

Linda grunted. "Your secrets are boring."

Marie's voice was hoarse, and one arm stretched behind her to the floor before she pulled it back in with a shiver. She then joked hoarsely, "I always liked things that went boom. But to be honest, I almost died. I lit the stove, and the flue was blocked. All the smoke came in the house. In a panic, I tried to pull out the wood. To put it all out. But then the rug caught fire. I inhaled so much smoke, I coughed for weeks."

Linda lay back down with a sigh and turned on her side.

Kitty brushed another roach away just before Marie coughed again. As she stroked the back of her friend's head, Linda asked in a bored voice, "Where were your parents when you were fighting the fire?"

Marie's voice was muffled beneath the blanket. "They were at a friend's. It was Shabbat."

Chills, like sharp needles, pierced Kitty. Had she heard correctly? She stared at Linda's figure but the Spanish woman was still. Linda had mentioned Germans.

Kitty reached over and grasped the woman's shoulder. "What did you mean when you said we should bribe you before the Germans bribe them? The Spanish guards, I mean?"

Linda slowly turned to face them again. Over Marie, she whispered, "Franco's *llepaculs* get money from a Gestapo man named Weiss. For turning people in. He comes from France once a month to purchase 'extra inventory'. That's what the guards call it."

"What kind of people?" Kitty's dread was thick in her voice.

"Spies. Allied airmen. Rebels from France." Linda moved her head, dark eyes flashing in the moonlight. In a low whisper, she added, "And Jews."

Kitty watched the stars slide past the barred window in their orbit. Suddenly, Marie jerked and flung an arm over her head.

She began muttering and Kitty leaned forward. She could not make out the words.

Linda also sat up, two dark shadows where her eyes were. She leaned closer to Marie. "I do not understand. What is she saying?"

Just then, Marie sat up. "*Eema! Abba!*"

Kitty froze and stared at the shape of Marie.

"She needs a doctor," Linda said quickly.

Kitty clasped a hand over Marie's mouth and made her lay down again. Linda tried to wrest it away, crying out, as if she thought Kitty was trying to suffocate the young woman. There was a sound at their door. Linda and Kitty dropped back down onto the mattress, but Kitty kept her hand tight over Marie's mouth.

The peephole opened up and Kitty saw the thin stream of light before it was blocked again. She pictured that cold, dark brown eye. It was there for a long time, Marie now twisting and turning in her fever.

"We need water," Kitty shouted. "*Agua.*"

At that moment, Marie thrashed again, calling for her parents once more.

Linda leapt up and went to the peephole. She spoke in rapid and authoritative Spanish. A few moments later the door opened. One of the guards stepped in, another one behind him, batons in hand. They dragged Marie up. Kitty cried out for them to stop.

"We'll take care of her. Please, leave her with us. Please!"

But Linda blocked Kitty's way. "They'll take her to the infirmary. She needs care. She's hallucinating."

Kitty stared at the woman in the half-light. Yes, Marie needed care. Yes, she was hallucinating. She had also spoken in Hebrew. Kitty tore herself away and threw herself on the door before it closed, but it was too late.

She turned to Linda, her heart pounding with terror.

The woman's arms were wrapped tightly around herself, but she jerked her chin at the door. "Now that *is* a dark secret."

Morning came. The light illuminated one corner of the cell and slid its way across into the other corner. Kitty sat shivering against the wall, every scuttling noise making her jump. For all her effort, Linda's words did not bring her comfort. The door opened twice more, once in the morning and once more in the evening. Brackish water. Hard bread. Gruel. And then night came.

"My lover," Linda said. "He will be here any day now. Any day. Maybe even tomorrow. And then I will go back to Barcelona."

But Kitty no longer believed her. The story was too far-fetched. At first light, she'd had enough. Kitty pounded on the door, demanding to know where Marie was. When her knuckles were raw, she clawed at the steel, kicked at it, slammed herself into the walls and cried out.

Linda leaned warily in the corner, as if watching a rabid animal.

When the guards came in again, they pressed Kitty up against the wall with a baton. One groped her, jeered at her. Kitty turned her head away, screaming her demands over the pain. Where were the men she'd arrived with? Where was Marie? She had a right to call the consulate in Barcelona.

One of them smacked her across the face and told her to shut up. Then they marched away and slammed the heavy door shut. Another night fell, and Kitty's despair wore her down to the bone. She slept deeply.

On the third day, the guards pushed open the door and deposited breakfast, then dragged Marie in. Kitty went to her on her knees, and grabbed her, examining her. Marie looked, for all intents and purposes, better.

"Did they treat you...?" She could not ask. Her breast still hurt where the guard had seized her. Her hands were mangled with scrapes and cuts, too.

Marie nodded. "They gave me medicine. Then when I awoke, they asked me many questions. Where was I from, and what was I doing here..."

"What did you tell them?"

"I told them my cover story, of course." She smiled weakly as Kitty took her to the far corner. "Why? God, Yvette, you look *awful*."

"You were speaking Hebrew, I think," Kitty whispered.

Marie's eyes grew wide, and she ducked her head. "You must be mistaken."

"No, Marie, you were. In your sleep. When you had a fever."

Marie was stock-still, her eyes skirted over Kitty's face before she dropped her head again.

Linda moved away from the wall and came to them, but Kitty grabbed Marie to her, whispering in her ear.

"Are you Jewish, Marie?"

Her friend whimpered and pushed away. In French, she began, "My name is Marie Sourisseau. I am a French national. I come from—"

Kitty bit her lip and stared wildly at her. Linda stopped and went back to her wall. "Did they say anything to you? God, Marie. Did they say anything to you?" Kitty pleaded.

A moment later, that scraping, that rattling and another man showed up at the cell, a bearded officer with a huge paunch. Linda leapt to her feet.

"*Capitán*," she cried and spoke in Spanish to the man, but his eyes were on Marie.

Linda suddenly pointed to Kitty and Marie. Kitty picked up *British*, and *American* but she had a hard time following anything else. The captain remained stony, then jerked his head at Marie, asking Linda an abrupt question.

Linda shrank back a little. "*Sí.*"

His eyes flitted to Linda, then back to Marie, then slid over Kitty. "*Muy bien.*"

And he left.

Linda went to the mattress, pulling at her skirt before kneeling down on it. She was avoiding Kitty's gaze.

"What is *muy bien?*" Kitty asked sharply.

Linda cleared her throat, a fake smile. "He is going to call my lover. And tell him to get me out. I promised him... a favor. I told you. Men will do anything for—"

"And us?" Kitty swallowed.

"I will do as I promised. As soon as I get out—"

"No!" Kitty snapped. She waved a hand between Marie and herself. "What did he ask about us?"

Before Linda could answer, the bolt slid across the door again. The guard who had molested Kitty earlier reappeared, a smirk on his face. A second one placed a bucket, a small mirror, a sliver of soap next to a fresh shift before waving Marie over to him.

"*Lávate. Vístete.*"

"What is this for?" Kitty asked.

But he frowned at her, the other one licked his lips. Linda made a hissing sound and made as if to charge at them, shoving Kitty away in the process. They jeered but left them, locking them in again.

Linda picked up the shift from the floor. "They want her to wash and get dressed."

"Only Marie?" Kitty went cold.

Linda nodded. "The captain wants to see her." She sucked on the bottom of her lip, before she said, "He said someone in Marseilles gave her away."

Marie gasped, whirling to Kitty.

Kitty crossed the cell and grasped Marie by the arms. "Listen to me, as soon as they take you out of here, as soon as they drag you down this corridor to wherever they are taking you, I want you to bite down really hard on your tongue. Really hard, you hear?"

Marie shook her head. "Why?"

"To make it bleed. Your lungs are still raw. You've been coughing. Now I want you to spit out blood. When they ask you what's wrong, tell them you have TB."

"What?"

But Linda snatched Marie by the arm, shaking it. "*Sí, sí.* You *must* do it. There is nothing they fear more than a prisoner with tuberculosis."

"They'll send you back. To the infirmary, at the very best," Kitty promised.

"But what if they have me checked?" Marie's eyes were wild-looking.

"She's right," Linda said. "When I complained of crabs, they fetched the doctor and he found that I was clean. The guards made me pay heavily for that."

Kitty bent down to look Marie in the eyes. "If anyone X-rays your lungs, they're going to find scar tissue. One, from your smoke inhalation when you were a child. And from your cough now, it will look like TB."

"How do you know, Yvette?" Marie cried.

Kitty hesitated. It took her a while to reach—even for a second—the memories of all those nights with Sam at the Larsson mansion; those memories she could hardly believe still belonged to her. It had been another life. Another world entirely.

"My brother," she finally said. "He is a doctor. I used to help him study."

They helped Marie into the fresh shift. The peephole opened first, then the two bullies descended on Marie with relish and marched her out. In horror, Kitty raced to the door and it nearly cut her hand off as it slammed shut. She yanked it back, screaming in pain.

Linda wrapped her hand with Marie's discarded blouse, but Kitty was distraught. As time passed, she paced and kicked the walls of the cell. Finally succumbing to Linda's care, she prayed with her, then called again for Celestin and Bonaparte, but still there was no answer. She felt alone except for the Spanish woman. Who else would they come for? Who else had the circuit in Marseilles given away? And who? Had it been Vladimir? Raymond? One of the French locals? Madame Keller? And would these *llepaculs* come for her next?

The sun had shifted by a couple of hours when the howling started. Kitty raced to the window.

"Marie!"

The screeches were coming from a distance but there was no doubt it was Marie. Kitty continued calling her name but stopped when a metallic banging sounded from below. The yard was empty, but the banging continued. Then more metal on the iron bars. Men began calling from below in protest.

"Those are the other prisoners," Linda said solemnly. Her dark eyes flooded with emotion.

Kitty grabbed the empty water bucket and also began banging, tears streaming down her face. "Marie!"

The screaming stopped. The silence that followed was heavy as, one after the other, the prisoners stopped banging whatever they had gotten their hands on.

Kitty listened at the window, her only comfort the stark gaze of the Spanish woman. Linda approached slowly, took Kitty into her arms and rubbed her back.

"We're going to get out of here. I know we will. My man is

coming," Linda whispered. "And when he does, I will tell the consulates in Barcelona that you are all here."

But Kitty was certain now that the woman was crazy.

That night, however, as Kitty slept fitfully next to Linda, she awoke to the voices of disgruntled men in the prison yard. Glass broke below, then a spotlight illuminated the yard.

Linda also stirred awake. Kitty could see her wide eyes aimed at the window. She turned her head to Kitty. "They believed the story about the TB, but..."

"But what?"

The Spanish woman moaned. "They're complaining about the Jew money they could have earned. They're saying your friend cost them a lot of money."

"Jew money? You mean... this Weiss? The Gestapo man?"

The voices of the Spanish guards rose again and Kitty went to the window. Linda joined her, her head cocked, a finger to her lips as she listened to the conversation.

Kitty waited, holding her breath.

There was an argument followed by someone placating the other. Linda clapped a hand over her mouth.

"They called Weiss again."

Kitty shook her head. "No. And what?"

"I don't know..." But the woman was lying.

Kitty grabbed her and pinned her to the wall. "Why?" she cried.

But the answer was unfolding outdoors. Two men crossed the yard to the large gates and they clanged open.

An engine revved outside before a black vehicle drove into the prison yard. It stopped, the engine running, and the back door opened. A tall man stepped out. Kitty could just make out the coat, and the hat on the man's head.

She yanked Linda to the window. The man was striding across the yard. "Is that... is this the Weiss you're referring to?"

"That's him," Linda said flatly.

Before Kitty could react, the Spanish captain marched out from beneath the arch. The German shook hands with him and they spoke in low tones before the captain waved a hand toward the building. The guards in the yard shifted as two others appeared, dressed in white coats and masks. They were dragging Marie between them.

Kitty wailed.

From a pool of light below, she saw Marie, like a child's rag doll, dragged over to the vehicle, the engine still idling. The German raised a hand and took a step back. Marie turned her head away from the blinding headlights.

"*Du bist eine Judin*," Weiss said, as if handing down a sentence. *You are a Jew.*

Kitty shouted, "She's a British civilian! *Sie ist britische Staatsbürgerin!*"

The Nazi's head jerked up toward her window. "*Wer ist das?*" Weiss demanded. *Who is that?*

Kitty was about to pull back, but there was a spark, like someone lighting a match. The crack of the pistol followed. Marie slumped between the two Spaniards, who then let her go. The one on the left held the weapon. Marie folded in on herself and onto the ground. Another flash. Two. Three. Marie's body jerked with each shot.

Weiss stood back at a cautious distance.

The Spanish captain suddenly strode over and pressed something into Weiss's hand. Kitty peered from the side of the window, and recognized the cards. French identity cards. All of them? Hers, too? Or just Marie's? Her pulse was racing. She'd spoken German and he'd heard her.

Weiss reached into his coat pocket, and handed something to the captain. Money. He then pointed to the window, but the captain steered the Gestapo man to the automobile. Weiss disappeared inside. The automobile motored out the gates. That banging and rattling of metal against iron began below as the masked guards dragged Marie's body after the vehicle and behind the gates.

When Linda's arms came around Kitty's waist, she fought the Spanish woman, clutching the bars of the window, and shrieked with each breath, until there was no sound left in her body, and the yard was dark and deserted. The other prisoners kept up the banging of pails and cups, and their outrage penetrated the night long after Kitty had sunk to the floor.

27

Spain

The day after Marie's murder, the guards came for Linda. That evening, Linda's lover arrived to drop the charges against her. She pulled away from the window where she'd been watching the limousine pull in, a triumphant expression.

"I told you, didn't I? Now I can keep my promise to you."

She reached to embrace Kitty, but Kitty backed away. She'd had too much time to think.

"What is it?" Linda dropped her arms.

"Did you turn her in?" Kitty asked vehemently. "Is that what you did? Did you tell those bastards out there that she was Jewish? That they should call Weiss? Wait. No. You're Weiss's mistress, aren't you? He gave you those shoes, didn't he?"

"A German's mistress? Ha!" Linda narrowed her eyes, her chest expanding. "I am a thief. I am perhaps even—as they say— a whore. But I am not a traitor."

"Then why?" Kitty cried. "Why would you offer to go to the consulate for us? For apples?"

"Apples? Apples. I think your question is why did your friend get murdered for positively nothing." Linda put her hands on her hips and huffed.

Kitty tossed the thin blanket off her shoulders. "No. I'm asking you what you gain from offering to help me."

"And? Now you want someone to blame so that you can lash out? Bloody your knuckles a little more? Would that make you feel better? Then go ahead. Hit me. Go on. Hit me!"

Kitty clenched and unclenched her hands, glaring at the woman. But she could not bring herself to hit her. Her suspicions were deep, but maybe Linda was right. Maybe it was not her fault.

"It had nothing to do with the apples," Linda added bitterly. "I am simply not a demon like those people out there. I'm going to help you, as I promised."

She grabbed her wrap, went to the door and shouted in Spanish. On the other side, the sound of the deadbolt sliding out.

Kitty threw herself at her. "All right. All right. Please. Please get word to the British consulate. Marie Sourisseau. Yvette Archambeau."

Linda repeated the names then grasped Kitty's shoulders. "Trust me, Yvette Archambeau. I know what it means to be lost."

And then, she was gone.

Weeping, Kitty sank onto the mattress and curled up into a ball.

The next days, in a blanket of fog and the rain, she passed the hours wavering between fury and deep despair. The temperatures dropped, and the cell was dank and cold. Twice she tossed her pail of waste out the window. She'd lost track of the days when two new guards appeared.

Kitty shrank against the wall, but all they did was deliver a fresh pail of water, remove her waste pail, place a clean wool blanket on the mattress, and hand her a bowl of hot broth.

Even when she stopped fearing them, and demanded answers, the new men did not speak a single word to her, as if they were deaf, or she did not exist.

She found herself talking to Edgar in her head, and sometimes aloud. Thoughts of him tortured her. She had no idea where he was. What had happened to him. And the fact that he —nobody at all—knew where she was, sent her into fits of rage and grief. But her howls fell on deaf ears.

Nobody was coming for her. There was no news from the outside. Nobody would tell her anything about Celestin or Bonaparte. As her cuts and scrapes healed, she derided herself for believing that a couple of apples could buy her freedom. Linda had not, could not or would not deliver the message to the British consulate.

One morning, two new guards led her out and to a shower. She was allowed to walk in the yard, but all Kitty could do was stare at the ground where Marie had been murdered. Not one of those men were around; not the captain, not the two guards. Not even the dirt—washed out by days of rain—revealed any evidence of Marie's brutal execution.

When Kitty returned to her cell, there was a bowl of rice with chunks of vegetables and tough meat.

Suddenly, she heard two men speaking French in the yard. She rushed to the window, her blood freezing at the sight of Bonaparte and Celestin below. Only when she realized that her friends were being allotted some time to exercise like she had, did she relax a little.

Kitty waved her hand out of the bars, and whistled softly. Bonaparte raised his head, his glasses reflecting the dull winter sun. She pressed herself closer to the window, standing on tiptoe as he shaded his eyes.

As Celestin slowly walked by, Bonaparte nudged him in the shoulder. Moments later, both maneuvered in a way so as to stand below Kitty's cell.

"Marie's been killed," she said hoarsely. "Some Nazi officer named Weiss."

Celestin lowered his head between his shoulders and faced the far wall. "We know. We saw it, too. They've got us two floors below you."

"Are you two all right?" She backed away from the bars in case the guards noticed her there.

"We'll be fine."

"I don't know what their plans are," Kitty mourned. "The worst is not knowing why they're holding us..."

"They're trying to figure out our worth." It was Bonaparte's voice.

The guards then whistled and when Kitty peered out, they were motioning for the men to come back. Soon, her two companions disappeared beneath the arch. She faced her empty cell, alone again.

There had been no sign of the captain or the old guards, the ones who had abused her, the ones who'd been responsible for Marie's death. Four days after seeing Bonaparte and Celestin for the first time since their arrival, and without ceremony, the door opened, and Kitty was led down the corridor in handcuffs. She tried to look over her shoulder, but the guard behind her ordered her to face forward.

When they brought her into a room, a tall man in uniform with a thick mustache rose from behind a desk. He muttered something and the handcuffs were removed. Kitty allowed herself a slice of hope when he motioned for her to sit down.

In English, he introduced himself as Captain Perez. He then steepled his hands under his chin and studied her.

"You have friends in high places, Miss Archambeau. Or whoever you are. And your two companions are benefiting from who you know. We regret the circumstances surrounding Marie Sourisseau's... accident. The guards and the captain who were responsible for not monitoring her more closely were accordingly disciplined."

Kitty leaned forward in the wooden chair. "Marie's accident? Is that what you are calling it? It was murder. We are on territory that has nothing to do with the German jurisdiction."

He looked down at the desk, one eyebrow cocked. "Perhaps. Except that Hitler and Mussolini supported Franco in the war. Regardless what your politics are, Spain has debts to pay. How do you say in America? They scratched Franco's back, now Franco scratches theirs."

"Scratching Hitler's back?" Kitty leapt to her feet. One of the guards reached for her elbow but she shook him off.

The captain waved him away. "Sit. Please. Cigarette?"

"No."

He sighed and tapped the desk with splayed fingers. "I would say it is time to look at your future. You are alive. We will feed you well. You will be dressed and clean. More than that, you should not expect."

He dismissed her then. Kitty was taken to a shower, then dressed in a simple shift, much like the one Marie had been given. Her rucksack and her coat were returned. She had a change of clothing and some essentials still in there, but the pistol was gone.

When the two guards led her outside, Kitty nearly laughed aloud at the sight of the car, her relief was that great. Bonaparte jumped out and Kitty gingerly got inside next to Celestin. The vehicle motored out the gates, and she patted the men's hands on either side of her. They had both received their personal effects, or at least their coats.

"Your report, Bonaparte?" She tenderly squeezed his arm with her good hand. "Do you still have it?"

He reached into his coat pocket and withdrew the pen. "All there."

She sighed and laid her head back, the smile of relief creeping slowly across her face.

An hour later, the driver came over a hill, and they were looking across the rain-splattered roofs and Barcelona's cityscape, the charcoal gray sea in the distance. They passed beneath broad palm trees on a main avenue and the driver finally pulled up at the British consulate. A guard at the gate threw open their door and a man in a trench coat peered in.

"Welcome to British soil, Miss Larsson," he said to her. "We're very glad to see you."

At the sound of her real name, Kitty gasped. It was like a punch to her gut and to her chest at once. She swiped at the tears before getting out and accepting the stranger's gentle handshake.

PART THREE

KITTY LARSSON

28

DECEMBER 1942

London, England

From Gibraltar, Kitty, Bonaparte, and Celestin returned to England by submarine. Vera Atkins and Major Buckmaster were both waiting at the harbor; two taxis were parked nearby.

"Welcome home," the major called, stepping forward to heartily shake each of their hands.

Vera embraced Kitty, as if she would break her, and Kitty hugged her tightly back to prove otherwise.

"I'm so glad to see you back," her mentor said. Then into her ear, she whispered, "That was close, Kitty. Far too close."

Kitty pressed her forehead into Vera's shoulder. The emotions were roiling, but there was business to be done now. The debriefing would take days, if not weeks, with Bonaparte's report needing to be transcribed and translated.

She turned to her two companions, the Polish officer and the radio operator. "This is Bonaparte, and you know Celestin."

Vera and Buckmaster greeted both men.

Bonaparte introduced himself briskly, thanking them all. "It is of the utmost importance that I report to the Polish government in exile."

"Of course," Buckmaster answered. "They are already waiting for you." He beckoned for Celestin to follow. "Come, I'll take you both to Orchard Court."

Kitty waited but he did not include her. She looked at Vera expectantly.

"You're taking the other taxi with me," Vera said. "To Trent Park. Colonel Kendrick and I would like to meet with you first."

This was odd, but she fervently hoped it meant that Kendrick had some news about Edgar.

Aware then that Kitty was not going with them, Bonaparte returned and shook her hand. "I cannot thank you enough. Without you—without your leadership—I don't know how far I would have made it. Thousands are counting on us, and you helped."

Kitty flushed. "I was only doing my job. Thank you. That report will finally come into the right hands." At least, she hoped so. There was much more to his story than met the eye; Kitty was certain of it.

She got into the taxi with Vera. "Have you heard about Vladimir and Raymond?"

"They were released. They had black marketeering charges brought against them though. Someone paid off the police. They have radio silence for their own good right now." She did not mention Marie. Instead, she said, "Rest now. We'll talk when you've had a moment to rest."

But Kitty was troubled. She wanted to know who—if it had been true—revealed Marie's identity to this German named Weiss.

When they arrived at Trent Manor, Kitty was shown to a guest room. Hours later, changed and with some food in her, she sat with Vera and Kendrick in the same sitting room she'd

been in when she'd first come to London and discovered that
Edgar was Pim. It was the same pale blue satin and walnut sofa,
the fire in the fireplace, the same tea service and even the same
brandy.

But for Kitty, everything had changed. It felt as if three
dozen years had passed since then, and not only three. She was
agitated. Nervous. Tears pooled easily at the simplest questions,
anticipating when she would have to recall the horrifying
escape from France, and Marie's murder.

When she did recount it, Vera came over to the sofa and
handed her a handkerchief, then offered her a cigarette. Kitty
took one only to prevent the sobbing. Her hand shook as Vera
lit it.

"You got Bonaparte out. As well as Celestin. We need to
celebrate the victories just as we mourn the losses," Vera said.
"But I grieve for each of my agents, and especially my girls."

"Bonaparte's report," Kitty directed her gaze at Kendrick.
"There is information in there that would be useful to the
Allies."

But the colonel briefly puffed out his cheeks and scratched
his neck. "I'm not sure how much of that information will be
accessible to us. The Polish leaders and our ambassador are not
on the best footing at the moment."

"Why not?"

Kendrick clicked his tongue. "Snobbery, admittedly, by our
British ambassador to Poland. And some very sore feelings from
his counterparts."

"They should get over it," Kitty said bitterly. "Politicians
can be so damned childish. People's lives are at stake here.
Jewish lives are at stake here. Something terrible is taking place,
serious war crimes that must be—"

"With all due respect, we have a war to win first," Kendrick
reminded her.

Kitty's teacup rattled as she set it down. "We can't wait that long. *They* can't wait that long."

Kendrick stuck his pipe back in his mouth. Vera was watching her, and Kitty turned contrite.

"I'm sorry. Please don't tell me that Bonaparte's efforts were for nothing."

"I don't think anyone sees it that way, Kitty." Kendrick shrugged. "It requires a special diplomatic touch."

"Then get Nils to assist," she pleaded. "I know for a fact that he has very good relationships on both sides."

Kendrick glanced at Vera. "That's not a bad idea."

His answer gave Kitty confidence again. "I'd like to meet with Edgar's current operational officers, if I can? Colonel, Edgar must get the information in that report. I can only tell you what he has shared with me, but I strongly feel there is a connection between what he knows and what Bonaparte's group witnessed in Auschwitz."

A cloud passed over Kendrick's face and she realized she might be asking for too much.

"Edgar suspected something months ago," she explained, remembering how her husband had struggled to get the overall picture. "A new deadly weapon perhaps made with a chemical gas, or poison. I believe Bonaparte's report will help him to continue piecing together what the Nazis are planning."

He and Vera both went still.

"I'm afraid that won't be possible," Kendrick said flatly.

Goosebumps rose on Kitty's arms in the silence. "Why not?"

Kendrick cupped his pipe in his hand and spoke slowly. "Edgar has vanished. We have not had contact with him in several weeks. It's why I'm meeting with you, Kitty. I need to know everything that has come to pass since you last saw him in Paris. We have good reason to believe his cover was blown or—"

"Because he was discovered?" Vera said and reached for her tea. "Or because he turned on us?"

Kitty stared hard at each of them. Were they serious? "That's not possible. That's not Edgar. He wouldn't do that."

"But it is possible," Vera said. "It wouldn't be the first time something like this has happened."

"I know he wouldn't," Kitty said sharply. "Not Edgar. He's very good at what he does. If he's off the radar, then it's for a good reason."

But she felt chilled to the bone. If he had truly disappeared... *Marguerite*. What had that Parisian woman's role been in all this?

"Miss Atkins believes he turned because he left a trail of destruction," Kendrick disclosed.

"What *trail*?" Kitty said angrily, stabbing out her cigarette. Her head was spinning and she felt sick. "What are you talking about?"

"You were his only connection to our F Section agents." Kendrick cleared his throat. "Which you exposed to him when you met him at his hotel in Marseilles."

Kitty shivered. "No."

Vera stood up and went to the fireplace before facing her again. "We believe he is the reason Prosper was infiltrated. Right before his disappearance. Then it was the Pat Line—the route you used. It collapsed. And the Sculptor Network did not go unscathed. All of them were sent running. And now we know what happened to Marie."

Kitty's heart lurched, and she clutched her stomach. "But why do you believe it is Edgar who betrayed me? He would never do that. Never."

"That's why we are here. To find out," Kendrick said gently. "I figured it would be better for you to meet with me first, rather than with strangers, but you will be meeting with his superiors as well."

Kitty buried her face in her hands, shaking her head. It couldn't be true. But something had gnawed at her about Edgar since Paris, hadn't it? As early as Marseilles, actually. But no. Not Edgar.

When she looked back up, she blinked back the tears. "What about Raymond? Vladimir? It could have been anybody. That first Spanish captain claimed that Marie had been ratted on by someone in Marseilles. Edgar knew nothing about Marie. Nothing. I promise."

Vera frowned, sighing heavily. "But Sculptor, Prosper and Circus, the escape line, they all collapsed long before that."

"If we're going to review every move, everything that was said, then we review *everyone*," Kitty demanded.

"How would you begin to do that?" Vera viciously stamped out her cigarette.

"I could go to France. Find out what happened for you." Kitty pleaded with each of them. "I could help rebuild Sculptor. Or Prosper, and get to the bottom of this."

Vera's expression turned to pity. "Kitty, we can't send you back in. You are involved. Even if you weren't, you'd be walking straight to your death. Especially if Edgar really has betrayed you."

"He wouldn't! Besides, it's my choice to make." She looked to Kendrick for support, but Vera folded her arms over her chest and gave Kitty a hard look.

"Regrettably, it is not. F Section decides who goes in and who does not."

Kendrick uncrossed his legs and leaned on his thighs. "Kitty, if he hasn't turned, then Edgar has been arrested and, well, under *Nacht und Nebel*..."

She stared at the man who had pulled her into this business —both her and her husband—and her anger was rekindled. "Tell me you'll help me to find out. No matter what. You owe us the opportunity to get to the bottom of this." She spun to Vera. "And investigate thoroughly."

Vera was stony but Kendrick shrugged and shifted again. Not for the first time, he was surrendering to her. She had to swallow hard around the lump of grief.

"I'll look into it, Kitty. I will. We both will."

She nodded slowly, gazing from Vera—who looked dubious —back to Kendrick. Had Edgar turned on Great Britain, or had the Germans discovered and arrested him? Regardless, he had disappeared.

But she was not prepared to accept any of their theories about her husband.

29

MARCH 1943

London, England

There was a wet swish from beyond the bedroom window and the sound of a bus motor accelerating. A weak light fought through the crack in the curtains. At the sound of a soft knock, Kitty pulled back beneath the covers and pressed her head further into the pillow, lying very still, hoping that whoever was at the door—Nils, Rose, or even Molly—would think she was still sleeping and would go away. No such luck.

She cringed at the sound of soft footsteps crossing to her bed.

"*Liebling?*"

She threw the comforter off her head, unbelieving. "Oskar? It's really you! What are you doing here?"

Kitty knelt on the bed to hug him. He was in a military uniform and wore his signature warm smile but the rest of him revealed concern.

"You are not looking well, *Liebling*," he said tenderly.

She shrank back, pushing her unwashed hair out of her face. In the mirror opposite she could see the faded red color. She'd let herself go in her grief.

"All right," she sighed. "I submit to your professional opinion."

She sat back down and pulled him onto the bed next to her. He put an arm around her.

"Corporal." She eyed the patch of his jacket. "You signed up. Special ops?"

He put a finger to his lips. "Top secret," he teased. But she knew he meant it. "Either way, it's what I need to wear for my job and is a bit more comfortable than the German one."

She took in his face, the brown eyes, the swath of dark hair left over from his buzz cut.

"I'm in London for a quick meeting. Then back to work. Kendrick told me you returned. Safe. But sound?"

She hid her guilt by straightening the comforter. "I should have called."

"No need for excuses, *Liebling*." He shifted on the mattress to look directly at her. "Your sister-in-law says you've been hidden away in this room for days. And that nobody knows much. I've been with you in the field. I understand."

Kitty swallowed but she was still hoarse. "I can't talk about it."

His eyes asked why but he did not utter the question.

She took in a long, shaky breath. "After this war—"

"After this war? Let's not revisit the things that made us lock ourselves up in a room. I know you well enough, Kitty. Whatever you were doing, you had good reason for it. And I can see that you are paying a heavy price for it."

She closed her eyes. If anyone knew how much of a price, it was Oskar. What if it was true that Edgar had betrayed her and Great Britain? "I am flailing."

He wrinkled his nose. "You do stink a bit."

Kitty pulled away and sniffed. "I do, don't I?"

"Don't worry, I still love you." He pulled her close to him before taking her hands in his. His eyes flicked up from her battered fingers and palms. They were now scarred from the walls of the Spanish prison. Softly, he said, "I don't know what it is that you have gone through, but to feel the sorrow and that pain I know you are feeling right now, and to keep going..." He kissed her knuckles, his eyes brimming with emotion. "To keep going, Kitty, that is real courage."

At the sight of her tears, Oskar laid her hands gently into her lap. "We should get you out of the house." He unwrapped himself from her, strode over to the window, and snapped back the curtains. "I wouldn't venture to say it's a beautiful day in London, but you are looking pasty, a little like white cheddar. We should get out there, at least into a warm tavern, put a pint in you."

Kitty laughed abruptly, but a tear escaped and rolled down her cheek. Doing something as normal as going out for a drink was obscene. Instead, she patted the mattress. Oskar sat down next to her and swung his legs onto the bed. They were quiet for a moment. Outside the window, the wind gusted rain against the pane.

"I nearly forgot, *Liebling*. I ran into Millie Hoffmann while you were away."

"Here, in London? When?"

"Around Christmas. I didn't know where you..." He took in a breath. "Anyway, she was visiting from Bern. Her boss was here for some meetings. Turns out, she's his right-hand woman and has become very important."

"I knew she wouldn't stop working," Kitty said.

"She wanted me to stress that you should go see her if you are ever back in Bern."

Kitty nodded but then frowned. "What do you mean, when I'm *back* in Bern?"

Oskar sounded uncertain. "Back in Europe? On the continent."

But it niggled her. Had Millie even known she'd been in Bern? She couldn't remember.

"She misses you," Oskar continued. "You know, we had some very good times, too. You must remember that, Kitty."

She did remember. She remembered it all too well. Her love affair with Edgar, their courtship, their marriage, and how it all descended into a hellish nightmare that left her alone in this very room, mourning him.

Kitty balled herself up and laid her head in Oskar's lap.

"Hey," he said again, stroking her head. "Is there anyone I can call for you?"

Edgar. She sniffed and wiped her tears. She could not even say his name aloud. *Edgar.*

"OK," Oskar said. "I won't say another thing, *Liebling.*"

He put an arm over her and she wept herself to sleep. It was the only way she found peace from her agitated thoughts.

Oskar made her get dressed before he left, and she joined the family for dinner. To spare her niece, Molly, the talk around the table focused on frivolities. Every few minutes, Kitty would inevitably think of Edgar. She had to bite the inside of her lip to keep from tearing up again and again.

Nils shot her a sympathetic glance, as if he sensed the silent torture she was going through. As he should. Nils shared the secret of who Edgar really was. There was nobody in her family except her big brother that she could talk to about her husband. But a signed document, swearing her to silence, stood between them.

That night, after tossing and turning in bed for hours, Kitty came down into the kitchen to find Nils warming milk and honey.

She felt jittery about being alone with him. Over the years, they had inadvertently developed a way of communicating via nuance. How high would they lift the lids of their Pandora's boxes before slamming them back shut?

"You couldn't sleep either?" She leaned against the doorway.

Nils faced her, then reached for the jug of milk and poured more into the pot.

"What's keeping you awake?" she asked.

His concentration turned into disbelief. "The position I find myself in right now, Kitty. Let me put it this way, it's painful being privy to nearly everybody else's business—private and public. Especially when you know it's affecting your family, the ones you love the most in the world."

"Stop it. You love Rose more than any of us." Kitty's half-hearted jest only earned her another one of his scowls. She took a seat at the table.

Nils clanged the spoon on the side of the pot before turning up the heat, then rested his elbows on the counter as they waited. "Maman sent me a telegram; it came after you went to bed. Sam is doing as well as can be in North Africa, and Aunt Julia is leaving France and joining Maman in St. Paul. Dad's seen to it."

"Thank God," Kitty breathed. At least that. At least Aunt Julia was safe.

"What about you?" he asked cautiously. "What are you going to do next?"

Kitty slowly shook her head from side to side. She didn't know where to start, her frustration was a hard, angry ball in the pit of her stomach. She'd been trained to trust nobody, except herself. And her innate trust in Edgar was now in question. She wanted Nils to have an answer.

Instead, she eyed the steam wafting from the milk. "I don't like it when there's skin."

Nils whisked the pot off the stove and poured them two mugs. She stirred in honey and cradled the hot cup. He put his mug down between his elbows and blew on it, eyeing her hands.

"Are you going to be OK, Kitty?" He was not talking about the scars he could see.

"On the record or off?"

His chest expanded. "OK. Off."

She had to whisper for fear of crying again. "I'm worried about Edgar. Something happened, Nils. He'd told me that he was dejected. Scared, even. You know about the Polish officer's report. Well, before I was sent to escort him out of France, Edgar told me about a Polish POW who was captured and killed in Paris, Nils. He had information that was compromising to the Germans. Very much so. And then Edgar warned me that things were changing at the headquarters in Paris; that he was letting his English communication channels grow cold."

Nils grunted and something flickered over his face.

She studied her mug, turning it in half circles, her chest painfully tight. Nils did not know that the SOE and MI6 suspected her husband of betraying them.

"I haven't seen Edgar or heard from him since September. The last time I saw him, he gave me information to pass on to England." She looked up. "Nils, are the Germans building a secret weapon?"

She'd just blown the lid clean off and the way Nils suddenly shifted, she knew she'd hit the mark on something. He hid himself behind the mug as he drank, turning his head away.

She pushed at the teaspoon sticking out of her milk. "What about the report from Auschwitz? Has it been translated, yet? I saw those delivery lists. I think there is a connection between what's going on in Auschwitz, and this... rumor."

Nils set his mug back down and added another teaspoon of honey before he answered. By the way his face was screwed up, he was conflicted. "I've talked to both sides, the Polish leadership and the British ambassador to Poland. They're going to meet to discuss options. And all I can tell you is this: there is no connection between Germany developing a new weapon, and the Jewish deportations. But there might be with those shipments of chemicals to Auschwitz."

So the rumor of a secret weapon was true. But the chemicals? Kitty held his gaze. "What are we going to do about it?"

"We?"

"Yes. We. Our governments?" She remembered Bonaparte's plea to bomb Auschwitz to oblivion, and that innocent men were prepared to die for it. "We have the information. Let's take action."

Nils folded his arms over his chest. "I'm not going to pretend I know what events are taking place on your turf, Kit. But I have only one question." He stirred the spoon absently before letting it fall to the side of the mug. "Do you know where Edgar is?"

Her heart leapt. She shoved away from the table and some of her milk sloshed over the rim. "You do, don't you?"

"I don't, Kitty. I only think that he might have tried to reach you."

"What? When?" She jumped to her feet, but her legs were shaky. She held on to the back of the kitchen chair.

"I was in Bern, and some man approached me. German accent. Just out of the blue in a park. And he said to me, 'He's on the move again. When it's time, he'll let her know about a return.'"

Kitty's head swam. "About a *return*. He used that word?"

Nils was grave. "Yeah. I'm pretty sure."

"When was this?" she whispered.

"I don't know. November? Early December, I think."

She stared at her brother. "And you didn't bother to tell me earlier?"

"Kitty..."

"Damn it, Nils. It's all I needed to hear. That he's alive! That there's still a chance he's alive!"

But Nils grabbed her wrist. "Kit, please calm down. I had no idea what he was talking about. I had no context. I didn't. You got here, tight-lipped, traumatized, and I have an inkling that something pretty horrific happened, but I couldn't know. I only connected the dots now."

Kitty paced to the boarded-up windows. Bern. Oskar had just mentioned Bern. *When you come* back *to Bern.* She did not believe in coincidences. She had to still her breathing. But how did Millie know then? *What* did she know? If she knew anything.

"Kitty?"

"I'm fine." She spun to Nils, trying to convince herself more than him. "I'm fine. I'll be fine." She walked over and kissed his forehead, her signal for them to close their boxes again.

She was grateful for the information, but she would harbor this secret, keep it close. At least until she got to the bottom of it.

Somewhere out there, Edgar was still alive. She knew it. Operating. Not caught in Hitler's Night and Fog. She had to trust her instincts. If she did, then Nils was right.

Edgar would send for her.

MARCH 1943

London, England

The next day, before Kitty could put together the entire puzzle —each piece was like trying to catch a wisp of smoke—Vera called.

"Can you make your way back to Trent Park?"

Kitty said she would. She had decided she would wait to hear what F Section and Kendrick had found out about Edgar, or the rest of the Sculptor circuit. She was very surprised to find Oskar gathering his coat outside Kendrick's office.

She pulled him down onto the leather sofa, suspicion flooding her. "What are you doing here?"

A shadow passed over his face. "Remember that meeting I was to go to when I visited you? I think I know what you were so sad about now." He leaned close to her and whispered. "I always wondered why Edgar had risked bringing me to you. It was against security policies. He was not doing it from the goodness of his heart."

"You're right, he never did anything without purpose," Kitty muttered. "It wasn't for me. He saw a reason to reach out to *you*."

"Exactly." Oskar poked his finger into her shoulder. "When Edgar found me in France, he cornered me and started asking me all kinds of questions. It was an interrogation. He terrified me. I was very defensive and protective of you. And then he sprang the plan about turning me into Vogels."

He spoke faster. "I thought he was insane, but he did not push it. He said we would talk more. We met a few times, and I started getting more and more comfortable with the idea. He was so damned convincing, Kitty. So sure! I then asked him if I could have a different name, and he said he'd chosen the name on purpose. I asked what he meant. And he just looked at me strangely and said, 'Sometimes you just need a little bird where it matters most.' When I met with Kendrick—"

Kitty seized his arm. Edgar's instructions were to get Oskar to Kendrick. On that last night in Marseilles with him, he'd said, *I just needed a bird's-eye view on this. And, Kitty, listen carefully, I got it. I found a little bird who could help me.*

She leapt off the bench and faced Oskar, but the office door flew open and Kendrick appeared. This was going to be a very official meeting. The colonel was dressed in full military attire.

"Miss Larsson. Thank you for coming." His eyes darted to Oskar. "We're ready for you."

With no time left, Kitty mumbled goodbye to Oskar, and followed Kendrick.

Vera was standing at a round walnut table. Kitty greeted her automatically, and took a seat opposite her, still coming to terms with the information Oskar had just shared. Kendrick took his position to Vera's left. She and Kendrick both had files on the table in front of them.

"What is Oskar doing for the Foreign Office?" Kitty blurted.

"Kitty," Vera objected.

She pleaded with Kendrick. "This is no time for games. What is Oskar doing for you? Because Edgar would have found out from you where he was placed."

Kendrick held her look. "Or he would have recruited Oskar for me."

Kitty laughed abruptly. "Of course!"

Kendrick eyed her curiously before finally saying, "I had a different idea for Corporal Liebherr. I asked him to be a stool pigeon."

"What is that?"

"Someone who is planted among POWs to win their confidence."

Kitty stammered, "What kind of POWs?"

Kendrick shook his head. "I can't and won't go into details. Only that we embellished Vogels's cover story quite a bit to make him convincing. He won their trust, and was privy to their conversations."

Kitty took in a sharp breath. "Did he find out about a new chemical weapon?"

"I'm not free to share that with you."

Kitty bit her lip, trying to keep her anger down. "I forwarded intel on that factory in northern France." She waited, expecting Vera to help confirm those strands of smoke slowly revealing something more tangible. "That intel was from Edgar. He gave that information to me to send to London. Don't you see?"

Kendrick winced. "Kitty, you were talking about Oskar. Anyway, he is no longer a stool pigeon."

"Why?"

Vera shifted, glaring at Kitty.

"He could not handle the bragging. He overhead conversations that were... They were talking about how they... Let's just say, the information left him distraught."

Kitty leaned forward. "Colonel, what was Edgar's request for Oskar?"

"Edgar's intention?" Vera cried impatiently. "What makes you believe he had any intention? Or any right to make that request?"

But Kendrick held up a hand, gazing at Kitty. He knew Edgar. Not as well as she did, but he was familiar with her husband's methods of operation. "Oskar is now typing up reports."

"Reports!" She couldn't believe it. Had Kendrick removed the one person who could have helped Edgar? "Reports on what?"

Vera once again protested, "Colonel Kendrick, this is the part that we must be careful about."

"Please," Kitty begged them both. "I have information that could help us to understand what Edgar might be doing or wanted to do. Maybe removing Oskar from—"

"The trouble is, Kitty," Vera said sharply, "that if we tell you, we'll have to send you to the cooler. *I* don't even have the authorization to know about this."

Kitty remembered the place where agents were sent to until the intel they had was obsolete. But if these two were going to clam up, she was going to hit a dead end before she'd even started.

Kendrick sat back and folded his hands on the desk. "I can only say that I finally sent Oskar to Danesfield House. The unit gleans intelligence from aerial photographs. It was what Edgar wanted but I can't—"

Kitty leapt to her feet. "That's it," she cried. "That's it!"

She went to the door, yanked it open, but Oskar was gone. She turned to the others. They were taken aback. *I found a little bird who could help me*, Edgar had told her. And he had purposefully chosen Oskar's cover name to be *Vogels*, which was the possessive form of bird—*bird's-eye view*. How was she going to explain this without sounding insane? Without sounding like she was just looking for meaning? *Was* she?

"I need access to those photos. Can I get access?"

Vera tapped a pen on the edge of the table and turned her head to Kitty. "We are only discussing obsolete intel with you. Kitty, the last thing I want to do is send you away."

She groaned. "Please. Please let me just ask a few questions."

"Kitty, we can't talk to you," Kendrick cried. He was losing his temper.

"I'm here to set things straight," Kitty argued. "Edgar was not the one who was responsible for Prosper's fall. Or Sculptor's. Or the Pat Line. I think he's still working for you."

"He most certainly is not," Kendrick bit back.

Vera cleared her throat and put her pen on top of the file.

Kitty forced herself to calm down. She leaned on Kendrick's desk. "OK. I'm going to tell you something you might not know. Edgar has gone underground."

Vera's look was severe. "Did he contact you? When? Why didn't you tell us?"

She had to be careful. "He did not contact me. But I've had time to think. When my husband was working as a legal adviser for Austria's Department of Economics, he had a lot of contacts in the country's industrial sector, and helped facilitate policies between Germany and Austria. Edgar knew nearly everyone who had a hand in manufacturing, from rubber to electronic parts."

Vera's expression was wary.

"This is true," Kendrick admitted. "It was one of the reasons he was so interesting for us."

"Last question. Regardless where the aerial photos are coming from, is the source the same? Is there a name? Code name? Operative? You don't have to tell me what it is, only if you know whether there is one."

Kendrick opened his hands. "That information is always redacted when it comes to us."

Kitty retreated, crestfallen. She faced Vera. "If my suspicions are accurate, then Edgar is still working for the Allies. Not Germany. But how, I'm not sure."

Kendrick sighed. "Your faith is admirable."

"No, it's not just faith. My husband was exhausted. He said he was tired of playing the diplomat, only so that he could save his skin. But he was also frustrated. He mentioned that he felt his information wasn't making a difference; or at least not fast enough. Something I could sympathize with." She paced the room, scraping up the bits and pieces from her memories.

"When I asked him what he had in mind, he said any drastic move on his part would have horrendous consequences. I assumed he meant from the Germans. Naturally, I thought, he couldn't break his patterns or he would create suspicion among his German colleagues. But what I didn't consider was that he might mean that if he broke any patterns with you"—she faced Kendrick—"the consequences could come from the British side. From the people who were meant to protect him."

Kendrick shifted uncomfortably.

"Colonel, you have to give him the benefit of the doubt." And she needed to get to Bern.

"Miss Larsson," Kendrick said. "We are pretty certain that Edgar is not involved with the intelligence we are getting."

"You've lost faith in him, haven't you? You were his *friend*," Kitty cried. She suddenly froze. *Most loyal friends have come to pass...* She could barely vocalize the thought.

"Are there orders to... liquidate him?"

Kendrick dropped his hands beneath the table and turned his head to Vera. Vera leapt up and strode around it, her hand out. It was so dismissive that Kitty could only gape at her.

"Thank you for your service, Miss Larsson," she said. "For your courage and bravery. Remember that you have had access to confidential information and you are obligated to the Secrets Act regardless what you do or where you go now. I don't want to send you away, Kitty. But anything more from you or from us, and we will be forced to put you in the cooler."

Kendrick rose slowly now, eyes on the floor. "I'm sorry to see you go," he said.

She did not know how, but Kitty willed herself to first grasp Vera's hand, then Kendrick's.

At the door, she turned back to them both. "I know my husband," she said coldly. "And he'll be back."

31

MARCH 1943

London, England

"Nobody will talk to you in Bern," Nils reprimanded. "You don't have the clearance, Kitty. You've been a British agent, not American. You can't just step on over to the other side and hope they share their intelligence with you."

They were sitting in his office at the embassy, and Kitty was fussing with the end of the shawl around her neck. She was always cold now. "Fine. But I could meet Millie in person, without opening my mouth about this, I'll know if she knows something. Like it is with you."

He rolled his eyes. "What are you going to do? Travel over Spain? France? To fly you in, we'd have to have you on official business. Kitty, there's a war—"

"Shut up, Nils. I know there's a war going on." He did not understand that she was terrified that Edgar was running out of time. If MI6 was now convinced Edgar had become a double agent, they were sure to be on the hunt for him. To eliminate him. And she was certain he'd be aware of that danger.

She tried again. "Get a message to Millie for me, will you? I think Oskar said her last name is Quentin, now."

Nils sighed. "All right. You can formulate it yourself. Listen, on another matter, I know you've been keeping a low profile, not feeling very social, but Rose and I are throwing a little soiree. Some Americans are on a junket. Wild Bill Donovan is here. They're coming the day after tomorrow."

Kitty dropped the end of the shawl. "Really?"

"Uh-huh. He did say that if you ever, you know, change your mind..."

Kitty tilted her head. "I think I can find something to wear."

If the SOE was not going to send her back into France, and was not going to give her any further access to reports and intelligence, she had no idea what she was doing in England any longer. But Wild Bill might know how she could be useful.

That Saturday night, when he walked in and shook out his coat, Kitty was lingering in the hallway, preparing to pounce. His dark eyebrows shot upwards when he caught sight of her.

"Well, this is a nice surprise." He beamed down on her.

Kitty embraced him and pecked his cheek. "Good to see you in person, Bill."

"Actually, Nils warned me you'd be here."

She flushed. "I heard about your promotion. Colonel now? Congratulations, sir. So, how are things?"

"Things?" He chuckled. "Things are fine, Kitty. How are things with you? Are you getting *things* done?"

Before Kitty could answer, Nils swept Donovan away with an apologetic glance at her and into the crowd of guests in the dining room. She went to Rose and asked how she could help.

"Nils tells me that Colonel Donovan's people are pretty active here in London," Rose said. "Didn't Wild Bill offer you a job once?"

"As his secretary," Kitty said. "But I'm sure that position has been filled."

"It's a war, Kitty," Rose said. "They need all the help they can get. Go talk to him. Surely he has something that you could do."

Kitty waited for a quiet moment before cornering Donovan again, this time behind the staircase and out of Nils's sight.

"Can we keep that conversation going? About things."

Donovan cocked an eyebrow at her. "We certainly can."

"I want to serve my country. You offered me a job once."

He wagged a finger at her. "Which you very promptly turned down."

"I had my reasons."

"I'm sure you did. Did they retire you already?"

"They?" Kitty challenged.

"The Brits, Kitty. I'm not alluding to knowing anything other than that."

She squinted at him. "Then let's cut to the chase. I could go back to the States."

"You don't look happy about it."

"I don't want to rest on my laurels. Isn't there anything you can think of for me? I realize I'm begging here."

Donovan leaned back against the stairwell and scanned her face, his bright blue eyes flashing amusement and, also, admiration. "All right, Kitty. Let me huddle with my team and we'll get back to you."

Nils stepped around the corner. "What are you two conspiring here?"

Kitty winced and pulled away. "I think it's time we all talk." She shot her brother a knowing look and his expression sobered.

Nils unlocked the door to his study. After they'd all arranged themselves in a semi-circle, Kitty held her brother's look.

"I think you should start. This is embassy business."

Nils turned to Donovan. "Bill, do you know the game telephone?"

Donovan frowned a little. "You mean the one where people whisper something into each other's ear?"

"That's the one. So, what I'm about to tell you has only come down the line to me." His eyes darted over to Kitty. "It's a confidential and sensitive matter. And again, I only have the bits and pieces that were shared with me."

Donovan glanced at her and she bit her lip. Whatever Nils reported now, he was doing it on official business. She was not allowed to say a word.

"Go on," Donovan said. "It sounds serious."

"A couple of months ago, the former prime minister of the Polish exile government here in London received a report that came from a resistance network inside the prison camp in Oświęcim."

"Auschwitz? In Poland." Donovan shifted in the armchair.

Nils lowered his voice. "Apparently the report originated from a group of Polish officers who are imprisoned there. It's the third report of its kind."

Kitty flinched. She only knew of two.

"Two of those reports made it to England," Nils went on. "The second was intercepted by the Germans."

Bill frowned. "Then how do you know about that—" He shifted in his chair to look at Kitty. She looked down at her lap. Donovan cleared his throat. "Go on, son."

"The first report was smuggled out by a released prisoner two years ago."

"Two years ago?" Kitty muttered.

Nils held her gaze. "He passed it on to a resistance network in Poland. They typed it up, had it smuggled to Geneva, handed it over to the Polish chargé d'affaires at the League of Nations, and that went on to a Polish station chief in Madrid. It arrived intact here in London."

Kitty sat back. She'd had no idea. Nils winced, his way of apologizing.

"The second report was, like I said, intercepted by the Germans. However, it apparently revealed the conditions in the camp, and alleged massive breaches to the Geneva Convention. According to my *source*"—his eyes darted back to Kitty—"the report detailed sheer brutalities and atrocities against the prisoners. The Germans are breaking international laws. The conditions, the prisoners reported, are so bad that many are dying of typhus. They are abused, tortured, even violated."

"But we don't know for sure?" Donovan asked cautiously.

"Just via a third source," Kitty hurried. "And an eyewitness who is here now, in London. He could corroborate the details of that lost report."

"But if we put together the information of all three reports," Nils said, "it paints a pretty grim picture. Most of all, it makes sense why the first report was asking for bomber command."

Donovan's forehead was furrowed. "The Polish officers wanted the Allies to bomb the camp? The one they are incarcerated in?"

Kitty's hand fluttered to her throat as she listened. Bonaparte had complained that if the reports had gotten through, then he should have died under a carpet of bombs.

Nils steepled his hands. "It detailed the coordinates, the ammunition depots, the factories, everything. Bill, these Polish officers were begging for the Allies to annihilate it all. They claimed that anyone who survived the attack would steal weapons and fight on the ground, but they absolutely stressed they were prepared to lay their lives down. I'll bet they still are."

Donovan looked down at his drink as if he'd just lost his appetite. "But nobody did? Why?"

"That's where this story goes bad. The Polish leader visited the English ambassador up in Scotland over Christmas two years ago. The request got battered and kicked around, and they hemmed and hawed about whether this had been planted by the Nazis or whether it was authentic. Finally, they decided that an aide-de-camp should send a summary of the report to the RAF directly with the bomber command request. And to give them credit, the RAF gave it serious consideration."

"Two years ago? British bombers..." Donovan mused aloud. Nils inclined his head.

"They can't carry that weight all that distance."

"Correct. The same conclusion the RAF came to. The load would be too great. You would need too many planes. And that presents great risk, and too few bombs presents likelihoods of inaccuracies. Plus, and this is where my source is frustrated, the moral principle of the message was missing by the time it was gleaned down to that RAF summary report."

Donovan shifted in his chair. "In other words, the RAF thought they'd be bombing *some* facility, with no understanding why. Or why so deep behind the lines. But we need lighter planes. More accuracy. Better technology. That much is certain." He looked at Kitty. "I'd like to hear this from you now."

"You mean about the third report?"

"She's not allowed to say," Nils interjected. He reached into his desk and handed Donovan a sheaf of papers. "But I am. Kitty got me involved. I just prepared a report today for D.C. The summary is on top."

Nils sat back and he and Kitty exchanged a grateful look.

Donovan read, then rifled through the pages. "This SOE operative, the one who got this character, Bonaparte, out..."

Nils cleared his throat. "Bonaparte's translated accounts of Auschwitz theorize that the Jewish inmates are being decimated. Not dying only due to awful conditions in the camp, but because they are forced to work with this pesticide."

Donovan balked. "That's preposterous."

But Kitty's anger boiled over. She'd had enough of the disbelief and the dismissals. They had not been there when

Marie was executed in cold blood. When Artur had been slain. When Judith disappeared into a Gestapo prison and never returned.

"It's not preposterous," she said acidly. "Not preposterous at all."

Donovan grimaced. "Do you know what that would mean? What you're accusing Germany of?"

"Yes," she said. "It would mean the Nazis are committing genocide."

He folded his hands and studied her. She straightened in her chair, daring him to contradict her again.

"Why are you coming home? If you believe all this, why would you return to the U.S.?" he asked.

Kitty bit the inside of her lip, the humiliation hot. "Because I've been retired."

"You were in France," Wild Bill said quietly. "I get that. And you lived in Vienna as well."

"That's correct, sir."

"I do have some *thing* you can do for me."

Kitty moved to the edge of her seat. If she could stay in intelligence, she might still have a chance of finding Edgar and figuring out what he was really up to. But she was not going to tell Donovan that. She cast a glance at Nils. Nils could read her, maybe, but he made no protest.

"We've cobbled together a group of about fifty operatives. We're training a number of them to infiltrate France. They are coming to England for orientation and guerrilla training. Last time we talked on the phone, you said that our European Allies have been paving the way for quite some time. We're depending on their experience now. We'd sent in some of our own operatives to France before, but the first few who landed in German occupied zones were promptly arrested. A bunch of cowboys who didn't talk the talk or walk the walk, if you know what I mean."

"As a matter of fact, I do."

"But you lived in France. You could train them to become invisible."

Kitty held his gaze, nodding slowly. "I could. I could teach them how to walk the walk, talk the talk, and I can tell them what to expect. I can share what I know. But..."

Edgar had been only partly right in Paris. He had told her she had learned the game. She had learned *about* the game, but she was far from a master at playing it yet. Carefully, she made her next move.

"What does it pay?"

Donovan looked baffled. "What does it *pay*? Well, I don't know Kitty—"

"Because I don't want your money, Colonel. I want to take part."

"Take part?"

"Yes. I want to be trained as one of your agents. I want to be able to take the whole course." She leaned forward. "We need to get behind the lines and get information from Germany. You don't only need agents in France, Bill. You need them at the source."

Donovan's eyebrows shot up. He turned to her brother. Nils cleared his throat, and she caught a flash of a smile, but his eyes were warning her that she might have gone too far. He saw through her now. But she could handle Nils. She had a hand to play with Donovan.

"She's a tough negotiator, Bill," Nils warned. "But I think you're going to find you'll get the better end of the deal in the long run."

Donovan scratched the back of his neck. "This isn't the first time I'm hearing this, Kitty, but setting up a network takes years. We don't have years."

"No, setting up a network doesn't have to take years. It only takes reigniting an old one..."

Both men now looked astonished. Donovan glanced nervously at her brother.

"You've got a lot of catching up to do with Kitty," Nils told him.

Kitty stuck her hand out to the American colonel. "You train me to be a full-blown agent, or I'm nothing at all."

"I'm not guaranteeing that we're going to put you in the field," he warned.

"Fine, but I guarantee that you're going to want me to be."

Donovan laughed, shrugged, and pressed his hand into hers. "All right. You do drive a hard bargain."

"It's not as hard as all that," Kitty retorted. "What is your organization called?"

"The OSS. The Office of Strategic Services."

"Fancy."

Donovan grinned. "When could you start doing this *thing* for me, then?"

"Tomorrow soon enough?"

"Let's get you through a background check first." He jutted out his big hand once more. "And then you'll head out with me, personally."

32

Great Britain

Pacing before the third wave of American officers, Kitty discreetly studied the faces and dynamics in the room. After going through the OSS training program herself, she was now responsible for leading the orientation on what awaited this new group over the course of six weeks. As she introduced herself, she recalled a remark Oskar had made.

"You've grown into your skin," he'd said.

It was a good analogy, because if there was something she was sure about, it was that she was right where she belonged: here, in this room. She was prepared—prepared to go find Edgar. All she needed now was to convince Colonel Donovan to put her out in the field. But she had to pay her dues, first.

"Welcome to your joint training on psychological and guerrilla warfare," she announced to the group. "The first thing you men are about to learn is that guerrilla warfare has very little to do with the military training you've had before."

She looked at the young, eager faces before her. A dozen first lieutenants and captains watched with a mixture of anticipation and admiration. But there was some doubt. She saw how some of the men's eyes traveled from her face to her ankles. They had not expected her: not just Kitty Larsson, but a woman.

Giving them the benefit of the doubt, these men were some of the fifty that the OSS had scouted out from a variety of army command stations and posts. They were coming to Great Britain in small groups in preparation for infiltrating France. They still had a lot to learn.

One of her jobs was to take them down a notch.

"Sabotage, espionage, paramilitary and resistance operations, counter-espionage," she listed, walking up and down the first row of prospects. "That's the order of the day, men. But there will be nitty-gritty details you will also be learning. You'll learn to fire and clean foreign weapons, including German arms. You'll continue your training as on any military base. Our obstacle courses will fire live rounds. You'll be learning to detonate different types of explosives so that you can measure their effects."

She faltered, the memory of Marie washing a wave of grief over her. She examined the men more closely. If they had any reservations about a woman being here, she was going to blow apart their preconceptions now. She would tell them the stories of women who'd already sacrificed so much: Guinevère's. Marie's. Mrs. Reboul's, and even Judith's, who may not have worked in the field, but marked the beginning of Kitty's journey.

"I had a friend," she said, her hands behind her back. "A woman, with whom I trained before going into France. Her code name was Mulligan. She was really good at making things go *boom*."

The men chuckled appreciatively.

"But the Gestapo hunted her down in a Spanish prison." She paused for effect. "That's right. A *Spanish* prison. While we were in transition, the guards took bribes from a Gestapo man. She was murdered, *sold* to the Nazis because she was a Jew."

She looked hard at one of the younger men, an agent named Rosenberg, before glancing down at her list. She cleared her throat and shared the rest of the curriculum.

The course was now much more professional, better organized since her own F Section training a year earlier. These candidates would learn how to live off the land. They would break into buildings and photograph or steal documents. They would practice sending intricately coded messages and decode the ones that came back on their radios. They would launch guerrilla attacks at all hours of the day and night, or set up shoot-and-run ambushes.

"You'll also all be tested on leadership," she finished. Again, she was reminded of her own lessons learned in Vienna. "If you don't think you are capable of leadership, you're wrong. Each of you is a leader. It's a quality and a discipline that can be learned if you lay your egos aside."

A few nodded understandingly, but one man smirked.

Wait and see, she thought. *Just wait and see.*

"Men, please follow me to the gadgets room." This was her favorite part.

Pooling together their resources of engineers and inventors, the SOE and the OSS now provided masterful tools for their agents and spies. She demonstrated how a baseball, a pipe and a hairbrush contained secret compartments where one could store messages or radio components. She revealed an array of miniature cameras, followed by compasses disguised as coat buttons.

"Thanks to the Geneva Convention, our POWs can receive parcels from the Red Cross," she explained. "So, we plant maps and escape routes into packets of playing cards, or foreign currency into Monopoly games."

The men admired the small board games and she peeled the top of a playing card off to reveal the map below. Picking up a box of Lucky Strikes, Kitty shook one out, offering it to one of the men she'd seen smoking before the orientation.

He reached for the cigarette, but Kitty pulled back at the last moment with a mischievous smile. "Kids are taught not to take candy from a stranger. You're about to learn not to take cigarettes offered by the enemy."

A ripple of nervous laughter followed.

"We're learning from some of the most sinister tricks that the German secret service is using. These cigarettes are laced with tetrahydrocannabinol acetate. The compound works similarly to morphine and is normally not lethal. But, offer it to an enemy agent and you're going to discover that the smoker will become an uncontrollable chatterbox. And this cigarette case?" She held up a beautifully embossed holder. "You won't want to open this up to just anyone."

She turned to the nearest engineer, a young man with tortoiseshell glasses and red hair. He indicated the room she should enter. The agents could see her through the wall of thick windows. When she was inside, she held up the case to them again then flipped it open before throwing it against a rubber panel. She covered her head. The case exploded. Against the panel, it did little damage. However, it was clear that, opened to a face, it would create serious if not fatal injuries.

When she rose, the men were cautiously applauding her. Kitty came out of the room and they eagerly followed her to the next exhibit. The last of the doubts and derision in the group were quickly evaporating.

With relish, she showed them knives that they could conceal within shoes, lapels, pencils, sleeves and even coins.

"And this ring," she said, removing the blue stone, "contains your L-pills."

One candidate with dark brown hair and a boyish face handled the ring. "Another pill that can get an enemy talking?"

"No," Kitty said, remembering how sobering it had been when Vera had handed her the cyanide pill. "These are for you to commit suicide. At capture, or during torture. You have forty-eight hours to endure incarceration so that the rest of your team can get away. If you don't think you can make it..."

A heavy silence fell over the group.

"Come on," she said after a pause. "I'll show you the big-boy toys, now."

The dozen men shuffled out onto the shooting range next door and she uncovered an array of weapons on a table, including the popular British Sten gun. However, the Allies had come a long way in adding to the mix.

First, she lifted a pair of soft leather gloves off the table. "This is the Sedgley OSS." The men looked satisfyingly perplexed. "It delivers one hell of a knockout punch. It's my favorite OSS weapon. Attached to this glove"—she revealed the secret—"is a single shot .38 pistol. You have one caliber round that will fire when the plunger is depressed. You can depress the plunger by just punching the bad guy."

Some of the men whistled quietly. Kitty continued the show.

"This pen is a covert gun. The OSS calls this the Stinger. It's designed to be disposable. Again, a single shot is all it has. This time, it is a .22 short round.

"Men, I'm showing you these because you must be prepared to kill a man at close range," Kitty continued. She looked at the reactions on the sea of faces before her. "Shoot, stab him in the kidneys with a stiletto, or strangle him with your bare hands. Again, this is *guerrilla* warfare."

The men took turns examining the weapons. Not for the

first time, Kitty felt chilled. These were the stealth weapons MI6 used, and she was not yet sure whether they were hunting for Edgar. She had to find him. She had to prove he was still on *their* side. On *her* side.

One of the aides suddenly strode in.

"Miss Larsson? Colonel Donovan has arrived. He expects you at his first meeting. It's time."

Kitty excused herself, taking one last glance at the group. As she gathered her things to go, the OSS agents clapped and cheered, thanking her for the tour. A number of them stepped forward and shook her hand.

In six weeks, these men would be sent in to Europe to find and infiltrate enemy intelligence. In eight weeks, she would be greeting the final round from America. And then a decision was due about whether she would be sent into the field herself.

Now that Donovan was back in Great Britain again, she would convince him of that.

As soon as Kitty entered the conference room, she knew that something big was happening. First, she was introduced to members of the Free French, and was surprised to not only see Vera Atkins and Colonel Buckmaster, but how warmly they greeted her. She was slightly amused when Donovan pressed a possessive arm over her shoulders and pointed out the seat next to his.

The SOE, the OSS and the Free French all in one room meant that something very exciting—and likely with roots stemming from military command—was developing. This time, she was sitting on the "American side" of the table.

"Thank you very much for your trust, sir," she said to Donovan.

He settled in, then said loud enough for the table to hear, "You've been doing a superior job, Kitty Larsson."

Embarrassed, she whispered, "I'd like to talk to you before you head back to Washington, then."

He cleared his throat and nodded, then directed his attention to Colonel Buckmaster.

The SOE chief opened the meeting. "We're all here to discuss a very interesting idea," Buckmaster announced. "The OSS is training its agents in Great Britain, and we are planning to send ops into France, Norway, and Belgium. The idea is to combine our intelligence efforts and expertise by establishing three-man teams made up of our men, the Yanks and a Belgian or French national. These teams will parachute behind enemy lines. They will assess the preparedness and necessary support needed for local resistance. That resistance will be trained to take counteroffensive measures against the Germans and Italians."

Colonel Buckmaster looked at Donovan, who leaned back in his chair before rising and taking over.

"These groups will report how many men and women are under arms in France, what targets are available for sabotage, and what stores are needed. France is an important area. These specialized teams will have to carry the ball. They'll disrupt communications and delay German troop movements. But we won't build up these areas with local rebels until we know whether there are sufficient numbers—and morale—to take on the Nazis." He dragged the *a* out. "The ground has to be fertile before we send in reserves and material."

Kitty raised her hand. "What about planting ops in the Reich?"

"How do you propose we do that?" Donovan asked, as if he'd never heard the idea before.

"Coordinating and drumming up local resistance efforts there. If we succeed in Belgium, France, Norway, even Italy, you can bet that the Germans will fight tooth and nail to prevent us from reaching the core of the Reich. We know that there are plenty of Abwehr and German agents in Bern, for example, who would be thrilled to help," she said. "We've just learned that there has been an uptick in resistance from within Berlin and Vienna.

Vera was watching her warily. Kitty's cheeks grew hot. Yes, this was about going and finding Edgar. But it was also a wholly legitimate strategy.

"Our focus is not Germany or Austria," Buckmaster said. "These men are going into the countries I have listed."

Donovan scratched his neck and winced. "Of course. But Miss Larsson's idea is possibly worth taking a closer look at."

Kitty looked down at her notes, smiling to herself. Millie had once told her that the secret to being a diplomat's wife was to give the men the impression that everything was their idea.

The meeting resulted in a vast to-do list for everyone involved. The SOE suggested a training ground in Scotland. The OSS would bring remaining prospects waiting in the States. Kitty warned that there might be cultural clashes, and that morale between the Brits, the French in exile, and the incoming Americans had to remain high. Her fellow compatriots were her greatest worry. They were brash and eager, and could rub the more modest Europeans the wrong way. Especially because the Yanks were coming late to the party and behaving as if they'd come to save the day.

When everyone began to disperse, she avoided Vera and cornered Donovan. He wagged a finger at her.

"What?" she asked with mock innocence. "Planting the idea about special ops in the Reich, over and over, is the only way it's going to bear any fruit."

"Kitty, I know you're eager to get into the field. And I am listening to you." He sighed, and her heart jumped a little. He was relenting. "I want you to go to Bern."

Her heart lurched. "Bern. Yes. OK. Why?"

"I think you should meet the station chief there, Allen Dulles. You two have a lot in common."

Kitty's gut was doing endless somersaults.

"Millie Quentin—"

"I know her. I worked with her in Vienna."

Donovan nodded, but a chill ran down her back. It had been three months and still no word about Edgar. She had sent Millie a telegram early on. It had been brief and used references from back when they first started their search for Pim: *You had a boy, once. Haven't heard about him since.* A brief telegram returned from Bern: *If I hear anything, I will let you know.* There had been no further communication.

"Millie asked for you," Donovan blurted.

Kitty was stupefied. "She did?"

"She said you and Dulles really need to meet each other. Go to it. Your part of the course ends in a few weeks. You can go then."

"And after that." Kitty put her hands on her hips. "We will talk about my first operation."

"After that, you've got one more round of training to get our men through, and then we'll talk about your next steps."

Kitty nodded automatically. Her mind was whirling with all the possibilities that Millie might be sending for her, and over Donovan. This was serious. And she was very sure it had to do with Edgar.

She had to get through the next weeks, but how much time did they have left?

33

JULY 1943

Bern, Switzerland

Kitty landed in Bern five weeks later. It was a hot July day. Donovan had arranged a car for her. Her driver showed her to the back and she settled in, but she was fidgeting.

"First time in Bern?" he asked casually.

Kitty shrugged in the rearview mirror. "It's been a couple of years."

As they motored toward the city, she peered out the window. "Why are all the street signs stripped?"

"In case of invasion," he said. "So that the German Wehrmacht won't be able to find their way. People are a bit on edge. Afraid of rockets and bombs. A few strays from the border have already hit. The town's built a fortification on the northern side of the city."

Kitty cocked an eyebrow and gazed out the window once more. As the car entered the city, she recognized the university's botanical garden. The driver crossed over the Aare River, and the landscape of Old Town's medieval structures opened before them. There was a lot of traffic.

"You're staying at the Bellevue?"

Kitty leaned forward, impatient to get there. "I am. Maybe you can just drop me off on the other side of the bridge?"

"Are you certain?"

She said she was. She wanted to walk. She had packed lightly and would carry her own bag.

Kitty entered the confines of the Old Town. She passed the ornate fountain with its mythical ogre in Kornhausplatz. People strolled along the arcaded streets. Across the Aare, beautiful villas and vineyard terraces dotted the hillsides with the Bernese Alps in the background. She reached the Zytglogge clock tower and checked the time. She was to meet Millie in half an hour at the hotel, and she was only five minutes away.

The Hotel Bellevue, overlooking the snaking Aare, was the equivalent to the Pera Palace in Istanbul. As she had once heard someone say, it was the place to "drink, sup and snoop." German Abwehr agents and legation workers, each with their personal agendas and a variety of affiliations, honed in on anyone looking remotely interesting or suspicious. Kitty had dressed conservatively, so as not to draw attention to herself. She went to the front desk, checked in, and went straight up to her room.

Her first affair was to search for bugs. She unscrewed the telephone, checked behind the painting over the bed, felt beneath the mattresses and frame, and traced the chest of drawers inside and outside with both hands. She was almost disappointed to find nothing. After freshening up, Kitty headed downstairs into the lounge. She spotted Millie at the bar right away.

At the sight of her, Millie's big green eyes widened and she squirmed off the bar stool. She was shorter than Kitty, curvier and just as dynamic as always. She wore her hallmark ruby-pink lipstick that matched the shade of her summer dress, and her dark hair had been done up in a pompadour. Her signature strand of pearls was replaced by a pearl brooch.

They embraced tightly, kissed each other's cheeks and Millie grasped her hand and pulled her close as she whispered, "I sent someone up to check your room."

"I just did it myself," Kitty whispered back.

Millie nodded coolly. "You can never be too careful."

They leaned against the bar together and Millie spoke with her normal New Yorker volume. "Gosh, how long has it been? You know, you were my favorite roommate when we worked at the legation together. Gin rickey?"

Kitty laughed, but she was nervous. "Yes, please."

The bartender mixed their drinks and Millie ushered Kitty to a table at the back of the room. They smiled at each other, but Millie mirrored Kitty's caution.

"Tell me about your husband, Mrs. Quentin," Kitty offered.

"Bob?" Millie's smile slid off her face for a second. "Bob is Bob. He's a good guy."

Kitty narrowed her eyes. "A good guy? That's all you have to say?"

Millie looked caught out. "You're prying."

"I'm sorry." Kitty took a sip of her drink. "So, you're an assistant to the station chief. Mr. Dulles?"

"Station chief," Millie huffed. Her eyes never stayed still. "Bob says everyone here knows that the only kind of chief Allen is, is a spy chief." She chuckled and leaned in, delivering her punchline. "Everyone, that is, except the Americans."

Kitty chuckled uncertainly.

"Which means," Millie whispered, "they all know that he's here to exploit any Germans remotely interested in removing Hitler from power."

Kitty raised an eyebrow and looked down at her drink. "That's a tough job if everyone knows about it."

Millie turned her cocktail glass around on the surface of the table. "I was so surprised to run into Oskar in London, Kitty. And he was so surprised, the first thing he told me was that he'd seen you as well. And I got to thinking, what is Kitty Ragatz—or is it Larsson now?—doing around Europe? I mean, I lost track of you after we talked about your divorce. You just... disappeared."

Kitty grasped her glass.

Millie placed a hand over Kitty's wrist. Her voice was very low. "Don't worry. He didn't tell me anything about what you were doing or where you were. But I started ingratiating myself with some of the folk around here in Bern, for Allen, that is. I kept catching the same name, a woman who threw some great parties here. An interesting woman who kept a revolving door open for all sorts of characters. She was a New York widow, from Boston, they said."

Millie raised her eyes to Kitty's. Kitty slowly slid her hands from the table and sat back.

"Elizabeth Hennessy?"

Kitty feigned ignorance though her insides went soft.

Millie smiled a little. "Anyway, she had an MO just like yours. Very similar. And I thought, wow, she and Kitty Larsson could have been twins."

Kitty pursed her lips. "Where is this going?"

Millie's face softened. "Oh, no. No, Kitty. I'm not..." She took in a deep breath. "Gosh, I'm scaring you." She peered at her. "I've just hit a sore spot, haven't I?"

Kitty reached for her drink and just held it in the air. "I feel a bit interrogated. I don't know this Elizabeth Hennessy. I don't know—" But it did explain why Millie had said to Oskar, *If Kitty ever goes* back *to Bern.*

Millie put a hand up. "Let me start over. I met Donovan in Washington, you know? We get along famously."

"I remember you play cards. I can understand why," Kitty said stiffly.

Millie looked as if she'd lost her footing. "Yes, we did play cards. And one day we were having lunch with him—Allen and I—and he mentioned you. Anyway... I promised to contact you if I thought something might be interesting. I asked Donovan to send you because Allen and I have been talking and..."

She leaned forward again and gestured for Kitty to take her hand. Kitty hesitated but put her palm in hers.

"You can trust me," Millie said, squeezing her fingers lightly. "I called you here because I think Allen might have found some of our old friends."

Kitty pulled back. *Edgar?*

But Millie made an O with her mouth and held up the five fingers of her left hand. "They've suddenly gotten rather active again."

The O5! Kitty's head swam, her nerves were taut. Millie had learned about Kitty's activities with the O5 during the Department of State meeting in Washington years earlier.

She took a quick drink, steeled herself and looked hard at her old friend. "When? When did they reappear? I want you to tell me everything."

Millie smiled gently. "That's why you're here. Drink up and then, when my guy comes by, we're going straight upstairs."

Half an hour later, the two of them were in Kitty's bedroom. They'd brought two sandwiches with them and a couple bottles of water.

"All right, my dear friend," Millie said. "Here's the story. I read the details of the training in Great Britain and it mentioned you; that you're helping our agents get oriented on France and such. I talked to Allen about you. And he got wind that you've been pushing for more ops in Germany or Austria. Thing is, Allen's been interested in the same thing and keeps running against a blockade. Then, something interesting happened."

Kitty was on tenterhooks as Millie continued her story.

"This spring, I'm having drinks at the Theater Café and one of the big shots at the British legation comes in. He strolls up to Allen and they start talking, then in passing, the Brit warns Allen that some character might come by the American legation looking to talk to them. The Brit describes this man as a German who is looking to dump a whole bunch of documents into Allied laps. For free."

Kitty frowned. "What kind of documents?"

"I don't know. Anyway, he said Allen should just turn him away. But I know Allen. Once, during the Great War, when he was working at an American legation, someone called and said they wanted to talk to him about Russia, and had information about Russian intelligence. Allen dismissed this. Later, he found out the man who wanted to talk to him had been—get this!—Lenin himself." Millie sat back, grinning. "Since then, Allen has a policy of listening to anyone who says they want to talk."

"And?" Kitty was digging her nails into the heels of her palms. "Did this German ever show up?"

"Eventually. Tells Allen he's got a guy waiting to meet him from Berlin. I don't know anything about what happened at that meeting. But, in the meantime, Allen has me babysitting a different German source he makes me call Dr. Bernhard. This Dr. Bernhard has written a tell-all book about the Third Reich, and I'm supposed to help translate it into English. Allen makes me report on everything Dr. Bernhard says. Everything. I figure it's to check the information he is giving in the book is consistent or will he trip up and contradict himself. Anyway, Dr. Bernhard suddenly starts talking about the assassination attempts on Hitler. And he mentions O5."

Kitty mirrored Millie's widening eyes.

"I tell you, I nearly had a heart attack, Kitty. But it gets even more interesting. He mentions one of the assets in this network." She looked hard at Kitty. "Pim."

Kitty gasped. "Edgar? He knows Edgar?"

Millie stood up and paced the room. "At least *about* him. I asked Dr. Bernhard—you know? Just to see how much he knew —what had happened to this Pim fella. Dr. Bernhard gets a look in his eye. 'Who says anything happened to him?' I said because he'd used the past tense. And he did not reply. He closed up for the day."

Kitty pushed her uneaten sandwich away.

Millie folded her arms and studied Kitty. "You're still in touch with Edgar, aren't you?"

Blinking back the tears, Kitty shook her head. "Oh, Millie! I wish I was. I wish I knew more... But I don't believe I'm at liberty to say what it is that I do know about him."

"OK," Mille said gently. "Not to me anyway. But Allen wants to meet you tonight."

"Where?"

Millie jerked her head toward the window. "Herrengasse 23. Be there at eight."

Kitty glanced down at her watch. Her heart was flipping about in her chest. She didn't think she could wait that long. Millie was preening in the mirror above the dresser, putting on fresh powder, then lipstick.

"I have to return to the office," she said. "But I'll see you tomorrow, all right?"

Kitty watched Millie snap the compact shut and drop it into her bag. "You keep referring to your boss as Allen. Not Mr. Dulles."

Millie looked up. "Oh? I didn't realize."

"Uh-huh." Kitty tilted her head. "You once asked me whether I moved to Vienna for love or money. You had a great job with the Department of State in Washington."

"Bob got the assignment in Bern, so I went with him. Then this position opened up. Bob recommended me."

Kitty nodded. "Sure. But *Allen*?"

Millie sighed, the purse dropping to dangle in the crook of her elbow. "It's that obvious?"

"Yeah."

"As obvious as your broken heart over Edgar?"

Kitty closed her eyes.

"I asked you to come here because your message was odd. But I understood it enough to know that you need help." Millie strode over to her and placed a hand on Kitty's shoulder. "And I convinced Allen that you are likely the one who could assist him with something. Don't be late, OK?"

That evening, Kitty went to the address Millie had given her. Off a busy cobblestone street in Old Town, she turned into Herrengasse and looked for number 23. She passed the American legation at number 26, where Millie's office would be, and stopped. The lamps were out along a good stretch of the street. Regardless, she quickly found the four-story Baroque building and rang the bell for the ground floor apartment.

A butler opened the door. "I'm Jacques," the man said.

"Kitty Larsson. Mr. Dulles is expecting me."

He led the way into a large reception room. She could see the apartment was luxurious and spacious. Jacques saw her past a living room and dining room, and ushered her into a cozy wood-paneled study. The red drapes were drawn over the windows. There was a table that served as a bar. Two leather armchairs and a traditional Swiss sofa were drawn around an empty fireplace. Above the mantel hung a portrait of a woman in a silver frame. That was certainly not Millie, Kitty mused.

"Mr. Dulles will be right with you," Jacques said. "May I offer you something to drink?"

Kitty shook her head. She wanted her wits about her. She would drink later.

No sooner had the butler gone than the door opened again and a man in glasses, sporting a mustache and holding a pipe, walked in. He wore a tweed blazer, his whole appearance that of a shabby professor.

"Miss Larsson?"

"Kitty." She took his hand. "Pleased to meet you Mr. Dulles."

"Please, it's Allen. Jacques said you don't want anything to drink. Can I offer you tea? Coffee? Water?"

"Thank you."

He showed her to the sofa. She lowered herself as he took the armchair to her right.

"Mrs. Quentin said you were in Vienna together. I worked as a foreign secretary there back in the day."

"Is that so? When?"

"It had to be, let's see, nineteen-sixteen. That's right. Nearly three decades ago." He chuckled. "Anyway, I did what you were likely doing there."

"Forging travel visas for Jews?" Her tone was saccharine.

Dulles removed his pipe from his mouth and uttered a one-syllable laugh.

"I'm kidding," Kitty muttered, though she wasn't. "I don't know why I said that. I'm not sure why I'm here. And it seems everyone knows everything about me anyway, so can we stop with the cloak-and-dagger dance and just get down to business. I'm certain that you and Millie have discussed my husband over pillow talk."

Dulles looked astounded. "I quite like the cloak-and-dagger dance, but this is also fine."

"I'm sure you're good at it," she said. "Better than me, at any rate."

His look softened. "A skilled intelligence officer is like a good fisherman. He prepares meticulously for his catch, scouts the waters patiently in which his sources swim, remains inquisitive and open-minded, but he is always aware that the person he hooked might be an enemy double agent intent on deceiving him. It's—"

"Are you talking about me, or my husband?"

Dulles raised both eyebrows and stuck the pipe in his mouth. "Millie warned me not to rile you."

He moved to a sideboard, unlocked a door, and reached inside. He returned with a large manila envelope. "I'm talking about both of you. Millie has told me about your history with the Austrian asset named Pim."

Kitty shifted to the edge of the sofa, her hand over her mouth. He opened the envelope. It had a broken red wax seal.

"I'm wondering if you can make something of this. These are photographs of the factories in Pennemünde. But it's this, in the bottom right-hand corner..."

She was looking at a series of aerial views. Her eyes darted to where Dulles was pointing on the first one, then the second one, and her heart stopped.

In the corner of each one, in white lettering: O_5P. She flipped through all of them. It was the same on each photo.

She stared up at Dulles.

"P, for Pennemünde," he said firmly.

Tears sprang to her eyes. "No. It's him."

The spy chief lowered his pipe. "Except Pim no longer exists."

34

JULY–AUGUST 1943

Bern, Switzerland

She dropped back onto the sofa. The photos scattered onto the floor. "Where is he? What's happened to him?"

Dulles gathered up the images then moved to the bar. "I think you prefer gin?"

She didn't want a cocktail. "Brandy. Please." Kitty twisted to watch him moving behind her. "Neat."

He filled two glasses, and brought one to her. "This is completely up to you now, Miss Larsson, but anything you can tell me might help me and even help you."

Her hand shook as she accepted the drink. "How? What do you need from me?"

"We had an interesting source come to us."

"You met him? In person?"

Dulles shook his head. "A man from Berlin showed up here, but Millie confirmed that this German was not your husband." He lifted the stack of photos briefly. "We do have reason to believe, however, that he is behind the information that has been filtered to us. But not as Pim."

It made sense. MI6 was looking for Edgar, likely any hint as Pim, but Edgar would have dumped all of his connections to his British counterparts, including the persona. Kitty tossed her brandy, trying to soothe her nerves.

"I can't tell you more," Dulles continued. "But Mrs. Quentin—Millie—has suggested that you might be the person to confirm whether he is... the genuine article. Or is he a double agent and trying to lure us out?"

"My husband is the genuine article."

Dulles set his snifter down. "We'll see. We're going to analyze this information. If it's viable, I will look to open up avenues with Rover."

"Rover?"

"It's the name I've assigned him."

Kitty suddenly lightened. Had Edgar switched over to the OSS? Like her, was he finding that the eager and ambitious Americans were holding the door open?

"I can tell you this one thing," Dulles warned. "Regardless who this source is, he will remain absolutely top secret. The information he has provided thus far appears to be invaluable. Neither you nor Mrs. Quentin will have the clearance for this. But, I will admit that the Department of State is so riddled with doubts about any German intelligence I get, that they keep blocking any action."

"Don't I know it," Kitty muttered.

Dulles cleared his throat. "Rover has an ally in me. I strongly believe it's information that needs to get into the hands of those who can take action on it. So, I am requesting that you help me to confirm that the source is bona fide. I figure, with your record, your name..."

Her dad's name, at any rate, Kitty thought. And Nils's.

"You could lend this the credence I need," Dulles finished.

"I'll do whatever you need me to do."

His gaze drilled into her then he took in a sharp breath. "Yes. Good. There is a contract you must sign first."

"The kind that could get me killed?"

He stuck the pipe between his teeth. "Well, Millie was right about you. You are a firecracker. Seasoned and sharp."

It was nearly a month later in August that Kitty received word from Bern. She was just finishing up the last training course in England, when Wild Bill Donovan called her in. He was about to return to the States.

"Allied bombers have destroyed the facilities in Pennemünde," Donovan reported to her behind locked doors. He opened a file and removed two images of a flattened landscape, and the ruins of a factory chimney. "The Germans were building V-1 and V-2 rocket bombs there. Production has been crippled for at least a few weeks."

"That doesn't seem like much," Kitty said.

"A delay is a delay. A lot can happen in the last few seconds of a ball game. If we stay on top of things, it will work in our favor."

"All right."

"Dulles's source sent the German reactions directly to Bern."

Kitty held her breath. Dulles's source. He meant Rover had sent the report, Rover who very well could be Edgar. "What's next?"

"Dulles wants you in Bern, on his team." Donovan stuck his hand out and pumped hers. "Congratulations, Kitty. Welcome to the field."

She was back in Switzerland a week later, back at Herrengasse with both Dulles and Millie. The lights were out all along his street, but now she knew why. With eyes watching everywhere, nobody should be able to see who was going in and out of Dulles's apartment.

Dulles had chosen the less classified documents for Kitty and Millie to review. "Rover sent us additional information about certain industrial facilities. But Kitty, are you *sure* that this is Dr. Ragatz? Your husband?"

She nodded. "It makes absolute sense. Edgar knows an awful lot of people in both Germany and Austria from his days with the Department of Economics. He dealt with industries from coffee to rubber, and from metals to electronics. I honestly believe that he is back there, and that's why O5 is now active, again."

"But where? Where would he be?" Millie asked softly.

Kitty glanced at her. "I don't know. That's the part I don't know..."

"Millie, would you mind?" Dulles beckoned for her to leave the room.

Millie's face darkened, but she lowered her head and excused herself. Dulles watched her go, then turned back to Kitty. He sat down at a chair across from her and leaned back, his hands behind his head.

"You mentioned all of these... industries. Someone from Austria sought out one of my case officers abroad. He told him a pretty amazing story about a small spy ring in Vienna."

"Yes?" Kitty leaned forward, her excitement growing.

"He fed my case officer with information and requested American support. He supplied the OSS with coordinates for certain industries, but one of the things that caused us to question the motive is that this man singles out companies in Germany, who are in the same industry as his company. So, we wonder why he appears to divert attention away from his own outfit."

"What industry, sir?" Kitty asked. She was mentally

running through all the people she'd met in Vienna, people that Edgar had had business dealings with.

"I can't tell you that."

She sighed. "But I could help."

"I want to return to something else. You told me about these reports from Auschwitz."

"Yes."

"This same source from Vienna sent a list of suppliers to our case officer. Shipments of Zyklon B being sent en masse to camps like Auschwitz. Treblinka. To Dachau. They warned that a large number of Jews are not just being executed, but that the trainloads are being decimated."

"Oh, God." Kitty stood up and paced the room. "That's what Bonaparte and his men also feared."

Dulles looked very troubled. "It's unfathomable."

"That's what the British said, sir. What Donovan said," Kitty said firmly. "But how many people have to come forward before we force ourselves to imagine the unimaginable? My own husband suspects that it's true!" She took in a shaky breath. "Sir, Edgar once said to me that he knew exactly how far the Germans were prepared to go. I need your help. I need the OSS to convince MI6 to stay any order they may have to execute my husband. Let me try and find him."

Dulles was nodding. "I want to send you to my case officer directly. He is the one who is handling seven, two, two."

"Seven, two, two?"

"Yes, Rover. I pick their names, and a three-digit number. But he's an infuriating asset. When we assigned him the name and the number I chose for him, he sent a message that the only digits he would accept would be seven, two, two."

Kitty flinched and dropped into the nearest armchair. "He picked it?"

"Yes."

"Rover wanted seven, twenty-two?"

Dulles grimaced. "That's what I said."

7:22. The hour and minutes when time came to a standstill for her and Edgar. The place where time stood still for just them... the place he wanted to return to.

Dulles started to put the papers away, but Kitty was remembering Edgar's whispers in the Sunrise Villa.

"Promise me that when it's time we'll come back here."

"Don't go," she'd said. "And then you don't have to worry about a return..."

A return. Aunt Julia's message; the message from the blond in Paris. They were the same. He'd been trying to tell her the same thing. Could he now be telling her how to find him?

"Mr. Dulles?" Kitty did not trust her voice.

He looked at her questioningly.

"If Rover proves to be Edgar, do you have the power to save his life?"

Dulles folded his arms, looking at her seriously. "I very well might."

With Nils's and Donovan's help, too, it could work.

"Where is your officer?" she asked flatly.

"Istanbul."

Dazed, Kitty slowly got to her feet. "In that case, I can guarantee that Rover is my husband. And I know exactly where I can find him."

35

SEPTEMBER 1943

Istanbul, Turkey

Istanbul was slipping into autumn, but the patio of Café Istanbul was soaked in sunlight. Kitty drained the Turkish tea, the slice of baklava untouched as she watched a man reach the intersection of the boulevard. The waiter quickly refilled Kitty's glass, and she shaded her eyes to get a good look at the stranger. He was bald on top, with thin dark hair along the sides, and a mustache. As he came closer, she noticed the pinky finger missing on his left hand, just as Dulles had described.

He stepped onto the patio and approached her table, holding a newspaper tilted so that she could read the beginning of the headline. Her jaw hurt from the tension. If the paper featured an Axis victory, Kitty was not sure she would manage to leave the cafe on her own two feet. If it featured an Allied victory, however, there was still hope.

Dulles's agent took a seat at the table next to hers and

unfolded the rest of the headline: *United States unveils new rocket launcher: the Bazooka!*

Kitty took a deep breath, her relief threatening to spill over. She drank the sweet tea hurriedly.

The man waited a moment before he said, "You want to get a message to Rover?"

"Have you ever met him in person?"

"He sends everything over couriers."

She nodded, gritting her teeth to keep the tears at bay. "Tell his couriers that Elizabeth has returned. As have old friends."

She rose, placed money on the table, and left. At the corner, Kitty waved down a taxi. She handed the address to the driver.

He eyed her red hair before grinning toothily. "This is Sunrise Road in English."

Kitty smiled stiffly. "Yes. That's where I'm headed."

He drove over the strait and Kitty kept her eyes on the pastel-colored houses piled along the hillsides like sugared Turkish delights. The vehicle turned onto a narrow road, and wound around the coastline for quite some time before going back up a rise. They rolled to a stop in front of a wrought-iron gate. Behind the enclosure was the Sunrise Villa, booked for the month for Elizabeth Hennessy.

She got out, paid the taxi driver and rang the buzzer. She recognized the butler, Nasir, as he hurried to unlock the gate.

He greeted her reverently. "We were expecting you, Mrs. Hennessy. Would you like me to give you a tour of the house? Refreshments first?"

He picked up her bags from the taxi driver and carried them to the front door. Kitty stepped inside and removed her sunglasses, looking around. The villa was as it had been the last time she'd been here.

"Thank you. I know my way around."

Something shifted on his face. "Of course. I remember. Is there something I could do for you?"

Kitty's pulse quickened. "I only want to know one thing. The man I was once here with. Has he been back at all?"

Nasir shook his head. "I'm afraid not."

Kitty tried to camouflage her disappointment and, when he offered to carry her bags, she followed him up the staircase. When she entered the sunlit room, she took in the tiles and mosaics representing the colors of the setting sun. The cornflower blue sheets were peeking out just below the colorful array of pillows. With a pang, she saw that the bronze sun clock above the bed was no longer stuck on 7:22, but had been repaired.

Nasir opened the balcony doors and threw back the curtains, revealing the bright blue of the Bosphorus Strait. The room filled with the timbre of cicadas and Kitty stepped out. Below her was the olive grove, and the narrow path Edgar had climbed after his swim. She heard the distant putter of motorboats, and a container ship blew its horn.

The soft click behind her indicated that Nasir had left. Kitty stared out at the landscape, prepared for the hard part, for the waiting.

A week later, she was going stir-crazy. After reporting to Bern that she'd still gotten no word, Kitty caught a bus and spent the day touring the city, trying to get her mind off the reason she was in Istanbul in the first place. It was early evening when she returned, the sun already slipping toward the western horizon. She let herself through the gate, and rifled for her keys at the door, but froze before she could unlock it.

It stood ajar. Only a little. But it was open.

Cautiously, she pushed inside. "Nasir?" Then she remembered it was Friday. His day off. He'd left after setting out her breakfast.

Her heart leaping, Kitty reached for the OSS 9mm she

always had with her now. She looked up the staircase first, cocking her ear. Not a sound. Everything was quiet, except that a breeze was blowing in from somewhere.

The dining room was to her right. Save for the regular tray of treats and drinks, it was empty, all the windows and doors shut. Tiptoeing, she headed for the expansive sitting room, over-looking the terrace and the strait. The French doors were flung wide open.

She inched her way to them and froze at the sound of splashing outside. Kitty lunged onto the patio, catching sight of a man's body in the water, and pulling away from the shore.

"Edgar!"

She was about to run down the path but stopped again. A suit was meticulously folded on the back of a recliner on the patio. The shoes and socks were neatly lined up alongside each other.

She placed the gun on the table and fingered the jacket. She lifted the sleeves of a silk shirt, and two silver cufflinks rolled into her palm. They'd been placed atop the shirt. These clothes were not something Edgar would normally wear. They were much too flashy.

She looked toward the water. The swimmer was near the buoys, and now veered left, disappearing behind the umbrella pines along the shoreline. She looked at the silver cufflinks again. Something was familiar about them. She examined the clothing more closely.

The fedora. The polished shoes. Her husband had never worn a fedora, but he'd always polished his shoes. She went to the top of the pathway leading down to the olive grove. Her heart was in her throat as the swimmer reappeared in the water.

Edgar! It has to be Edgar!

She pictured the last time they'd been here, how he'd slid out of the water. Her chest swelled as the swimmer headed back for the shore. She hurried down the path, anticipating the reunion with her husband.

But as the figure neared, she froze. The strokes were different. Edgar's shoulders always rolled a little when he did the crawl. This was a sloppy stroke. And when the head lifted out of the water, the hair was dark and glossy, the skin too brown.

Kitty backed away from the path. Whoever this was, he'd broken into the villa. She ducked behind the trees, and glanced back up at the house, swearing under her breath. The pistol was still on the table.

She scrambled deeper into the grove, finding the thickest trunk, and waited. The man suddenly appeared on the path, and passed by her. She pressed herself against the tree, and watched. He was toweling himself off as he strode up, and by the time he was done, he was on the patio and had his back to her.

He wrapped the towel around his waist and slipped out of the wet suit, before quickly pulling on his bottoms and then his trousers.

Kitty's heart was broken but she was also very afraid. What was this stranger doing here? Why was he swimming on her rented property? Had he broken in to do so?

He was slipping on the shirt, and as he put an arm through one of the sleeves, his back stiffened. He went to the table. He lifted the gun.

"Hello?" The man stepped toward the French doors. "Hello?"

Kitty's heart tumbled to her stomach.

He raised the pistol and turned to face the sea. She could finally make out his face. Her mouth dropped.

It was Khan.

· · ·

Khan, the street-smart Kazakhstani who'd squirreled away with Big Charlie on the Vienna Woods property. Khan, the genius, who'd fashioned vegetable crates with false bottoms so that they could smuggle falsified documents to Jewish families. Khan, turning his face to the sun after a night of forging ration coupons in the dark and dank cellar.

She remembered the cufflinks now from the night she had met the whole gang. Millie had introduced Kitty to Khan, and when they danced together, those cufflinks had flashed beneath the lights of Akhmed Beh's nightclub.

The memories were muddying her reflexes now. How could she have been wrong? She couldn't have been. Everything had led her here. But had Edgar reignited the O5, or was it...

"Khan?"

Khan dropped the pistol to his side. He squinted, studying her as she came out of hiding. He was seeing her red hair. The freckles. The woman who was Elizabeth Hennessy. The woman who covered up Kitty Larsson Ragatz, and her broken heart.

His smile came slowly and he replaced the pistol onto the tabletop behind him. But she was all business. She eyed it, measured the distance between him and her, the route she would have to take to retrieve it.

"You are the last person I expected to find." Another two, three steps. "What are you doing here?"

Khan opened his arms to her. "Good to see you, too."

She came forward, trying to decipher what her instincts were telling her.

Khan's smile wavered. "You sent me a message."

Realizing what he meant, she had to blink back the tears, her focus still on the gun. Kitty inched forward, slowly shaking her head. "I sent Rover a message. You're not..."

Khan glanced back at the weapon, and picked it up. She

flinched, but he turned the handle to her, his look softening. "If it makes you feel better, take it."

She maneuvered around the furniture, reached for it, grasped it. He let go. It felt heavier than usual, but she held it, prepared to take aim if she had to.

"I'm one of his couriers," Khan said.

"I don't understand," Kitty said hoarsely.

"You wouldn't be here, Kitty, if you didn't understand."

"Please," she begged. "Is he here?"

"He only wants to know one thing." Khan's gray eyes flashed.

"What?" she asked impatiently.

From the French doors, a smooth voice, that Viennese accent crisp and warm. "Well, for one thing, are you planning to use that gun on me?"

Kitty staggered backwards, the pistol loose at her side. "Edgar!"

He was coming to her, but it was too much. Kitty doubled over and sobbed. Her husband swam before her eyes as he led her to the nearest chair.

Edgar soothed her, calling her name, then instructed her to breathe. "That's it, Kitty. That's it."

"I knew... I knew you had to come!" she stammered.

He was gripping her shoulders, her arms, stroking her head. Then he was on his knees in front of her. "I trusted you would, too. I prayed and hoped you would understand."

"But I don't! I don't understand!" Her hands on his face, she pleaded with him. "What are we doing here?"

"Many things, Kitty. Many things." Edgar kissed her palms. "But for now, this is where we can stop—"

"Time," they both said together.

"At least for a little while," he said gently.

She sobbed, still disbelieving, and shoved him away from her.

Khan moved toward her, and she wiped her face.

"And you?" she asked. "What about you? How did you two come to be here? Together?"

The men shared a look.

Edgar stood up, pulling her up with him. "We're here to deliver the war to the Allies, darling. And, Kitty, we need your help."

A LETTER FROM CHRYSTYNA

Dear reader,

Thank you for reading *An American Wife in Paris*. If you enjoyed it, please consider recommending it to other readers and leaving a review. If you'd like to keep up to date with all my latest releases, just sign up at the following link. Your email address will never be shared and you can unsubscribe at any time.

www.bookouture.com/chrystyna-lucyk-berger

Part of the fun of writing historical fiction is hunting for inspiration among real accounts. I love learning which parts of a novel were historically accurate, and which were fiction. For this reason, I write a blog that details the background stories that inspire my plotlines. You can read all about this series in my blog on www.inktreks.com or sign up to receive bi-monthly highlights by subscribing to my newsletter at www.inktreks.com/#newsletter.

By the way, we're not finished yet! Join me on Kitty's and Edgar's next journey!

Chrystyna Lucyk-Berger

KEEP IN TOUCH WITH
CHRYSTYNA

www.inktreks.com

facebook.com/inktreks

twitter.com/ckalyna

instagram.com/ckalyna

goodreads.com/ckalyna

bookbub.com/profile/chrystyna-lucyk-berger

AUTHOR'S NOTE

Kitty Larsson and Edgar Ragatz are products of my imagination and composites of many different people whose lives and history have been well documented. Many of those inspirations stemmed from my research at the DÖW (Dokumentation-sarchiv des österreicheschen Widerstandes/Archives of the Austrian Resistance) in Vienna. As for the events related to the SOE, MI6, and OSS, my resources included: Walter Douglas's extensively researched and wonderfully written *Disciples: The World War II Missions of the CIA Directors Who Fought for Wild Bill Donovan*; Helen Fry's *Spymaster*; C. Turner's *Cassia Spy Ring in World War II Austria*; Kate Vigurs' *Mission France*, and the jackpot that is Richard Heslop's memoir, *Xavier*, based on his work with the SOE. It contains a goldmine of anecdotes, including the one about the woman who biked many miles with plasticine in her bloomers, the jailbreak, and the intelligence smuggled out in a baguette.

Without dedicated historical curators, we authors would not be able to bring our worlds to life. I am indebted to the dynamic team at the Musée de la Résistance nationale in Champigny-sur-Marne and the meticulous collection at the

Liberation of Paris museum in Paris, both very much worth a visit.

Many thanks go to all those who helped me during various stages of developing the manuscript: Ursula Hechenberger-Schwärzler, the Thelma to my Louise; Genevieve Montcombroux, Olga Nohra; Theresa König; Lesya Lucyk; Jessica Vander Stoep; and my editor, Jess Whitlum-Cooper, the entire team at Bookouture and Anne O'Brien. Without the support of my husband and son, I would not have gotten the job done. Your sacrifices were not in vain.

All real historical figures are fictionally portrayed in this novel. I am especially grateful to Jack Fairweather's enormous undertaking in bringing Witold Pilecki's story to life in *The Volunteer*. The reports from Auschwitz depicted in this novel are loosely based on the Polish underground's efforts to bring the Holocaust to the Allies' attention before it was too late.

Unfortunately, heroism is considered an exceptional act—worthy of the page and the monuments—because cowardice and self-interests are much too common.

Printed in Great Britain
by Amazon

25526695R00192